DECEPTION OR PERCEPTION

ELLEN CARRON

Black Rose writing

© 2014 by Ellen Carron

All rights reserved. No part of this book may be reproduced, stored in a retrieval system or transmitted in any form or by any means without the prior written permission of the publishers, except by a reviewer who may quote brief passages in a review to be printed in a newspaper, magazine or journal.

The final approval for this literary material is granted by the author.

First printing

All characters appearing in this work are fictitious. Any resemblance to real persons, living or dead, is purely coincidental.

ISBN: 978-1-61296-374-7
PUBLISHED BY BLACK ROSE WRITING
www.blackrosewriting.com

Printed in the United States of America

DECEPTION OR PERCEPTION is printed in Times New Roman

I want to thank family and friends who have been supportive physically, mentally, and spiritually through the duration of my writing *Deception or Perception*. I could not have accomplished this achievement without your help and prayers. Thank you from the bottom of my heart. - Ellen

DECEPTION OR PERCEPTION

Chapter One

Like any other small town with a population of about twelve thousand, Ellisville, Illinois has its average number of churches, taverns, schools, businesses and, of course, a hospital. One of the town's most outstanding historical sites is the Ellisville Hotel where Lincoln stayed overnight when making a trip from Springfield, Illinois to St. Louis, Missouri.

My name is Shannon Whitney. I am thirty-two years old and described as brown-eyed, tall, lean, and handsome. Well, I don't know about handsome, but I'll accept any compliment.

After graduating in 2004 from the Louisiana State University School of Veterinary Medicine, I returned home to Illinois to start my own practice. I was fortunate to find an old farmhouse on six acres of land with a large barn and a corral in the pasture. The property is located on a slightly slanted hillside, just far enough out of town to be considered country. The long driveway leading up to the house was lined with lilac bushes years before, but they'd been badly neglected since then. I decided to trim the old branches off as far back as possible without damaging the plants. In no time, they began turning green and looking like small trees.

To maintain my privacy, I hired a contractor to build a tall fence between the clinic and my home. Having a gift for carpentry, I began working on the first floor at the northwest corner of the house. I then tore out the old interior and completed the living room with a fireplace on the south wall and added a large bath to the reconstructed bedroom. Because of the kitchen's location, I formulated and assembled a beautiful staircase between it and the living room. The second floor already had two bedrooms and a bath. This project took several months, but I completed it before opening the clinic the fall of 2005. Looking back, I can say that all the work and money was well worth it.

The following few years taught me that the town veterinarian hears a lot of gossip, and Ellisville has a great deal of that and plenty of ears to listen. One day in March, around 7 in the morning, I was sitting at my usual table in Millie's restaurant (the local hangout for serious coffee drinkers) and having coffee with my two best friends, Grant Carrolton and Hank Nikensary. Grant, our town pharmacist, is a good-looking black man who dresses like a nerd. His perfectionism in pharmaceuticals is unquestionable, and he has the reputation of being a highly intelligent man. Hank, on the other hand, works as the manager of a nearby power plant. He is also extremely intelligent and hides it by looking and acting like a redneck. Hank often uses very descriptive language that can be smutty, crude, and tasteless, and this makes some people uncomfortable. However, friends and family who are closest to him see his compassion, honesty, and loyalty.

As we were having our morning coffee, Hank leaned over the table and, in a low voice asked, "Have you heard about Brian Avis and the blonde teller he hired at the bank?"

Grant chimed in, "Yeah, but tell us what you heard!"

Hank continued his story, "Well, ol' man Jenkins decided to go down to the river late last night to check his trot lines. When he got there, he saw somethin' shinin' through the willows, so he eased on through the trees and what do ya thank he saw? Brian Avis and the blonde teller were in the back seat of a car gettin' with the program." I asked, "Hank! You're not saying they were having sex?"

"That's exactly what I'm saying,"

I shook my head in thought. *Why would a man do something like that? He is taking a chance of losing his wife and two sons who love him very much.*

Grant broke into my thoughts, adding to the gossip, "I heard he knew her before she moved here from Kinsworth."

As we were finishing our second cup of coffee, a bundled up woman who looked like an Eskimo came through the restaurant door. Carrying the "help wanted" sign that Millie had placed at the entrance the day before, she walked over to the counter and set it aside. Then glancing around, she removed her winter apparel and placed it on a stool near the counter. From where we were sitting, we had a clear view of the most beautiful woman I had ever seen. She had green eyes, red hair, and a figure a man would die for.

Picking the 'help wanted' sign back up, she asked, "Is the owner here?" Everyone in the restaurant turned around and stared, especially the men. Finally, when the people stopped gawking at her, someone yelled, "Hey, Millie! Somebody out here wants to talk to you."

Now, Millie is an attractive woman with blue eyes and blonde hair, who stands approximately five foot five and weighs about one hundred thirty pounds. She sometimes has a very colorful vocabulary and the voice of a drill sergeant. Also, she can be tough as a merchant marine, especially if a person gets out of line. However, having a heart of gold, she would go to the ends of the earth for anyone who might need help.

Millie came through the swinging doors from the kitchen and walked to the counter where the young woman stood. Looking as though she were sizing up the pretty young redhead who stood in front of her, she asked, "You wanna talk to me?"

In a soft, timid voice, the young woman answered, "Yes, if you are the person who does the hiring." (And she pointed to the sign.) I would like to apply for the job if it's still available."

Millie, with her tough manner asked, "Well, the sign was still on the door, wasn't it?"

"Yes, ma'am," The young woman answered.

With a haughty attitude, Millie abruptly snapped, "Then, the job is still available!" The young woman became very nervous as Millie, with one hand on her hip asked, "What's your name?"

Answering timidly, the young woman said, "Cheryl Lee Canton, but you can call me Lee for short."

"What's your experience in the restaurant business?" Millie then asked.

Nervously looking around, Lee answered, "Well...I can clean." Then slightly fidgeting, she slowly brushed her fingers across the counter and said, "Looks like the place could use a little of that." Then, Lee sheepishly smiled at Millie, and several people began giggling. However, when Millie gave them a dirty look, they all got as quiet as mice. Suddenly, it dawned on Lee what she had just said. She began to stammer saying, "Oh, I- I- I- I ...didn't...mean ...your... restaurant was dirty; I just thought...it looked dirty...." Looking down, she paused and said, "Right here," pointing to a spot on the counter. Trying to cover her blunder, Lee continued, "I'm sorry, ma'am, I shouldn't have said your restaurant looked dirty. What...I meant to say...was that someone must have missed this spot."

Millie, with her arms folded, glared at Lee and asked in a huffy voice, "Is cleaning all you can do?"

"No, ma'am," answered Lee. "I can cook, wash dishes and wait tables. I am reliable, and I *really* need this job!"

Millie, with her arms still folded, tilted her chin to her chest, and looking at her said, "Sundays and Mondays off, forty hours a week, seven, seventy five an hour."

"Have I got the job?"

"Yep, for now."

Lee's face lit up like a Christmas tree, and as Millie started to walk back to the kitchen, Lee asked loudly, "When do I start?"

By this time Millie had gone through the swinging doors of the kitchen, and she yelled, "Tomorrow. 7:00 A.M."

With a big smile on her face, Lee bundled up in her neck scarf, heavy hooded jacket, and gloves, then turned and walked out the door. I stood up from the table and watched through the restaurant window and saw, much to my surprise, that her transportation was a bicycle. My curiosity got the best of me. Telling Hank and Grant that I had some errands to run, I quickly left the restaurant and got into my truck, determined to know her destination.

Lee headed towards the Old Ellisville Trail, which is the main blacktop out of town. I cautiously kept my distance for about a quarter mile. Then she turned left onto a gravel road. Still being very careful, I stopped the truck long enough to be able to continue following her without being seen. After about another quarter mile, she turned left onto a narrow dirt lane, just wide enough for a vehicle, which led into a grove of large trees with thick underbrush. I asked myself. Where in the world was she going? I had lived in this area all my life and never knew of anything other than a big patch of woods.

I parked the truck and walked parallel with the lane until the undergrowth thickened enough to hide in. Just beyond, Lee's bike was parked in a clearing against some steps attached to the porch of an old mobile home. I stood there for a few minutes in disbelief. The rusting seams gave the appearance that it could fall apart at any time. The collapsing porch foundation looked as though the least disturbance could cause it to crumble. To the right of the mobile home stood an old, rusting hand pump, and a worn path led to an outside toilet.

Still amazed, I returned to my truck and drove back to town with questions racing through my head. *Why would anyone want to live in a place like that? And why would she choose such a desolate area?* I had no answers to my questions, but one thing was for sure. I felt a deep attraction to this woman and wanted to get to know her.

Entering the driveway to the clinic, and glancing at my watch, I realized how late it was, and muttered sarcastically to myself, "Oh, well! After the cow is out, there is no sense trying to fix the fence." I walked through the door and found the waiting room full of small animals and their owners.

My receptionist, Ronda, in a concerned voice asked, "Where have you been? I was beginning to think that I may have to send everyone home." I told her not to worry and requested that she begin filling the exam rooms. Annoyed, she remarked, "You know, you could have called me!"

My guilt made me feel defensive and my thought was, *I am not in any mood to defend myself for being late,* and gave her a glance as if to say, *that is enough.* Ronda responded promptly with a "kiss my butt" glance.

I went into the office, put on my scrubs, and grabbed a stethoscope, but was still thinking about Lee and how it would feel to hold her in my arms. Ronda interrupted my thoughts with a knock on the door and said, "Dr. Whitney, your first patient is ready in exam room one."

Shaking my head brought me back to reality. *What is wrong with me? Why am I fantasizing about this woman?*

As the day progressed, it became long and tiring. After saying goodbye to my last patient and his owner, I went into the office, sat down, and closed my eyes. Thoughts of Lee once again appeared in my head, looking over her shoulder at me with a happy-go-lucky smile. The phone rang, and in the depth of my illusion, I almost jumped out of the chair. It was Mr. Carter calling to ask about the results of the biopsy I took from their son's pony a few weeks before. I told him, "I am happy to say that Rickey's pony does not have anything seriously wrong. The lab results came back and reported that he has an allergy to corn, so tell Rickey to feed him oats or alfalfa." Mr. Carter thanked me and we hung up.

When I stepped out of my office to lock up, the clinic door flew open. In walked Mrs. Myers and her daughter Justice with a poodle on a leash. Mrs. Myers blurted out, "Dr. Whitney, would you please take a look at Cherie? I realize you're ready to close, but there is something wrong with her. She's not eating much at all, and, furthermore, she has gained a lot of weight. She also seems to be sleeping too much!"

"Bring Cherie into the examining room."

After checking the poodle's vital signs, I checked her mammary glands. While listening to her abdomen with my stethoscope, I could hear at least three tiny heartbeats. "Mrs. Myers, Cherie is going to be a mother."

As Justice let out a squeal and jumped up and down, Mrs. Myers said, "That can't be. During Cherie's heat period, we only let her out to do her business in a fenced back yard!"

I smiled and said, "Doesn't your neighbor, Mr. Fillmore, have a male Pomeranian?"

She answered sadly, "Yes."

Then I asked, "How closely were you watching *his* dog?"

Answering in an unhappy tone, she said, "Evidently, not close enough."

Mrs. Myers, her daughter and the poodle left about 6:30 P.M. Feeling very tired, I locked the clinic and retreated to the house. After taking a shower and putting on some sweats, I walked over to the fridge and searched around for something to make a sandwich, but all I saw was a package of outdated bologna and a slice of mold-covered cheese. However, there were a couple of beers on the back of a shelf, and they looked more appealing to me than food. Taking one from the fridge and migrating to the couch, I sat down to relax and turned on the television. There, before my eyes, I saw a man and a woman, lying on a bear-skin rug in front of a fireplace, making out. Watching the hugging, kissing, and touching, I began to fantasize about Lee. *Stop it!*

Ellen Carron

You don't even know her! Damn that little redhead! Why does she have to be so beautiful!?

I am, almost thirty three years old, and this is the first time I have ever obsessed over a woman. I switched off the TV, picked up my beer, and walked out onto the porch, slumping down on the swing.

After sitting there for a while and emptying the bottle of beer, I looked up at the moonlit sky. I had never noticed how beautiful the stars were until tonight. All of a sudden, one of the stars streaked across the sky. Watching it disappear into the darkness, I realized how restless, lonely, and empty my life had become and memories came rushing back like a nightmare. I remembered returning home from LSU to bury Mom, Dad, and my little sister, Jess. Between my confusion over Lee and the memories of the loss of my family, all kinds of emotions began flooding my head. *Oh, no, I'm not going there!* I jumped up from the swing and practically ran back into the house, then headed straight to the clinic office, and dove into a pile of paperwork to silence my thoughts. Hours later, when the exhaustion became greater than the work, I got up and went to bed and, thank God, fell asleep without the mind chatter.

The next morning, I awoke to the sound of footsteps outside my bedroom. As I sat up in the bed, the door opened, and Lee came walking through. "W-W-What are you doing here? And how did you get in?"

She came over to my bed, and reaching down, she softly touched my face with her fingertips. "You probably didn't think I noticed you at Millie's yesterday, but I did." Then she knelt on my bed, moving as close to me as she could. By this time, I didn't care how she had gotten in. I swallowed hard and could feel her breath on my face. In a very sensual voice, she whispered, "Shannon, you have no idea how long I have waited for a man like you and how much I." BEEP! BEEP! BEEP! The damn alarm clock woke me up and made me jump as though I had been shot out of a cannon! I took a deep breath and headed straight to the shower. Only this time, I chose a cold one. After stepping out of the shower with a towel around my waist, I walked to the mirror, stared at my reflection, and thought, *who is that man? He has to be crazy to think a woman like Lee would be interested in him.* I terminated my conversation with the man in the mirror and opened the medicine cabinet to remove my razor.

After shaving, I splashed some of my best cologne on my face, searched in the closet for just the right shirt and jeans, got dressed and left the house for Millie's. Arriving at the restaurant parking lot, I wasn't surprised to see it full of cars, trucks and SUVs. As I said, news travels fast in Ellisville. It looked as though everyone in town had turned up at Millie's to check out the new waitress. I managed to find a parking spot on the street and had to walk only about a block to the restaurant. Grant and Hank had gotten there early and managed to get a table. I worked my way through the crowd and thanked them for saving me a seat.

Grant looked at Hank and said, "Puy-wee! Hank, what's that smell?"

Hank responded while sniffing the air, "I don't know, Grant. It's hard to describe." Then, sniffing the air again he squinted his eyes, as if needing to define the odor, and he continued his assessment by saying, "Well, Grant, it kinda smells like something between a rose… and a pair of dirty socks."

I tapped Hank on the back of his head with the palm of my hand and responded, "Maybe you need to keep your nose to yourself. I'm sure you wouldn't want me to share with some of Ellisville's finest gossipers the antics you did to get Vickie's attention." Trying to keep the humor in all this nonsense, I continued, "Besides, friends don't cross each other's boundaries by making fun of their best cologne."

Hank and Grant began laughing. Grant, trying to calm his laughter, remarked, "Boundaries, hell Whitney! If everyone here wasn't so charmed by Millie's new waitress, your smell would have cleared out this place when you walked in the door."

The two of them just wouldn't let it go. Hank, grinning like a Cheshire cat, reached over and brushed his hand across my shirt sleeve and said, "Hey, Whitney, how come you're all slickered up this morning?"

Grant spoke up, "Oh, Hank! Can't you see he is trying to impress Millie?"

While both of them snickered, I stared at them and said, "You two think you're real funny, don't you?"

About that time, Millie looked over at our table and yelled, "Hey, Doc, you want some coffee?"

I yelled back, "Yeah!"

"Then, get your skinny little ass over here and pick it up! Can't you see how busy I am?!"

By the time I worked my way around the tables to the counter, Millie had a hot, steaming cup of coffee all ready for me. "By the way," I retorted, "I've been told that I have a nice tush, and it is not skinny at all!"

With a smirk Millie answered, "I guess it's all in a person's perception."

I returned to the table with my coffee and sat down. The restaurant door opened, and in walked Lee. I began to stare at her, and Hank began waving his hand in front of my face in an attempt to break my trance.

Lee's long red hair was pulled back into a ponytail. Her navy blue sweater and white jeans were just tight enough to be ladylike, yet she looked kind of sexy. It's usually hard for a man to describe a woman's clothing, but somehow for me, it became easy after seeing Lee.

When Hank's gestures didn't affect me, Grant started snapping his fingers in front of my eyes. Finally, I stopped staring at her and glanced around and didn't say a word. Picking up my cup and taking a drink of coffee, I noticed that Hank and Grant seemed confused. Why shouldn't they be confused? From the moment Lee walked through the restaurant door, I had acted completely out of character.

Grant, with a serious look on his face could see my confusion. He leaned back in his chair and remarked, "Good grief, Whitney! Surely you're not thinking what I think you're thinking! You've only seen this woman one time, and you're acting like a lovesick schoolboy! Of all the women you've dated, I've never known you to be this infatuated with any of them."

It was quiet around the table for a while. Eventually, I spoke up. "It is not an infatuation, Grant! It's something that goes a lot deeper than that. It's like wanting to be…I don't know what I'm feeling. I can't explain it!"

Hanks, scratching his chin, leaned toward me and commented, "Hey, man. You ain't gonna come unhinged on us, are you? You know, maybe all you need is a cold shower."

Grant spoke up. "Hank, stop your assumptions! Can't you see he has a lot of sorting out to do?"

Hank gazed at me for a few seconds, and then said, "Whitney, if your hankerin' fer this little lady is an infatuation, you'll know it when you go out with her. But if that old 'love bug' has bitten you…well, all you can do is go with the flow. There ain't no pill you can take and nothin' you can do that will cure the 'love bug flu'".

I let out a big sigh, not understanding what was going on with me. "Thanks for the advice. I really appreciate it. But I need to get out of here and go to work before Ronda fires me."

Driving to the clinic, I thought about what Hank had said. And going out with Lee would surely let me know if what I felt was more than an infatuation. But being honest with myself, I knew this guy wasn't ready to take the step of asking her out. Also, my gut told me to be patient. The right moment would come. Perhaps going out of town for four days to a veterinary medical convention would give me some time to think about the situation and gain some perspective.

Chapter Two

After returning home from the convention, I headed straight to Millie's and was eagerly greeted by Grant and Hank. Grant asked, "Hey, sport. How did you like the convention?"

"It was great. There are so many new developments and treatments for animals today. And it's amazing how far science has come with the help of computers. The resources given to me is going to be very useful."

Sitting down at the table, I could see Hank "champing at the bit" to tell me something so I asked, "What's been going on with you, Hank?"

"Never mind about me," he answered. Hank then leaned over the table and, almost in a whisper, continued, "You know what, Whitney? Lee is a mysterious woman."

I sarcastically remarked, "No kidding!"

"No, Whitney. I ain't kiddin'! All she does is come to work, and when she's finished her job, she leaves and no one has ever seen where she goes. I asked a lot of questions of the people around town, including the sheriff, and nobody knows anything, not even where she lives. She jes gits on her bike and rides off."

Teasing him, I remarked, "Are you saying that *you*, Hank Nickensary, a man who has a nose for the news, couldn't find out *anything* about Lee? Man, you are slipping."

He wasn't very pleased with my teasing, but it didn't stop him from expressing his opinions regarding the mystery surrounding Lee.

Getting a "know it all" look on his face, Hank said, "Lee is a strange one! I was thinkin' that…maybe…she just might be a witch."

Grant spoke up, "Hank, you must have a screw loose! Just because you have drilled everyone in town trying to find out who she is and still don't have a clue, you have come up with a lame-brained idea that Lee is a witch!? You are unbelievable!"

Interrupting Grant, I asked, "You honestly believe in witches, Hank? And, even if you do, how in the world could you ever think Lee might be a witch? That is the most asinine notion you have ever come up with." Grant and I sat there staring at him in disbelief.

Hank didn't respond at first. Suddenly, his face broke out into a silly grin. Then he hit the table with the palms of both hands and said, "Gotcha!" He then began laughing so hard he almost choked. Trying to calm his own laughter, Hank commented, "Boy, I wish you coulda seen your faces when I said Lee might be a witch! I wouldn't take a hundred dollars and miss that!"

"Okay, Hank! You got us! You can calm down now, everyone in the restaurant is staring, and it would be embarrassing if Millie threw us out."

Hank became a little more civilized. However, Grant got into the action and remarked, "Whitney, I don't understand why you won't ask Lee out."

"Grant, I don't know her well enough."

Looking directly into my eyes, he said, "That's a bunch of bullshit and you know it! I've heard you ask women out for a date just from an introduction. What's so different about Lee?"

I had no intention of answering him, but of course, Hank spoke up again, "Grant is right. You ain't never had a problem askin' women out, and somethin' that puzzles me is, you ain't ever gone this long without a piece of …"

"Hank, that's enough! You and Grant seem to have the idea that either of you can meddle in my love life any time you want to. And I'm beginning to get a bit resentful! So, I am going to say this one time! Yes, you are right! Asking women out has never been a problem for me. However, I have told both of you, when it comes to Lee, my feelings are different. I do not need to be reminded about my past dating. My fullest intentions are to ask her out to a movie or take her to a Cardinal game. You guys can see how badly I want to go out with her, and you should know that nagging me about the issue is not going to promote the process. So, do not pester me about Lee again!"

Grant and Hank didn't say a word, but I could tell by the body language and their attitudes that everything I had just explained to them went completely over their heads. Sure enough, Grant sarcastically spoke up, "Great idea Whitney! Take her to a ball game.

That should really impress her."

I leaned back in my chair, looked at the ceiling, and lifted my hands in the air. My breath was wasted, and I thought, *I guess if a person can't lick 'em, then they have ta join 'em.* So I responded, "Okay, what do you suggest, Grant?"

"Well...first you've got to ask her out you know, and then choose a proper place to take her. I think she is a classy lady and isn't the type of woman to accept just any kind of invitation." Snapping back, I asked, "Oh yeah?! And how do you know what kind of woman she is?" Grant opened his mouth to answer my question as Lee stepped through the door into the restaurant. She removed her coat and scarf, hung them on the coat rack and immediately began picking up dirty dishes and cleaning tables. I couldn't help watching her every move until Hank poked my arm with his bony finger. When I tried to ignore him, he poked me again. In an exasperated, angry and somewhat loud voice, I turned toward him, and asked, "WHAT?!"

"Well, you don't have to bite my head off, Doctor Asshole!" Hank snapped. "I jes' thought this would be a good time to ask the little lady out fer a date!"

Almost gritting my teeth, I replied, "Like I would ask her out in front of you!" Emphatically shaking my head no, I gave him a look as if to say, "Keep your big mouth shut!"

Hank completely ignored me. Raising his hand, he waved at Lee to come over to our table. As she approached, she smiled and asked, "What can I do for you, Hank?"

Trying to be cool, he responded, "You know my name!" Teasingly, she said "Why, everyone knows you. You're a popular man in this town."

Hank appeared very pleased with himself as his face broke out into a silly grin. However, his next unadulterated stunt was the most unacceptable, inexcusable behavior he had ever displayed. Leaning back in his chair, he said, "Lee, I'd like fer you to meet my two best friends in the whole wide world. Over here is Grant Carrolton." Then, putting his arm around my shoulders, he continued, "And this is Shannon Whitney. Not only is he good lookin, he ain't married."

Lee reached out to shake our hands, one at a time, saying. "Glad to meet you." Because of my embarrassment, it seemed as though my hand weighed 100 pounds, but I did manage to respond. Backing away from the table to leave, she asked, "Do you boys need anything else?"

Hank started to open his big mouth, but before he could say a word, Grant and I kicked his shins at the same time. It happened to be exactly what was needed to release the tension of my embarrassment, but it was all I could do to keep from exploding into laughter. Hank grabbed the seat of his chair and sat straight up, stiff as a board. His eyes began to water, his cheeks turned blood red and puffed out like those of a constipated bullfrog. Grant, trying to keep a straight face, answered her, "No thanks. We're just fine." The minute Lee got out of sight and hearing distance, Grant and I burst into laughter.

Hank mocked Grant with, "No thanks, were jes' fine! Fine as hell! Wha'd you kick me fer?" Pulling up the legs of his jeans, he continued, "That hurt bad! Look here how hard you kicked me! I'm gonna have big bruises on my shins! And the one you kicked, Whitney....well, I jes' might have ta go ta the doctor!"

When we finally calmed our laughter, Grant told him, "Hank, if you would stop letting your big mouth overload your face, maybe we wouldn't have to go to such drastic measures to shut you up!"

It got really quiet for a moment. Then, Grant turned toward me, kind of looking sideways, and asked, "When *are* you going to invite that little girl out, Whitney?"

Hank, still rubbing his shins, angrily said, "It's 'cause he's a chicken! He ain't never been turned down before and he's afraid this little lady will be his first."

Grant, going along with Hanks evaluation asked, "Is that right?"

Hank, still feeling anger responded, "Yer damn tootin it's right!"

Those two were beginning to get on my number one nerve. Even though Hank gave a correct evaluation, I would never admit to either of them that they knew me like a book. I began to question their motives for pushing me into asking Lee for a date. "Are the two of you having a problem with my attraction to Lee? Or, maybe, you're jealous of my freedom to enjoy looking at a beautiful woman without a wife's watchful eyes."

Grant quickly spoke up, "Hell no Whitney! I'm glad for you to have the freedom to watch pretty ladies. I try to sneak a peek every once in a while myself, and you're right about having a wife to catch me. I have to be very careful not to let Ellen see me sneak that peak. If she did, you would hear it on the evening news, 'Irate wife Ellen Carrolton shoots husband after catching him watching pretty women.'"

Hank added, "Vickie would do somethin' a whole lot worse than that. She'd cut me off fer a year, if ya know what I mean!"

"Both of you are exaggerating," I responded.

Grant quickly spoke up, "You don't know our wives."

I teasingly replied, "I won't tell your wives about you sneaking peeks at pretty women if you two will cool it about me asking Lee out!"

Grant, indignantly responded with, "Damn, Whitney! That's bribery!"

I closed my eyes, shrugged my shoulders, and said, "That's the deal!"

Hank chimed in, "I'm gonna tell you this Mister Smart Ass. I ain't gonna share anything personal with you again."

"Is it a deal?" I asked.

They agreed, "It's a deal!" I didn't know how long the "deal" would last, but if it got them off my back about Lee for a few days, it was worth the whole conversation and Hank's name calling.

After Hank and Grant left for work, I remembered that I didn't have any patients scheduled until 1:00 p.m. As I sat at the table shuffling my coffee cup back and forth, Lee walked up behind me and asked, "Shannon would you like a refill of coffee?" I sat there like a dunce, staring down at the table and swallowed a big gulp. Stepping in front of me she asked again, "Would you like a warm up?" Lifting my eyebrows the thought occurred to me: *Sweetie, if I were any warmer, you would have to call the fire department.*

Then she slightly bent over, and her breasts barely peeked out of her bra. There is no man in the world who would not notice to some degree a picture like that staring him in the face. I swallowed another big gulp, and she asked a third time, "Shannon, do you want any more coffee?"

Not being able to say a word, until my eyes finally decided to look up, I stammered." Shshshure, the coffee is great here!" While she filled the coffee cup, my face burned like fire, and I thought: *Stupid, stupid. What a stupid thing to say!*

Adding to the drama of my embarrassment, Millie yelled from a nearby table, "It must be good coffee. You're in here every morning drinking it!" Her remark made me feel even more like a dunce.

It took several days for me to work up the courage to go into Millie's. Walking into the restaurant and making my way to the table, I prepared myself for the two "dreadful darlings." As I sat down, Hank spoke up first. "Hey there, Casanova. We were beginnin' ta thank you had been kidnapped by some aliens."

"Don't go there, guys," I said, and gave them a look that would make an iceberg want to wear a jacket. They glanced at one another and settled back in their chairs. Having no conversation for a few minutes, Grant shook his shoulders and made a "burrrr" sound as though my presence gave him a chill. It was easy to make up my mind that I didn't care what they did or said, as long as they left me out of it.

After a few minutes, Hank, angrily voiced an opinion. "Whitney, there ain't no use in you havin' yer bowels in an uproar, 'cause that ain't never fixed anything. Right, Grant?"

Of course, Grant agreed with him, saying, "You know something, sport? You have set yourself up since you were a teenager to be a woman charmer and flirt. Well, what do you know…you haven't measured up to your expectations as the 'world's greatest gift to women.' You need to get over yourself! Come on, Hank, I'm ready to leave!"

Pushing themselves away from the table, they stood up to leave. I asked them, "Please sit down. I'm sorry for being such a shithead. But, this is a hell of a place I am in and I don't know what to do, and it's driving me up a wall!"

"Man, we're yer friends," said Hank. "You don't act like a spoiled liddle kid jes because someone teases you a bit."

Grant spoke up. "Yeah, Whitney, we would never hurt you intentionally. There isn't a man in this world who hasn't embarrassed himself trying to impress a beautiful woman, but that does not give him the right to be rude to anyone, much less a friend."

I shook my head up and down and said, "You're right. I have got to figure out what to do. You two have never let me down when I really needed you, and again, I am sorry to be such a shithead."

Hank gave me a silly grin and responded, "Man, that's all right, like Grant said. We LOVE ya!"

"Okay, Hank!" I replied, looking around to see how many people heard him professing his love for me. I then whispered, "I am ever so grateful to have yours and Grant's love. Can we keep it to ourselves and not announce it to the world!? I have a love problem with a woman right now, and the gossip is already floating around like cotton balls on a lake. You know what? I'll handle OUR love problem next week. But, for now, let me see about solving the problem with Lee first!"

The three of us burst out laughing. Looking at them and shaking my head in disbelief of what had just been said, I asked, "What am I going to do with you two?"

Grant spoke up. "You know we can't be mad at you for very long. We are buddies."

Confirming his statement, I said, "Yes we are."

They stood up from their chairs to leave for work, each giving me a pat on the shoulder. Grant reassured me with, "Hang in there, buddy. You will know what to do. See you tomorrow." I knew those buddy feelings between us would be short lived, but if Grant and Hank should ever stop their teasing and hassling me, it would be a pretty boring world for me.

Several days had passed since "The Good Coffee" incident at Millie's and when I walked through the door of the restaurant, a reoccurring embarrassment engulfed my mind just knowing that Lee was there. I had two choices, either turn around and leave before anyone saw me, or face the demon of stupidity and recover my dignity. I chose to recover my dignity, and that gave me the courage to walk through the restaurant as though nothing had ever happened. I hurried to the table and sat down. Lee brought a cup of coffee over to me, and placing it on the table, she commented, "I hear you are a veterinarian."

Feeling my knees starting to shake, I leaned both of them against the left leg of the table and tightly anchored them with my right hand.

Deception or Perfection

The nervousness caused my stomach to give out a loud growl, but I managed to clear my throat and respond with a raspy yes.

She then asked, "Do you know of someone who might have a puppy to give away? I would like one if there are any available."

By then, I had calmed down somewhat and told her, "Yes, I do. Mrs. Myers's poodle had a litter a few days ago. Only, it will be about seven weeks before they are ready to leave their mother. Would you want to wait that long?"

She responded excitedly, "Oh, sure. There isn't any hurry. It will give me time to buy supplies for the little guy....or gal, whichever the case may be. Would you mind letting me know as soon possible when a puppy is available, so I can pick it up?"

"What would you prefer? A boy or a girl?" I asked.

"Either will be just fine."

A couple of months or so passed, and the usual schedule at the clinic kept me busy. I did, take time to go to Millie's every morning. I always tried in some way to say something to Lee that might get her to talk about herself. It wasn't easy because she always had her guard up and controlled our conversations, keeping them strictly impersonal. Sometimes, I could get by with teasing her. One day, I asked. "Is it true that redheads are hard to get along with?"

She came right back at me and said, "As long as you don't cross them."

Smiling my boyish grin I remarked, "Sure hope you will remind me if I should ever cross you!"

She chuckled and tilted her head saying, "Believe me, you won't need reminding."

As I watched her waiting on the other customers, the emotions inside me reached the pounding of my heart, and I knew, beyond a shadow of a doubt, I loved this woman.

Thursday morning arrived and after being up all night on two emergency calls, I almost didn't go to Millie's. I asked myself, "Are you going to feel any better if you have a short nap and wait until opening the clinic? Probably not." Needless to say, I decided against taking a nap.

I then drove over to the restaurant, determined to stay cool, calm and collected if Grant or Hank began to annoy me. And I thought: *This is a very good decision, Dr. Whitney!*

However, when I sat down at the table with them, and before I could say a word, Grant opened his big mouth. "Hey, bud. Are you still procrastinating asking Lee for a date? You have not gone out with anyone for weeks."

Hank, with a big grin on his face, had to add his two cents worth. "Ain't it gittin a little HARD ta sleep at night?"

That did it! Calm, cool, and collected went out the window. My blood pressure must have shot through the roof as I snapped at both of them. "You know, I had the fullest intensions of ignoring you guys, but this kind of teasing is totally unnecessary! I don't have to answer either one of your weak-minded moronic questions, but I will say this much. If...Lee goes out with me, you two will be the last to know! My feelings for her are real, and I DO NOT APPRECIATE your wisecrack, Hank, or you keeping tabs on my dating, Grant! It is none of your business as to who, what, when, where, or why I date anyone. Furthermore, if either of you is concerned about how much sleep I'm getting and how long it's been since I have had sex, why don't you tell me how long it's been since you had sex. Just maybe, you need to take care of your wives and stop sticking your nose into my affairs!"

Hank's eyes got as big as quarters, and he seemed upset. "Hold on there, pal! I didn't realize this kinda teasin' wud upset you like this. Didn't we talk about teasing the other day?"

I said to him, "Yeah, but the two of you should also realize that there are limits to certain subjects, and you just passed them up!"

"Hey, man, we're real sorry if we offended you," Hank responded nonchalantly.

"Yesiree, Bob," added Grant. "We are sorry, Whitney! What can we do to make up for being so insensitive?"

Shuffling around in my seat there was a long, dead silence and it was starting to get a bit uncomfortable for me. Then the two of them watching my discomfort, suddenly, burst into laughter. I looked down at the table, shaking my head and told them, "I surrender. You guys are impossible!"

Hank let out a big "Aww!" Then, he shoved his chair next to mine, giving me a big hug in front of God and everybody.

"Stop it! I yelled," trying to get away from him. "You are like a wad of gum stuck to the bottom of my shoe, Hank!" Swinging my arms, I yelled again, "Get out of here! Are you crazy!?" I thought: *Those are the two most harebrained people in the world, but I wouldn't trade their nonsense for all the gold in Alaska. In the past, if I needed a friend, both of them would drop everything to be at my side, or if something happened that shattered my life, I could always depend on their strength to help me to pick up the pieces and get through another day.*

After the two "wise crackers" left Millie's for work. I ordered breakfast, and when Lee brought it to me, she commented, "You are such good friends with Hank and Grant. How long have you known them?"

I answered her with a smile, "Since we were kids in kindergarten." As she set down my breakfast and handed me the silverware, I questioned her. "What about you Lee, do you have any kindergarten friends around?"

Responding cautiously, she answered with, "Define 'around.'" When justifying her answer she smiled and seemed a bit nervous as she continued with, "If President Clinton can evade a question by asking what the definition of 'is' is, surely it's okay for me to ask you to define 'around.' As Lee walked away from the table, I felt totally confused, but she did cleverly evade the question, leaving my mouth wide open.

To top it off, then she walked away and turned around with a helpless look in her eyes, saying, "Shannon, someday we can have a long talk, and I will answer any question you ask."

Even more confused, I had a fleeting thought: *Give it up, mister. No matter what you say or do, you are not going to penetrate that wall she has built around herself.* I had never walked away from a challenge before when I wanted to attract a beautiful woman's attention. However, I sensed that no one could get past Lee's obstinate attitude--not even me!

After drinking the last of my coffee, I reached around the back of the chair to grab my jacket. Before I had the chance to put it on,

Thelma Hoggan flopped herself down at the table. "Dr. Whitney," she asked with an annoying little girl's voice, "Could I impose on you to work in a ticket booth in the September Fall Festival?"

Astonished by her question, I sat for a few seconds not knowing what to say. It was the first time anyone asked me to do anything for the festival in years. I had always come up with good excuses that got me out of it. Finally, I answered, "It's kind of early to commit myself for a festival job, Mrs. Hoggan."

She eagerly responded, "My, my, Dr. Whitney, September will be here before you know it. I need to line up workers for the festival. Are you willing to work or not?"

Stammering, I told her, "Look, I would like to help out, but…"

She clapped her hands and patted my cheek saying, "Thank you, Dr. Whitney." Then, jumping out of the chair and backing away, she said, "You're so sweet. Thank you again." And before I could blink my eyes, she had disappeared.

Shaking my head, I asked myself, "What just happened?!" I quickly grabbed my jacket to leave, and stepping up to the register to pay Lee for my breakfast, Suanne McBride, an old high school lover, walked through the restaurant door. I had not seen her since the summer of our graduation. I turned my back to her, hoping that she didn't see me.

Chapter Three

Suanne and I began dating during our junior year of high school, but neither of us experienced a "good time" until our senior year. One night we had a discussion and decided to give "it" a try. Needless to say, we participated in lots of "good times" after that. We enjoyed the first one so much that we continued them in cars, trucks, barns, a boat on the Meramec River, and even under the Ellisville High School football field bleachers. As a matter of fact, the last one, before we left for college, took place right there under the bleachers, which happened to be our favorite hideaway to have a "good time." Everyone believed we were in love but that was the furthest thought from our minds. I wanted to be a Veterinarian and Suanne wanted to become a lawyer. Not long after our last "good time" we said our goodbyes, left Ellisville for college, and lost contact with one another.

As I stood at the register trying to be discreet, Suanne yelled from the entrance door, "Hey, Shannon!"

Thank goodness, the restaurant had emptied by this time. Out of the corner of my eye, I could see Suanne hurrying toward me with a big smile on her face. My thoughts were running wild. "Uh-oh," I mumbled to myself. "Okay, Whitney. It would be wise to handle this carefully."

"It's been a long time, Dr. Whitney! How have you been?"

"Well, hello to you, Suanne. How are you after all these years?"

She flashed a flirty grin and remarked, "Better now than five minutes ago! Damn, it's great seeing you! You're as handsome as you ever were." After I thanked her, she asked, "What are you doing tonight?"

Still standing at the register, I pulled a twenty dollar bill from my wallet and handed it to Lee to pay for my breakfast. I also noticed she was giving Suanne a dirty look. I wondered if it had anything to do with my old high school lover's interest in me. *Naw*, I thought. But... what if ...just maybe she could be a little jealous. After seeing Lee's reaction to Suanne, my acting kicked in, and I began to play a part. Too bad Lee was the only one to witness my acting skills. I could have won the local theater's "actor of the year" award for sure. Flashing Suanne a flirting, dimpled smile, I answered, "I'm doing whatever you're doing."

Suanne then stepped forward and pressed against me so close that her breasts indented my t-shirt. In a soft sexy tone, which I knew Lee could hear, she said, "How about meeting me at the football field tonight. Say... about seven?"

Laying my arm around her shoulders, and whispering in a sensual voice just loud enough that Lee could hear, I said, "Best invitation I've had all day."

"Well then, my friend, don't be late. We're going to have a good time," she promised. "See you tonight."

Watching Suanne walk out the door, I thought, *Wow, not only is she cute, her body has filled out in all the right places.* I began to fantasize about having sex with her under the football bleachers.

Suddenly, Lee interrupted my thoughts with, "Shannon, here is your change."

For some reason, I felt angry toward Lee and gave her a dirty look and said, "Keep the change, and you can consider it your tip."

Tears gathered in the corners of her eyes as she placed the bills and coins in the palm of my hand and softly replied, "No, but thanks anyway."

After realizing the type of behavior I had just exhibited, it hit me like a ton of bricks. There was absolutely no excuse for the way I treated her. I asked myself, "What the hell is wrong with you? You love this woman! How could you hurt her pride to the point of tears with such an insult?" And yet, I justified my behavior. There was no way I was going to let her sad eyes sway me from having sex with Suanne tonight. My insides have ached since the first moment Lee walked into Millie's, yet she wouldn't give me the time of the day. Besides, this might be exactly what I needed to get her out of my head.

While driving to the clinic, I noticed how warm the weather had become. Usually, Illinois is on the chilly side during the last part of April, but, the daytime temperature had been in the upper-seventies for over two weeks already. The grass had turned green and the trees were filled with new leaves. For the first time in months, I strolled into the clinic and worked all day with a smile on my face.

I closed the clinic at six and hurriedly showered, shaved, and dressed to meet Suanne. When I arrived, I found a discreet parking spot behind the school where a vehicle could not be seen from any direction. As I pulled into the space to park, I felt a twinge of guilt. After convincing myself it was all right to be there, I thought, *Why not enjoy myself tonight? I'm not committed to anyone. Not only that, I haven't had any sex since the first time I saw Lee at Millie's, and I am going to soak up every minute of it tonight.*

Taking a deep breath, I rolled the truck window down, and sat there for a few minutes, looking at the old surroundings. I then opened the glove compartment to take out a condom and stepped out of the truck. While closing the door Suanne's hands covered my eyes. "Guess who?" she asked. When I turned around, we were face to face, and I wrapped my arm around her waist with a rough, urgent tightness, pulling her into my chest. Reaching to the back of my head, she squeezed a handful of my hair; and slightly bit my lower lip with an intense kiss.

That's all it took to arouse my needs. I quickly reached through the window of the truck, grabbed a large Mexican blanket from the seat, and threw it over my shoulder. We ran across the parking lot and darted under the first open section of the football field bleachers. As we stood in front of each other, Suanne began unzipping my jeans with the eagerness of a child opening a long-awaited gift. She had on a low-cut, very accessible, short, tight dress of a jersey fabric. Reaching down to the hem of the dress, I pulled it up and over her head. Simultaneously, we removed the remaining clothing, and I put on the condom. Her breasts had developed considerably since we were in high school, and for a moment, I stared at them. When she saw my expression, she almost laughed.

I picked up the blanket from where it had fallen when we entered the bleachers. Holding it between Suanne and the plank wall, I hung it on the hooks that had been secretly positioned there years before. She backed against the wall and said breathlessly, "This is going to be a treat for me Shannon, so... let's do it the way we used to when we were in high school." And that's what we did. Stepping toward her, I wrapped her arms around my neck as she leaned against the blanket and we made the connection. A few moments later, our lustful needs were satisfied. After separating from each other, we looked at the blanket-covered wall and smiled. Even after all these years, we were still good together. I removed the condom and disposed of it where no one would find it.

After we got dressed, Suanne picked up her shoes and we walked around to the football field where we sat down on the bleachers. The slight illumination of two pole lights at either end of the field helped us feel comfortable sitting out in the open. Not saying a word, Suanne reached into her dress pocket, pulled out a pack of cigarettes, and offered one to me. "No thanks," I said. "I've never smoked and have no desire to start now." I watched her as she lit one up and drew in a deep breath. "When did you start smoking?" I asked. "You hated it when we were in high school."

After releasing the smoke, she answered, "Right after I left Ellisville. Really don't know why I started. Most everyone smoked at college. I guess part of it...I don't know... the loneliness would be so bad sometimes, I decided that it might help."

My response to her was, "I'm sure glad I never tried it."

Suanne gave a crooked smile and in a disgusted tone said, "It's a hideous, offensive, nasty, and dangerous addiction! I wish I had never bought that first pack. You know...that's all it takes to get hooked!"

I nodded my head in agreement, "Yeah, you're right about that." We didn't say anything more until she smudged out the cigarette in the grass. By then, my curiosity prompted me to ask, "What happened with your life after you left here?" She remained silent at first and then all at once she opened up.

"Well, the first four years I went to classes, studied, and worked as hard as I could to keep my G.P.A up so that I could get into law school. I didn't even date. I also realized that my expectations of men were very high, so I dismissed any thoughts of having a relationship at that time. My lovers were books, the library, and classrooms."

I responded with a question. "You did get into law school, didn't you?"

Smiling, Suanne said. "Yes, I did. It was during my second year that I met Eric. I fell in love the first time I laid eyes on him. People say that doesn't happen, but I know better." My thought was, *I know better too.*

"We hit it off on our first date, and after about six months he asked me to move in with him. We loved each other so much. We stayed together through law school, and afterwards, both of us found jobs. We worked for a year, and he asked me to marry him. The days I spent planning our wedding were some of the happiest days of my life."

"Where is Eric now?" I asked.

She reached into her pocket and took another cigarette out of the pack. After lighting it up, she continued, "One night Eric had to work very late. When he left his office building and headed to the nearby parking garage to get his car, he heard a woman screaming. Down an alley he saw two men dragging a girl by her hair. Dropping his briefcase, he ran to her rescue. When Eric tried to stop them, one of the hoodlums hit him several times in the head with an iron bar. When they threw the woman down and ran away, she managed to crawl to the street where someone saw her and called 911." Suanne paused for a moment and swallowed hard with frozen tears in her eyes. After taking a deep breath, she continued her story. "The doctor at the hospital told Eric's mom, Olivia, and me that if Eric lived he would be a vegetable. After three months in the hospital, he had to be placed in a nursing facility. His intellect is that of an eighteen-month-old child."

"What happened after that, Suanne?"

Taking one last drag off her cigarette and throwing it down she answered, "I buried myself in my work. Olivia would tell me, 'Honey, you have to go on with your life. You know that's what Eric would want you to do.' Two years later, I sent my resume to a firm in New Orleans. After only one interview, they called and made me an offer, which I accepted. And here I am. I wanted to visit my family before starting the new job."

"I'm sorry you had to go through so much sorrow alone. When I lost my family several years ago, I thought the excruciating agony would never go away."

She looked at me with compassion and said, "Mom called me right after it happened. I wanted to get in touch with you, but at the time, all I could focus on was my studies for the mid-term exams. Later, so many other concerns cropped up..."

I quickly butted into her explanation. "Hey, it's alright. I never took the time to ask about you, much less call. I understand."

Suanne started to cry. Pulling a handkerchief out of my back pocket and handed it to her, she blew her nose and wiped her eyes. Her chin quivered as she continued the–conversation. "Thank you for listening to me. This is the first time I have shared my grief about Eric with anyone. Also, I want you to know that you and he are the only men I have ever had sex with." She giggled like a shy little girl and teased, "You are a great lover Shannon, but Eric could have given you a few pointers for making out."

I put my hand over my heart and sadly vocalized, "Wow! You know how to hurt a man. ....Wait a minute! Don't you think you're a mite prejudiced! You were in love with the guy! And besides, considering my short notice, I think you owe me an apology!"

Suanne gave me a big grin and acknowledged, "I am still in love with Eric. I didn't realize how long it had been since the last time he and I made love. And coming back here, driving by the high school, I remembered making out with you under the bleachers. I have to be honest; it made me hot. My amorous needs burned inside me like a furnace." I turned my head side-ways with a frown, and almost laughed. She glared at me and blurted out "What!?"

Quoting her with a question, I asked, "'*Amorous* needs?' That is the most refined word I have ever heard for horny. "

She burst out laughing, saying, "I will never be able to use that word again with a straight face. Can't you see me questioning my opponent's client in court? Mrs. Smith, are you saying it was your amorous feelings that induced your sexual relationships with, not only your husband, but also...Mr. Chan, Mr. Clark, Mr. Julio, Mr. Jones, plus Miss Congeniality, your husband's secretary?"

"Yea," I said. "But I think you would definitely make your point." And both of us laughed.

When our laughter settled down, Suanne turned to me and asked. "It's been a while for you too, right?"

"Yes, it has!" I exclaimed.

"Why?" she asked. Trying to evade the question, I came back with a "Why what?"

She then specifically asked, "Why has it been so long since you,... had sex,...made out,... screwed,... had a fu....?

Personally, I don't like that four-letter word, so I quickly snapped, "The right opportunity has not presented itself, that's why!"

With a disbelieving glare, she leaned into my face and said, "Liar, liar, pants on fire!" Pausing for a moment, she then began peering at me with that "lawyer-look" and seemed to be trying to figure out the truth. Not saying a word, I nonchalantly reached down, pulled a blade of grass, and stared around at nothing. Suddenly, she inhaled a quick breath and put her hand over her mouth with eyes as big as quarters and blurted out, "Oh... my...God! You are in love!"

I didn't say a word.

Still staring at me, she continued her analysis. "I cannot believe it! Shannon Whitney is in love," she went on. "That's why you have been celibate for so long. You are waiting for her to respond to you."

I gave her a crooked smile saying, "Ok, Miss Suanne. You have solved the motive for Shannon Whitney's celibacy. And just so you know counselor, yours truly will not be guilty of that crime after tonight."

I smiled at her and she ruffled my hair with her hands and said, "I am sorry, my friend!" Putting a big grin on her face, she let out a "Wow! The realization just hit me how lucky I am, to be the one to receive all that pent up sexual hunger you had."

"I could have sworn you were pretty hungry yourself."

Suanne got a serious look on her face and said, "I can see how you are hurting, Shannon. And if I wasn't still in love with Eric, plus a dedicated career woman, I would stay here and make it my full time job to take you away from her! At least seeing you in this state of mind makes it easier for me to admit that we are at the football field for the same reasons."

"Are you saying my needs were...amorous ones?" I asked.

She responded, "Yes indeed, you heard me right!"

All at once, Suanne jumped up from the bleachers and sat down on the grass in front of me. Reaching for the zipper on my jeans, she asked, "How about one for the road?"

Quickly grabbing her hands, I told her, "I don't have another condom."

Reaching into her other dress pocket, she pulled one out and handed it to me, remarking "Remember...I'm like a Boy Scout...always prepared."

She unhooked my belt buckle and pulled the jeans past my hips. She began kissing my belly, and touching me in places that would make any man respond to her invitation. We took off our underclothes, and I hurriedly put on the condom as Suanne threw the blanket across the grass. Our needs were ablaze as I lifted her up by the buttocks, and we connected once again.

After completing the "one for the road," we dressed and I noticed the air had become a bit chilly. Grabbing the corner of the blanket and draping it around Suanne shoulders, She spoke up saying, "This has been the greatest night since Eric..." Not finishing her sentence, she glanced at her watch, and informed me, "I have to catch a plane in three hours for New Orleans. I am starting my job the day after tomorrow."

I didn't know how to respond as she stood up and she softly said, "I will remember this night, my friend, for the rest of my life. You have given me a reminder of how it feels to have a man's arms around me again. Perhaps another Eric will come into my life someday. But, until then, will you promise me something?"

"If I possibly can," I answered.

"If you are single when I come back here, and if I should come down with a chronic amorous attack, will you be my doctor and treat the symptoms?" Suanne then gave me a childlike look, and I laughed heartily. Smiling really big, she bragged, "See, I can still make you laugh even when you are sad."

"Well, Miss McBride. It would be my pleasure to treat your amorous symptoms anytime you may have them."

We stood there for a few seconds. Finally, Suanne took a deep breath, kissed me on the cheek and said, "Thank you, my friend."

"You are very welcome," I said. "And I thank you."

I put my arm around her shoulder and she began to tear up. Walking away from my embrace with her shoes in hand, pausing, she turned around and waved goodbye. After blowing me a kiss, she disappeared into the darkness.

Standing there in the night chill, I recognized a feeling I had after the funeral of my family…total aloneness. Staring at their graves that day, I had made a conscious decision that I was not going to allow myself to care deeply for anyone for the rest of my life, and I didn't until Lee came along. But I learned something very important about myself after spending the evening with Suanne. I discovered that all the sex in the world cannot fill the emptiness of a heart that had forgotten how to make room for a faithful and joyful love.

After leaving the football field, my head began to spin. When turning into my driveway, apprehension and guilt came over me for having sex with Suanne. Strange thoughts began to saturate my mind. What was happening to me? This was irrational. Did it make me a bad person for wanting to get it on with a woman when the occasion arose? If marriage never came into my life, were these feelings going to crop up again after making out with a woman? Knowing that giving up sex would make me less of a man, I thought, *God help me! A man needs sex! How do I know for sure what's right or wrong regarding casual sex?* My mind was in turmoil.

By the time I parked and turned off the truck, I felt emotionally exhausted and on the brink of tears. Overwhelming fear swept over me, and I felt unable to get out of the truck. Then, something unexpected happened. There was a voice in my mind and it said "Son, don't feel guilty for any of yesterday's happenings. You have been awakened to the truthfulness of loving someone unconditionally. Your encounters with women in the past were nothing more than the gratification of releasing the urge for sex. Now, you love a woman from the depth of your soul. Now, you know how beautiful it would be to enter into the divine reason for sex between a man and a woman." I knew that the voice inside of me belonged to my mom.

A peaceful feeling came over me as I stepped out of the truck.

Entering the house, I undressed and went straight to bed. Then, laying my head on the pillow, a soothing thought entered my mind. *Shannon, everything is going to be all right.*

When I woke the next morning, the first thing that caught my eye was a sparrow building her nest in a tree next to my bedroom window. It seemed to be a deed of love with no thought of any return for her labor. I watched her carefully flutter around a chosen spot and place strings of grass and twigs to build a secure nest for the next generation. Perhaps, this little sparrow was giving me a good lesson—that patience and love can be my strings and twigs to build a future with Lee. Feeling good with that revelation, I got out of bed, went through my morning routine, and headed for Millie's.

By the time I arrived at the restaurant, Hank and Grant were on their second cup of coffee. I approached the table and sat down. Grant immediately said to me, "You are looking mighty rested, Whitney. You must have had a good night."

Responding to his observation, I replied, "Sure did." By that time, Lee had brought me a cup of coffee, put it down on the table, and quickly walked away. Watching her, my heart sank to my belly button. But, at the same time, I said, "Everything is gonna be all right."

Hank, noticing Lee's rapid retreat to the opposite side of the restaurant, remarked, "She sure's ta hell got outta here real fast!" Then he got a big grin on his face and asked, "By the way, Shannon Boy, did Suanne find you yesterday? Didja have a real 'good time'?"

Not giving him the information he wanted to hear, I answered with a big smile saying, "It's none of your business."

By then, Grant couldn't stand it any longer. Looking disappointed, he tried to coax me into telling them about last evening with Suanne. "Aw, come on Whitney. Tell us what happened last night! Did you and Suanne…get it on or not!?"

"It's none of your business, Grant," I snapped. "How many times do you two have to be told? It's none of your business!"

Hank, not being able to stand my reluctance to share what had happened between Suanne and me, squirmed in his chair. He leaned forward over the table and spoke with an annoyed voice. "You ain't gonna tell us a damn thang, are ya? It wuz you and Suanne makin' out that kept the school gossip goin' ya know. Not only that, when Suanne told a bunch of her friends about how much fun you an' her had, it opened up a new idea fur the girls ta be more agreeable with their boyfriends. You shore never kept nothin' quiet about you and Suanne when you were in high school."

Being frank and with serious look on my face, I teasingly explained to him. "Hank, we are not in high school. Surely, you understand. As we mature, or maybe a better phrase, as some of us mature, we shouldn't think of casual sex as a conquest. We should be glad that there are women who come into our lives who need release from tension just as badly as us. We should always think of them as giving, not as conquests. Do you understand what I am saying?"

Hank sat for a few seconds and stared at me. Then, he shook his head, leaned back in his chair and said, "You're so full of bullshit, Whitney, I can smell your breath frum here! And that is the most ridiculous thing you have ever said!"

Laughing, I told him, "Well, Hank, you're as smart as I knew you were. So....why don't you cool it with the questions!"

Under his breath Hank muttered, "Jes like a doctor…Gives his patients double-talk when he don't wanna answer their question. I jes wanted ta know if you and Suanne renewed some old memories." With folded arms across my chest, a big smile on my face, and trying to keep from laughing I said to him, "Why, Hank, you're a pervert! Ask Suanne if you want to know what happened between the two of us." I have to say, it gave me satisfaction to be able to stop Hank and Grant with their prying questions.

Chapter Four

An hour had passed since Grant and Hank's inquisition about my evening with Suanne. After glancing at my watch, I realized the clinic had to be opened in a short time. As I made a move to leave, Grant asked, "Hey man, have you ever been on a gambling boat?"

Shaking my head, I answered, "Nope...never have. Why do you ask?"

"Well, because Hank, Vickie, Ellen, and I are planning on going to a gambling boat near St. Louis Saturday night, and we were wondering if you would like to ride along with us."

"Sounds good to me,"

"Then, we'll pick you up Saturday evening at 5:30,"

Hank grinned and added, "Tell ya what, Whitney. Stick with me, and I'll show ya how ta win some money."

Grant asked quickly, "And how much money did you *lose* the last time we went to the casino, Hank?"

Becoming a bit indignant, Hank replied, "I am here ta tell ya, Mister Butt Fink, the reason I lost that150.00 is because the moon happened ta be full! If ida known it wuz gonna be a full moon, you wouldn'a seen me at that boat!"

Grant gave Hank an "Oh, Brother" look and reassured me, "Don't depend on either of us showing you the ropes. My losses were230.00 the same night. By the way, it would be all right to invite the pretty little lady who just waited on us if you want to."

It was obvious that Grant's invitation was an excuse for me to ask Lee out, and if she turned me down, it would save me embarrassment. Knowing my friends, they probably formulated the whole trip just for that reason. I wondered about the best way to approach her. A plan began to manifest in my mind.

I closed the clinic early that day and went straight over to Millie's to hang out and get up enough nerve to ask Lee out. I took a seat at the counter and felt as nervous as a cat when I ordered a glass of iced tea.

After bringing me the tea, Lee asked, "What are you doing here this early in the afternoon?"

Looking down at the table and trying to be calm, I whispered, "I'm here to talk to you." When I didn't get a response, I looked up to see that Lee had not waited for my answer. She had already walked away and taken off her apron to leave work for the day. As she headed to the coat rack to get her sweater, I immediately got up from the counter, walked over to the door, and opened it for her.

Giving me a strange glance, Lee said, "Thank you" and went down the steps toward the parking lot, with me following closely. Realizing I was behind her, she stopped abruptly and asked, "Shannon, are you following me?"

Nervously, I nodded my head and stammered in a voice that seemed an octave higher than my own, "Y-y-y yes! Have you ever been to a casino? I-I-I…if you haven't…the…uh… Hank, Grant, and their wives invited me to go with them Saturday night and wondered if you would like to ride along with us? We would leave Saturday afternoon somewhere between five-thirty or six!"

While unchaining her bike from a telephone pole, Lee accepted my invitation. "Sure, that sounds like fun," But you have got to understand something, Shannon. I am not your date. We're just friends, okay?"

Taking a deep breath and trying to stop my heart from beating so fast, I reassured her. "Right. It won't be a date. We'll go just as friends. By the way, Grant has a van, and we can all ride together. Would you like for him to pick you up at your place?"

"Oh, no! No," she replied. "Millie doesn't close until seven. I'll bring a change of clothes to work that morning, and you guys can pick me up there."

With my excitement mounting higher, I stepped away from her bike and fell backwards into a shrub. Lee acted as though she didn't notice. Quickly regaining my composure, I responded, "That's great! It's, it's really great! I'll see you then! No, what I-I meant to say is tomorrow…..at Millie's….for breakfast is when I'll see you!"

As she rode off on her bike, she turned her head slightly toward me and smiled as she yelled, "See you in the morning!" After watching her go out of sight, I held my left arm up and with the other in front of my chest (as though there was a partner in my arms,) began dancing around yelling, "Yes! Yes! Yes! Thank you, God!"

Finally, Saturday evening arrived. When Grant pulled into the driveway, all I had to do was grab my jacket and head out the door. Climbing into the van, I greeted everyone with a hello. Grant then drove to Millie's and parked the van in front of the restaurant. When Lee came out of the door and walked toward us, Vickie asked, "Is that Lee?"

Hank, Grant, and I chimed, "Yes!" all at the same time.

Ellen exclaimed, "Wow! She sure is pretty!"

Sitting in the back seat, everyone was visible to me, and I noticed Hank watching Lee as she approached the van. In a shrill voice, Vickie asked him, "What are you staring at!? And why haven't you ever mentioned anything about Millie's new waitress being so beautiful?"

Hank knew he had just been caught staring at a pretty woman, and he responded quickly, "Hell, Vickie, she ain't new anymore!" Before Vickie could ask another question, Grant jumped out of the van, ran around to the passenger side, and opened the door for Lee. She squirmed her way to the far back seat and sat down beside me. As we pulled out onto the highway, Grant and Hank introduced their wives to Lee, and before we had traveled five miles, the three girls were talking up a storm. Listening to them, a person would have thought they had known each other for years.

When we arrived at the casino, Grant drove the van up to the entrance and we were met by a vale. As we walked through the doors of the casino, we were bombarded by the clinking, clacking, and musical sounds of slot machines. We broke off into couples, agreed to meet back at the entrance around 9:00, and went our separate ways. Grant and Ellen went to the south of the casino. Hank and Vickie took off toward the escalator that went to the second floor. At first, Lee and I just stood there, feeling a little awkward.

"What would you like to do?" I asked. "I've never been to a casino before. Have you? Oh, I'm sorry. You've already been asked that question the other day in the parking lot at Millie's." I felt embarrassment with the questions I had just asked but, for some reason, it struck my funny bone, and I began to giggle.

Lee looked offended and asked indignantly, "What are you laughing at?"

"Nothing...honest...It's just that I am so damned nervous, I'm about to pee in my jeans!"

At first she stared at me in shock. Then, she began laughing and with a snicker asked, "Are you saying that.....little ole me makes you nervous"?

Nodding my head, I replied, "As hell!"

With an astonished expression on her face, she questioned, "Should I be flattered

or insulted "?

"Please believe me; it is *not* an insult!"

Then, with a big smile on her face, Lee took my hand, and with excitement in her voice she instructed me, "Let's go this way! Just follow me!" My thinking was, *Baby, I would follow you to the ends of the earth!*

The first place she led me was to the men's restroom. When I returned from relieving myself, she grabbed my hand again. We stopped a server and placed a drink order. Lee ordered a pink lady, and I ordered bourbon on the rocks. When our drinks were delivered, we noticed a clown behind a table with three empty nut shells on it. Lee watched with intensity as the clown placed a folded 100.00 bill under one of the nut shells. We moved closer to the table as a crowd gathered behind us. The clown pointed to Lee and then to the shells as if to say, "Come play my game." She stepped closer to the table, and I handed the clown a 5.00 bill. According to the sign next to him, that was the price for a person to play the game. He began to move the shells slowly, and all at once, his movements were unbelievably fast. Then, he stopped his illusionist activity and looked at Lee. She stood there, trying to figure out which nut shell contained the 100.00 bill. Starting to point to one, she shook her head "no" and jerked her hand back. Finally, she settled for the far left shell. Slowly, the clown lifted it, and no 100.00 bill could be seen. Looking at Lee with a sad face, the clown shrugged his shoulders as if to say, "Sorry."

Lee took my hand again, and we walked to the far side of the casino where she saw a counter filled with bowls of gourmet fruit, chips and nuts. There was just about every kind a person could imagine. She bought what the sales lady called the "Dukes Mixture." Sitting down at a nearby table, Lee ordered another pink lady and bourbon on the rocks for me. When the server brought our drinks, we gulped them down and gorged on the Dukes Mixture. After eating our fill, Lee mischievously squinted her eyes and with a big smile announced, "We're going to win some money!"

Reluctantly, I shook my head and said, "Don't think so!"

With a determined look on her face, she assured me, "Oh, yes, we are!"

I smiled at her and asked, "What do you want to bet that we don't win back our investment?"

She gave me a stare and said, "I bet ,...that if we cover our losses, you are to serve coffee at Millie's, wearing my apron for at least three days in a row and for five minutes each day."

"Ok," I said. "And if we don't cover our losses, what will be my pay for winning?"

Going into deep thought again, she came up with, "How about,.... me giving you a grand curtsey for three days in a row every time I serve your first cup of coffee."

After I asked about the rules, she began to explain, "We start out with the same amount of money, and we put our winnings into the cup with our investment. After the hour is over, we count what is in both cups. If we have less than our original investment, you win the bet. But, if there is more money or the same as our investment, I win the bet. Shall we shake hands to seal the agreement?"

After the hand shake, we went to a cashier cubical where we bought four rolls of nickels, and the game began. I put nickels into the slot of my machine and was hitting a good run. Noticing that Lee was also filling her cup with winnings, I had to come up with another strategy. When the drink server showed up at my machine for a drink order, I slipped a roll of nickels under the tab as a tip for the lady. Now some people call that cheating, but my definition is strategy.

In less than thirty minutes, my nickels were gone. And two minutes before the hour ended, Lee needed twenty cents for us to break even. She gave me another hand shake and said, "Congratulations." Even

Deception or Perfection

though technically my strategy was cheating, there came a sigh of relief, knowing I had narrowly escaped the "dreaded apron wearing and coffee serving."

We played on our own for a while, and after losing forty dollars, it occurred to me that the machine I used had a never ending appetite. By then, it was time to meet with our friends. Lee came over to me, and as we walked away to meet the gang, I could have sworn the slot machine let out a satisfying burp.

No one seemed to have much to talk about on the way back to Ellisville except for a couple of complaints from Grant and Hank about losing money. I reminded them, "Hey, guys, you should know the casinos are going to win. The only way I can justify losing 40.00 is to consider it as entertainment."

Ellen and Vickie looked at each other, and Vickie asked, "Forty dollars is all you lost?"

Reluctantly, I answered, "Yea, that's how much the damn machine ate. Why do you ask?"

Vickie shouted demandingly at Hank, "Tell them how much you lost, Mister Know-It-All!" He wouldn't say a word.

Then Ellen spoke up. "Tell them about your gambling adventure, Grant." Grant just glared out the windshield, not blinking an eye.

Nearing Ellisville, the tension cooled down. I ever so slightly stretched out my arm over the back of Lee's seat. She gave me the sweetest smile and politely removed my arm. I thought, "Oh, no, Whitney! You have goofed up!" However, she removed it with a smile, and that did give me some comfort.

Lee spoke up. "Grant, would you mind driving over to Millie's house? She asked me to stay with her tonight."

"Sure will."

As Grant pulled up in front of Millie's home, Lee told everyone good night. She left her seat to step out of the van, and I leaned forward to get up to walk her to the steps of the porch, but she turned around, smiling, and said, "No, no, no, I'm a big girl. It's quite all right for you to sit right here."

I sat back into my seat feeling a bit disappointed, but I watched Lee until she entered the door of the house. As Grant drove away to take me to my place, Ellen remarked, "Shannon, Lee is a sweetie. Not only that, she is intelligent and beautiful."

Vickie also gave her opinion about Lee. "I agree with Ellen. She has a great personality; and her character shows honesty and sincerity. Compared to all the other women you have brought around us, she is a keeper, and you need to hang onto her, Shannon!"

I reminded them, "It takes two to tango. I'm ready to dance, but she has to accept my invitation."

Grant dropped me off at my place a bit after 10:00 P.M. Knowing it would be a while before I'd be able to sleep, I decided to go to the office and straighten some of my files. Trying to concentrate on the work became difficult because I kept reliving the evening over and over in my head. Every glimpse of Lee made me more aware of her inner beauty. I saw an openness that she had never revealed before tonight. In my thoughts, I prayed, "God, you know how much I love her. Please help her to love me back!"

As I put away the last file, the phone rang. *Don't let this be an emergency call*, I thought. It was Mrs. Myers.

"Dr. Whitney, do you still want a puppy?" she asked. "Cheree has weaned her litter, and we have only two left. If you want one, you need to pick it up tonight."

"Ok, Mrs. Myers," I said. "I'll be right there." After locking the clinic, I got into the truck and drove over to the Myers's home as quickly as possible. As I entered through the gate of their fenced-in back yard, two puppies ran over to me. One was a cute male with a curious personality and the appearance of a blonde fuzz ball. He walked around my shoes, sniffing and looking up as if to ask, "Who are you?" That's all it took to make my choice.

Returning home, I realized that Lee's days off were Sundays and Mondays. Also, there was no way to get in touch with her. After placing the pup in a small kennel, my next move was to go to bed.

Waking up Sunday morning and still debating what to do about the puppy, I made the decision to surprise Lee by taking it to her. Driving down the lane to the mobile home, my imagination reflected a picture of Lee running toward me with an "open arms" greeting.

After parking beside the porch of the mobile home, I took the puppy from the back seat and walked up the steps to the entrance. I stood on the porch, held the dog with one hand, and knocked on the door with the other. Glancing in a window, I noticed a shadow of someone darting into the hallway. A woman's voice on the other side asked, "Who's there?"

"I'm Shannon Whitney."

The voice didn't belong to Lee, but the woman nervously yelled, "What do you want?"

Trying to get the lady to open the door, I told her, "Look, lady, I brought Lee a puppy that she asked about a while back. He is a baby, and it would be dangerous to leave him out here on the porch by himself. Something could happen to him!"

She slowly made a small gap in the door and with hesitation, opened it enough that I could see her. Much to my surprise, she was a very pretty black lady and appeared to be about Lee's age.

I asked, "Is this where Cheryl Lee Canton lives?"

Glancing over toward the hallway, she yelled, "Lee, there is somebody out here who says he has a puppy for you!"

A minute later, Lee stepped out onto the porch, closed the door behind her and with a shocked look on her face asked, "What are you doing here?!" I told her the whole story from Mrs. Myers' phone call to my standing on her porch with the puppy. All at once, she became very angry, and I backed away as she made a step toward me. With a glare in her eyes, she said, "I told you when the puppy was ready to let me know, and I would pick it up!"

Still holding the pup and sheepishly responding in the manner of a question, I answered, "I'm letting you know....now?"

Lee grabbed the pup out of my arm and asked, "By the way, how did you find me?" I tried to stall for time to come up with an answer while she stood there with an impatient look. Suddenly, she butted into my thoughts harshly, yelling, "Well, answer me! How did you know where I lived?"

Looking down at her, I felt perspiration popping out on my forehead, and burning heat in my face. In the excitement of having an excuse to drive out to her place, my brain completely forgot about my following her home from Millie's. My first thoughts were to make excuses, but knowing that it just wouldn't work, I blurted out the truth!

"I followed you home the day you applied for a job at Millie's."

While standing and watching her reaction to the confession, a cold chill began to run down my spine, and Lee's face turned blood red as she gasped a dismayed breath. And her eyes looked like those of a dragon ready to shoot fire out of its nose!

"What gives you the right to be so grossly insensitive that you come here...uninvited! Just because you're a 'somebody' in Ellisville, doesn't mean you're above rudeness. I don't know if you realize it or not, but there are people who get arrested for doing what you have done. It's called stalking!" I butted in a couple of times to try and calm her down. She came toward me like a hell cat, and her anger increased even more as she continued. "I'll tell you what Mr., Mr., Dr.! Here is the deal...*do not ever*, set foot on this property again, and I won't have you arrested for stalking! I nodded and slowly stepped backwards away from a beautiful woman who had just turned into a verbal terrorist before my very eyes. Forgetting how close the steps were behind me, I lost my balance and tumbled to the ground. Lee came over to the steps and looking down at me, she asked in an annoyed tone, "Are you hurt?"

Mumbling a "no" and managing to stay upright, I then hobbled to the truck, turned the ignition with the key, and took off like a bird with his tail feathers on fire. On the way home, the thoughts shuffled in my mind. "Sure hope she's in a better mood Tuesday morning. She may be beautiful, but that temper is one from hell. All I wanted was to find out where she lived."

The next morning, which was Monday, I went into Millie's and sat down at a table with Grant and Hank, but couldn't say a word to either of them about the misunderstanding at Lee's the day before. However, both of them knew that my mood wasn't in any place for idle chit-chat. Thank goodness, they were sensitive for once. Finally, the time came to leave the restaurant for work. Knowing my schedule would be a short one gave me comfort. Later, it turned out to be a blessing because by mid-afternoon, fatigue began to hit me hard.

After closing the clinic early and going into the house, I felt a letdown sensation in my gut. I glanced around, hoping to find

Deception or Perfection

something that would terminate my emptiness, but there wasn't anything in sight that could accomplish such a goal. Feeling exhausted, and slumping down on the couch, I went to sleep. Waking up an hour or so later and realizing how late it was, I jumped up from the couch and quickly drove over to Millie's for a sandwich and fries. After hurrying into the restaurant, I sat down on a stool at the counter and placed an order to go. Millie gazed at me intently then remarked, "You don't look so good, Doc. Are you sick?"

Hardly looking at her, I impatiently answered, "No, Millie, I'm just fine."

Making a huffy sound under her breath, she sarcastically said, "Oh sure, frustrated, insecure, negative and, evasive. Of course, you are just *fine*! But you sure look to me like you're coming down with something!"

Leaving the restaurant with my food, I drove over to the city park. After sitting down on the grass and taking the sandwich out of the sack, I noticed that the sky, above the sunset had an eerie orange color. In Illinois, when you see an orange-colored sky, it usually means there is a major storm somewhere. I hoped it wasn't as major as the one in the pit of my stomach. Taking a sip of Cola and leaning back on my elbow, I relived the Sunday incident with Lee. Not taking any responsibility for my part in making her angry, my thought was, "Well, one thing about it, there is no need to daydream about her going out with me someday. She can have all the privacy she wants! Anyway, who gives a care?" Even though I didn't believe those thoughts in my subconscious mind, it helped me to have a good night's sleep.

When Tuesday morning came, and going over to Millie's, I sat down with Hank and Grant, not noticing Lee until she walked to the table with three cups and a pot of coffee. She had a smile on her face as she sweetly spoke to Grant and Hank and chatted with them while she sat their cups down. After serving their coffee, she rounded the table to my side and sat the last cup very close to edge of the table, right in front of me. When she poured my coffee, it gushed out of the pot and doused my jeans from the belt to the crotch. I stared down at the spill with a surprised glance then raised my head as she put her fingers up to her mouth and uttered "Oops, I missed!" Then, like a graceful princess, she gave me a curtsey and walked away, leaving the empty cup on the table.

Hank and Grant started laughing like a couple of hyenas in heat. Hank managed between holding his breath to keep from laughing to ask in an astonished tone, "*What* have you done to that little woman?! She wouldn't do anything like that if you ain't doin' somethin' to her!"

Then, Grant took up where Hank left off. "Yea, Whitney. What have you done to her?" By then, everyone in the restaurant was staring at us, and I felt like disappearing.

Millie came over to the table, threw a towel at me, and remarked, "Wow, Doc. She is pee-owed at you! What did you do to her?!"

That was the straw that broke the camel's back. Not caring what anyone thought, I loudly said, "Why is everyone assuming that I did something to her?"

Hank spoke up with a self-righteous attitude. "Because a sweet little thing like Lee ain't gonna deliberately spill coffee on a person unless they did somethin' terrible to her!"

Getting a mite pissed-off and thinking *you should have seen her last Sunday*, I began to defend myself. "I'm going to tell all of you what you can do with your opinions, and I'll clean up my language because there are ladies within hearing range. Why don't you ask the 'sweet little thing' the reason she spilled coffee all over me?! I'll have all three of you know that I went *out of my way, at eleven o'clock at night* to pick up a puppy for her…that *she* asked for! And do you think she gave me a 'thanks?' No! What she gave me was a chewing out, a sprained ankle, and a gallon of Carlos's Best Columbian Coffee dumped on me from the bottom of my shirt to the crotch of my jeans! Also, it will be a frickin' cold day in hell before *'that little lady'* ever…" Stopping in mid-sentence, I noticed Lee across the restaurant talking and smiling with a couple of kids who were sitting at a table with their parents. It suddenly occurred to me that I should stop making excuses and be honest with myself. I did in fact follow her home to find out where she lived, which could definitely be considered stalking. I deserved everything from the chewing out to her dousing my lap with coffee.

I was deep in thought feeling remorse over my blunder with Lee when Millie stepped up to the table and said, "Before what?"

I gave her a puzzled look, and she continued her inquiry. "It will be a fricken' cold day in July before what?"

All three of them were staring at me as though a crime had been committed. (Their stares were accurately defined because I did a terrible thing following Lee home from Millie's that day.) Knowing they were waiting for me to fill in the blank, I finally made a stammering attempt and came up with, "A-a, before she will ever serve me another cup of coffee."

Millie huffed under her breath and went back into the kitchen. Suddenly, Grant and Hank had chores to do before going to work. I just sat at the table, looked down at the empty cup, and then tried to soak up some of the drenched mess on my clothes with the greasy towel that Millie had thrown into my lap and thought to myself, "Well, Whitney, that's, that! There is nothing you can do or say to make up for your inexcusable, deranged behavior that you have displayed toward Lee."

Feeling like a useless piece of dog crap and pushing my chair away from the table to leave, I looked up, and there stood Lee. She pointed to the chair across from me and asked, "Is it all right for me to sit down?" Blinking my eyes in shock and swallowing a big gulp, I jumped up and pulled the chair out for her, then swiftly settled back down into my chair.

After pausing for a few seconds, she took a deep breath and with sincerity said, "First of all, I want to apologize for spilling coffee on you. But everything that was said to you Sunday, well, you deserved that.

"Lee, please accept my apology. You had every right to say those things to me, and if there is anything that can be done to make it up to you, just name it. There is no reason for you to accept any apology from me and certainly no excuses. It would be understandable if you hated me! Again, I am so sorry for everything!"

She smiled and touched my arm saying, "Shannon, I don't hate you, and I never could. You are not the only one who has done some very stupid things. There are a few episodes in my life that I wish would have been done differently. And believe me, they were not actions to be proud of, but you can do me a favor."

"Tell me what you need! Anything, just ask!"

"Okay, please don't tell anyone where I live.

"Lee, if anybody finds out, it will not be from me! And again, I apologize."

She butted in with a smile and responded with, "Apology accepted. Now, there is something that you need to be told. This morning, before you came into the restaurant, my anger had not gone away, and I spouted off to Millie about you invading my privacy. That's all I said to her. Then, Millie told Grant and Hank that you had hurt my feelings real bad. Well....the two of them were very vocal about the whole thing, and agreed that you should not get by with hurting my feelings. So they suggested spilling coffee in your lap and that's all it took for me to run with the idea. I asked Millie to put some ice in the pot of coffee, and you know the rest. Don't get mad at Grant and Hank. It was a surprise to them as well as it was to you. They didn't dream I could do such a thing, but I did. And I'm the one who should take responsibility for the whole incident. I'm sorry, Shannon."

Sitting and blinking my eyes in disbelief and in total shock, it felt as though my mouth was taped shut as Lee touched my arm and asked, "Do you accept my apology, Shannon?"

"Absolutely! But you don't owe me an apology. As far as I'm concerned, you don't owe me anything." When Lee left the table, a big sigh of relief emerged from the depth of my stomach. What Grant and Hank didn't realize was that they did me the biggest favor of their lives. Lee's confession about their contribution in her drenching my jeans relieved me from guilt, and I could be at ease with her again.

The next day after the "Big Spill," I joined Hank and Grant at our usual table. Lee came over with a pot of coffee in one hand and cups in the other. Pretending to be scared of her, I jumped up and said, "Please be careful with that pot of coffee, Miss Lee!" She smiled and set all the cups in their places. Then picking mine back up, she carefully filled it and put it down in a safe spot toward the center of the table. After giving Hank and Grant their coffee, she turned to leave. All at once I cleared my throat loudly, and Lee immediately stopped and turned around. When she looked at me, I asked. "Lee, I'm sorry to bother you, but...didn't you forget something? You remember? Ch-ching!?"

She muttered under her breath "Oh, yeah!" She sat the pot on a table next to her and walked around in front of me where I had a clear view. Stretching her arm out to one side, Lee bowed her head to the waist and, with one bent knee, gave the most beautiful curtsey I had ever seen.

Grant and Hank sat staring at me with their mouths wide open. Hank blurted out, "What ta hell wuz that all about!? She wanted ta kill ya yesterdee. Taday she's bowin' to you!"

Smiling, I corrected him, "That wasn't a bow. It is called a curtsey."

Hank, in an extremely arrogant tone, said, "Aw, shit, Whitney. Bow, curtsey, it's the same thang. Jes' tell me why ta hell she wuz doin' it!?"

"If you want to know, ask Lee,"

Not being happy with my answer, Grant responded, "Damn, Whitney, you sure like having your secrets and keeping me and Hank in the dark, don't you?!"

I leaned my chair back, rocking a bit, with my arms folded against my chest and smugly asked, "Oh! You don't mean like....some people make plans and encourage others to dump coffee on some individual... isn't a kind of... "keeping dark secrets?!" Neither of them said a word. Suddenly, it seemed as though they had important things to do, and both of them left the restaurant as quickly as they could.

Lee came back to pour me another cup of coffee. She backed away to give me a curtsey and I stopped her. "Can you sit down at the table for a little while?"

She sat down and asked, "What's on your mind?"

Smiling my boyish grin, I told her, "You don't have to curtsey to me anymore."

"Oh, but I want to," she responded. "When a person makes a bet, they should live up to it. Besides, did you notice Grant's and Hank's faces after my curtsey? That was awesome!"

Both of us chuckled, and I remarked. "Yeah, and they have no idea what it's about."

Lee got an impish expression on her face and suggested, "Don't tell them. It will be fun to watch their faces each time I give you a curtsey. Try to drink at least two cups of coffee the next couple of days."

We shook our heads in agreement, and I said, "You are right! That is going to be fun!" Lee started to get up to leave the table. I quickly stopped her and asked, "Lee, are you comfortable enough to share with me why you don't want anyone to know where you live?" Her eyes widened, and she had a frightened, serious look on her face when she abruptly answered, "*No*, Shannon!" The tone in her voice became sad. "I can't. Please don't ask me again!"

During the following weeks that passed after the "Big Spill," as hard as I tried, there were no responses from Lee that gave me an opportunity to ask her out. She always seemed to be friendly enough, but would only let me get just a little close to her, and then the walls would go up. I thought, *It's okay, pretty lass. Patience is one of my virtues. Especially when I know something is worth waiting for. So, build all the walls you want, because someday, you're going to run out of brick and mortar, and I am going to be there to fill in the gap.*

Chapter Five

After waking early Monday morning, I got dressed, jumped into the truck, and headed over to Millie's for a coffee to go. It was about 7:15 when I arrived at the clinic. Having a full schedule, I glanced over the medical history of the sicker animals which would give me more time to prepare for their special needs. After taking my first sip of coffee, the sound of the reception room entrance door being unlocked caught my attention. Listening to the footsteps, I recognized the gait and stride and knew it had to be Ronda. After all, she is the only person who had a key to the clinic besides me. When she peeked into the office doorway and saw me, it scared her so badly that she grabbed her chest and gasped, "Oh, my goodness, Dr. Whitney! I wasn't expecting you to be in here so early! You like to have scared me into a heart attack! How come you are at your desk at this time of the day? We don't have any patients coming in until ten a clock."

Stretching back in my chair with a big yawn, I replied, "Good morning. What are you doing here so early?"

She began to chatter. "Well, I remembered an order of supplies that had come in last Friday, and they needed to be put in the storage cabinets. Once the patients start coming in, there won't be any time for me to get that job done, and this would be my only chance to do it before leaving for vacation Friday." I looked at her with an "oh, no" expression on my face, and in an exasperated tone, she exclaimed, "Dr. Whitney! ... Don't tell me you forgot! Don't you ever check your dates for future commitments? It's been on the calendar for six months now!"

"Please accept my apology," I said meekly. "But don't worry about it. This is not your problem."

Shaking her head from side to side, she remarked, "Dr. Whitney, you are not going to be able to take care of the patients and work my job too."

Watching Ronda and seeing the genuine concern for the mess I had made for myself gave me a different perspective about this attractive lady. It made me realize that she didn't deserve a boss who had taken her for granted. She had been a loyal, dependable, and a dedicated receptionist. No matter how uncomfortable her job became, she was always trustworthy and reliable, especially with anything that pertained to the clinic or my patients.

Observing how worried she seemed, I had a flashback of the first time she walked into the clinic, clutching the help wanted ads from our local newspaper. Her face had the elegance of a queen with big brown eyes, olive complexion, turned up nose, full lips and a friendly smile. A man would certainly take a second glance at her figure.

She looked me straight into my eyes and said, "I am here to apply for the job that is in the newspaper. Are you the person who is hiring a receptionist?"

I nodded my head and she continued, "My name is Ronda Haysure, and here is my resumé. I'll be glad to come in for an interview if you are interested in giving me one, and I thank you."

She turned away suddenly and was halfway to the door when I yelled, "What's your big hurry?" When she turned around toward me, she replied, "Well...any person seeking a job wouldn't want to interfere with a prospective employer if he should be busy." Needless to say, I gave her the job before she got out the door.

Ronda got married about two weeks after coming to work for me, ending any thoughts that were on my mind, other than an employer and employee relationship. Even though she was a few years older than I am, I had some hopes that we might get together and let nature take its course. Today, it is easy for me to admit my real motive for hiring Ronda, and thank God she turned out to be the professional person that matched her resume'. However, I learned later that she would never have allowed herself to step over any boundaries with me, other than a working relationship. Even if she was available to do so, and I had asked her for a date, she would have said. "Why, Dr. Whitney, you know that wouldn't be ethical! But thank you for the compliment of asking me out." She always had a way to keep people from being embarrassed when they made a major blunder with her.

Smiling, I told Ronda "You know what? We have made it through bigger problems than this one. If you don't mind, can you reschedule all the follow-up appointments? Perhaps that would lessen the load."

Waving her hand at me, she replied, "I'm on my way boss."

I glanced at my watch and knew it would be at least two hours before our first appointment and hoped that Ronda might be finished with the schedule by then. To my surprise, she had it on my desk within an hour. She came into the office and began to explain the changes.

"We are going to have extra patients this afternoon, so that means you and I may be working late. Wednesday and Thursday will also be busy. Now, the week I am on vacation is still too full for you to take care of everything by yourself. There are a few…Dr. Whitney, you don't know of anyone that could help you?"

I shook my head. "No, can't think of anyone, Ronda."

She stood for a moment, tapping her pin on the appointment book. Suddenly, her eyes lit up and she suggested, "Why don't I take the list home with me and see if there is something else that can be done to lessen the appointment load for next week? Would that help?"

"Whatever you do will be a tremendous help, thank you so much."

I could tell Ronda was beginning to worry again and was concerned about the predicament of not having anyone to help me during her absence. "Dr. Whitney, it's still going to be almost impossible for you to work next week by yourself," she expressed.

I got up from my desk, put my arm around her shoulder, and said, "Ronda, don't you worry. This is my problem, okay?" She smiled and walked out of the office.

We had a busy day but when Ronda left, she promised to let me know what solution she came up with to alleviate the load while she was gone on her vacation.

Later that evening, she called me, excited. "Guess what, Dr. Whitney!? I was talking to a neighbor and mentioned I was going on vacation next week and that you needed someone to help you out while I was gone. Well, she has a daughter who has had some experience in a vet clinic, so I called the daughter, and she said she would be glad to help out until I'm back from vacation. Isn't that great?"

"You are a saint, Ronda," I said gratefully.

She responded with a giggle. "To tell you the truth boss, it's knowing that if some of this scheduling isn't straightened out before I leave, well, by the time I get back, things will be so screwed up, it would take me weeks to straighten it out. So you don't need to call me a saint. The reason I'm doing all of this is as much for me as it is for you."

Teasing her, I said, "Ronda, you know there isn't a receptionist in the world that would come to their boss's rescue like you have me."

She agreed by saying, "Ooookay, Dr. Whitney. Flattery will get you everywhere, and on that note, I'll wish you a goodnight!"

When Ronda came back to work from her vacation, I welcomed her with open arms. "Did you have a good vacation?" I asked. And that's all it took for her to begin chattering.

"Oh, Dr. Whitney, we had such a wonderful time! When my sister and brother-in-law got here from Chicago, we went sightseeing all over St. Louis, from the arch to the zoo. We included the Botanical Gardens, the Old Cathedral, and a couple of other nice places. Then, we took a day to visit the Cahokia Mounds. Have you ever been there?"

"No, can't say that I have," I answered.

She continued chattering, describing every detail of her vacation. "You really should go to the Mounds museum! There is quite a lot of interesting history about the Cahokia Indians. We also heard about a huge painting just north of Alton, on a rock cliff, and we decided to go looking for it. We followed the Great River Road north on Highway 100 and sure enough, there on the side of the bluff we saw a painting of the Piasa Bird. It's amazing that it survived for so many years. I don't know much about the history, but I understand that the exact age of the painting has not been determined. However, Lewis and Clark recorded a description and the location of the painting in their journals after seeing it when they were exploring this area.

"Didn't realize Illinois had so many fascinating and historical places to see. It would be really nice to visit them,"

"Just let me know, and I'll be glad to give you directions to anywhere you choose to go!" I started to turn around and walk back to

Deception or Perfection

the office but Ronda stopped me. "By the way, Dr. Whitney, my sister and I went into Millie's the other afternoon for a sandwich. She thought the waitress looked like someone whose picture appeared in a Chicago newspaper several months ago."

I thought for a few minutes and responded, "Surely, if Millie hired a person from Chicago, someone would have said something by now!"

Ronda shrugged her shoulders and answered, "Darned if I know! Perhaps my sister could have been mistaken."

After working until 6:00 and locking up the clinic, I felt a bit disturbed at what Ronda had said about Lee. It was already the end of May, and there would have been some indication by now if she once lived in Chicago. But, she was very closed-mouth about her past. It didn't really worry me though, because I hadn't yet gotten the nerve to ask her for an official date, much less try to nose into where she came from. But I knew someday the right time would come and I fully intended to invite her to go out with me. Grant and Hank would say I was making excuses by waiting for the right moment, but that was okay too.

Little did I know that the very next day, while buying gas at a nearby truck stop, the opportunity would present itself Heading into the station to pay for the gasoline, I saw Lee's bike parked at the corner of the building. It occurred to me that this could be the moment, so I decided to go for it.

After hurrying to pay for the fuel, I looked around but there wasn't a sign of Lee anywhere. My hands were soaked with gasoline, so I decided to rush into the men's room to wash off some of the odor. When I came out of the restroom and closed the door behind me, I walked out into the service station hallway. Lee was standing at a public phone with her back to me. I didn't want to interrupt her, so I decided to hang around until she finished with the call. However, I was uncomfortable because I could hear her entire conversation. I honestly did not want to eavesdrop but stepping back and away meant I would lose sight of her. Not wanting to take a chance of missing her when she left, I just stood there in the hallway, waiting.

"Are you sure that Brandie, Jaden and I can't be traced?"

Who in the world are Brandie and Jaden? I thought.

She continued, "Oh, that's wonderful. You have no idea how grateful I am. She paused for a moment and said, "Then, I will see you Monday morning when I bring the Mercedes to the car dealership. You are going with me, aren't you? ... That will work. Thank you so much. Goodbye for now." She didn't even look my way as she turned from the phone and walked out the back door of the station.

Heading for the truck, a little puzzled, I asked myself, "What in the hell is going on with Lee and this person she was talking to?! And who is Brandie and Jaden?! A *Mercedes*!? She is living in a dump and has a *Mercedes*? There wasn't anything I could do about it, but it sure didn't make any sense to me.

After leaving the truck stop, I went back to the clinic and put in a full busy day's work. At closing time, when I walked into the front of the reception room to lock up, there was a light tap on the door. I peered out the window to see who would be coming to the clinic so late and, much to my surprise, Lee was standing there with her puppy on a leash. Without delay, I opened the door, and she began apologizing, "I'm sorry for coming here so late, but this is the only chance for me to bring Goggy into the clinic for a check- up."

Waving my arm in a welcoming gesture, I told her, "It is okay. Just come on in."

Stepping into the reception room, she began to chatter nervously like she was trying to make conversation. "I think he is old enough to start his vaccinations. Guess he should have been brought into the clinic a long time ago just for a check-up, but...oh, well...you know how it is…"

I put my hand on her shoulder and with a big smile, butted in saying, "It's alright." I pointed to the counter where Ronda's computer sat and Lee followed me. I then began to ask her information for the pup's health record. "What's his name?"

"Goggy."

"You call him…Goggy?"

"Yes, you heard me right! That's his name!"

While typing the puppy's name into the computer and trying to keep from laughing, I teasingly asked again, "Goggy is what you named your doggie?"

Grinning slightly and trying not to laugh, she answered in a serious tone, "YES! Goggy is his name. Is there anything wrong with that?!"

"Oh, no. No, that's...that's a fine name," Then, not being able to hold back any longer, I began to apologize with a sputter of laughter, saying, "I'm sorry. It's just that in all the years of my veterinarian career, I've never heard of a doggy named Goggy."

After looking down at her feet, Lee glanced up at me, trying to keep a straight face, and both of us burst out laughing. When our laughter calmed down to a snicker, she admitted, "Well, since you put it that way, his name can certainly bring a smile to a person's face." For the first time we seemed to have a definite connection between us.

After recording all the information that was needed for Goggy's medical records, I took a step toward the hallway and motioned for Lee and the pup to follow me. After entering the exam room, she lifted him onto the table and took off his leash. After giving the pup a thorough examination from the tip of his nose to the tip of his tail, I announced, "It is my pleasure to inform you that your puppy is just about as healthy as they get."

"That's great, he is loved very much, and it would really upset me if there had been anything wrong with him." For a few minutes, neither of us said anything. I began to busy myself by hanging the stethoscope in its proper spot, then washing my hands.

All at once she nervously spoke up, "Shannon, you sure have a nice clinic. As well as appearing professional, it has an inviting, relaxed atmosphere with a comfortable refinement. You must be very proud."

Lee and I became somewhat apprehensive again and neither of us was able to make eye contact, but I did manage to smile and say, "Thank you so much. You complimenting the place has given me the confidence that the hard work, time and money spent fixing it up wasn't wasted. It really feels good to have someone notice. You are the first person to say anything complimentary about the clinic."

With a surprised look on her face, she said, "No kidding! These people around here don't know how lucky they are to have a good vet and this kind of service!"

Then a thought entered my head. *"Could she possibly be nervous because of me?"*

Dismissing that thought I told her, "Lee, if you'll excuse me, I'm going to the med cabinet to get you a couple of flea and tick packets plus heart worm medication. Also, he needs to begin the first of his round of vaccinations. I'll be right back."

She smiled, waved her hand at me, and said, "You go right ahead. We aren't going anywhere." Returning to the exam room, I handed Lee the packets of medication and quickly gave the puppy his first distemper and rabies vaccines. We stood for a few awkward seconds before Lee broke the silence. "Thank you again for seeing us on such short notice. Guess you want to call it a day, so Goggy and I will scoot out of here and let you close up."

With a big grin, I responded, "I'm not in any hurry, and it isn't necessary to thank me. It's a pleasure to come to the rescue of a beautiful woman and her doggy."

Aiming a shy, flirty grin at me, she responded, "What a nice thing for you to say."

Lee picked Goggy up from the table and sat him down on the floor. Holding the pup tightly, she began to snap the leash to his collar. Suddenly, the puppy gave an unexpected hard jerk, causing Lee to lose her grasp on him. Before we knew it, he was off and running. When turning to try and grab the pup, Lee somehow stumbled, which caused her to have a collision with the door facing. The impact knocked her to the floor, flat on her butt, and down the hallway went Goggy, straight into the reception room. I quickly helped Lee to her feet and we took off down the hallway. Standing at the entrance of the reception room, we saw him darting towards the door. All at once he turned around and headed back for the hallway. Lee stepped in front of him, but she wasn't able to catch the rascal.

He jumped on the couch and darted back and forth from the couch to the chairs. We slowly tried to close in on him. Watching our every move he made the decision to leap from the back of one of the chairs and dove onto the coffee table and then slid into a belly flop onto the floor. Recovering quickly, he hunched down on his forelegs with his tail wagging ninety miles an hour and sticking straight up in the air. Whispering, I told Lee, "Sneak up behind him and I'll attract his attention. Then, maybe you can grab the little scamp!" Slowly creeping towards the pup, I tried to coax him to come to me by softly saying "Here, Goggy, be a good boy, come on, I'm not going to hurt you!"

In a playful manner and with his tail still wagging, he ducked his head down, let out a ferocious puppy growl and began barking. Lee made a quick effort to seize him and yelled, "I got him!" She grabbed one of his hind legs, thinking her grip was tight enough to hold him, but the pup managed to slip out of her hand and made a lunge into an end table next to the sofa. He knocked over the table with a lamp, which fell into the magazine rack, then shattered as it fell to the floor. The noise must have scared him because he made a tragic mistake and ran behind the counter. Lee and I stepped to the end of it and trapped him. By this time, Goggy knew the counter was impassable. I squatted down and clutched him with a firm grip. Lee rushed to the exam room to grab the leash and promptly returned to hand it to me. After snapping it to his collar, I pulled him from behind the counter, with all four of his paws digging into the floor. The poor little guy then began to tremble. Lee gently picked up the puppy as she softly said, "You're okay, sweetie." She held him close to her chest until he stopped shaking.

After the chase, we stood for a moment, surveying the disorder around the reception area. "Oh, no," Lee said. "The room is a disaster. Please, let me know how much it will cost to fix and replace the furniture. I promise to cover all the expenses. Please, forgive Goggy and me!"

I told her, "There is nothing to forgive! Do you think this is the first time something like this has ever happened?! Besides, my insurance will cover everything. Goggy is not the first runaway pup in this clinic, and you can be assured he will not be the last."

Almost in tears, she asked, "Are you sure you wouldn't like for me to at least clean up some of the mess?"

"You are not to worry one bit about this."

She glanced up at me and softly uttered, "Thank you so much! But I wish you would let me do something to help."

Putting both my hands on her shoulders, I shook my head and said,

"Please, don't let this bother you. It is going to be taken care of."

For the first time, when I stared into her eyes, she didn't look away, and when the distance between us began to close, she didn't move muscle. Slowly, I leaned a bit forward and could feel her breath on my cheeks. She lifted her chin with closed eyes, and just as our lips were about to touch, there was a loud knock at the door. Grace Jinkens, a lady who lived just out of town on a farm, stood outside the door. She began yelling, "Dr. Whitney, are you in there?!" When I opened the door, she spoke frantically, "Dr. Whitney, I tried to call you but something is wrong with my phone so I drove over here as fast as I could. Sweet Pea is trying to foal, and her colt doesn't want to come out!"

"How long has she been in labor?"

"I don't know. Greg and me had come out of the field from working all afternoon and noticed that she had some drainage, so we put her in the barn! Then, my phone went dead when I was trying to call you. That's when I came over here!"

Quickly running to the instrument closet where I stored my emergency gear, I grabbed several things that might be needed to deliver the mare's colt. Lee came in behind me and began to help. I remarked, "You seem to be familiar with veterinarian instruments."

Under her breath, she softly uttered, "Somewhat." I untied Goggy and handed the leash to Lee. After locking the clinic and running to my truck, I realized Lee was right behind me. "Where do you think you're going? You can't go with me!" I said sternly.

In an indignant manner, she asked, "Why, is there a law against it? Maybe you could use a little help. It's for sure the lady here is not in any shape to know what to do, and I am sure that if her husband is in the same shape she is in, he sure isn't going to be any help."

After Lee made her point, I told her to tie the puppy in the back close to the cab for wind protection. Then, jumping into the truck, we took off for the Jinkens' farm like a bat out of Hades. Watching in my rear view mirror, I noticed Mrs. Jinkens was following so closely that there couldn't have been enough space between our bumpers for a blade of grass. "Sure hope a deer doesn't decide to cross in front of us! Mrs. Jinkens is right on my tailgate, and it could cause a major collision," I remarked.

"The lady probably has no idea how close she is to you. The only thing she has on her mind right now is the mare."

"You're right. The Jinkens have already lost one horse a couple of years ago. She developed a serious case of pneumonia, and I had left town for a convention in Chicago and was on my way home when she got sick. The vet they called lived sixty miles from here, and at the same time the Jinkens needed him, he had an emergency in his own district. When he finally did get to their farm, it was too late to save the horse. Have you ever been to Chicago, Lee?"

Seeming a bit shook up from my question, she turned her face toward the side window and replied in a raspy voice, "No!" By this time, we had arrived at the farm, and driving onto a road that led to the pasture, I could see that Mr. Jinkens had the gate and barn door open. I parked next to the large barn entrance, and Lee quickly got out of the truck and reached into the bed, taking out the instrument bag. I immediately grabbed the other equipment. We slowly entered the barn and approached the stall where Sweet Pea stood. I could tell by her restless movements, she was having a contraction. Lee carefully set the bag of instruments down beside me and stepped away. Steadily, reaching down into the bag, I took out the stethoscope, placed it around my neck, and put on surgical gloves. Lee, looking around, noticed an old wooden crate, and carried it as close to the wall as she could to Sweet Pea's adjoining stall. I patiently waited outside in the service hallway of the barn until the mare completed her contraction. When I stepped into the area with the horse, her hips faced me. Nevertheless, she began to pace around and with an angry snort, backed into a corner of the stall. As I tried to maneuver myself to a place behind her, she turned with another snort and barely missed me with a back hoof kick. "Okay, baby girl," I whispered, "Settle down." Knowing Sweet Pea and recognizing her warning, I realized that she could have kicked the daylights out of me if her intentions were to be hurtful.

Lee stepped onto the crate, and by stretching one of her arms over the divided wall, it gave her access to Sweet Pea's ears, and she began to scratch between them with soft strokes. The mare calmed down enough that she let me rub her neck underneath the chin, and I cautiously checked her heart rate. Moving around to the back of the stall, I began a soothing chatter. "You're a good girl. You need to settle down now." The horse became a bit nervous, so I continued the chatter. "Whoa there, girl. I'm not going to hurt you. It's going to be all right." Patting her body, I eased toward my destination and managed to examine the cervix and evaluate the progress. With a sigh of relief, I concluded that everything was normal and announced to Mr. and Mrs. Jinkens, "She is doing great. I don't see any reason your little girl should have a problem delivering her foal."

Lee, still standing on the wooden crate, glanced around the barn and saw an old blanket lying on a stack of straw. She picked it up and folded it over her arm. About that time, out of curiosity, Sweet Pea turned her head toward the adjoining stall. This gave Lee the opportunity to lay the blanket carefully over the mare's head and eyes, and this gesture helped to calm her down even more.

Watching closely and noticing Sweet Pea's breathing becoming more intense, I whispered to Lee, "Grab me another pair of surgical gloves! Our little lady mare is getting ready to have a contraction." Lee went to the bag and carefully reached in for the second pair of gloves. Stretching out my hands toward her, she slipped them on and walked back into the adjoining stall. I slowly stepped behind Sweet Pea. The contraction came fast and hard, and she gave out a painful coughing groan. I began to talk to her as though she was a young woman. "It's gonna be all right! Go with it and push. Let's bring that little guy or girl into the world!" Checking the cervix again, I could see the foal's front hooves. Mr. and Mrs. Jinkens nervously stood outside the stall, and I whispered, "She is doing fine!" They seemed a bit relieved, but they were not completely convinced that their Sweet Pea was all right.

I began to rub the mare's hips near the birth exit and talked to her again. "You are doing great, sugar! Your baby is almost here!" Her breathing began to deepen, with faster intervals between the breaths. When the contraction hit, she shook her head and let out a loud whinny. It was so painful that she staggered and almost fell to her front knees. After the contraction subsided, she gained her composure, and her breathing calmed down. I began talking to Sweet Pea again. "Okay, girl, the next one is it! All you need is one more!" The sentence barely got out of my mouth and the next contraction hit her with no mercy. She whinnied so loudly it seemed to rattle the tin roof over the barn. Flouncing her neck back, eyes bulging, she gave forth a painful groan and whinnied again. Weak from the pain, she lay down. Her breathing became harder, and she made a grunting sound as the foal's hooves slowly emerged, then the nose. Sweet Pea floundered and again whinnied with a groan. In a loud demanding voice, I said to her, "Come on girl! You can do this! Sweet Pea…push!" Reaching into the area of the colt's head, I gently gave a tug and said encouragingly, "Push, girl. This baby wants to see its mother. Come on, girl! You can do it! Push!" The mare gasped for breath and groaned again as the head emerged, then the stomach, and at last, the hind hoofs. I yelled, "It's a boy!"

Lee, stepping into Sweet Pea's stall, picked up the blanket that dropped to the ground during one of the mare's contractions. She began to rub the colt down vigorously, then wrapped the blanket around his stomach for warmth. I finished-working on Sweet Pea and she lay for a few more minutes, catching her breath.

About the time I finished my job, the colt let out a squeaky sound, and the new mother's ears perked out. With determination, she stood up and turned around toward the colt, and it was love at first sight. The colt raised his nose to his mommy and she gave him a deep-throated grunt. He began to struggle, trying to stand. Finally, he stood up on his legs. When Sweet Pea gave him a loving nuzzle, the colt wobbled to his dinner.

Lee, with tears in her eyes, smiled at me and remarked, "Isn't the miracle of birth awesome? And you, Dr. Whitney, are amazing!"

All of us stood, staring at the mom and her baby. I unconsciously reached over to Lee and put my arm around her shoulders, saying, "No, Sweet Pea is the amazing one. And by the way, you are quite amazing yourself. I have never seen an amateur so knowledgeable about horses when they are giving birth. Thanks for the assistance. You have no idea how much it helped."

We were still standing and watching the nursing colt when Lee, with no hesitation, turned toward me. Tiptoeing, she laid a kiss on my lips. I could have been knocked over with a wet noodle. Mr. and Mrs. Jinkens just stood there quietly smiling at us. When Lee noticed them and realized what had just happened, she became so embarrassed that she instantly stepped back from me and stammered, "Please d-don't take that personally. As…as you can see, I am a very emotional person! You do understand that, don't you?"

Smiling to myself *little lady, you have no idea how long the wait has been for me to see the slightest sign of your liking me.* But I only said okay and gave her a big grin.

Still embarrassed, Lee headed out of the barn and passed the Jinkens, saying, "Please understand I am a very emotional person." After almost running to the truck, she jumped into the seat and slammed the door as though the devil was after her.

I said goodnight to the Jinkens, gathered up the instrument, and headed for the truck. Lee was very quiet on the way back to the clinic and I reassured her. "You don't have to be uneasy about the Jinkens. They will not tell anyone that you kissed me. They don't gossip and I won't take it personal.

When we arrived at the clinic and stepping out of the truck I noticed Lee was having a hard time opening the door. Walking to the passenger side I realized the damn door had jammed again. After several hard jerks, it jarred loose. Trying to keep the situation impersonal, I apologized, "Sorry about that. The crazy thing wants to stick sometimes! Been meaning to get it fixed, and I just keep putting it off."

She started to scoot from the seat. I was still trying to keep things from being personal and was reluctant to help her out of the truck, not knowing what the reaction might be. Nevertheless, she reached for my hand and stepped down to the ground. Her face had the same look as it did at the Jinkens' farm just before the kiss. I no longer resisted expressing my feelings.

We took a slight step toward each other and she stared into my eyes, not making a move. Circling my left arm around her waist, and placing my right index finger under her chin, I gently lifted it just enough that our lips touched. She closed her eyes, and our bodies seemed to melt into one. She responded to the kiss with the sweetness of innocence, and the intensity began to increase. It must have become evident to her how deeply she cared for me because with sadness in her eyes, she pulled away from our embrace, shaking her head. "I can't do this, Shannon as much as I want to!" Then she reached into the back of the truck, grabbed Goggie, and placed him in the basket of her bike. Turning around she mounted the bike and road away. Watching her ride out of sight I thought, *Baby doll, you will never convince me that kiss wasn't personal.*

Chapter Six

After getting out of bed the next morning, I quickly got dressed and left the house, heading straight to Millie's. I fully intended to be there before Grant and Hank left for work. After arriving in record time, I made my way to their table and sat down. Grant gave a wave, and Hank sort of grunted a "hey." Then, Millie came over with a cup of coffee and asked, "What's up Doc?"

"Not much Millie. Would you bring me your breakfast special?"

As she wrote on her check pad, she repeated the order. "Okay, Doc. One breakfast special coming up."

Glancing around the restaurant, I made eye contact with Lee on the other side of the room and she smiled and waved at me. As I smiled and waved back at her, Grant seemed to sense something different about the two of us; however, he didn't say a word.

We chatted and exchanged useless information as I ate my breakfast. There wasn't one question or hint about me asking Lee out, and that made me a bit suspicious. On the other, hand, maybe it was a good thing. Going to work today without having to defend myself from the two of them nagging me about Lee was an improvement.

The work day wasn't a busy one, so I closed at 2:00 p.m. and sat around the house, bored and restless for several hours. Eventually, I decided to email an old friend. However, all my thoughts were on Lee, wishing there could be a way to spend some time with her and yet not wanting to be pushy, and make her angry with me. Finally, I emailed my friend Taylor, asking him to meet me for dinner, beer, and a movie. He immediately responded, accepting my invitation. Taylor lives in an area called Clareview Heights, which has a cinema and all sorts of shopping centers, restaurants, and other businesses. We needed to get together early because he had a date at eight that night "with a great woman," as he put it.

Taylor's sister, whom I dated for a while, was the one who introduced us. Because we had so much in common, we hit it off right away. His interests pertained to research and development in finding economical and alternative ways to distribute food supplies to animals in the wild, especially the ones that were stranded in areas of natural disasters. A short time after our introduction, his sister broke up with me. She had the crazy idea that the words 'committed relationship' weren't in my vocabulary. Nevertheless, Taylor and I remained friends.

During my drive through Clareview Heights, I relived the kiss that Lee and I shared the night before, and that gave me renewed hopes that the two of us would someday be a couple. If only Lee knew the depth of my love for her. I wished she could see in my eyes how much I loved her. Maybe then she would give us a chance.

After a prolonged stop at a green light, a honking horn startled me out of my fantasy. Looking in the rear view mirror, I realized that the Sizzling Sassy restaurant, where I was supposed to meet my friend, was three blocks behind me. After making a u-turn, I arrived at the restaurant. Seeing Taylor waiting in front of the entrance brought back some fun memories. I got out of the truck, met him at the door, and eagerly shook his hand. With a big grin on my face, I said, "I'm so glad you're getting to see me!"

"You shyster!" he said. "How the hell are you? Man, it's been a long time since we did this! I'm sure glad you contacted me!"

After sitting down in a booth, the two of us began sharing what we had been up to since the last time we saw each other. During dinner and a couple of beers, he told me about his lady friend and said that he planned to ask her to marry him. I told him about Lee and he remarked, "It sure has taken you a long enough time to finally meet a woman who could sweep you off your feet, Mr. Romeo. I'm hoping the best for you, man, and it sounds like you might soon be heading to the church altar."

Looking at him sideways with a frown, I reminded him, "Look who's talking! What about this fascinating lady you've been talking about! Besides, a man of your age shouldn't wait too much longer before getting hitched. Remember, you're older than me! Would you like to bet you'll be standing in front of the parson and the altar before me?"

He smiled, and responded, "No! Now that I have told you about my girl, it's obvious who will be *standing in front of the parson first!* BESIDES, KNUCKLEHEAD, I'M ONLY TWO WEEKS OLDER THAN YOU!"

After eating like pigs at dinner, we left the restaurant and took in a movie. When the movie ended, and both of us stood up, Taylor shook my hand, saying, "Hey, bud, this has been great. Let's not go so long before doing this again."

I put my other hand over his with a firm, solid shake of friendship and told him, "That sounds great to me, Taylor."

He smiled, gave me a light pat on the shoulder, and walked away. I grabbed my jacket from the back of the seat and slipped it on, deciding to linger a while to wait for the crowd to thin out. Finally, I walked out of the theater and into the hallway. When glancing down to zip my jacket, I bumped head-on into someone. Quickly making my apology, I lifted my head to see Lee standing right there in front of me. Astonished, I blurted out, "Lee!" I also recognized the woman standing next to her as the same woman who answered the door at Lee's mobile home. I began to stammer. "W-w-what are you doing here?"

Beside the woman a little boy stood holding her hand, who looked to be about four years old. Lee stared at me with a stunned expression. Finally, in a shaky voice, she began her introductions. Touching the arm of the lady, she said, "Shannon, this is my roommate, Jaden Harris. And this beautiful child… is my son, and his name is Brandon."

Nervously, I said to Jaden, "Glad to meet you." I knelt down and offered my hand to Lee's son. He lifted his and we gave one another a hi-five. Smiling, I said, "Glad to meet you Brandon." Still in shock after the introductions, I glanced helplessly at Lee.

Finally, Jaden spoke up. "What do you say, Brandon, shall we go find some good seats?" When they walked away, the little guy turned around and gave me a big smile. Smiling back at him, I said "He *is* a beautiful child."

As the two of them went through the theater doors, Lee began to confess. "Shannon, there are things about me that need to be explained! I'm truly sorry for keeping so many secrets! Do you remember how angry I was the day you came to the mobile home with Goggy?"

Indignantly, I answered, "Yes! And a person who is the recipient of that kind of anger doesn't easily forget it!"

Glancing down at the floor, and in a regretful demeanor, she said, "You're right, but that can't be changed. That's why, if there is a chance you could come to my place tomorrow, I will explain everything and answer any questions you ask. If you do…maybe you can make it for lunch, say about twelve thirty?"

Nodding my head, I answered, "You can depend on it."

Lee touched my arm, and in almost a whisper, asked, "Please, Shannon, whatever you do, don't tell anyone about seeing me here tonight. I feel that you can be trusted, and that is the reason I have decided to tell you everything about us!

I reassured her, "You have my promise not to say anything to anybody. But, if you are in any kind of danger, perhaps I should stay with you tonight."

She smiled, saying, "We're just fine. By this time tomorrow, you will understand my request."

Needless to say, after returning home, the mind chatter ran-through my head like an Indianapolis car race. Going to bed did not make it any better. I tossed and turned all night. I finally dozed off at about six in the morning when, all of a sudden the phone rang. One of Mr. Landry's calves had managed to get through a broken fence and foundered himself on green clover.

After coming back home from the emergency call, I fell across the bed and went sound asleep. All at once, I woke up. Jumping off the bed and glancing at the clock, I noticed the time was 11:50. Scurrying to the bathroom, I shaved, showered, and dressed in twenty minutes.

During my drive out to Lee's, all sorts of feelings welled up inside of me, and questions bustled through my mind. Could she be married? Surely there would be some sign, like an indentation on her finger. Then I remembered she wore a birthstone on her ring finger. Maybe she was gay. But then she wouldn't have kissed me like she did the other night. Nonetheless, she could have been "testing the waters," so to speak. Or she may be hiding from an abusive x-boyfriend.

Finally reaching the mobile home, I parked in the clearing, slid out of the truck and took a deep breath. As I walked toward the door, someone opened it and stepped out onto the porch. There stood the most gorgeous woman imaginable! Suddenly, it dawned on me that it was Lee! Her complexion was olive-toned and perfectly clear, with no make-up on. She had dark brown hair, with big light brown dreamy eyes, that could hypnotize a man if he looked into them long enough. I felt paralyzed as I stared at her with my mouth hanging open. Finally, I stammered, "Lee, I-I can't believe…you're so beautiful. N-not that you haven't always been beautiful; B-but you look…look…"

She interrupted with an invitation. "Please, come on in." Glancing down at herself with opened arms she added, "Like it, or lump it, Shannon. This is the real me."

Swallowing a big gulp and looking at her with an approving grin, I said, "I like it!" She gave me an "all right, wise guy" smile as I made my way into the living room.

"Lunch is on the table. Please come and eat. That is, if you are ready."

Still grinning, I told her, "Well, the body is willing but the legs are still trying to recuperate from the vision I'm experiencing!"

Trying to keep from giggling, she dropped her head and thanked me. Then, she took my hand like a child and led me to the dining area. I apologized to her for being late, and she responded "it is no big deal. You are not that late." After I sat down, she called out, "Brandon, Jadan, lunch is ready!" The two of them came from the hallway, and when they joined me at the table, Lee gave the blessing and sat down. She had prepared chicken salad, broccoli and cheese soup, and homemade chocolate chip cookies for dessert. After a few bites of food, my breathing settled down, but I couldn't take my eyes off of Lee. Passing the food around, she smiled as though she didn't notice.

When we finished our lunch, Brandon became restless. Jaden asked him, "Hey, little one, would you like to go for a hike after we help your mom clear the table?"

He answered Jadan with a big "Yes," and asked Lee, "Is it okay, Mom?"

She kissed him on his forehead and told him, "Don't give Jaden

Deception or Perfection

any trouble" Then he ran to the back bedroom for his jacket.

Scooting myself from the table, I told Lee, "Thank you for your invitation. It isn't often that someone invites me to come to their home for such a terrific lunch. And I haven't had any homemade chocolate chip cookies like that since…I don't know when. They were the greatest."

"You are very welcome. Glad you could make it."

I began helping Jaden and Lee clear the table, and just as we sat the last dish in the sink, the dog came running from the hallway, with Brandon right behind him. Both of them headed for the door and Brandon, looking over my way, asked, "Did you see how fast Goggy can run? He is the fastest runner in the whole land!"

Glancing over my shoulder at Lee, I gave her a big smile as I answered him with, "I sure did! He is a fast runner, all right!"

"My mommy says that he is the best puppy in the whole wide world because you picked him out."

Lee turned away from us and seemed a bit embarrassed that Brandon shared her comment about me. As I looked at him, a memory came to me of years past when a dad gave a little boy his first puppy. This stirred indescribable emotions down in my soul. Glancing at Lee with a smile, I also couldn't help remembering our evening when she brought Goggy to the clinic. I knelt to the floor at Brandon's level, saying to him, "Well, Little Man, there must have been something in the back of my mind that made me realize that Goggy should belong to a special person."

Grinning from ear to ear, he yelled out, "YEAH, ME! AND BECAUSE HE IS MINE, I GOT TO NAME HIM!"

I smiled at Lee and said, "So that's why the doggie's name is Goggy." She returned a silent glance that seemed to say, "Yes, now you know!"

Lee walked Brandon and the pup to the door and kissed him again on the forehead. By then, Jaden had taken his hand and said, "We will see you later."

Lee came back to the table and sat down. After a few awkward seconds, we spoke up at the same time. She quickly offered, "You go first!"

"No," I said. "You go first! Whatever it is you have to share with me may answer my questions."

She sighed, and after taking in a deep breath warned me, "I hope you are prepared to be here for a while because what I am about to tell you is as unreal as it gets." Then, taking another deep breath and glancing around at nothing, she asked herself out loud, "Where do I start? I guess at the beginning….. First of all, Shannon, I am a licensed veterinarian."

Not being too surprised, I remarked, "The thought occurred to me the night we helped Sweet Pea deliver her colt. You seemed to have too much knowledge of the equipment. Besides, the way you knew how to handle Sweet Pea during the delivery proved to me that you were no amateur. I'm sorry. Go on with your story."

"Okay", she said. "Well, in March of 2000, I received a notice that I had been accepted for an internship at a local clinic in Denton, Texas. I only had about two-and-a-half months of school to finish before graduating in June. One day at work, while I was entering medical data into a patient's record, a very handsome man walked into the clinic. He excused himself and asked "Could you tell me how to get to I-35?" After I gave him directions, he started for the door, but suddenly turned around and walked back to the counter. Leaning toward me, he asked, "Will you have dinner with tonight?" and I said to him, "I don't know you from Adam. Why should I go out to dinner with you?" Reaching to shake my hand, he smiled and introduced himself as Amon Joseph Costa, but I could call him Joe. He said he was twenty-nine years old, intelligent, had a good job, liked horseback riding, golf, having dinner with a beautiful woman and he was single. Then he asked my name. A little shocked and smiling at his forwardness, I told him," Christina Rogers." He took my hand and replied, "Glad to meet you, Christina Rogers. Will you have dinner with me tonight?"

"Needless to say, he swept me off my feet, and two days after my graduation, we were married. I was so young and naive. On our wedding night, when I told him that I had never had sex before, he was floored. But, it was as though he became more deeply in love with me. The next day we flew to Chicago…. before you say anything, Shannon, God knows I didn't want to lie to you when you asked me if

I had ever been to Chicago. You are going to understand after I have told you everything."

I reassured her, "It is okay, Lee. Please go on. I'm listening."

She stared down at the table and glanced out of the window. It seemed that she was having a hard time looking at me. Nevertheless, she continued her story. "When the plane landed in Chicago, there was a limo waiting for us. Thirty-five minutes later, we turned into a gated driveway and I couldn't believe what I saw! The landscaping looked like that of a fairyland, with gardens, shrubs, water fountains, statues...and the house...it wasn't a house. It was a two-story mansion! Over the next few months, I met a lot of people Joe introduced to me as "business associates." They were okay, but because of their snobbish attitudes, I had no desire to encourage any friendships with them or their wives. In August of 2002, I had a beautiful baby daughter, and we named her Brandie Jo Costa. I'd never been happier and felt like the luckiest woman in the world. Not only did I have a handsome husband who adored me, now God gave me a beautiful baby girl."

Stopping Lee again, I asked, "Wait. Lee, you have a daughter!?" Then the light bulb switched on in my head, and I asked, "Brandon is a girl?"

She replied, "Yes." I was at a loss for words and sat there in dismay. My head was spinning. She continued, "There is a lot more, Shannon. I have hardly touched the surface."

Nodding my head, I told her, "Go on, Lee. You need to tell me everything!"

She took a deep breath and continued her story. "Where was I? Oh, yeah...in July 2006, I began plans for Brandie's— that's what we called her—third birthday party. Joe had been overly sensitive and ill-tempered for months. I had hoped that the party would cheer him up, and it did. We began going out more and socializing, especially with Keith and Rachel Ferguson. Keith, a tall, good-looking black man, was Joe's best friend. Rachel and I had hit it off immediately. We went to expensive night clubs and swanky restaurants. Sometimes, we would fly to New York and go to a Broadway show. Rachel and I became best friends and were always doing things out of the ordinary. One time, she even suggested we go skydiving and we did. Later, we learned to skateboard and shoot clay pigeons. And, I might add, she became an excellent marksman. She also taught me how to fish."

"One day, Rachel and I went shopping. When we got back, she dropped me off at the front entrance of my home, but before I could put my key into the lock, the door swung open and Joe stood, staring at me with a big grin on his face. He said, 'Hey, Sugar, our daughter is asleep and I have something to show you!' After taking the packages from my arms, and setting them down, he grabbed my hand, and led me upstairs to our bedroom."

"When he opened the door, I was speechless at what I saw. There were rose petals everywhere, and candles on the night stands, dresser, and chest in the bathroom. There were also silver streamers hanging over our bed. But the most amazing thing was a bird cage with two doves hanging in the center of the room. With wide-eyed excitement, he asked, 'What do you think, Sugar? Ain't it great? I did this all by myself to surprise you.' Then, he looked at me very seriously saying, 'There are no words that can express how deep my love is for you and Brandie. The two of you mean more to me than life itself. I don't deserve it, but will you accept my apology for acting like a jerk for so long?'

Personally, I felt that the room looked gaudy. Kind of like something a kid had put together, and it was all I could do to keep from laughing. But Joe was so excited and remorseful for his past behavior; I never let him know my real thoughts of his decorating skills. After I forgave him...he took me in his arms..."

Suddenly, Lee got up from her chair and asked. "Shannon, would you like something to drink?"

Shaking my head, I told her, "Please go on with your story. I'm not in need of anything right now."

She responded, "Well, just let me know if you want a drink or something. How about another cookie?"

"Lee, are you stalling because you don't want to say anything more about your past?"

With tears welling up in her eyes, she admitted, "The story is getting to some painful memories and I guess...maybe you're right to say that I'm stalling. Even so, my intentions are to tell you everything Shannon, to the best of my ability."

Reaching for her hand, and holding it, I tried to reassure her. "Lee, take all the time you need. There isn't anything you can say that would make me judge you or that would keep me from respecting you. Go on with your story."

Blinking back the tears, she responded with a sigh and said, "Okay, here goes. December came and we had a beautiful Christmas. One night after the holidays, we were stretched out on the sofa in each other's arms in front of the fire place. Joe gave me a kiss and I teasingly asked him what that was for. He looked at me with deep sincerity and said it was because he loved me so much. Then he told me. "If anything should happen to me… ,

"Nothing is going to happen to you."

Then, the last Saturday of February he came downstairs with his work-out bag because every Saturday morning he and Keith went to the gym. Anyway, slipping on his jacket, he motioned for me to come to the door with him and then he did something strange. He reached into the athletic bag and handed me a little black book and told me to put it in a safe place.

I butted in again with a question. "Wait, Lee, for just a minute! Didn't you ever ask what kind of work Joe did or what his business consisted of?"

"He told me that he was in the shipping business; and I visited his office at least once a week and there wasn't anything out of the ordinary. It just looked like a normal office to me."

Another question came to my mind. "Where were his relatives all this time? And his parents…where were they?"

Lee looked slightly upset and answered defensively, "He told me he was an orphan and talked about the orphanage quite frequently! I didn't ask about any relatives because he didn't know who his relatives were!"

I gently said to her, "My God, Lee. His shipping business had to be something that wasn't on the up and up! The way you have described yours and his life style … well, it sounds as though he could have been into smuggling!"

Tears filled her eyes and she began criticizing herself. "Yes Shannon, I know that now. All that can be said about me is that I'm a stupid woman!"

Handing her a napkin from the table, I tried to console her. "Don't cry, Lee. I'm the one who is stupid! I have no doubts that you were a good wife to him, and you certainly are not stupid. Please, go on with your story and I will try to keep my mouth shut."

After wiping her eyes with the napkin, she reminded me, "It's okay, Shannon. The promise I made to you before starting my story was that you could ask anything you wanted to ask. So don't you hold back on any questions you have."

"Yes, I know you did. But if my questions cause you any pain, then maybe I need to keep them to myself."

"It's not the questions that hurts," she reassured me. "It's resentments of the events that took place in my life from the time I met Joe. When I'm finished telling you everything, you will know what I mean. And I don't want to leave anything out, so please just be patient with me!"

"Anyway, he told me to put the little black book in safe place, and if something happen to him, it should take care of Brandie and me for the rest of our lives. I kissed him on the cheek and told him to have a good workout. By that time, Keith had pulled into the driveway to pick Joe up. After stepping into the car, Joe watching through the window, waved at me. I waved back, closed the door, went to the foyer closet, and put the little black book into my coat pocket. After walking to the lounge room and switching on the television, I went about my chores with the plan that when Brandie woke up, we would go over to Rachel's and have breakfast with her."

"After finishing my chores and walking back into the lounge, a news break came on the T.V. The announcer said, *"Ladies and gentlemen, we just receive a report that two well-known gangsters, Amon Joseph Costa and Keith Ferguson, have been shot to death at the front entrance of the First Class Fitness Club! All we know at this time is that it was a drive-by shooting. There will be a full report on the news at noon!* Then, the station flashed a scene at the First Class fitness center where Joe and Keith had gone to work out. I remember falling to my knees on the floor in disbelief and screaming, *'No! No! I'm having a horrible dream! Let me wake up!'* I began crying hysterically and everything started spinning and..."

Lee's eyes were filled with tears. I picked my chair up and sat it down next to hers and she reached for me. I put my arms around her until she stopped crying, and asked, "Lee, are you sure you want to go on with this today?"

After taking a deep breath, she wiped her eyes. With a quiver in her voice said, "Yes Shannon. This has to be done! I have bottled up these feelings for months! Not only that, I'm sick and tired of hiding my past from you! I-I can't stand it any longer!"

"Ok, if you are sure that's what you want to do,"

She began her story again. "I must have blacked out. I don't know for how long. Struggling to get up from the floor, still in a daze I heard the phone ringing. I answered it with a shaky hello. It was Rachel. She was sobbing so hard that I couldn't understand her. Then, I started crying again and told her this had to be a nightmare. Finally we gained our composure somewhat. Still crying, she blurted out, 'Christina, someone just called me! He...he wouldn't give his name, but he said that you and the baby and I must get out of Chicago, immediately! He...he told me he was a friend and that the Ted Tardino mafia family had us on their hit list.'"

"I can remember screaming at her how crazy all this was. Mafia... gangsters...what's going on here?" None of this made any sense! We weren't gangsters! Why would anyone want to kill us? Rachel began to cry again and said the man told her that we needed to change our identities, and not to let anyone know where we were going."

"And you believed him?" I asked.

"She then asked me, 'Christina, would you have ever believed our husbands were gangsters who were going to be shot to death?!' Then, reality hit me. Everything began to make sense. I was remembering Joe's behavior, the trips out of town, and the strangers coming to the house. Then I said, 'Oh my God, Rachel. It's true! The mafia must think we know something that could hurt them. What are we going to do?'"

She told me to pack the largest suitcases we had for both Brandie and myself, and to get as much of my jewelry together as I could, and put it in my car.

I immediately did what she instructed me to do. After packing the suitcases and throwing them into the trunk of the car, I ran back into the house, took Brandie out of bed, and grabbed my coat from the foyer closet. By the time I put Brandie in her car seat, Rachel was in the driveway. I threw her belongings into the trunk and we took off. Driving straight to I-55, I asked her which way we should go. Rachel reminded me that it might be a good idea to get off the interstate as soon as possible, because there could be state cops on the mafia's payroll watching for us. The next exit we came to, I got of the interstate and turned south on a black top road."

"Lee, stop just for a minute. From what you have been saying, you didn't see Joe's body? And Rachel! Is she Jaden?"

"Answering your first question, Shannon, no, I didn't see Joe's body. And yes, Rachel is Jaden. I'm not nearly finished. It gets even more bizarre!"

I smiled and told her, "Go for it! I'm past being shocked!"

Chapter Seven

Lee continued her story.
    "After a few hours of driving, Brandie became fretful and restless. Seeing a mile-marker sign, I knew we only had a few minutes to the next town. Rachel saw a service station, and–thought it looked like a safe place for us to pull off for a break and a cup of coffee. After parking the Mercedes at a pump, Rachel climbed out of the car and proceeded to fill the gas tank, while I took Brandie into the restaurant and bought her a package of peanuts. Returning to the car, and trying to find a napkin in one of my coat pockets to wipe Brandie's nose, I discovered the little black book that Joe had given me earlier before he was killed. I opened it up and saw it was a savings account book that showed a balance of more than twenty million dollars. I handed the little black book to Rachel for her to take a look."
    "When she saw the balance, her eyes got as big as quarters. Putting her hands over her mouth, and with a surprise look on her face, she asked me where it came from. I told her about Joe giving it to me earlier before he left for the fitness club and suggested that we find an ATM. She was worried it could be traced but we figured, since it was Saturday and the banks were only open until noon, any transactions wouldn't post until Monday. We'd be far away by that point."
    "I drove around in the little town looking for an ATM. Rachel finally saw one in front of a Wal-Mart store. After pulling up to it, I punched in the account number. A message saying no record of this account number could be found. I tried again, and the same thing happened. I opened the glove compartment and threw that stupid little black book in it as hard as I could and slammed the door shut, adding a few angry words. As we left the parking lot, I asked Rachel to check our purses and every inch of the car to see how much cash she could find. After her search, she came up with192.37."
    Rachel had picked up an Illinois map at the truck stop, and after looking at it, we decided to drive south on the Highway 127 black top,

as far as the money would take us. Our only stops were to grab a bite to eat, to buy fuel, and go to the restroom. It was so hard on Brandie, but she traveled like a trouper. Once in a while she would ask, 'Mommy, where are we going?' or, 'I'm tired of riding' and finally, she fell asleep.

It was about 8:30 P.M., Rachel counted our money, and we had a little over30.00. She asked, 'What now, Christina?"–I saw a country service station and pulled into the parking lot. I shook my head and told Rachel, 'I don't know what to do. Maybe, God will hear my prayers and something will turn up.' She hugged me and said, 'Me, too, I've been praying all day and we are going to be just fine Christina. God hears our every prayer. All we have to do is believe they will be answered.'"

About that time, there was a peck on the car window, and an old gentleman stood there, bending his head level with the car. After I rolled the window down, he asked, 'Can I hep ya lady?' I told him that he could and asked what part of Illinois we were in.

'"He smiled real big and said, 'Be glad to. Yer in Bond County.' Pointing, he continued, 'And Saint Louis is about sixty-three miles that a way. Yer welcome to sit here if you like but, I'm closin' about twenty minutes frum now. Are you and yer friend okay?"

"We're just fine. Thank you for asking."

"He gave us a final nod, saying, 'Take care, ladies, and a good night to ya,"

"After rolling the window up, I leaned back in my seat. Rachel could see that I was about to burst into tears."

"'Stop it, Christina," she said. "Let's think for a minute.'"

"Full of anger and about to have a panic attack, I hit the steering wheel with my fists. 'Did I hear you say let's 'think a minute?' Good heavens, Rachel! It's bitter cold outside, and we are broke and sitting in a dark parking lot of a closed service station!' Lifting my hands toward the ceiling of the car and completing my point, I said, 'Oh, yeah. And we only have a half tank of gas. What the hell is there to think about?' She reached over, and we held each other and cried."

"Finally, running out of tears, Rachel spoke up. 'Maybe, we can hock some of our jewelry.'"

"For a few seconds, we thought that could be the solution to our money problem. Then it dawned on me that the jewelry we brought with us was registered with serial numbers. Rachel started to cry again, but I interrupted her, telling her that if she started again, so would I. She was right—we needed to calm down and think. We sat in the parking lot of the service station, not knowing what to do or where to turn. We both started reminiscing about our dreams as children and how far off the path we'd veered. I suddenly recalled that my best friend had moved to Illinois. We had been friends from kindergarten until her dad's company transferred him to Illinois in our tenth-grade year. Rachel stared at me with a puzzled look, until I told her I had stayed in contact with my friend until I met Joe. Rachel asked if I had an email address or phone number. I told her, "I didn't know if she had changed her email address or phone number. Besides, I thought email addresses could be traced."

She seemed a bit discouraged. 'I don't know, Christina. Surely, there is some way to contact her without being traced. That is, if she is still in this state.'"

"Excitedly, I told Rachel, "In the last email she sent, she said that their family had settled in Clinton County. Rachel reached in the pocket of her seat for the map and began the search for Clinton Count. Then, she said enthusiastically, 'You are not going to believe this! It is the next county south of where we are right now!'"

"I opened my mouth, took in a deep breath, and muttered, 'You are kidding!'"

"She shook her head and said, "No, here it is on the map." I leaned over Rachel's shoulder and looked at the map she was holding. We stared at the spot above her index finger and discovered that the Clinton county line was only a few minutes away from where we were. I put the car in drive and headed for Highway 127 South."

"After crossing the county line, we began to watch for signs that would give us some idea how far it would be to the next town. And, sure enough, Rachel saw one that advertised a motel only seven miles away.

Driving into the town, we looked for a restaurant and immediately found a fast food place. After parking the car, I dug into my purse for change and managed to come up with enough to call directory assistance. Plus, Rachel handed me a couple of dollar bills."

"I went into the restaurant and inquired about a public phone. The cashier pointed to the rear of the building. After making my way to the booth and digging some change from my coat pocket, I put the money into the slot, and dialed the phone for information."

"Thank God she gave me a number that had the name of my friend. Taking a deep breath and shaking like a leaf, I dialed the number. The phone began to ring. One ring...two rings...three rings, and a prayer went through my mind. Oh, please, God, let this be her, and let her answer the phone! Almost hanging up the phone after the fifth ring, I heard a woman say hello and I recognized her voice right away."

"Is this Millie Sterling?"

"Who the hell wants to know?'"

"My knees were about to buckle when I said, "Millie, this is Christina Rogers! Remember, we were friends in school...when you lived in Texas..."

"Now, just a minute, Lee! You knew Millie before coming to Ellisville? What are you saying? What in the world?" I stared at her in disbelief.

"Yes, Shannon. Please, be patient. I'm almost finished. Then, you will understand everything. That's a promise!"

"Okay, Lee. But you need to know something. You are freaking me out! Well...what did Millie say?"

"Nothing for a few seconds. Then, suddenly, she blurted out, 'I'll be a son of a biscuit-eater. How are you, Charlie? You know, I had you on my mind just today, wondering whatever happened to you!'"

"That's all it took for the flood-gates to open and I told her the whole dilemma about Joe, Brandie, and Rachel." "It's ok, Charlie. I know exactly where you are, and I'll be there in about thirty minutes."

Upon returning to the car I told Rachel that we must have had an angel on our shoulders. Not only did I talk to my friend, she is coming to get us!" Rachel uttered under her breath, "Thank you, Jesus!'"

"Millie showed up in about twenty-five minutes. When she got out of her van, she met me with a big hug. I burst into tears again, and Millie kept her arms around me until I stopped crying. She comforted and reasured me. 'It's all right, Charlie. Shush now, honey. I'm going to see to it that you, the baby and your friend are going to be safe.' Hearing my childhood nickname calmed and comforted me."

Stopping Lee again, I asked, "Why did Millie call you Charlie?"

"Well, the first day we went to pre-school, she couldn't say my name. And when she tried, it came out 'Charlie.' Even when she could say 'Christina,' she never stopped calling me 'Charlie.'"

"Sorry for the interuption," I said as I got up to get a glass of water. "But do you realize what you have been telling me sounds like a movie or a T.V. mini-series? I'm baffled!"

"There is more if you can handle it."

Nodding my head, my answer was, "Oooh yeah, tell me e-ve-ry detail!"

"All right," she said. "Here goes."

Millie said, "I have a place in mind to take you that hardly anyone knows about except a friend and me. "It isn't much, Charlie, but it will be a roof over your head and a warm safe place to stay until we can come up with something better. Get in your car and follow me. We're only a little way from it." She walked with me back to my car and Rachel rolled down her window for a quick introduction.

"I got in my car and over hills and dales we went until we came to a sign that read *Welcome to Ellisville, Population 12,620*. We took a street through town and out again to a country black top, then onto a gravel road, and down a dirt lane that led us into a patch of woods. Finally, we saw a clearing and the mobile home. Rachel took Brandie out of her car seat, and we all went inside. Millie turned on the heat and apologized that the place was so run-down. I told her it looked like a castle to us and that we were so grateful to be there and have a safe place to stay."

"I hugged her and said, "Thank you, dear friend." As Millie turned away from me, it looked as if tears began to puddle up in her eyes. She took the tail of her shirt and pretended to wipe her forehead. Millie cleared her throat, and looking at Rachel and then pointed toward a door saying, 'the small bedroom has clean sheets and pillows if you want the little one to sleep in there.' Then she asked.

"How much money do you have?

"Less than thirty-six dollar,"

"You are going to need money and some transportation,' she said. 'But the first thing we're gonna have to do is hide that Mercedes in an old shed out back. A car like that can be spotted from the air. I guess you know you can't drive it around either! It would attract too much attention. I'm making a trip into town. I'll be back as fast as I can.' It was almost an hour and a half before Millie returned. Looking out the window, I saw her take two large bags of food from the van. After bringing them in and setting them down on the kitchen counter, she motioned for me to follow her to the van. Millie opened the doors and we began setting boxes down on the ground with all sorts of linens, hand towels, wash clothes, toothbrushes, shampoo, hair brush, make up, and all kinds of other things. We carried them in, and she began digging into one of the boxes, stating "I know it has to be here somewhere". She pulled out a red wig and then some little boy's clothing. She handed them to me and said, "I'll be back in a minute."

"When she came back in, she motioned for me to come with her again to the van. Millie opened the back door, and I peeked in. There was a girl's bike with all the frills and a basket on the handle bars. I asked, "Millie! Where did you get all of this stuff?" She told me, "I had it in my garage and attic, and now there's a use for it."-We took the bike out of the van and parked it next to the porch."

"The night had become very cold and we headed back into the mobile home. Millie apologized to me. 'Charlie, the bike is all I could come up with right now. But we're going to work something out, so don't you worry.' Then she asked me where I had put the wig. Seeing it on top of one of the boxes and picking it up, she walked over to me and began fitting the wig on my head., it looks a hell of a lot better on you than it ever did on me! Wish there was a way to cover those big brown eyes.' I told Millie that I had a pair of green contacts, she said, "You have got to be kidding me! That'll be perfect." I rummaged through my stuff 'til I found the contacts and went to the bathroom to take out my clear lenses and put the green ones in my eyes."

"When Millie saw me, she said, 'You're already looking a lot different, Charlie, but we still need to do more.' After that, Millie widened my eyebrows and made my lips larger with heavy make-up. I went to look at myself in the mirror and was amazed by the change. 'I don't look like myself at all, Millie!' She smiled and agreed. 'No, you don't! But that's the idea! It is perfect, and you are beautiful. Charlie, I think you and Rachel should get a couple of days rest. But tomorrow after work, I'll bring you some real warm clothing for you when ride the bike. I have some other ideas about how we can shorten the ride to town. Now, this is what we are going to do...'"

"Well, Shannon, that's it. You know the rest of my life."

Dumbfounded and shocked by Lee's story, I leaned back in the chair, crossing my arms over my chest and remarked, "You and Millie deserve an Academy Award for your performance. You have everyone fooled."

Lee spoke up quickly in a defensive mode. "Shannon! That was the only way for me to get a job and to keep my identity a secret. I couldn't use my driver's license or any other identification. You have no idea how much it bothers me to have to live a lie. Please understand. There are two other people who depend on me to keep them alive! I'm not being a drama queen here! There are gangsters who are out to KILL us, Shannon!"

I stood up and began to pace the floor, trying to mentally digest the information she had shared. If she could fool me and everyone else with her little scene at Millie's, what if everything she had said today was a fabrication? But, seeing the expressions of fear and the sadness in her eyes, I somehow knew she was telling the truth. "Is Millie the only one who knows who you are?"

"Yes, and I can't stress it enough to you that this is the way it has to be. It's a matter of life or death for Brandie, Rachel, and me! Can you understand? We have to be so careful because one slip and...." Lee began to cry.

I sat back down, reached for her hand, and tried to reassure her. "Your secret is safe. I would never reveal anything that you have shared with me about your past."

With tears running down her face, she slumped in the chair as though a ton of bricks had been lifted from her shoulders. Taking her other hand in mine, I said firmly, "Look at me, Lee! Know this! If anyone tries to hurt Brandon...excuse me...Brandie, your friend, or you, it will be over my dead body because it is going to be my business to protect you."

Getting a scared expression on her face, she warned, "I'm not so sure that wouldn't be arranged, especially if we become good friends!"

"Don't you think the kiss we shared the other night qualifies us to be a little more than friends?"

She smiled and asked, "Are you serious, Shannon? Even after everything I've told you?"

Lifting my eyebrows and flashing my boyish grin at her, I asked in a quiet voice, "Does a bird shit on a clean car?"

At first, she smiled. Then, suddenly, she laughed, saying, "Thank you again, Shannon. You have a wonderful sense of humor. I haven't laughed like that in …. I can't remember when!"

I responded, "Good! There is a lot more where that came from!" I got up from my chair and walked over to the back window. I saw a shed and pointed to it. "Is the Mercedes in there?"

Lee answered with a yes and said, "Millie has a friend in St. Louis who is trying to find out how the car could be sold without being traced back to me. He has no idea about the circumstances of my ownership. She told him that I couldn't find the papers to the car. I don't know of any way to sell it that would be legal. Does a person have to send a title or something to a state office of some kind when they purchase a car or sell it?"

Putting a down-side to her hopes, I told her, "I'm afraid so."

With a concerned frown, she mumbled, "There has to be a way to get rid of that car. It is so dangerous to have it here. I don't know what to do."

"Maybe there is a possibility of getting it taken care of. But, right off hand, I don't know of anything."

Lee assured me, "Shannon, there are no expectations on my part that you do anything. I just appreciate having someone who cares."

We sort of looked at each other and decided that it was time for me to leave. "Better be on my way, Lee. Jaden and your daughter are probably ready to get back from their hike. Make me a promise that if you need anything…"

She nodded and said, "I promise! You have no idea how much

Deception or Perfection

pressure has been taken off me now that everything is out in the open with you." Lee followed me to the door and, just before I stepped out to leave, she kissed my cheek and asked, "Shannon, do you think we can pull off keeping my identity a secret?"

I gave her a reassuring smile and said, "Lee, there isn't anything on this earth that we can't accomplish together, with God's help."

As I was driving down the lane, I thought, "I wonder just what might be on the Mercedes title that Lee has stashed in the shed? There might be something which could clear it enough to be legal! Not likely, but, what if?" I turned around and headed back to the mobile home. Lee saw me parking in the clearing. She rushed out the door and onto the porch and asked "something wrong?"

Heading up the steps, I answered, "No. But it did occur to me that perhaps there is something on the registration.... Do you know where it might be?"

"It could be in the glove compartment or in one of the back seat pockets. I don't know for sure." After I suggested she take a look, she asked, "Would you go with me?"

The two of us went out to the old shed and pulled back the branches from the entrance. After opening all four doors to the car, we frantically began our search for the registration. I reached into the back pocket of the driver's seat and found a large envelope. We went back into the mobile home, and sat down at the table. I opened the envelope and found there were several papers. After carefully examining each one, I said, "Lee, there is nothing that even looks like the registration in here!" She couldn't believe it. We searched again with no luck.

With a concerned tone, she remarked, "I don't know where it could be! A person just assumes their car has at least papers that state who it belongs to."

"Is it possible it could be someplace else?" Shaking her head in disbelief, she said, "That registration could be anywhere."

Feeling very disappointed, we just sat there. Neither of us said anything for a few minutes. Finally, Lee spoke up. "I'm going back to the shed to see if we missed something." When Lee returned from the second search of the car, she handed me a yellow sheet of paper saying, "Shannon, this is all I found. It was under the driver's side sun visor. It isn't the registration, but it should be looked at."

Glancing at it, I asked, "Were you with your husband when he bought the car?"

"No! It was a surprise Christmas gift. Why do you ask?"

Smiling at her, I announced, "Because this piece of paper is a contract for the Mercedes, and neither yours nor your husband's name is anywhere on it. The car has been leased and the owner is Diamond Back Rental Service in Las Vegas, Nevada. Let me show you."–I pointed and moved the paper towards Lee. "Do you know a Carl Nester?"

"No!" she replied. "I've never heard of him!"

Pointing to where the name appeared on the contract, I told her, "Look here…his name is on the line as the person who leased the vehicle."

"What does that mean?" she asked. "Well, that means there is no way this car can be traced to you, Lee! All that needs to be done to dispose of the Mercedes is to take it to a Diamond Back rental place and drop it off."

She beamed as her excitement grew. "You don't mean it!"

"Indeed, I do, Lee."

"Are you sure?!"

As both of us stood up, I responded. "As sure as God made little green apples!"

She let out a big squeal as she came to my side of the table with open arms. As I stood up, she put her arms around my neck and gave me a grateful kiss. I picked her up, swung her around, and just as our lips were about to meet again, Jaden burst into the door and screamed! "Christina, are you ok? What is going on in here?"

As I set Lee back down, she quickly reminded her friend, "You forgot, Jaden, it's Lee! And I am just fine! Shannon has discovered a way we can get rid of the car, and I'll tell you all about it."

Brandie walked through the door with a big smile on her face. I sort of brushed at my jeans and Lee ran her fingers through her hair trying to regain her composure. Jaden took in a deep breath and said, "When I heard you squealing Lee it scared me! I'm sorry for bursting in like that."

"No, I should apologize to you. It's just that...for the first time in months, maybe we can regain some normality to our lives." After Lee and Jaden hugged each other, Jaden gave me a wave and retreated to her bedroom. Brandie asked her mom if she and Goggy could have some peanut butter and crackers in her room, so Lee fixed them some cracker sandwiches and kissed Brandie on the cheek. Then Brandie headed to her bedroom with Goggy trailing closely behind.

Lee was ecstatic and said, she was going to drop the car off, first thing in the morning, and I told her, "Don't you, worry, Lee. You, Brandie, and Jaden are going to be safe, okay? So...will you have dinner with me Saturday night?" Without hesitation she said yes, and we set the time for me to pick her up.

The next day my heavy schedule did not allow the pleasure of my usual coffee break at Millie's. At about ten o'clock, Lee showed up at the clinic. I smiled, pointed toward the hallway, and she followed me into my office. After closing the door, I asked her, "How did it go? And how did you get back to Ellisville so fast?"

"It went great! The lease had been paid in advance for eighteen months and they refunded six of the eight months that was left on the lease. And what is amazing Shannon, they didn't ask one question! To answer your second question, Millie called one of her friends who lived in St. Louis and he brought me here. You know, if it hadn't been for your knowledge and persistence, I would still be scared about that car. Thank you so much!"

"No thanks are necessary," I told her. "I'm just glad something worked out for you. It's hard for me to understand what the whole thing was about, but it worked, and that is all that matters. And I'm sure glad Millie could come to your rescue."

Lee took a deep breath and said, "Guess I'd better get out of here. Jaden is expecting me home in about twenty minutes." As she walked out the door, she turned, smiled, and waved, saying, "See you tomorrow."

As I grinned and waved back, I responded, "You betcha!"

The next morning after arriving at Millie's, instead of waiting to be served I walked to the end of the counter where the pot and cups were sitting, and poured my own coffee. After seating myself at the table with Hank and Grant, I took a sip and placed the cup on the table. I then leaned back in the chair with crossed arms over my chest and gave the two of them a big smile.

With a one-eyed squint, Hank pointed his finger at me and remarked, "Now, there's a contented man, Grant."

"Yep, Hank. He sure looks like a contented man all right," I'd say he has more on his mind than coffee."

I just kept on smiling, not saying a word.

Finally, Hank couldn't stand it any longer and blurted out, "Hey, Whitney. Ain't you got somethin' ta tell us?"

Before Hank could say anything else, Lee approached the table with a big smile and asked, "Would any of you guys care for breakfast this morning?"

Grant and Hank passed on the food and said they had to leave for work shortly. Leaning toward the table, and giving Lee a big grin, I reached for the menu. After glancing through the breakfast section, I said, "I'll have a stack of pancakes, two eggs over easy, hash browns, ham, and a large glass of O.J."

Smiling sweetly at me, Lee responded, "Your breakfast will be here shortly."

Grant and Hank were fit to be tied, but they kept their cool even though they knew there was something different between Lee and me.

"What's going on with you and Lee, Whitney?" Grant asked suspiciously.

"If it was something I wanted you to know, you would have already heard about it." "Then, Hank chimed in with, "Okay, Mr. Doodle Dip! You jes go ahead and keep yer little secret. If you don't tell us... well, somebody else will! So, why don't you jes spit it out?"

Teasing them, I said, "You know what? The problem here is that the two of you want to be the first news carriers in this town. I'm sorry boys. Guess you are going to hear about Lee and me through the grapevine just like everyone else."

Grant got out of his chair in a huff, saying, "I've got to go to work!"

Hank muttered under his breath to Grant, "His mouth is tighter then a rectum with diarrhea. He ain't gonna tell us a thang!"

Deception or Perfection

When Lee delivered my breakfast and realized what was happening, she added the icing onto my cake with sexy body language as she cooed, "Shannon, is there anything else I can do for you?"

"Don't think so, baby," I told her. "With everything you have already given me, who could ask for anything more?"

When Lee walked away from the table, Grant bent over into my face and said smugly, "You and Lee think you are pretty cute don't you?"

Hank, trying to console Grant, told him, "They think their jes a couple a comedians tryin' ta git our goat. Don't pay no attention to 'em, Grant!"

Teasing them again, I said, "We're so cute we had a poster made. I'll lease you one real cheap if you are interested."

Hanks face turned blood red as he blurted out in anger, "You arrogant prick! You know, asshole, what goes around comes around, and I'm gonna be there when you git yers!" Scooting out of his chair, he motioned to Grant and continued, "Let's get out of here! We don't have ta stay around this fart-head and git insulted." With that they left Millie's.

Over the next few days, Grant and Hank made themselves scarce. Finally, Friday came around, and as I entered Millie's, I could see Hank sitting at the counter. I walked over to him, put my hand on his shoulder, and asked, "Hey, Champ! You and Grant still pissed off at me?"

Hank glanced up and admitted, "A little." Then, he smiled and said, "Nevertheless, we will git over ourselves. Go on and sit at our table. I'll be there in a jiffy." Glancing at Millie, he smiled at her and added, "Jes' as soon as Millie gits my cup of joe."

When Hank got to the table he also had a cup of coffee for me and sat down. I asked, "Where is Grant?"

"He's been sick with the flu fer a couple of days now," said Hank.

"Wish Ellen would have called me," Maybe there is something I could do to help him or Ellen."

"He's gonna be fine, Whitney. It ain't any thang serious." We sat for a few minutes. Finally I opened up. "Hank, Lee…we…well, we are getting closer. And I'm taking her out for dinner tomorrow night."

Hank grinned real big, "It's about time. She's a good woman, and I thank she likes ya a bunch, man."

Hank had no more than finished his statement and Lee came to the table. When she refilled our coffee cups, I told her, "Lee, Hank knows about our date tomorrow night. It hasn't been easy keeping it to myself. Hope it's okay."

She smiled and responded, "I'm sure looking forward to it!"

"Me and Grant had a suspicion the two of you might have become more than jes friends. I jes told this pup that she is a very a good woman; he had better treat you right. If he don't, he's got me and Vickie to answer to! I can't hardly wait ta tell Grant!"

Hank and I finished our coffee and decided we needed to get to work. At the register, I reminded Lee that I would call her before she left for work and confirm our date. She looked at me shyly and said, "That's great. I'll be waiting."

Walking out the restaurant door, Hank asked, "Will ya tell Grant and me how yer date went?"

Looking him straight in the eyes, I asked firmly, "Hank, did you or Grant tell me about your first dates with Vickie and Ellen?"

Hank admitted, "That wuz a dumb question, Whitney. Don't pay no attention to me. It's jes that we have seen you lonely and sad for a long time, and we're as excited about you and this little lady as you are."

Responding to his concern, I promised, "Tell you what, my friend. You are going to hear everything that is appropriate. There are a lot of things that a man can't share if he thinks it would embarrass his date. How does that sound?"

Hank nodded and gave me a knuckle bump on the shoulder and said, "You have a good, wonderful, great time. It's my hope that she is the right one. Okay, bud? See you Monday."

We gave each other a wave and went on our way to work. Of course, I knew when the time came for sharing, he and Grant were not going to be happy with me, but that would be their problem.

Chapter Eight

After waking up Saturday morning, my first priority of the day was to sit down at the computer and make reservations at the Blue Skies, a romantic restaurant in St. Louis. During my lunch break, it occurred to me that I needed to call Lee to confirm our date before she left work. We talked and planned to leave Ellisville by six. After hanging up the phone and taking a deep breath, I thought, *this is really happening!*

The day passed quickly and closing at three, excitement began to fill my thoughts. After getting all spruced up for my date and leaving to pick up Lee, it hit me. I didn't have to fantasize about asking her out anymore. The fantasy had become real, and she said "Yes." *God, thank you for helping me make this happen. Even though there wasn't much footwork done on my part, you still came through for me.*

I drove into the clearing at Lee's place, and she opened the door as I stepped out of the truck to meet her. She smiled and greeted me with a kiss on the cheek. She looked so beautiful and seemed five years younger without the heavy makeup and the other disguises. Her hair was curled around the face, which made her eyes appear larger and almost hypnotic. She was wearing a blue, low-cut, off-shoulder dress. Kind of short, it fit snugly to her body and just below her waist it flared out like a fluffy cloud. The fabric was shimmery with little dark red rose buds that appeared puffed up and made a complete circle around the bottom of the dress. She wore what looked like three-inch heels of a dark red, the same color as the rose buds, and she carried a little purse that matched her shoes. Her perfume had a very light fragrance of honey and fresh rain. That sounds like a weird combination, but it was the most haunting fragrance I had ever experienced in my life. I thought to myself, *you're the most awesome woman in the world, and it's unbelievable that you are standing next to me.*

I opened the passenger door of the truck and Lee settled into the seat, giving me a sweet smile. After stepping into my side of the truck, the first remark out of my mouth was, "You're a knock-out, beautiful lady! All the men will be jealous of me tonight for having the most beautiful women in the two-state area on my arm!"

Lee teased me, "Why, Dr. Whitney, only two states?" Then she giggled and said, "Thank you. And I will be very proud to be hanging onto the arm of a handsome man such as you."

After backing out into the lane, I put the shift in the go-as-fast-as-you-can gear and we were on our way to the Blue Skies restaurant.

We shared pointless chatter for a while, and then I asked, "Lee, what would you say to helping out at the clinic now and then when you are available? It's understandable if you can't."

"I would love to help out. But my licenses and Texas college transcripts are in my maiden name. It would be dangerous for me to try to have them mailed to my address. There isn't any way for me to obtain them without possibly being traced."

Changing the subject, I asked, "Jaden sure doesn't get out much, does she?"

Thinking for a moment, Lee answered, "No. She is still grieving over the loss of Keith… Oh, yes, Shannon…just a reminder. Don't let our real names slip during any conversation with others. Brandie is a boy named Brandon. I'm praying that somehow soon things will change. Keeping her and Jaden hidden from people has become more difficult. Plus, when August comes, she will be old enough to go to pre-school. It seems like Brandie has become Jaden's life. I've questioned her several times about getting a job or volunteering, but she's told me she has a job babysitting Brandie. Plus she can work on her book. She does worry that she is a financial burden, but, as I've told her, she cooks, cleans, and cares for my baby like her own."

Leaning towards me, Lee said, "And you know what, Shannon? Millie has been the most wonderful friend to us. She would come late at night and take us to movies, shopping, or any place we needed or wanted to go. By the way, she was the one who brought us to the movies the night you bumped into me. She had to go to the ladies' room after we got to the theater. She saw you as she was coming out of the restroom and jumped backwards so fast that it almost slammed the door on a woman trying to enter." Lee then began to giggle. "You should have seen your face that night!"

"Well, you should have seen yours!" Both of us giggled, and I mentioned again about her working at the clinic. "Look, what would be wrong with you helping me on Mondays, your day off. It wouldn't have to be all day. I could use some help, and the pay isn't bad."

"Are you serious?"

I began to answer her with one of my old cliché. "As serious as..."

"Yes I know, as serious as a heart attack!" Lee butted in.

Under my breath, I mumbled, "That wasn't what I was going to say, Miss Smarty."

With a big smile, she added, "By the way, I accept your offer to come to work for you."

"That's the best news I've heard since you said 'yes' to our dinner date tonight."

By this time, we arrived at the restaurant, and it wasn't easy finding a parking spot. Finally, a space opened up after we circled the lot several times. Then jumping out of the truck and hurrying around to the passenger side, I opened the door and offered Lee my hand. As she turned to step out of the truck, she somehow got the toe of her shoe caught in the hem of her dress. All at once, she began to fall forward. Making a fast grab, I managed to keep her from hitting the asphalt. With the toe of her shoe still in the hem of the dress, I held her steady as she leaned against the truck. When lifting her foot to release the hem from the shoe, Lee completely lost her balance. There was a sound as though her dress was being ripped to pieces. And again, I caught her before she tumbled head first onto the parking lot. After gaining her composure, Lee looked down and saw the skirt of her dress hanging half-way off the waist. There she stood with shoe in hand, staring at her torn, beautiful dress dropping from the waist. Her chin started to quiver when she frantically announced, "There is no way I can go into any place looking like this."

"It's okay, don't be upset," I told her.

In a hurt and disappointed tone, she exclaimed, "Don't be upset? All the trouble you went through making reservations and driving all this distance for a nice dinner and the "klutz-master" of the year ruins everything." Tears began to fill her eyes.

"Look, there are some clean sweats behind the truck seat. I keep them there just in case some farm animal happens to get me dirty when I am on the job. They may be too big, but at least," I said with a grin and a snicker, "you won't have a draft around your waist."

With tears still in her eyes, Lee gave me a chin-up, cockeyed confrontational glance and with a demure, complacent grin she said. "So I'm to understand that you are not into the "drafty look"!"

"Who, me? Honey, I'm into anything you want me to be!"

She took a deep breath and with disappointment in her voice, remarked, "It's too early to go home."

Pointing to the truck, I suggested, "Why don't you go ahead and put the sweats on. We can stop off some place where you can feel comfortable, have a bite to eat, and visit a while. Then, we can go on back to Ellisville."

"That's just about all we can do for now," she said. "How about getting something to go so that I can stay in the truck?"

"Would you feel comfortable going into a fast-food place for a hamburger or a chicken sandwich?"

"Yes, that sounds fine."

"You can get the sweats out from behind the seat and change in the truck. It's dark and no one will see you." Then, putting my hand up like a traffic cop, I teased her by saying in an authoritative manner, "I'll even stand guard so that if someone should walk up, I can say give me a dollar and I'll let you see a beautiful woman who is undressing in my truck."

Looking at me with squinted eyes, Lee responded, "You wouldn't dare!"

"Of course, I would!"

She smiled and teased me back. "Okay, maybe it will open up a new career for me."

After Lee changed I climbed into the truck. We were crossing the Eades Bridge back into Illinois when Lee remarked, "I'm sorry that I ruined the evening."

"Well, I'm sorry to disagree with you, but you have not ruined our evening," I said quickly. "The night has just begun! And, as far as being a klutz, well join the club. I have tripped over patterns in a carpet. Sometimes, we have no control over becoming unbalanced when a heel, toe, or anything else decides to become tangled in our clothing."

Lee scooted next to me, closing the gap between us. Laying her head on my shoulder, she said, "Thank you for being so understanding. You are a kind person. Most men would have taken me straight home and not looked back."

"You bring out the best in me."

Lee smiled saying, "What a line, Shannon Whitney! I'll bet you say that to all the girls you have dated!"

"Oh, no! You are the first woman to hear that from me. Honest, Lee. I *do not* say anything that isn't the truth to a female. My dad used to tell me, 'Shannon, never lie to a woman unless you are ready to pay the consequences.' So, dear heart, you can take that to the bank. I will never lie to you!"

After about thirty minutes of traveling, we got off the interstate to get a bite to eat at a fast food restaurant. When Lee got out of the truck, I couldn't help smiling at her. She looked like a cute little girl who had been swallowed by my sweats.

We went into the restaurant, sat down, and ordered our food. While we waited for our order, neither of us did much talking. Finally, I spoke up. "In case you haven't guessed by now, I'm almost a pure-blooded Irishman. My dad's great-grandfather came from Ireland and settled in St. Louis, where he met my Irish great-grandmother. So my dad was pure bred Irish, but my mom was three-quarters French, one-eighth Irish and one-eighth Italian."

"No one would have ever guessed you had any Irish blood in you," Lee teased. "Unless the name Shannon disguises your Irish heritage."

Giving her my boyish flirty grin, and taking her hand, I kissed it and said to her with a silly French accent, "Boot sum time when I am with a bou-ti-fill lady, de French purr-son coums out in me. And, olso we ore ver-ee sin-shue-el louveers."

Lee turned her head side-ways and glanced at me, saying, "I don't know how sensual you are, but your accent needs a lot of practice."

"Oh, mon Cherie, you con say an-nee-thing, and it melts mye hart," Suddenly, it looked as though she was about to cry. I was stunned because I had never experienced a woman tear up when I was showing off with my French accent. It had always gotten a laugh. Lee blinked her eyes and smiled as I tried to lighten the moment.

"Well, little lady, wait till you hear my John Wayne impersonation! That'll pud-da a bee in yo-ur bonnet."

She finally laughed then gave me some advice. "Don't try to make a living with your impersonations, especially if you want to put a bee in someone's bonnet."

Smiling at her, I had to admit, "Okay, so it needs a little more developing. Give me time, and I'll sound just like John Wayne! Now tell, me beautiful lady, shall we head for Ellisville? You're not ready to go to your place yet, are you?"

"No!" she said quickly.

"Would you like to have a glass of wine at my house? The evening is still young."

"Only if it's imported French wine," she answered.

Not wanting to lie I replied, "Is there any other kind?"

She smiled as though she knew I was evading her statement and said, "It would be wonderful to go to your home for a glass of wine!"

On the way back to Ellisville the two of us talked up a storm. But after arriving at my house, I became uptight, and got very nervous while trying to unlock the door. For some reason, my key just didn't seem to fit the lock. Lee gently touched my hand that held the key and asked, "Would you like for me to try and unlock the door? After all, you have had a very traumatic evening."

Turning around and looking into her hypnotic eyes, I asked with a smile, "Oh? And you haven't?"

The first time Lee put the key in the lock and gave the door a little push, it opened. "See how easy that was," she said. "You know, Shannon, a woman's coping skills are much better than a man's."

I thought to myself, *sure,* but my response was, "I will tuck that away in my memory bank just in case it is needed at a later date."

She gave me a condescending smile as if to say, "Good for you!"

Both of us were feeling a bit awkward as we walked through the foyer into the living room. Nervously, I pointed toward the couch, and with a voice that sounded like a thirteen-year-old boy going through puberty, I stammered, "P-p-p- please sit down and m-m-make yourself comfortable. D-d-do you like music?"

Lee nodded,

"W-w-would you like to listen to my favorite CD?"

"That sounds great,"

When going over to the stereo and putting the CD into the slot, I pointed toward the kitchen and said, "I'm going to g-g-get the wine. I'll be back in a jiffy."

Walking into the kitchen, I felt my knees shaking like a willow in a wind storm. Then, after grabbing two glasses from the cabinet and taking the wine from the refrigerator, I took a deep breath and heard my mom's voice: *Shannon, just be yourself. Everything is going to be all right.* That thought brought a smile to my face as I entered the living room.

After setting the glasses down on the coffee table, I noticed Lee looking at some of the pictures from my family photo album. As I stepped over to the couch, she glanced up at me and patted the cushion as though she wanted me close to her. After easing myself down, I opened the wine bottle, filled our glasses to the brim, and handed a glass to Lee. As I was taking a sip of wine, she put her index finger on one of the pictures and asked, "Are these people your parents?"

"Yes, they are."

She curiously directed her eyes to the picture again and asked, "Where are they now?"

"You mean no one has told you about my parents?"

She answered with astonishment, "No, Shannon! Is there something you don't want to reveal about your parents?"

"Not at all," I said. "It just amazes me that Millie hasn't told you all about my family. My mom, dad, and little sister were killed in a head-on car collision."

As she took my hand, compassion came over her face, and she said, "I'm so sorry! That has to be very painful for you. How could anyone emotionally survive such a horrendous tragedy? That is an ultimate loss."

Swallowing hard and clearing my throat, I told her, "I've got a lot of great memories that have been helpful."

Lee released my hand. "Would you be comfortable sharing any of them?"

At first, I was afraid that talking about the loss of my family might cause me to have an emotional outburst. However, it occurred to me that this might actually help to ease some of the pain. "Sure, there are a couple of memories. At about eleven years of age, I remember getting off the school bus in tears. I entered the house, ran past my mother, and headed straight up the stairs into my bedroom. Mom yelled from the bottom of the steps, 'Shannon, are you okay?' and when I didn't answer her, she followed me upstairs."

"She asked me again, 'What's wrong Shannon?' Not wanting her to see me crying, I jumped on the bed and buried my head in the pillow. Mom stood at my doorway and asked 'What's wrong Shannon? Did something happen at school today?' I shook my head no, and she continued to question me. 'Shannon, did something happen on the bus?' After coming over to my bed, she sat down beside me. She gently smoothed back my hair and kept questioning me. 'Are you crying?' she asked."

Trying to hold back the tears, my throat began to hurt, and, in a muffled voice, I said, 'A little!' She put her arms around me and gently asked, 'You want to tell me what happened?'"

"I swallowed hard and rubbed my sniffly nose with my shirt sleeve. All at once, I started to cry and blubbered out, 'The boys on the bus say I have a girl's name! They call me a *sissie* and *girlie* and some other ugly names that I can´t even repeat to you, Mom!'"

"She cuddled me close and placed her cheek on top of my head and sort of rocked me in her arms. And, with a soft, consoling voice, she whispered, 'Shush. Shush, now. Everything's gonna be all right.' Then, pausing for a moment, she asked, 'Shannon, do you know what your name means?'"

"Wiping the tears away, I told her no."

"'Well, 'In Celtic, it means ´Big River´. And, in Hebrew it means, ´Blessed be God.´ Have you ever heard the Mississppi River called the *The Mighty Mississippi*?'"

I shook my head no. And looking straight into my eyes, she continued,'When you were born, I told myself that I want my son to have a name with power and might as well as the sensivity of God. Because I knew someday when you grew up to be a man, you would have both Godly qualities and the strength of a great river. How many of those silly boys at school can say they have a name like that?'"

"After a moment of reflecting on what she said, I told her, 'Heck, Mom! None of them has a name that means *mighty*!' She gave me a kiss on my head and said, 'That's right! Now, go wash your hands. Dinner is almost ready.' And, from that day on, I have never been ashamed of my name."

Lee smiled for a moment, then softly said, "That is the sweetest memory I have ever heard. Tell me some more!"

Smiling back at her, I asked, "Tell you more of what?"

Lee kicked off her shoes, turned toward me, crossed her legs Indian-style, and made her request again. "Tell me more of your memories about your family!"

Not quite understanding her interest, and still smiling, I asked, "Is there a reason you want to know more about my family?"

"Yes. It's because you're a great story-teller. Plus, it gives me a deeper understanding of who you are. Tell me about your sister."

"Okay, if it's not boring you! One of my favorite memories with my sister, Jessica, was around the same time as the episode with the name calling. Maybe, that's where she got the idea. Anyway, she was about six years old. We all sat down for dinner one night, and Dad blessed the food. Before we filled our plates, Jessica began squirming around in her chair. With elbows on the table and her chin cradled in her hand, she announced, 'I want to change my name.'"

"Mom blinked her eyes in astonishment and asked, 'You want to change your name?' Jessica, still in the same position as before, continued to cradle her chin with her right hand, as she began twirling her hair with the left hand. She started swishing her feet back and forth under the table as she nodded her head yes. Then, Dad asked her, 'Why do you want to change your name, Jessica?'"

"Looking at Dad as though he had asked the dumbest question in the world, she answered him in an aggravated and indignant tone. 'Because, it's boring!' I was minding my own business but began to feel really annoyed, which was apparent by my body language. Plus, by that time, my stomach was growling for food. Then, mom asked me, 'What do you think about your sister changing her name, Shannon?'"

"My patience was at an end. I threw my hands into the air and snapped, 'How should I know? She can change her name all she wants. It don´t make no differance to me!' Mom gave me a stern look then turned toward my little sister and asked, 'Well, Jessica, what would you like for your name to be?' Standing up, and with full confidence, she announced, 'Jess!' That's what I want my name to be, 'Jess!'"

"A little shocked at her request, Mom and Dad looked at one another from across the table, and dad stood up. 'This matter must have a vote from all members of the Whitney family who reside in this household,' he said. Taking a spoon he lightly clinked a glass three times and made a proclamation. 'Hear ye, hear ye. Being of sound mind and the oldest of this family, I move to make a motion that the complete Whitney household is to take a vote as to who is in favor of one Jessica Whitney changing her name to Jess. Do I hear any nays to this motion?... There are no nays to this motion so, if any of you are in favor of the request of Jessica Whitney to change her name to 'Jess Whitney,' please raise your hand.'"

"Mom, Dad, and Jessica raised their hands and I just sat there. Mom gave me a look as if to say, *Raise you hand, Shannon*. When I didn´t respond, she grabbed my hand and lifted it up to show a *Yes* vote. Dad, still standing, clinked the glass again and announced, 'The Whitney family has voted unanimously that one Jessica Whitney, from this day foward, shall be known as 'Jess Whitney.'"

I paused for a moment because a lump the size of a baseball was in my throat, and its pain helped to take the focus off the emotions I was feeling.

Suddenly, Lee spoke up. "That is a remarkable memory. What did Jess do after your dad announced her new name?"

That question from Lee also helped to get the focus off of my feelings. I ended the story with, "Oh, she stood up from the table and jumped around singing, 'My name is Jess, my name is Jess!'"

"She must have been a great kid," Lee remarked.

After clearing my throat, I told her, "Yeah, and boy did she love horses. By twelve years old she had won blue ribbons and all sorts of trophies riding in professional rodeos."

Lee seemed a little sad and with a forlorn tone in her voice said, "You have been so blessed to have a wonderful sister and parents who loved you deeply. Not only that, they seemed to be aware of your individuality and abilities. And, from what you have shared with me, the two of them were sensitive to the needs of a child, even if they didn't understand them. Those are amazing qualities in parents."

After thanking Lee and pouring us another glass of wine, I noticed that she had her arms around herself as though she felt chilly. I asked, "Are you cold?"

She nodded and said, "Yes, a little bit."

"I can remedy that problem." After lighting the fireplace, I noticed that its flickering flames, the soothing music, and the dim lighting added a tender, warm atmosphere to the room and sat back down beside Lee.

She picked up her glass of wine and after taking a sip, asked, "What did your dad do for a living?"

Stunned by her question, I remarked, "It's hard to believe that Millie hasn't mentioned to you anything about my family!"

"Oh, I asked, but she told me, 'Charlie, someday an opportunity will come up and Shannon, himself, will tell you about them.' So, here I am, sitting in the middle of an 'opportunity.'" Millie did say, however, that you were a workaholic, you were not gay, and that she really respected your values. Now, tell me about your dad."

"Well, I'm sure glad she cleared it up that I'm not gay."

Both of us chuckled and again, she insisted, "Please, Shannon, tell me about your dad."

Looking straight into her eyes, I asked, "You really want me to talk about my family all evening?"

"If that's what it takes to hear about your dad, yes!"

I cleared my throat again and shared a special memory about my father. "My dad raised pure bred stallions for stud services and also sold stallions to people who used them for racing. There were people all over the U.S. and Canada who used his services. He and my mom owned 220 acres just a few miles southwest of here. The Meramac river was the southeast boundary of the farm that my dad called it the Bottom Land. He fenced 125 acres for pasture. The house and a large barn was located on the other 100 acres. Actually, this place looks a lot like it but, of course, on a much smaller scale. We raised a lot of our own feed, and with dad's gift for horse breeding and finances...well, the business flourished." I stopped talking and asked Lee, "You really want to hear all about my..."

Butting in, she replied, "Yes! Please, tell me more about your dad!"

Pausing for a moment and smiling at her, I continued my story. "On one of my visits during a summer break from school, my dad decided to buy a new truck and invited me to go along to help do the shopping. We went to three or four car dealers, looking for a truck with a bench seat. When we couldn't find one, Dad began to get pretty agitated. Finally, I told him, 'Dad, pick-up trucks don't have bench seats anymore. All of them today are equipped with bucket seats and a console between them.'"

"He mumbled a couple of curse words and angrily said, 'What the hell is with these manufacturers! Who wants their ass sitting on the floor while their driving! I hate them bucket seats! And if I can't get a truck that has a bench seat, I'll just keep this one until it falls apart!'"

"On the way home, we saw a Ford dealership and pulled in. I hoped they might have something that dad would like. But, when he requested to look at a pickup with a bench seat, the salesman, almost snickered and said, 'We dont have trucks with bench seats, sir. They are obsolete.' My dad got so angry that his face turned blood red. Dad stepped toward the young man, got in his face, and yelled, 'Obsolete, hell!' The salesman turned almost ghost white from fear. Dad continued shouting, 'Why, you little redneck asshole! Who do you think you're talking to? If you're too stupid to know what I'm talking about, then you had better get somebody who does!'"

"The salesman slowly backed away, and, in a consoling manner, stutterd, 'O-o-okay, sir. I-I'll do just that, sir!" And he headed for the main office. Right away, an older black gentleman came toward us. With a smile, he shook my dad's hand and introduced himself. He said, 'I am Richard Mason, and you sir, are...?' 'Whitney,' my dad said,

'Michael Whitney.' Mr. Mason began apologizing. 'I'm sorry, Mr. Whitney, for the misunderstanding. You are looking for a truck with a bench seat?' Dad firmly verbalized, 'Yes I am!'"

"The man then explained, 'Mr. Whitney, we don't stock any trucks with bench seats. However, we can special order one for you. Just tell us exactly what you want. But it will take eight to ten weeks to get it to you.' Dad told him, 'That's just fine, Mr. Mason.' And, by the time we were getting ready to leave the Ford dealership, Dad was teasing Mr. Mason and they gave each other a pat on the shoulder as we walked out the door."

'I went back to school the next day and, two months later, my phone rang with the news about my family's accident. About a week later, a card came through the mail saying that my dad's special order truck had arrived and was ready to be picked up at his convienence. Dad never got to see his new truck."

With empathy in her eyes, Lee softly said, "I'm so sorry, Shannon. Nothing in the human vocabulary can be said to ease your pain. There is only one power that can do that, and it is God, when you are ready. I have found that it takes time. Even though Joe's death was only a few months ago, the first twenty-four hours of grief after losing him felt like a lifetime. The first day when I walked into Millie's, my decision was to live again! Jaden is still having a rough time of it, but she has had a noticable change just in the last couple of weeks. If I were given any wish for you, it would be, 'Please let me take away Shannon's pain.'"

The emotion was so great it was difficult to choke back the tears. After settling back into the couch in order to regain some composure, I said,"Having you here sitting next to me is a beautiful gift. I'm feeling like I'm the luckiest man in the world. Now, tell me some of your memories."

Lee smiled and looked at me sort of sideways and said, "Shannon Whitney, you have a line that makes a woman think she is the only one you have said these things to!"

"First of all, what will it take to convince you that what I say to you isn't a lie or line? You are the only woman who has ever touched me in a way that makes me want to be with you all the time. And don't try to change the subject. What are some of your memories?" With a sincere look on her face, she took a sip of wine, and in a soft voice began to talk about her childhood. "I was born in Dallas, Texas, and my dad didn't want any more children, so I'm an only child. Dad was a veterinarian and spent most of his time working in the clinic or in his lab. Two weeks before graduation from high school, I decided to follow in my his footsteps. And, three months later, he left us for another woman and divorced my mom. He then moved to Canada without a goodbye to either of us. My mother was devastated. She had clinical depression and was in such denial that perhaps she made mistakes, too. She showed me affection only if I could do something for her. And, basically, for several years, I became a loner. There were very few dates. But, between my shyness and my belief in celibacy until marriage, the guys were not interested in me. And that's about it. You know the rest of my memories."

Shaking my head, I remarked, "Lee, what you have told me about your childhood doesn't sound like memories."

With sadness in her eyes, she explained, "Shannon, those are all of the memories I have. I don't have your kinds of memories. My mother and father were very sterile and unaffectionate. If they did have any kind of love, they kept it to themselves."

Then, out of nowhere, she changed the subject and made a comment about my truck. "Your truck has an unusual seat. Is it the one your dad ordered?"

"Yep, and I'm going to keep it until it starts falling apart. And when that time comes, she will be parked for the rest of her life. And it will be put where I can see it at least once a day."

Holding her glass of wine, she leaned forward from the couch and glanced around the room. With a mischieveous smile, she asked, "How come a good looking man like you hasn't been snatched up by a woman?"

"Well," I said teasingly, "there hasn't been a woman who had an intoxicating effect on me until now."

Lee grinned and responded with another question. "Are you saying that there is someone who might give you that feeling?"

"Yes!" I said. Then I boldly stammered, "Sh-she's sitting next to me." Again, Lee glanced around the room and nervously blinked her eyes as though my statement shocked her. I thought, *Oh no! I've stuck a foot in my mouth all the way to the shoe laces! And she's getting out the brick and mortar!* I quickly apologized."I'm sorry, Lee, for overstepping my boundaries."

"No need to apologize," she said. "Your boldness is becoming. And I'm seeing an honesty about you that makes me feel safe."

"I'll never lie to you. Remember?" Then, taking her hand in mine, I reminded her, "My promise still hold's true and it will never be broken." As I held her hand in mine, she laid her head on my shoulder, and we quietly sat for a while, watching the flames in the fire place. Then my favorite song came up on the CD. Standing up and offering her an arm, I asked, "Beautiful lady, would you like to have this dance with me?" She stood up from the couch and slipped into my arms like velvet gloves. I held her with a China doll eloquence and she responded to my lead like a dream. Encircling my arms around her waist and drawing her closer into my body, I felt that we moved with the precision of a sparkling flawless diamond. Her perfume made my knees weak, as I tried to concentrate on the dancing instead of how good she felt against my body. I tightened my arms around her waist and began singing the words to the music. "Pardon the way that I stare, there's nothing else to compare, the sight of you makes me weak, there are no words left to speak, and if you feel like I feel, please let me know that it's real, you're just to good to be true, can't take my eyes off of you. I love you baby..."

Suddenly, she stopped dead still as if her feet were frozen to the floor. Standing on her tip-toes, she lifted her chin to my face and gave me the most sensual kiss that I had ever experienced in my whole life. It was as though I was receiving an invitation to seventh heaven. Trying to lighten the intensity of the intimacy, I asked, "Miss Lee, are you trying to seduce me?"

Kissing me again, as though she was searching for my mouth, she asked, "Is it working?"

Making an effort to stabilize my breathing, I answered, "Is it ever!" I returned the kiss with the kind of passion that only a man in love could give, leaving the two of us almost breathless. Holding her ever so close, I whispered in her ear, "What do we do now?" With a stunned look, she stared at me. Trying to keep my temperature under control, I added, "Well, it's been such a long time between kisses, I'm a bit out of practice."

All at once, she thumped my nose, and when I gave out a screeching "OUCH,'" she squinted her eyes and came back at me saying, "Shannon Whitney... if you haven't gotten the clues by now, then don't ask me what to do! "

Grinning like Hank, I softly whispered in her ear again, "Gotcha!" and swooped her up in my ams and headed for the bedroom.

Lee began to giggle as I carried her over the threshold of the bedroom and, wouldn't you know, the cuff of my shirt sleeve got caught on the door knob. Struggling to get it loose, I thought, *Oh no, this can't be happening*! And down we went to the floor! When I sat up, the first words out of my mouth were, "Are you okay, Lee?"

Trying to keep from laughing, she indicated *yes* by nodding her head. Then, looking up to the celing and lifting my hands, I yelled, "What the hell is going on here? Is there some kind of conspiracy trying to keep us apart?" As I shook my head in disbelief, Lee sat up and began to snicker. "Oh, you think this is pretty funny, huh," I said to her. Then we both burst into laughter. "Well it's a good thing that the carpet is a plush one," I said. "It would be a castastrophe if you would have been hurt. Lee gave me a seductive look. We got up from the floor and I lightly caressed her cheek, and we leaned toward each other with a longing stare. Then, I began slowly kissing her forehead, then her eyes, and her chin as I led her to the bed. Then when placing my lips tenderly on hers, she met them eagerly and began unbuttoning my shirt. I finished the last two buttons and discarded it behind us. Lee drew back from our kiss for a few seconds and took off her sweatshirt and bra. Leaning foward again, she lifted her chin, and I kissed her neck and continued downward to her breasts, enveloping them with my lips. First one, and then the other. Lee quickly unzipped my pants and we slipped off our remaining clothes. We kissed again and Lee settled back invitingly on the bed. I reached in the night stand and took a condom from my top drawer and quickly put it on. Looking down at her, I felt she was the most beautiful woman in the world, and my heart skipped a beat as I positioned myself over her sensual body. Slowly raising her head, she gave me another warm, sweet, and tender kiss. Then, she laid her head back down and closed her eyes. I carefully placed my hands on her hips, pulling her closer to me. When our bodies met, we not only became as one, we knew that our lovemaking would be the union of our souls. I wanted to tell her that I had never felt these kinds of emotions with any other woman, that she was in my every waking thought and dream. And, oh, how long the wait had been for this moment to arrive for me to physically express my love for her.

Lee must have read my thoughts because she lifted her arms over her head in a relaxed manner as though she was completely surrendering herself to me, body and soul. By this time, our desires began to soar and, with every breath, I could feel her breasts lightly brushing against my chest. Eagerly, she began to stir her hips as each deepening motion intensified, and we kissed with the splendor of our movements. We never wanted it to end. Pausing for a moment, I cradled one of her breasts in my hand and gave her another caressing kiss. As we continued to make love, I wrapped my arms slightly around her back and lifted her to angle her more perfectly with my body. We held one another even closer, and she began to meet me with an urgent craving. I then encompassed her buttocks with my hands as the strokes deepened into ecstasy. The exhilaration of our movements became more rapid. Lee began to gasp with short, elated breaths as we devoured each other's lips, and we fulfilled the appetite of our lovemaking. Catching our breath, we disengaged our bodies but continued to cuddle for a while. Finally, we sat up and slipped our clothes on. Lee smiled at me, and I gave her a quick kiss.

Lee quietly went to the bathroom, and when she returned, we walked back to the couch. As we sat next to each other, it seemed natural to put one arm over Lee's shoulder. I thought that this would be a good time to tell her how I felt. "Lee," I began, "Surely by now you know that I'm in lo…" Lee quickly and gently put two fingers across my lips. Then, removing them, she kissed me.

"Shannon, there is something you can be sure of! Our lovemaking was the most magnificent experience I have ever had. There was never any occasion with Joe that made me feel love like you have given to me tonight. But this—this intimacy that you and I have shared is beyond words, and I'm confused with my feelings right now. I can't say that my love for Joe was even real. I question what kind of love I had for him. However, I do know there has to be some kind of closure, and I-I don't know how or when that is going to take place. Doesn't that sound crazy?"

"Not at all. My head has been spinning ever since we met."

After staring down at nothing for a moment, she then looked at me like a little girl who was about to reveal a secret and said, "There is something else I need to tell you. I didn't dare let you know how I felt about you because all my energy and thoughts needed to go into keeping my little girl and Jaden safe. The first day at Millie's when we met and I had to bring coffee over to your table, my knees got weak. The menus received a lot of damaging abuse as I fanned myself with them in the kitchen. If you got within reaching distance of me, it was so frightening that…that my emotions churned inside me. It was unbelievable how much I was attracted to you. One day, Millie teased the daylights out of me, and asked her if there was something wrong with me. My husband's body is barely cold and, here I am, sexually attracted to Shannon! At that time, thinking about love was the farthest thing from my mind. And Millie said. "He is a good-looking, sexy man. I just wonder what your real feelings are. Perhaps it goes a lot deeper than wishing you could spend an hour in bed." A bit shocked, but very pleased with Lee admitting her attraction for me, I smiled boyishly and asked, "Are you saying you had the 'hot's' for me?"

Lee smiled back with a shy expression on her face and answered, "Well, I guess that interpretation is as good as any! Whether you knew it or not, the day you showed up at my place with the puppy was a reality check for me. It took everything within my mind and body to keep from reaching down to help you when you fell off the porch."

"What stopped you?"

"There were several reasons," she explained. "For one, I was trying to convince myself that my feelings for you were nothing more than an infatuation. Well, that didn't help. And after watching you struggle to pick yourself up from the fall, it became evident how much you meant to me. The second reason was, I've often heard it said that the 'best defense is the best offense.' Consequently, if you weren't allowed to explain yourself, then there wouldn't be time for you to notice my hands shaking."

Raising an eyebrow, I chimed in. "It's for sure you are good at hiding your nervousness. All I could see was how pissed off you were!"

Lee giggled and remarked, "It worked, didn't it?" Then she resumed her explanation. "I also thought it was dangerous to get close to anyone because the more people who become acquainted with me, the more likely Jaden's, Brandie's, and my identities could be revealed."

Pausing for a moment, Lee glanced at me with a puzzled look on her face and remarked, "I thought for sure you caught on to my jealousy the day Suanne came into Millie's."

Hearing her remark about Suanne surprised me, and I replied, "Then you did get jealous."

"Yes. You didn't notice the tears?"

Remembering what happened that morning, I asked, "How in the world can you forgive me for the way I treated you that day? There are no excuses for my shameful behavior."

Looking at me with a smile, Lee responded, "Shannon, what kind of behavior did you get from me for months, besides my ignoring you, evading your questions and, oh, yes, and here's another thing you can add to the list, avoiding you. There were times when Millie took your order because you made me so nervous. And even after our trip to the casino, there was no doubt in my mind that you cared a lot about me, but the fear of my identity being discovered kept me from responding to you. Now, who do you think needs to apologize? Hank and Grant have consistently hinted about how much you liked me. They also revealed that you stopped dating the day I started work at Millie's, and that yours and Suanne's relationship was strictly, as they put it, 'a good time friendship.' It's understandable why you jumped at her invitation. Believe me, Shannon, it is okay. Okay? If there is any reason we haven't gotten together any sooner…well, that's on me!"

After kissing her hand, I said, "You're quite a woman, Lee!"

She came back at me. "Yeah…and I'm a woman who has a request. It's my understanding that there's a certain place you and Suanne used as a play house quite often when you were teenagers."

I smiled at her and reluctantly said, "Yes…there is."

"I'm very curious to see what kind of place a couple of teenagers called their play house."

Blinking my eyes in disbelief, I asked, "Are you kidding?"

"Absolutely not! Why should Suanne be the only one to enjoy this unique place?"

Her request really caught me off guard. "Lee, when Suanne and I were in high school, we only cared about feeling good, and she trusted me. There's a great deal of difference between you and her. I never loved Suanne in a romantic way or thought about a future other than having a sexual friendship with her. She and I set boundaries as far as our commitment level went. And that was a load off my shoulders because my feelings for her have never, ever been anything more than friendship. Please believe me! When looking at you…well, I know that you don't want me to say this, but, I'm going to say it anyway. When looking at you… I, I can't imagine my life without you. You're the only woman that I have ever thought of spending the rest of my life with."

Lee touched my cheek, and in a reassuring voice, she said, "Shannon, you don't have to justify any of your past relationships with me. It's not in my nature to expect you to be anyone other than yourself. And there is something you can count on. There will be absolutely no other man in my life but you." She gently kissed my lips. Then, the two of us got up from the couch and migrated to the bedroom. We lay down on the bed and made love again. Afterwards, she settled into the curve of my body, and I whispered to her, "My dreams have come true."

With a yawn, she responded, "Mine too," and we fell asleep in each other's arms.

Chapter Nine

The next morning, I woke to the smell of fresh-brewed coffee. As I rose up on my elbows, squinting my eyes, I could hear Lee shuffling around in the kitchen. After I put my head back down on the pillow and closed my eyes, she walked into the bedroom and sat down beside me. She gently touched my cheek and softly said, "Good morning, sleepy head. It's time to get up."

Groaning and stretching, I grabbed her around the waist and pulled her down on the bed beside me and said, "Good morning to you, beautiful lady!" I kissed her passionately and Lee bent over me and returned the kiss sweetly. It suddenly occurred to me that this wasn't a dream! So I kissed her again.

After the kiss, Lee drew away from me saying, "We don't have time for any love-making now. You know darn well kissing me like that makes my heart start racing. I should have left five minutes ago! The coffee is ready and there is a filled insulated mug on the counter."

"Okay," I'll get dressed and have you home in a jiffy."

While we were driving to her place, Lee asked, "Shannon, do you know of anyone who has a good used car to sell—cheap, at around3,000?"

Even though I knew she was asking for herself, I inquired, "Well, just who is this person that is looking for a car?"

Seeming a bit perturbed, she responded, "Again, you missed the hint, Shannon Whitney. It's me! I'm the 'person' who is looking for a car. I'm going to need one before winter!"

Smiling at her, I remarked, "Why didn't you say so in the first place?"

Lee hit me on the shoulder, annoyed, and replied, "Men! You're all alike. Needing everything spelled out for you. Anyway, with the refund from the Mercedes and a few dollars in my dresser draw, surely that is enough to buy a fairly decent used car. Wouldn't you say?"

Not responding at first, I finally said, "I know where one is, and it's the right price. It's hardly been driven and is in good condition."

Excitedly she asked, "Where and when can I see the car? This is Sunday. Is there any place open today?"

"Do you want to see it today?"

I barely got the words out of my mouth when Lee, bubbling with enthusiasm, asked, "Do you mean right now? That is if you have the time for us to pick up Brandie and Jaden, so they can see it, too. Oh, but what if someone sees us?"

"Not to worry," I said. "We will take country roads and hardly anyone goes to this place on Sunday."

"Are you sure?" She asked.

Using a John Wayne impression, I answered, "Stick with me, little lady, and you will have a horseless carriage before sunset!"

Her enthusiasm grew higher. "You mean it, Shannon? We can see it today?"

Still in John Wayne mode, I answered, "You got it right, little lady. Today is the day!"

The minute the truck was parked Lee jumped out, ran into the mobile home, and in no time, came back to the truck with Brandie. After they climbed into their seat, I asked, "Where is Jaden?"

"Oh, she was watching a movie on TV and didn't want to miss the ending."

After driving on country roads, we finally pulled into the driveway of my place.

A bit surprised, Lee asked, "What are we doing here?"

Getting back into my impression of John Wayne, I answered, "Well, little lady…" Immediately, she butted in, "Shannon, stop that and tell me what we are doing here!"

Having a sad look on my face, I responded, "You don't care for my John Wayne impression, do you?"

"Oh, so he's the one you are supposed to sound like?"

"You just broke my heart and doused all my dreams of being a famous impressionist."

"I'm sorry if your feelings got hurt, but you still haven't answered my question."

After parking the truck in the driveway and requesting that Lee and

Brandie follow me, we walked toward the barn. I opened the two large doors and said, "I've got something to show you." I went over to the dusty tarp covering, yanked it off, and announced, "There she is!"

Lee's eyes got as big as quarters and, putting her hands over her opened mouth, she yelled, "Oh, my God. It's a Jeep! And it is the cutest one I have ever seen!"

Brandie ran to the passenger side, opened the door, climbed into the seat, and shouted excitedly, "Mommy, I like it! Can we go for a ride?"

Lee grinned, slid into the driver's seat, took a firm grip on the steering wheel, and asked, "Will it run?"

Acting as though I was astonished at her question, I responded, "Of course it will run!" I then reached down under the floor mat, took the keys out from under it, and dangled them in front of her. Lee snatched them from my hand and stepped out of the jeep. After sauntering around it she took a good look. Then she stopped at the driver's door, pulled her shirt sleeve across the palm of her hand, puffed her breath on the mirror, and gave it a swipe. "How much will you take for her?"

Teasingly, I answered, "When someone wants to buy a vehicle, you never ask the price until you drive it!"

Still holding the keys, she asked boldly, "Can we take it for a drive?"

"I don't see a problem with that, except we do have to stay on the country roads because it doesn't have any tags."

With Lee at the wheel, we all went for a quick drive. After we returned to the barn, the three of us stepped out of the Jeep and Lee walked around it again, kicking the tires, and opening and closing all of the doors. She then turned to me and, with hands on her hips she asked seriously, "How much do you want for her?"

Trying to hide the smile on my face, I scratched my chin and replied, "Well...You can see she is in excellent condition."

Turning around and glancing at the jeep again, Lee cautiously said, "Yeah, we can agree on that."

Resuming my sales pitch, I said, "Also, I'm sure you noticed it has very low mileage. And the tires have been replaced with new ones just three months ago."

Squinting her eyes a bit, she shifted her body and impatiently demanded, "Okay! How much do you want for the Jeep?"

Lee looked so cute in her bargaining stance that I could hardly keep a straight face, and Brandie was intently watching her mom. It was a perfect picture of a daughter's eagerness to store in her mind her mother's negotiating abilities that she might use herself someday. With a serious look, I walked over to Lee and stood directly in front of her. Then I smiled a really big smile and gave her my price. "How about a kiss and a hug every day for the next ninety years?"

Lee stood for a few seconds, staring with her mouth open while computing my asking price. Then, all at once, she squealed, threw her arms around my neck, gave me a kiss, and proclaimed, "You drive a hard bargain!"

I grinned again and responded, "You have very good collateral!"

Brandie grabbed her mom's leg and blurted out, "Mommy! You kissed Shannon!"

Lee bent over and kissed Brandie on her cheek saying, "I sure did, sweetie. That's an advance payment on our Jeep!"

Brandie came closer to me and began yanking at the leg of my jeans. I glanced down at her and she raised her arms for me to pick her up. When I did, she put her arms around my neck, gave me a big hug, and kissed me on the cheek. "Is that okay, Mommy, to give Shannon another payment?" she asked Lee.

We burst out laughing and Lee told her, "We need all the help we can get, sweetie!"

During the drive back to the mobile home, I mentioned to Lee, "You know what? It just dawned on me that you can't get a license for the jeep without an I. D."

"You're right, Shannon! I'm going to have to find a way to become legal and keep it a secret. The reason it hasn't been taken care of is because I didn't know where to start and, at the same time, feel safe. I honestly don't know what to do!"

After thinking for a moment, I told her, "There's a friend of mine who went to school with me from kindergarten through high school graduation. He, Grant, Hank, and I were known as the 'Fearsome

Four.' I haven't talked to him for a while but he may be able to help us. He is the head of the Vehicle and License Bureau of Illinois. He just might know what we can do."

Lee stared at me and her eyes puddled with tears.

"What's wrong?"

"You said, *we*. Do you have any idea how that makes me feel? Never in my whole life has anyone said *we* when discussing a problem that was bothering me. For the first time, I don't feel alone. Thank you. Are you sure it is safe telling your friend about me? I sure don't want to take any chances on someone accidentally or purposely revealing my identity. It could be dangerous." By this time, we were parking the truck next to the porch of the mobile home. Lee leaned over, kissed me on the cheek, and asked, "Would you like to come in?"

"No. I've got to get home and call Bill."

"You're calling him on a Sunday?"

"Sure. He'll be glad to hear from me. It's been a long time since we've been in touch and we have a lot of catching up to do."

Brandie spoke up and asked, "Mommy, can I go on in and play with Goggy?"

After Lee gave Brandie permission to leave the truck, she turned to me and again asked, "Are you sure you can trust this friend?"

I reassured her. "Lee, I have known William Dillard all my life. He saved the 'Fearsome Four's butts many times from getting burnt. He had a sixth sense and always knew when we were about to go too far with some of our escapades. His level head, truthfulness, and integrity would remind us of right from wrong. He was the one that kept us honest and morally centered. I would trust him with my life."

Lee, biting her thumb nail in thought, nodded and softly uttered a prayer, "God, please let this be the right decision." After her prayer, she took in a deep breath and said, "Okay, Shannon. Let's go for it. I'm going to trust your judgment."

Arriving back at the house, I immediately headed straight for the phone and called Bill. When he answered, I teasingly said, "Oh, great leader of the Fearsome Four, your friend needs some help with a problem."

He laughed and responded. "How have you been doing, Shannon?

Believe it or not, just yesterday I told Cindy, 'One of these days, I'm going to call Shannon. We haven't had a bull session in months."

"Well, my friend," I said, "A lot has been going on, and that's the reason for my call tonight."

He was astonished by Lee's story when I told him everything. "Whoa, man! You must really love this woman. You could be in as much danger as her!"

My voice cracked when I told him, "Yeah, she fills my heart just thinking about her."

Bill paused for a moment and then asked, "Is it all right for me to do a background check on her?"

"Absolutely, That is, if you can do it safely."

He reassured me, "You have got my promise, man. This will be the most discreet background check on record in my career. I'm not going to take any chances with your sweetheart's identity. This is the safest way to use the Witness Protection Program."

"Bill, remember there are three lives that I have put in your hands!"

"Hey, bud, I'm counting four! Don't you worry! Have I ever let you down? Trust me! However, I do need to know her full legal name, weight, height, date of birth, color of her eyes, and her real social security number. Also, her new full name and a recent front face photo. Be sure and send the information to my home fax."

"I'll send all of the information to you tonight."

"Shannon, go to another town and get a post office box," I thanked him and then asked, "By the way, how are Cindy and the kids doing?"

"They're doing great!" But, tell me about you. I thought you would be a bachelor all your life. This woman who has snagged you must be extraordinary."

"She is remarkable! And beautiful, smart, caring, and…"

About that time Bill jumped in "I get the picture, man. You've finally met the woman that you have been looking for and I wish you two lots of happiness."

We continued talking for another hour or so and finally I said, "I've got to get off the phone if I'm going to get that information to you tonight."

Deception or Perfection

"Okay," he said. "We'll pick up our conversation where we left off the next time we talk. And, don't take so long, Prissy, to..."

Butting in before he said another word, I told him, "My friend! This is a promise! And if you *ever* call me that in front of anyone, I'm contacting all of the Springfield newspapers and telling them your nickname is *Dildo*, Bill Dillard!"

Both of us got a chuckle from our childhood nicknames. When we were about to end our conversation, Bill reassured me, "We are going to get things fixed up for you and your beautiful lady. And again, don't be a stranger. Call and let me know how you're doing." I thanked Bill again, and we said our goodbyes. After-hanging up the phone, I jumped in the truck and headed for Lee's place.

Jaden answered the door with a welcoming smile, "Hello, Shannon. What are you doing coming out at this time of the night?"

I asked Jaden, where is Lee? She replied, "Millie came and picked her and Brandie up to do something. Don't know what they had planned. Since I've been working on my book, I've not taken the time out to go places with them. Can I help you with anything?"

"Maybe you can, Jaden."

After telling her about the conversation with Bill, she assured me, "I can get all of the information needed for your friend." Then, she began to go through drawers, closets, shelves, and came to me with everything I asked for.

Giving her a big hug, I remarked, "Perhaps it's a good thing Lee isn't here. If it turns out that my friend's plan doesn't work, it's better that she doesn't know anything until everything is finished. So, if you don't mind, Jaden, let's keep this to ourselves." She agreed and I left. I returned home and faxed the information to Bill.

Getting up early Monday morning, I drove in to St. Louis to the nearest post office, rented a postal box, and immediately went to an office supply store to fax the box number to Bill. After arriving home and entering the clinic, I heard the sound of my fax machine. I couldn't believe it. Bill was already coming through on his promise. The fax included a copy of a birth certificate for Cheryl Lee Canton, plus a social security card, an I.D. card, and a driver's license in Lee's name. There was also a note that read, "Hey, Mr. P., The originals will be coming to the post box number that you sent me. Don't be a stranger, and be sure that we get an invitation to your wedding." The note was signed, *Mr. D.*

By this time, the clinic doors were unlocked, and the patients poured in. The day was a busy one and seemed to pass quickly. After locking up at six, I drove out to Lee's place with the faxed information in hand. By the time I parked next to the porch, Lee was out the door to meet me.

"Hi Shannon, is everything okay?"

"More than okay, sweetheart! Look here, what my friend sent me on the fax this morning!"

After seeing the papers, she asked, "Is this what I think it is?"

Grabbing and hugging her, I said, "Yes! And the originals will be in St. Louis by Wednesday in a post office box that I rented today." Suddenly, Lee's eyes filled up with tears. "What's wrong?" I asked her.

"These are happy tears," she responded. "How did you do this?"

"With a lot of help from the Man upstairs and a good friend named Bill!"

She touched my cheek and kissed me, saying, "This is the most awesome blessing anyone could ever receive. Can you come in for a while?"

"Sure!" After entering the mobile home and noticing that Jaden and Brandie were not around, I asked, "Where are your two roommates?"

"Oh, Jaden turned in early and Brandie went to sleep before Millie dropped us off. Shannon, thank you so much." I slowly stepped into Lee's space, put my arms around her waist, and passionately kissed her. When she began to respond, I slowly started guiding her toward the couch. Pulling away from me she exclaimed, "Shannon, what do you think you are you doing? Jaden and Brandie are two doors away!"

I abruptly straightened up and said in an all-knowing voice, "I knew that. So why were you trying to get me to the couch?!"

In a frustrated tone, she responded, "Shannon Whitney! *You* were the one heading to..."

"Uh-uh, I know what you were trying to do! You wanted to make out!"

She slightly punched me in the belly with her fist and, said in a whisper, "Yeah, I know"...*punch*..."After last night"...*punch*..."you can't get enough of me can you?"

Grabbing her hands, I whispered in her ear with my John Wayne voice, "That's right, little lady, so what are ya gonna do about it?"

She quickly kissed me on the cheek and remarked, "That will have to do you for now, superman."

I grinned at her and said, "At least, I know there is going to be a next time. By the way, do you think Millie will let you off Wednesday to go to St. Louis and pick up your legal papers? If you can, then I'll have Ronda reschedule my appointments."

"I'm sure that can be arranged. Millie can call her friend to fill in for me. There's also a woman who helped Millie before I came to work for her."

Lee was able to get Wednesday off and we headed for St. Louis. Neither of us had a problem with conversation during the trip. She talked about how wonderful it would be to have a place large enough to house wild animals in their natural habitat. People could drive through and children could play with domestic animals. "I think there is one in Missouri," she said. "It would sure be great if there was one here in Illinois. That's my dream. What is your dream?" Lee asked.

"You know, Lee, to be honest, I haven't thought that much about the future. But it would be wonderful to have a family."

Smiling and taking my hand, she closed the gap between us. "You know what? That's a dream both of us can share." We were quiet for a few more miles and then Lee asked another question. "Shannon, how come the jeep only has 455 miles on it?" I didn't answer her question right away, and she said, "You don't have to tell me if you don't want to."

I bit my lower lip until it hurt, cleared my throat, and explained. "You've heard the story about dad's truck. Well, about three weeks before that, Mom and Dad had bought the jeep as a graduation gift for me and had it hidden in a neighbor's barn. After my family's funeral, the neighbor came up to me and it was six months before I asked him if he would bring the jeep and park it in my barn and he did. Over the years, I just couldn't make myself sit in it, much less take it for a drive.

So, asking different friends, mostly Hank and Grant, to take her out once in a while to keep her in good shape, she hasn't been moved. They would take her to the car wash and to Ron's Repair Auto Service to lubricate, change the oil, and other maintenance as needed." Clearing my throat again and trying to keep from crying, I smiled and added; "now it's clear why I hung on to her."

After picking up Lee's papers at the post office, she noticed a gourmet Delightfully Delicious ice cream shop down the street from where we were parked. We decided to celebrate by pigging out on large ice cream cones, topped with chocolate, pecans, and sprinkles. While sitting at a table and thoroughly enjoying ourselves, Lee spoke up. "I've just thought of something. Now that we have agreed on a payment plan for the jeep, I can afford to get some new clothes for Brandie. I can also buy Jaden a pair of boots at the Shoe Shine Shack that she has been admiring for a long time!" I asked her if there was anything else she wanted to purchase and she paused, in deep thought. Then, a light bulb went off in her head. Her eyes sparkled and her voice bubbled with excitement, as she exclaimed, "Oh, oh, Shannon! Guess what? I can have some repairs done on the mobile home. And not only that, it's safe for me to get a cell phone!"

Leaning toward Lee and taking her hand in mine, I remarked. "That sounds great, baby-doll!"

Tears began to pool in her eyes and it took all that was in me not to wrap Lee in my arms right in front of God and all the people in the ice cream shop. I thought, *she has been through hell, and it is time for her to have some peace and happiness.*

It was like Lee knew my thoughts because she placed her index finger softly on my chin and said, "You are becoming my life-line, Shannon Whitney. I can't think of anything I could do to ever repay you."

Plastering a big grin on my face, I whispered, "Just give me some time, baby-doll. I'm sure I can come up with something!"

She responded, "Well, Dr. Whitney, that just might be arranged!" We both chuckled and headed out for home.

After getting back to Ellisville, I drove straight over to Millie's because we wanted to talk to her about our restoration plans for the mobile home. After we talked, she said, "Don't see any problems with that, but my friend who owns half of the property has to be notified. I'm sure he will not care one bit, but I'll know by tomorrow if it's okay with him."

The next day, when I arrived at Millie's, there were only a couple of customers in the restaurant. Lee came over to me and whispered, "Guess what? My boss says she has something to tell us."

About that time, Millie came over to the table. She pulled out a chair, sat down, and motioned for Lee to sit in the other one. Excited, she smiled and softly told us, "Got good news for the two of you. My friend said you can do anything you want to the mobile home. But, after talking to him for a while he asked me about buying his half out. I made him an offer and he accepted it! I am now the owner of the ten acres, the mobile home, and a small lake that borders the property. So, go for it, Charlie! Do anything you want to and I will foot the bill. No sense in you spending your money." Millie winked at me and added, "Who knows, you may not be living there too much longer any way."

Lee glanced at me, then turned toward Millie and said, "Millie, you're an angel!"

"Charlie, I just wish you wouldn't have had to live in that piece of junk this long,"

Lee put her arm around Millie and said, "It isn't junk to me, my friend. I'm grateful to the Man upstairs that He worked through you to provide a safe home for Jaden, Brandie, and myself. No, it isn't junk. It's a castle to me."

Millie quickly and nervously jumped from her seat, exclaiming, "Better get to work! Nothing's getting done sitting here with all this sentimental, mushy, improvised adlibbing around here!" Lee just smiled at her.

"I think I've witnessed a first with Millie." I said. "Was it my imagination, or did she have tears in her eyes?"

"It wasn't your imagination."

Lee sat at the table a little longer and we talked about how Millie thinks she is hiding her soft heart.

When the last two customers walked out of the restaurant, I reached across the table and took Lee's hand and, flirtatiously asked her, "How would you like a big celebration of the good news that we have been given today?"

Leaning close to my face, she answered, "Sounds great! However, I do have a suggestion. After the celebration, perhaps you can show me yours and Suanne's old play house?"

"Well, what are you doing tonight?" I asked her.

Bending even closer she replied with an impudent smile, "That's a good question. I'm doing whatever you are doing!"

For a moment there was a sick sensation in my gut, as the blood drained from my face. It felt like *déjà vu* as I remembered the conversation with Suanne a few weeks before. Lee's response to my discomfort was to lean toward me and, with a soft kiss on my forehead and a satisfied-smile, she said, "Gotcha!" Then, giggling like a school girl, she confessed, "I'm sorry, but you stepped right into that"

Lifting my chin, and leaning back in the chair trying to look pitiful, I confronted her. "So…you're sorry! Then why are you laughing at me?"

Still giggling, she responded, "If you could see yourself, you would be laughing, too."

"Okay, I deserved that. Now, when are we going to celebrate the good news?"

Looking at me apprehensively, she asked, "Would you mind if we celebrated next weekend? I promised Brandie that the two of us would go shopping and do a movie tomorrow night. She needs to spend some quality time with me." I agreed that her little girl did need special time with her mom.

Chapter Ten

Saturday mornings are always slow at Millie's, so I jumped in my truck and arrived at the restaurant just as she was opening up for business. As I made my way to the counter, Millie asked, "How come you are out and about so early this morning?"

"I'm here to talk to you about Lee."

"Okay, Doc, what do you want to know?"

"Well... everything. I did find out that her birthday is July eighth and she was born in 1977, but what is her favorite color? And what kind of jewelry, food, and other things does she enjoy?"

Millie gave me a short answer. "Blue, 18 karat gold, chocolate, and going to the movies." Thinking for a few seconds, she added, "You know what? I overheard her talking to some customers the other day about the Muny Opera in St. Louis and that she would like to go there some time. She is also crazy about baseball."

"Really?"

"Yah, she played softball in high school. She made the first team when she became a freshman and played all four years."

In shock, I responded. "Lee played *softball?*"

"Oh, yes, she played the third-base position like a pro. And, not only that, she had the highest batting average of the whole team from her sophomore through senior year of high school."

"How about that! Lee played softball! It's unbelievable! I can't wait to rub this information in Grant's face! Thank you, Millie!"

By that time, Lee was driving into the parking lot, and I wanted this conversation to stay between Millie and I. "Don't mention anything to Lee about the conversation we just had, okay?" Millie made a zipping motion across her lips. I quickly walked to a table and sat down. Lee came into the restaurant, went straight to the kitchen, and didn't notice me at all. Cautiously getting out of my chair, I eased over to the swinging doors and backed snugly against the wall. As she came out of the kitchen carrying a tray of cups and making a beeline for the coffee maker, I stepped in the shadow of her footsteps. Completely focused on her destination, Lee approached the counter and carefully set the tray down. Just as she turned around, and we were toe to toe and face to face, I quickly let out a deep voiced, "Boo!"

Lee jumped like a jack rabbit and let out a blood-curdling squeal. Millie came running out of the kitchen yelling, "What's going on in here? Shannon, are you harassing Lee again?"

I made a second big mistake by laughing at the whole scene, and Lee turned into the hell-cat I witnessed when taking Goggy out to her house. With an angry look on her face, she picked up the carafe, squinted her eyes, and growled in a threatening manner. "You haven't had coffee poured in your lap lately, have you?"

"I-I-I'm sorry, Lee!" Following her as she rushed around cleaning tables like a mad woman, I then stepped between her and a table, and with humility and a contrite heart said, "I'm so sorry, Lee! Are you okay?"

She put her hands on her hips, stared me straight in the eyes, took a deep breath, and said very seriously, "That was a dangerous stunt, Shannon! What if I hadn't set the tray down and suddenly turned toward you? What do you think could have happened? That is, if you have the ability to think two inches past your nose!" I didn't say a word. Lee pointed her finger in my face and continued her tirade. "I'll tell you what could have happened, so you understand!" Waving her hands all around she continued, "The cups would have been knocked off the tray and shattered all over the floor to... to... who knows where!"

I began to apologize again. "I'm sorry, Lee. You are right. My thoughtlessness could have been a mess. Lee turned her back to me and, went into the kitchen. I asked loudly, "Will you please forgive me?" She didn't answer my plea for forgiveness. As I stood there, in the center of the restaurant, waiting for Lee's absolution, I heard her mention my name and then she and Millie started laughing. Now, that embarrassed me! Then, to top it off, I turned around to see the "two stooges" standing there, snickering.

"How long have you two been standing there?" Hank, still snickering, answered, "Long enough, Joker Wild!"

Glaring at both of them, I uttered a warning under my breath. "Don't either of you dare say a word!" The three of us went to the table and sat down. There wasn't a person in the restaurant who didn't notice the smile on their faces. It was quite evident that Mr. Pill Pusher and Mr. Grinner were eating up the scene between Lee and I.

Grant spoke up first. "How are you and your Juliet getting along, Romeo?" Of course, Hank, grinning from ear to ear, chimed in. "Yeah, man, it looks ta me like she's a bit pissed off at you. How are ya gonna git out of this jam, bud?"

As I looked straight into Hanks eyes, it occurred to me what Lee had said a short time ago: "The best defense is a good offence." So I shot back, "Define 'gonna,' Hank!" It worked because he just stared at me for a few moments blinking his eyes, not saying a word.

Finally, Grant broke the silence, and asked, "Why are you so huffy, Whitney? We feel awful the way she talked to you."

Hank spoke up again. "Now, come on, Mr. Hot Shot..." both of them began to giggle... "You know you can tell us any thang you want to, 'cause we're on yer side, man."

"Do either of you know how monotonous it is to constantly defend my personal life?" I responded, angrily.

Hank lifted his eyebrows and, in a tantalizing manner, said, "But, your life is a whole lot more exciten than ours!"

"Hank, Grant, why don't the two of you find a different hobby besides heckling me? Just maybe you should take your ladies out to the river and give them what you think I'm getting!"

"Well, Dr. Whitney, that advice is as useless as tits on a boar hog. First of all, our truck ain't designed for that kind of entertainment! Second of all, I'd have to git Vickie to the river. And third of all, we would need a babysitter!"

Shaking my head again, I leaned over the table, got right in his face, and whispered loudly, "Hank Nikensary, those are the most pathetic excuses I've ever heard! If you really want an exciting time with your wife, be creative, and make it happen!"

Hank sat for a while and didn't say anything. Then, peering at me and scratching his chin, he remarked, "You know what? Vickie and I ain't done something like that since the kids were born." And, grinning from ear to ear, he hit me on my shoulder, saying, "Thanks, Dr. Whitney. This weekend, I'm gonna give my wife a hard round of lovin' like she ain't never had before. How about babysittin' fur us, doc?"

"Sorry, bud, you're going to have to be more creative than that to find a sitter. Besides, my weekend is already taken.... You sure are quiet, Grant. Don't you have anything to get off your chest about my relationship with Lee?"

"A man like me needs all the hair he can get!" Grant must have thought his answer was funny because he got a nerdy facial expression and laughed. Hank and I just stared at him as he began to explain his joke. "You know, hair.... on my chest." When Hank and I ignored him, Grant frowned, then, responded to my suggestion. "You are right, Whitney. Ellen and I...well...we could use some spice in our life." Sounding as though he liked my suggestion, Grant went on to say, "You know what? I'm going to make reservations at a five star hotel in St. Louis weekend after next. What I'll do is buy a dozen roses, a box of fine chocolate candy, and take her to a fancy French restaurant. Then, when we arrive at the hotel, and she is in the bathroom preparing for bed, I'll get out some he-man clothes! You know, like a black leather vest and trousers! What you want to bet that will turn her on!"

Hank huffed and laughed. "He-man clothes, huh? Where ya gonna git some he-man muscles ta fill them out?"

Grant didn't like Hank's insinuation. To him, it sounded as though he was making fun of his body. Of course, that's what Hank was doing. And it was the first time I had ever seen Grant get really angry. "I'll have you know, butthead, I'll match my muscles with anyone's, including yours!"

Wow! Grant sure told him off, I thought. And it was all the two of us could do to keep from laughing at him. However, Hank gave me a 'hold it' glance and it became evident that Grant was struggling with something. His voice and body language seemed overly defensive at Hank's remarks. Usually, Grant would come back at us with a rebuttal and laugh about it. But, for whatever the reason, he leaned back in his seat and crossed his arms, as if to say, "Knock it off, *now!*"

Looking at my watch and noticing the time, I stood up to leave. By

Deception or Perfection

then, Lee had come over to our table to pour us a refill of coffee and asked, "Leaving so soon, Shannon?" Sorrowfully, I answered, "Yeah, got to go to work. Are you still mad at me?"

Lee quickly glanced around the room to make sure we weren't too conspicuous, came to my side of the table, and planted a big kiss on my cheek. She then patted my cheek and proceeded to talk to me as though I were about five years old. "No sweetie, I'm not mad at you. But I hope you'll think twice before pulling another stunt like that. It could have been dangerous."

I raised my right hand, as if taking an oath, and said, "I'm so sorry, baby doll. I'll never do anything like that again, scout's honor."

Grant leaned forward and smiled, while Hank just sat with his usual silly grin plastered on his face. It was clear to see that the wheels were turning in their minds thinking of ways to tease me at our next coffee break, which was their favorite pastime. Watching-them looking so cocky, I decided to strike first and asked Lee, "Does Millie still sell those energy drinks that older gentleman and teenage boys request when they come in?"

Nodding her head, she answered, "Yes, why do you ask?"

"Well, you might want to send a six-pack home with Grant and Hank. Make it my treat. They are going to need them for some jump-starts with their wives over the next two weeks!" Not giving anyone a chance to respond, I left as fast as a rabbit eating a carrot, and told Lee, "I'll call you later!"

After I arrived at the clinic, Ronda greeted me with a reminder. "Dr. Whitney, we have a light patient schedule today, so it's the best time to work on a load of stock that was delivered yesterday. Several boxes came this morning too. Maybe you can give me some idea where you want the merchandise to be stored."

Smiling at Ronda I responded "Well, let's file our patients out the door like they have an invitation to board Noah's ark. With the two of us working, it shouldn't take long to get those supplies put away. Ronda, I've got a favor to ask, if you have time. Would you please check the internet for the July dates of the Cardinals home games?"

"Sure will, Dr. Whitney."

We dismissed our last patient at about-a quarter to five. When we finish stocking the shelves, it was six and I retreated to my office. On the way out of the clinic, Ronda handed me the Cardinals baseball schedule. I thanked her, and she left and locked the door of the clinic.

I called Lee just to hear her voice. We talked about the mobile home and what project we should start first. Winding down our conversation, I asked, "You haven't forgotten our Saturday night celebration have you?"

"Not a chance,"

After hanging up the phone, I retreated to the kitchen, opened the fridge, and grabbed a bottle of beer. About that time, my housekeeper stepped out of the bedroom with a basket of laundry under her arm.

Her name is Debra Blais, and she had worked for me a little over three years. She and her husband moved to Ellisville from Clermont, France. After the last big flood in Illinois, the Corps of Engineers had hired her husband to come here for his advice and expertise in constructing stronger devises to divert flood water.

Debbie had worked several months as my housekeeper before she told me that she had a master's degree in teaching but couldn't get a job until she improved her English. Her dream was to teach first or second graders because she loved children so much. However, there were times that Debbie's nosiness would get on my nerves. After letting her know that she was over stepping her boundaries, she would say, "Oh, Docture Whitney, I'm so sar-ree!" And all my frustrations about her inquisitive manner would disappear.

Setting the basket of laundry down Deb commented, "You muss have had com-pa-nee."

"No one has been here except me."

Picking up a wash cloth from the basket, she asked, "Docture Whitney, you use make-op now?" I blushed because she had just caught me in a lie. She then remarked, "You cannot lie, Docture Whitney. Da face tells on you. You all-waighs get cought." And she laughed. "You ne-vur hov bean carr-less leeving ev-i-dence of com-pa-nee before."

Butting into Debbie's chatter, I reminded her, "Debra, it's time for you to tend to the basket of clothes in your arms."

When she finally left the kitchen, I made myself a sandwich and grabbed another beer. I was sitting down at the counter and eating my food when Debbie came back into the kitchen. She began her jabbering again, telling me that everyone in town was talking about my being involved with Lee and how pretty she was. Hank and Grant talked about Lee as though she were the most delightful woman to hit the town of Ellisville in a long time. I hadn't expected that, so I asked, "What do you mean about Hank and Grant?"

Debbie quickly informed me that the two of them had total respect and loved me like a brother. Then she added, "Hank and Grant are glad to see how ha-pee you are, and they had not seen you like dis een a long time." I didn't say another word, and Debbie went on about her work.

The next day, when Hank and Grant arrived at Millie's, Lee had just given me a second cup of coffee. Grant spoke up first. "Hey, sport, what's going on? You've got a serious look on your face. Is everything all right?"

Glancing at both of them, I responded, "No, it isn't, Grant! You know how I feel about the two of you, but there is something we need to talk about. Debbie told me the gossip going around town about Lee and me. And she mentioned that you guys have also expressed your opinions about our relationship." Hank started to open his mouth, but I put my hand up toward him like a cop directing traffic and continued, "Hank, let me finish. Then you can say anything you want. Look guys, I don't care how you talk about me to other people, but Lee has shared some very personal things about herself and family. She has also experienced an enormous amount of pain during her childhood. If someone should say anything that could be embarrassing or hurtful, it would devastate her, and you know there are people who have no scruples when it comes to gossip. Evidently, she never received any emotional or recognizable love from her parents, which, in my opinion, has made her very vulnerable. So, please take what I'm saying seriously, for Lee's sake. Don't say anything about her to anyone." For the first time, Grant and Hank were very quiet and listened to me.

Lee came over to our table and filled their coffee cups. Not noticing our quietness, she quickly walked away to take a customer's order. Grant picked up his cup, took a big gulp of coffee and, with all sincerity, said, "You have my word, Shannon!" When he called me Shannon, I knew he meant what he was about to say. "I'll not say a word to anyone unless you give me permission."

Putting one of his hands on my shoulder, Hank spoke up and gave his promise. "You shore nuff have my word, bud. Thar ain't no stupid gossip in tha world worth you or the little lady gittin' hurt. But that don't mean we cain't talk among ourselves, does it?"

I told him, "Not at all. But what we say to each other stays with each other!"

Then, the three of us shook hands to seal the agreement, and it was time to go to work.

The next morning when getting out of bed, excitement filled my mind, and I exclaimed aloud. "It's just twenty-eight hours until Lee and I will be together again,"

After getting dressed, and heading over to Millie's, the breakfast hour had passed. I entered the restaurant and, there was a noticeable emptiness. After sauntering over to the counter and taking a stool, I noticed the only sound was Millie and Lee chattering away in the kitchen. Evidently, they didn't hear me come into the restaurant. So, I got up from the stool and silently strolled over to the swinging doors of the kitchen to eavesdrop.

Millie said to Lee, "Charlie, you have got to tell Shannon how much you love him." You're right, Millie," Lee responded. "But those three little words won't come out of my mouth. When we're together, there are no boundaries. I have shared the most intimate moments of my life with him, and I will continue doing that so he knows how much he means to me."

Millie's response was, "Lee, what is wrong with...?"

I quickly went to the front of the restaurant and opened and closed the door so that it looked as though I had just entered the building. I walked over to the stool and sat down again. Lee then came out of the kitchen and noticed me sitting at the counter.

Smiling, she said, "Good morning, handsome."

I whispered, "Sure do like you, beautiful lady." She leaned over the counter very close to my face. And when I did, she kissed me seductively, and it awakened a part of my body that should remain somnolent, except at appropriate times. When the kiss ended, I gave her a quick grin and settled snugly back on the stool and told her, "Baby doll, that is unfair. Now I'll have to take a cold shower before going to work!" She patted me on my cheek and turned away, going on with her business as if nothing had happened. *You have no idea the affect you have on me! If women only knew the power they have!*

Lee broke into my thoughts by setting a cup of coffee in front of me and asked, "Aren't you seeing patients today?"

"Yeah, but not until one. What are you doing when you get off work?"

"I promised Brandie and Jaden that we would go to the pond and take a dip," she answered. "When we are through swimming, Brandie is looking forward to me reading some books to her. They have such little entertainment; it's the least I can do for them. What are you doing after closing the clinic?"

"I have procrastinated on some paper work long enough and that will take up most of the evening." Lee went back into the kitchen and I sat there, sipping my coffee. Suddenly, the door opened and in walked Gerald "Jerry" Spencer, the county sheriff. Jerry is slightly younger than I am and, according to some women around town, he is-a six foot, knock-down, drag-out, good-looking black man with a physique Arnold Schwarzenegger would envy. He swaggered over to the counter and sat on the stool next to me. Offering his hand for a shake, he asked, "How are you doing, Dr. Whitney?"

Shaking his hand, I responded, "Call me Shannon. And I'm doing great. How is the law business, Gerald?"

He answered, "Well, Shannon, you can call me Jerry. And the law business...it's S.O.S."

Lee came over to us and seemed a little nervous. She asked the sheriff what he would like to order, and with the smile of a hungry wolf, he responded, "What do you suggest?" She handed him a menu, naming several kinds of drinks. And, with a flirtatious smile, Jerry placed his order. "Well, how about a tall glass of lemonade? It seems to be getting a bit warm in here."

Lee responded nervously, saying, "One lemonade coming up."

When she delivered his order, he watched her every move. After she walked away, he remarked, "Now there goes a gorgeous dame!"

With a harsh tone, I quickly told him, "Her name is Lee. Yes, she is a beautiful woman and, not that it's any of your business sheriff, we are dating!"

He got a crooked grin on his face, leaned over the counter to get another look at Lee, and remarked, "It's kind of a waste to only…date a woman like her."

It took all that was in me to restrain myself from mopping the floor with such a sorry ass of a man. And it would have been total embarrassment for Lee. Realizing that I could wind up in the hospital and jail also helped to keep my temper from getting the best of me. I'm not a coward. Nevertheless, it was common sense to hold my anger for the time being.

Then, to top it all off, he gulped down his drink, and stood up, stretched his posture and flexed his shoulder muscles so that they protruded through his uniform. Hitting me on my shoulder, and almost knocking me across the counter he said, "Good seeing you, Doc. Excuse me, Shannon. I've got to tend to law business." After paying for the lemonade, he tipped his hat to Lee as a goodbye and left the restaurant.

Glancing around, I noticed that she was leaning against the side of the register shaking like a willow tree in a wind storm. I got up from the counter, walked over to the register, put my arms around her and asked, "Hey, baby, what's the matter?" She turned around and snuggled into my chest. I embraced her until a couple of customers came into the restaurant. Quickly, she pulled herself together and whispered, "Call me when you are through with work at the clinic." Then she walked away to wait on the customers.

Later that evening, I called Lee, and she sounded much better. After we chatted a bit, I asked her, "What happened this morning that upset you so badly?"

"It was so scary, Shannon. Knowing that anyone could be a danger, even a sheriff, and for whatever the reason, it made me nervous! But Millie told me not to worry. Jerry could be trusted."

I thought to myself, *Millie didn't hear his remark about Lee. And, if he hadn't been a sheriff, I would have invited him outside, muscles or not.* Trying to reassure Lee, I said, "No one is going to hurt you or your loved ones. As far as the sheriff goes, I think that he is up to something."

"He's okay. Millie reassured me that Jerry is..."

Butting in, I said, "Oh! So you're on a first name basis with him?"

"Shannon! Millie says he and his family used to come into the restaurant a lot, and he had always been a very polite kid and seemed very intelligent. She called him Jerry, so that's what I called him!"

"You can do what you want to, Lee, but I'm keeping an eye on him!"

She teased me saying, "My hero. What would I do without you?" Lee then began to talk about her special outing with Brandie and Jaden. "It was an outstanding time for us. First we went shopping. Not only did I buy some clothes for Brandie, there was a pair of boots that Jaden had been admiring in a store window, so I bought them for her. Then we went to a sports shop and got us some fishing gear. And, besides all of that, Goggy now has a comfortable bed to sleep in. After the shopping, we went to the lake and had a ball pulling one another into the chilly water." She got quiet for a minute. "After I tucked Brandie in bed, she asked about her dad. It was the first time she's mentioned him since we left Chicago. I told her that he was in heaven, watching over her every day, and he loved her with all his heart. That pretty well wraps up our afternoon and evening."

"If we are still on for tomorrow evening, is it all right to pick you up at your place about six?"

"You betcha!" she replied.

Chapter Eleven

Driving out to Lee's place the next evening, and looking in the rearview mirror, there seemed to be a car following me. I continued to watch the vehicle and switched from one street to another, but it stayed right on my bumper. However, when I approached a stop sign at the black top that led out of town, it made a sudden turn and sped away.

The thought of another full evening with Lee quickly dismissed any apprehension of the tailgating car. Wanting to spend as much time with her as possible, I began to press-harder on the accelerator. The old truck was rolling so fast, that it rattled from the tail pipe to the hood ornament.

After I parked in the clearing by the mobile home, Lee stepped out of the door just as the sun was setting and a stream of light shined behind her. In a split second, she appeared to be moving in slow motion as she came toward the truck. She looked like a beautiful princess walking in the rhythm of a symphony.

Shaking myself into reality, I jumped out of the truck, hurried to passenger side, and opened the door. She spoke a sweet hello and positioned herself comfortably close to the driver's side of the seat. After walking back around the pickup and climbing in, all I could do was stare at her.

Tilting her head a bit she frowned, giggled, and asked. "What"? I told her she was breathtaking. Smiling she responded, "Why, thank you, Dr. Whitney. You are pretty good-looking yourself."

As we approached town, I inquired, "Are you ready for that glass of wine we talked about earlier?"

She nodded, and said teasingly, "That sounds great! It's my hope that you might have some of your 'French' wine left over from our last date."

By that time, we had come to the entrance of my driveway. There was a man alongside the road, squatting by a vehicle and holding a tire tool as though he was fixing a flat. What bothered me was that it looked like the same car that had followed me earlier on my way over to Lee's place. I didn't want to frighten her, so I hid my suspicions. It was then I truly realized how vulnerable Lee, Brandie, and Jaden were living in such an isolated and desolate area. One of my concerns was the lack of security lights around the mobile home, which gave me the idea to make a suggestion to Lee.

"Lee, I've been thinking. You need some brush and trees cut down around the mobile home to give you better visual access to your surroundings. Also, the lane could use a trim, and it wouldn't hurt to have a couple of lights installed at each corner of the clearing. Would you be okay with me calling a friend who runs a tree trimming service? His name is Dylan Moss and his work is excellent. Besides, he owes me a favor. He could probably get someone out to your place tomorrow and have an estimate of the cost before evening. I'll pay for it."

"That would make Jaden and I feel a little more secure, Shannon. But, do you think he will come out to my place on a Sunday?"

"Sure, as long as he isn't busy,"

It was a little after six when the two of us walked through the door of my house. Smiling at Lee, I said, "Make yourself at home, sweetie. I'll be back shortly with our wine. Turn the stereo on if you like and we can visit for a while. I'm going to give Dylan a call to see if we can set up a time for him to come to your place tomorrow. Are you sure you're okay with that?"

"Sounds like a plan to me!"

I gave Lee a kiss on the cheek and went off to get in touch with Dylan. After hanging up, I called out from the kitchen, "Dylan will be able to come at one-thirty tomorrow!"

"Thank you so much Shannon. You have no idea how much I appreciate you doing that!"

Grabbing the glasses and wine, and migrated back to the living room, we made ourselves comfortable on the couch and I filled each of us a glass of wine. Lee sat quietly for a moment and laid her head on my shoulder. Then, with a very serious expression on her face, she looked into my eyes and nervously said, "Shannon, there's something I want to discuss with you, and it's embarrassing to talk to you about this, but it's very important to me."

I shrugged my shoulders and responded, "Go for it, baby. You can tell me *anything*."

Lee glanced around and took a deep breath. She then bit her lower lip in a thoughtful manner, and with a straight-forward tone in her voice, she blurted out. "Shannon… have… have you always used condoms with all of your sexual encounters?"

I was taking a sip of wine at the moment Lee asked the shocking question. Getting choked, I began coughing, causing the wine to spray all over the coffee table. Lee gave me a startled look and began patted my back. Still coughing, I jumped up and ran to the kitchen to retrieve some paper towels. After returning, and in a scratchy voice, I cleared my throat, and made an effort to answer her question.

"Lee, I have always used condoms. The women I've dated were also adamant about using condoms. They were grateful that a man cared enough to provide protection. I'm not the kind of person to take any chances with venereal diseases or the possibility of pregnancy. Using protection has always been a priority when it came to my sexual activities. Why do you ask?"

She looked down toward her hands and gripped the glass of wine tight enough to crack it. "This is hard to talk about!" Mumbling under her breath, she asked herself, "How can one ask this appropriately?" Then, without hesitation, she again blurted out another question. "Honest to goodness, Shannon…you have always used condoms?" Quickly reassuring her, I said, "Yes, Lee! I've always used protection!"

She quizzed me again. "For sure, you've never had unprotected sex?"

In a mild, yet forceful tone, I answered, "*For sure,* sweetheart. I've *never* had sex without using a condom!"

Lee set her glass on the coffee table and turned toward me. She began sharing her sexual history and continued pressing me for answers on the subject. "I was a virgin until my wedding night with Joe. He told me that he always used condoms but it was to protect himself from getting a woman, as he put it, 'knocked up. I believe with all my heart that Joe was never unfaithful to me, which brings me to another question. I know that I'm safe from any sexually transmitted diseases. Are you absolutely sure…and be honest with me…that you are positively safe?"

Staring into her eyes, I responded "Lee, my job requires the handling of all sorts of animals and blood samples and it is my business to take every precaution that no one is exposed to any kind of diseases. There are animals that can transmit some infections to humans and, being a vet yourself, you know nothing is ever positively secure. But, to be extra safe, I go once a year for a complete physical exam and full blood work up, and the Red Cross gets a pint of my blood."

Then, with a serious look on her face, she said, "I trust you completely now that we have talked about our sexual safety." I immediately gave her an apology. "I'm sorry. Please, go on with your questions. I'll answer them as best as I can."

Pausing for a moment and taking a deep breath, she seemed unsure of herself. She finally spoke up. "There is no tasteful way to say this, so I'm just going to come out with it. Would you feel safe making love to me without a condom?"

You could have knocked me over with a wet noodle! Blinking my eyes like a frog in a hail storm, I stammered and asked, "B-b-but what about pregnancy?"

Sitting straight at the edge of the couch, she smiled, saying, "The Monday after you and Suann reunited, I made a doctor's appointment and requested a prescription for birth control pills. There is no need to be concerned about me getting pregnant." Looking embarrassed and turning her head away from me, she leaned back into the couch and softly repeated, "Would you consider not using condoms when we make love?"

All at once, my entire body became strained and taut. There was no way she could have asked a more shocking question. Bewildered, I replied, "You never cease to surprise me with your boldness, Lee. Give me a minute to recover from your first question! Are you sure you are not kidding?"

"No, I'm not kidding. We are both adults and I thought we should seriously discuss this. Sex without condoms is amazing. So…since you've never had sex without protection before…are you willing to try it or not?

It took a few seconds for me to digest what she was asking and shook my head in disbelief saying, "I g-g-guess so, Lee."

"Shannon, there is no guessing to it. It's either a yes or a no!"

Finally, swallowing hard, and with a nod, I answered her. "Sure…ah…y-yes. We can make love without a condom."

Sitting straight up from the couch and smiling from ear to ear, she let out a nervous "Wow!" She scooted closer to me and, bumping my body with hers, she stated in a self-confident tone, "I have never been able to be an assertive person. See what you do to me? I never could have talked to Millie or Joe about something that personal."

I leaned forward, gave her a light kiss, and remarked, "You sure shocked the hell out of me, lady!"

"You have a delightful evening ahead of you, Mr. Whitney," Lee said teasingly. And we kissed again and again and again.

Then, nibbling on her ear, I whispered, "You realize this could lead to an early celebration."

She backed away from me and asked, "Is it time to play house?"

I stood up from the couch, presented her my hand, and eagerly announced, "I'm ready if you are!"

Driving into the parking lot by the football field, I couldn't help but notice the two florescent pole lamps that were just bright enough to make a perfect light through the bleachers. In all the years of going there, I had never seen a more beautiful night. As I parked in my safety zone, Lee looked around and commented, "Shannon…this does *not* look like a lovers' nest to me!"

"Good things sometimes come in disguised packages. Trust me, sweetie, it's alright."

Because Lee looked as though she might be changing her mind about our adventure, I quickly jumped out of the truck, ran to the passenger side, and opened the door for her. She stepped down to the sidewalk, and I quickly grabbed the blanket from behind the back of the seat. Lee stood for a few seconds, checking out the surroundings and seemed a bit reluctant to move any further.

"Come on, baby, follow me! It's alright. That's a promise," I told her.

Darting her eyes to the bleachers, she asked me, "Could there be any spiders or snakes under there?" After I reassured her that there were no spiders or snakes, she sucked in a nervous breath, squeezed my hand, and said, "Okay, let's go."

The two of us quickly arrived at the bleacher section and we stepped into the entrance. Looking up at the under-side of the seats, Lee commented, "I got dressed up for this? Shannon, this place doesn't..."

Before she finished her sentence, I kissed her...and kissed her again in a way that lit a fire in her.

When we withdrew from the kiss, she had a sweet, trusting look on her face. I took the opportunity to hang the blanket. Putting my arms around her waist, I slowly nudged her against the wall with my body. Lee reached for the bottom of my sweatshirt, slipped it over my head, and discarded it on the ground. We kissed again, and then she removed her top and bra and dropped them to the ground. I took her hands in mine and raised her arms until they were above her head. At first, she looked like a frightened little girl, so in a loving tone, I softly assured her. "Lee, you don't have to be afraid. Look at me, sweetheart. I'm a gentle man and never, never in this world would I hurt you in any way. Please, trust me."

She completely relaxed against the blanket and we gently began to kiss again. Lee suddenly responded to me and we hungrily kissed one another several times. Letting go of her hands, I continued to kiss slowly downward to my beautiful lady's breasts and caressed each one with my lips. After we took off our remaining clothes, she looked into my eyes and lovingly touched my cheek, and I continued kissing her upper body. She placed her hands on each side of my head, and guided my kisses back to her breasts. Devouring them with my lips, I could feel her desire escalating. She arched her body into mine and, when our eyes met, I whispered in a husky voice, "Lee, I'm so in love with you."

She smiled and softly said, "All I can give you right now is this." Then she kissed me with passion, and love. With tears in her eyes and a quiver in her voice, she said, "If there was a way, at this moment, to make myself say the words you want to hear, they would be from the depths of my being and you would be hearing them now." Whether Lee knew it or not, she had just declared how much she loved me. Then, we barely touched our lips in a kiss while closing the small gap between us. As we united our bodies, she gave in with an accepting gasp.

I made my movements a slow, short, deliberate tease and Lee hungrily responded with a sweeping motion. Back and forth. Back and forth. It almost sent me over the edge. Pausing for a few seconds, I whispered, "Baby, you are so beautiful, and it's hard for me to believe that I'm here making love with you!"

I put my hands around her waist and pulled her body closer into mine until her breasts were snug against my chest. Strengthening my grip around Lee's waist, I lifted her higher against the wall. She put her arms tightly around my neck and encircled my thighs with her legs. This allowed our movements to become deeper with every stroke. After a few moments, Lee began a rhythmical up and down movement and our sexual craving became more intense and electrifying. We kissed opened-mouthed, devouring each other's lips, and our breathing began to elevate. Wanting to prolong the ecstasy, we paused for a short while and just looked into each other's eyes. After a moment, we resumed our love-making and our passion transcended itself with an exorbitance of emotions. Lee gasped a profound breath between her lips, and I held my breath through the process of our souls uniting once again. Clinging to one another, our breathing became gasps and we reached the fulfillment of our celebration.

Lee put her head on my shoulder and we didn't move for a while. I held her tight until she dropped her feet to the ground. Catching our breath, we parted our bodies but continued to hold one another. Lee still had her arms around my neck and said softly, "I don't want to let you go!"

After kissing her cheek and forehead, I swallowed hard and teasingly said, "Baby, I'm going to need twenty counts to become fully conscious! Give me a few minutes. I can't handle another round like that right away!"

She giggled and pinched my belly. Letting out a big 'ouch,' I smiled at her and took the blanket from the wall. After getting dressed, Lee followed me to a private spot on the football field. After placing the blanket on the grass, we lay down and cuddled. I held her close as she curled up closer into my arms, clutching my hands and drawing them up to her chest I began to kiss the back of her neck, she said, "Shannon..."

"Yeah?"

I continued kissing her as she began to share. "I would never have believed in a hundred years that my feelings for someone could be so profoundly beautiful and perplexing at the same time. This is totally and completely new for me!"

"You don't have to understand your feelings, baby, just believe them!"

She turned around until we were face to face. Then, in a shocked tone, she said, "It's real! Your love for me is real!"

Responding from the depth of my soul, I said, "I would give my life for you, Lee!"

She stared straight into my eyes, saying. "I'm committed to you, Shannon, from the depth of my being! And there will never be any man but you in my life! My heart was yours the first time we made love!"

"From the first day you walked into Millie's, there was a knowledge in my heart that you were the woman I wanted to spend the rest of my life with," Raising up on my elbow, and resting my head in the palm of my hand, and giving her a delicate kiss on the lips, I asked, "Would you like to go to the house and have a glass of wine? It's still early and my intentions are to keep you with me as long as I can." She smiled as I took her hand and helped her to her feet. After another soft, gentle kiss, I tossed the blanket over my shoulder. As we headed back to the truck hand in hand, my thought was,-*Whitney, you are a blessed man to be with a woman who is beyond belief. Treasure her, because very few people ever experience the kind of love you and Lee share.*

When we got back to my place, Lee just wanted ice water. After giving her the drink she requested, I poured myself a glass of wine and sat down on the couch beside her. We made ourselves comfortable and she cuddled up next to me and asked, "Shannon, do you believe in

God?"

It sort of surprised me, but it shouldn't have because she had already shocked me with her other questions. "Absolutely. And my faith is without any doubt!" I could tell that she had another question coming and my thought was, *Here we go again!*

"Do you believe that pre-marital sex is a bad sin?"

Now, this question was one that needed careful forethought. Pausing for a moment, I answered, "Actually, Lee, I have researched the interpretation of the meaning of the word 'sin' as it is presented in the Bible. My findings were that the original Hebrew definition of 'sin' is 'missing your mark.'"

"Really?' she replied.

After nodding my head and taking a sip of wine, I continued. "It's my conviction that mankind has set the standards of the rights and wrongs that we do. That's why Jesus came to try and straighten things out. He gave us two rules to live by. First, to love God with all our heart, soul, and might, and, to love other people like we love ourselves. Lee, do you remember the story in the Bible about a woman who was married and got caught making out with another man?"

She said, "Yes, I do.

" Well…I guess someone caught her making out with another man... Anyway, he dragged her out to a courtyard and a bunch of people showed up. They intended to throw rocks at her until she died. But that didn't happen. Jesus was sitting on the sidelines watching the whole scene, and he asked all the guys and gals, 'Is there any one of you who hasn't goofed up at some time or the other?' Those guys and gals just stood around. Some of them hung their heads and others looked at each other as though they didn't know what to do. Then, Jesus spoke up again. 'If any of you people feel you have never made a mistake or did something wrong,' Then, Jesus picked up a rock and handed it to some jerk standing next to him and said, Go ahead! Chuck them rocks at the little lady until you kill her.' You know what? Not one of those people threw a rock at her. They all left and she was standing all by herself. Jesus never looked at her. He fiddled with a stick in the dust, and he told her. 'Little lady, you go on home now, and don't make the same mistake again. I don't think you are a bad person.'

"That's it. Jesus went on with his business and the woman was left stranding in the court yard"

Lee giggled and hit me on my shoulder saying, "Shannon Whitney! I have heard that story all my life and it was never told in such a unique and colorful manner. You are quite a storyteller."

Looking at her with all sincerity, I felt I made my point. "Yeah, I'm quite a story teller. But my interpretation of the scripture is that God loves all of us more than we can imagine. He loves us more than you love your little girl. Would you, no matter what your little girl did, condemn her to suffer eternal pain? Lee, I know as far as myself, I make my own hell. Now...to answer your question. No, I do not believe that pre-marital sex is a 'sin' as man has interpreted it. It is also my belief that sex between two consenting adults is a growing experience. Believe me, there are a lot of people who would come down on me like the plague for that opinion. But, stop and think. Had you not married and had sex with Joe, you would not have known the difference between having sex and making love.

That is the difference. I'm not saying 'make out' with every Tom, Dick, or Jane is okay. And I'll be the first one to say that my experience included a lot of Jane's. However, they were absolutely there just to fill a physical need. You are my soul-mate, and my love for you is beyond description. Making love with you is different than making out, having sex, getting it on, or whatever a person chooses to call it. Our lovemaking will always take us into a spiritual realm of peace, beauty, love, sweetness, and joy. If we described God, wouldn't that be the words we would use? The two of us were meant to be together from the beginning of time. To me, we are already married in the sight of God. When it comes time for you and I to be ready to stand in front of a man or woman and recite vows and sign man's legal papers, then that is what we will do. I'm sorry, my love, I didn't mean to get on a soap box. But was your question answered?"

Lee didn't respond right away. And, when she did, she said, "You have given me a lot to think about. I have never thought of God in that perspective. My guilty feelings for making love to you our first time kept me awake that night. But, hearing you describe God in that light lifts my heart and it helps me realize that my caring for you is different than how I felt about Joe, and I don't just mean in a sexual way. Just the nearness of you calms my whole inner self. Your sense of humor is so cute and it makes me laugh. The way you hold your coffee cup, the way you take care of our four-legged friends and your dimpled smile when you're flirting. And my favorite is when you are trying to imitate John Wayne."

We laughed, and then she became very serious. "Shannon, I don't want to miss any part of us being together and loneliness sets in when you are not around me. What I'm saying is enough for you to believe me until…"

Putting my finger on her lips, I told her, "There is no need for you to say anything else.

And, if you do come to a place where you can express your love in a different form, then I'll always be receptive when that time comes."

Chapter Twelve

After waking up on Sunday morning, my first thought of the day was to flip on the air conditioner. After going through my rituals of showering, shaving, and slipping on some sweats, I hopped back on the bed and called Lee to see what she had on the agenda for the day.

She sounded a bit out of breath when answering the phone. "Right... at this moment... Brandie and I are giving Goggy a bath. We haven't planned anything else for the remainder of the day. Why do you ask?"

"Well, I was thinking about coming over to do some carpenter work on the mobile home."

"That sounds like a good idea to me. But what kind of a carpenter are you?"

I lapsed into my John Wayne voice. "Why, I'm the best carpenter in these here parts, little lady. Don't tell me you haven't noticed the beautiful woodwork at my homestead. Yours truly is the one who did all of that work."

In a sultry tone, Lee said, "Okay, Mr. Wayne, come on over here with your tools. I'll see to it that they are put to good use. Just... come and show me your stuff."

Still using my John Wayne impression, I informed her, "If you are going ta see to it that my tools will be put to good use, what if I'm too tired to do the carpenter work, little lady?"

Lee had a big laugh at my imitation. Still giggling, she asked, "What in the world enticed you to come up with imitating John Wayne? Didn't he die a long time ago?"

"John is my hero. And I watch his old movies at least twice a week."

Giggling again, she replied, "All I can say is that you need to watch them a whole lot more often."

"There you go, hurting my feelings."

She laughed again and asked, "It didn't hurt your feelings bad enough to keep you from coming over to work on the mobile home, did it?"

"Well, I'm tough and can handle insults. However, I need an apology with a kiss. And, if you are willing to do that, I'll be there before you know it."

"An apology with a kiss will be here waiting for you."

About two hours later, I pulled up at Lee's place with lumber, nails, and my tool box. I jumped out of the truck to unload the material and looked up to see Lee standing on the porch. She came down the steps and headed toward the truck to greet me "Hey, there. Could you use some help?"

I motioned for Lee to come to the tailgate where I was unloading and reminded her of the promise she made. "You are in debt to me and I'm here to collect, missy!"

Lee stepped in front of me, smiled, and put her arms around my neck. "I'm so sorry, John, for hurting your feelings." Knowing I couldn't do anything about it, she gave me a kiss that might be interpreted as a come on, but she knew her boundaries and just when to back off.

After the kiss, I looked at her with a surprised expression and remarked, "Lee, I'm... I'm Shannon!"

Placing her hand across her heart she began to snicker. "Oh, my goodness, Shannon! Did I call you John?"

"Sweetie, you can call me any name you please, as long as you make sure it's this man you're kissing."

Then we kissed again, and she asked, "You're jealous of yourself?" She started laughing. That's the funniest dilemma that I've ever heard a man get himself into."

Starting to unload the truck, I confessed, "Okay... you're right. So, make sure you're kissing me and not him!"

She smiled at me and said, "No one could take your place. Not even John. But how are you at mimicking Brad Pitt? Just kidding, dear heart. You know how hard it is for me to walk away from you when we kiss. It's sort of like that potato chip commercial. I can't kiss you just once."

Giving her a sly smile, I commented, "Well, here's hoping that you never lose your appetite."

I worked for a couple of hours, and heard Lee yell out the front door, "Shannon! Why don't you come in and drink something cold? It's getting pretty hot out there! I made a pitcher of iced tea!"

Responding to her invitation, I put down my hammer and went into the mobile home. Lee handed me a paper towel as I took off my hat. Wiping the sweat off my forehead, I asked, "Where is Brandie and Jaden?"

"Oh, Jaden took Brandie to the pond to fish but brought her back when she got bored and tired. I put her down for a nap and Jaden went back to the pond to work on her book. She says that sitting next to the water is peaceful and gives her inspiration."

"Are you sure there are fish in the pond?' I asked.

"Absolutely. Jaden brought back enough fish for two meals."

Lee handed me a glass of tea as I sat down at the table. Just when I was about to take a drink, two little hands started poking me with their fingers. Lee lifted her eye brows, smiled, and gave me a nod from across the table. About that time, a little intruder yelled, "Boo!"

With squinted eyes, I jumped out of the chair, grabbed Brandie, and we landed on the floor. The little rascal then jumped onto my belly and began punching me while laughing and yelling, "Boo! Boo! Boo!" I picked her up, got on my knees, and did a pretend slam dunk and she squealed again.

By this time, Goggy entered the action by growling and tugging at the leg of my jeans. But that didn't stop me because the "tickle torture," was my next move. I warned Brandie. "This is what you get for scaring me, Miss Brandie! Do you give up?"

The tickle torture did the trick. She screeched out, laughing and pleading. "I give up, Shannon! I give up!" I asked her a second time if she was *for sure* ready to give up, and again she squealed out in laughter, "Yes, for sure, Shannon, I give up!" We scrambled to our feet from the floor, turned around, and flopped down on the couch. Brandie scooted in right beside me and Goggy jumped on my lap. With beautiful brown eyes, Brandie looked up at me and said, "You are so much fun, Shannon." Scrambling up on her knees, she put her arms around my neck and gave me a big hug. Then, she laid her head on my shoulder, saying, "I'm so glad Mommy likes you because I like you, too, very much!"

Now that melted my heart. Honest to God, it took all that was in me to hold back the tears; and when looking up at Lee, I quickly made a remark. "My work is waiting on me, I'll grab my tea, and skedaddle out of here"

After working a few more hours on the porch, I noticed the sun was about to set and decided to put my gear away. After packing up, I knocked on the door and Lee and Brandie stepped out for us to say our goodbyes. Lee put her arms around me. "We had a hard time leaving you alone to do your work. Brandie wanted to help, but after telling her that you liked working by yourself," Lee winked at me, "She was okay with that."

Squatting down to give the little munchkin a kiss on the cheek, I stood up, gave Lee another goodbye kiss and headed home.

It was 6:30 the next morning when the telephone woke me up; it turned out to be an emergency. Needless to say, it was almost nine by the time I got back to the clinic, and patients were already in the waiting room. I also found out that Lee had called and left a message on the answering machine thanking me for the work I did on her porch. She asked me to call her back when the clinic closed.

After a very busy day, I locked the doors of the clinic and dropped into my office chair. Almost immediately, the phone rang and it was Lee. "I'm so sorry for not waiting for you to return my call," she said, "but I was anxious to find out about something. Would you be free to come over for dinner Friday night? Brandie told me that we should invite you over to our place more often. So, what do you say?"

Leaning back in my chair and parking my feet on the desk, I answered, "Well, she's right. Three invitations a week isn't too much, is it?"

Lee laughed and responded, "Wait a minute! Your practice doesn't allow you that much freedom. If anyone understands the vet business, well... it's me. Being around you that much might distract me from my responsibilities to Brandie and Jaden. You know how you affect me. I might be tempted to do something inappropriate like... giving you a kiss."

"There's nothing inappropriate about that. But it is nice to know when I'm around you, kissing me is on your mind. Hmm. Could it be... that we're thinking the same thing? You are so irresistible. What should we do about this predicament?"

Lee paused for a moment and said, "We can decide later about our *predicament* but perhaps we need to keep a little distance for a while." We giggled at our nonsense because we simply loved teasing one another. Then she said, "Seriously, can you make it Friday night?"

"Yes, I'll be there with a healthy appetite. And I'll also be hungry for food."

Lee laughed and came back with, "Let's take care of the hunger for food first The other appetite, well...that will have to wait for another time. So, can you come for dinner somewhere around six-thirty or seven?"

"That would be perfect. But Lee, you will have worked all day. You shouldn't be bothered to fix a meal, too."

"I won't be. Jaden is going to make the dinner."

The rest of the week seemed to pass quickly. Finally, it was Friday and time to go to Lee's for dinner. On the way to her place, I noticed a car following me again. After quickly pulling off the road and stopping, I watched it speed around me like it was going to a fire. I saw a man who looked like the same guy pretending to be changing a tire in front of my driveway. This concerned me a bit, and I knew that this wasn't a coincidence. Even though it was suspicious, the only thing that could be done was to be more aware of my surroundings. I didn't notice anything else out of the ordinary for the rest of the journey.

After knocking on the door at Lee's place, I heard, "Come in, it's open." As I walked through the doorway, Brandie came running towards me. I picked her up, and she gave me a big hug. About that time, Goggy ran out of the hallway and attacked my shoes, growling and barking. Lee stood up from the couch, with a sparkle in her eyes, and said, "You sure look nice tonight, Shannon."

"Thank you, my lady, for the compliment. Of course, you are *always* beautiful." She smile and thanked me as we walked to the dining area. Carrying Brandie and dragging Goggy, who was attached to my jean leg, I finally made my way to the table and was able to sit the little princess down in a chair. Jaden yelled at Goggy to get out of the room and go to his bed. He seemed to mind better than some children.

Lee had the table all set, complete with lit candles, which gave it a touch of elegance. We sat down to a Caesar salad, sirloin steak smothered in gravy, mashed potatoes, and steamed broccoli with a hollandaise sauce.

We finished dinner, and Lee brought out a hot fudge cake topped with ice cream. She also made a pot of coffee to drink with our dessert. By the time it was all over, I backed away from the table so full, it felt as though my butt was glued to the chair. I eased my way across the floor to sit down on the couch, nearly sitting down on top of Goggy. He had sneaked back into the living area and was lying on the couch. Lee yelled at the canine to get down and he reluctantly hopped to the floor. Then she sat down beside me and asked, "How was dinner?"

After telling her that it was great, I leaned back for a few minutes. It was all I could do to keep from loosening my belt buckle. By that time, Jaden came to the living room area and we visited for a while. "You're a fantastic cook, Jaden. And I'm sure the scales are going to tell me to stop eating so much. There is no way a person wouldn't eat like a pig around that kind of food."

"Thank you, Dr. Whitney. It's so nice to have a guest for dinner. Besides, you could use a few extra pounds."

"Jaden, please call me Shannon. You are a friend, and friends call each other by their first names."

She smiled and said, "Okay, Shannon. Well, it's time for me to clean the kitchen." Lee and I both stood up to help but Jaden quickly said, "No, you two sit back down. Lee bugged me all evening wanting to help with the cooking, and I finally got her to keep her mouth shut, and the rule still goes. And if it's alright, I'm going to excuse myself and go to my bedroom as soon as the kitchen is cleaned up."

While Jaden did her cleaning, Lee and I sat on the couch, Brandie played with Goggy on the floor and talking to one another for a while, we suddenly noticed a rank odor in the air. Jaden peeked around the room divider with a questioning look on her face and Lee shrugged her shoulders while I pretended not to notice. All at once, Brandie jumped up from the floor and yelled, "Goggy! Shame on you! Mommy, Goggy just farted again!"

Lee looked mortified and just sat there for a few seconds. Jaden stepped from the room divider holding her nose. Then Lee stood up, pointing her finger toward the hallway and demanded that Goggy go to bed. The canine, with his head down and tail tucked between his legs, retreated to the bedroom.

Lee sat back down, and with a 'what can I do' embarrassed look on her face, said, "That was not in the plan for the evening. Suddenly we both burst out in laughter. Jaden took her hand from her nose and began laughing, too.

Brandie thought we were being insinuative and began to defend her pet. "Goggy is not a bad doggy! Sometimes I fart too!" We all glanced at each other and began laughing again. Brandie ran to her bedroom to console Goggy and returned to the living room with a teddy bear under her arm. Crawling up on the couch she laid her head on my lap, and asked, "Shannon, do you think Goggy is a bad puppy?"

"Absolutely not! Didn't you notice that he went right to bed when your mom told him to? And he has stayed there." Brandie must have been okay with my answer because she yawned and, in a few minutes, went sound asleep.

It was about eight-thirty by this time. Jaden had already excused herself and withdrew from our company. Lee left the living room to fetch the little one's pajamas. After returning to the couch, she slipped them on Brandie and we walked together to carry the little princess to the bedroom. After helping Lee tuck her in, we stood for a moment, just staring down at the beautiful little girl sleeping safely and soundly in her bed. I put my arm around Lee's waist and whispered, "What would you want to bet that my dad and mom felt the same way we are feeling, when seeing Jess and I sleeping in our beds? She is a treasure." Lee smiled and sweetly commented, "That's one bet I'll pass on. I'm sure your mom and dad did exactly what we are doing right now. That's what parents do. And from the things you have shared with me, they evidently adored you and Jess."

I quickly suggested we return to the couch because the emotions in my gut were causing my eyes to tear. We headed back to the couch and sat down. I put my arms around Lee and we cuddled for a moment. Then, in a whisper, I asked, "Lee, if you're not doing anything next Monday, would you like to come over to the clinic and help out for the day?"

She straightened up from my arms and said, "That sounds great to me."

"Maybe you can teach me a few things," I told her.

Condescendingly, she replied, "Just maybe." She kissed me sweetly as I pulled her closer.

Still whispering so I wouldn't wake Brandie and Jaden, I warned her, "A little more of that kind of behavior and you are going to get carried out to the wood shed, missy!" Kissing my face, she challenged my threat as she whispered, "No, I don't think so. It is not only too close to Jaden and Brandie, it is also too early. No hanky panky is going on if there is the least bit of a chance that one of them is not asleep."

"Okay, then. Let's cool it. It's no fun leaving you and having to go home to a cold shower. I've already had my shower for the night."

She smiled and continued to smother my face with kisses, saying, "Well, maybe one of these nights when you are having a shower, I can wash your back."

"Lee! That kind of talk really turns me on." I got up from the couch and was trying to tell how she was affecting me but she continued the taunting. She stood up grinning at me, and began twirling her finger on my face.

"Damn it, Lee! I'm serious as hell!" She didn't listen to me and began rubbing my chest. That was it! I grabbed her up, threw her over my shoulder, and headed for the bathroom that was located off of the kitchen.

Agitated and helpless, she whispered, "Shannon, put me down! Now Shannon, put me down! Are you crazy? PUT ME DOWN! Now!"

Just after we entered the bathroom doorway, I sat her down, smiled real big, kissed her on the forehead, and whispered, "Gotcha!" Oh, my! There was mad all over her face! She said in a loud whisper, "Just for that, Shannon Whitney, I have something *I'm* going to show you!"

With excitement in my voice, I asked, "What are you gonna show me, baby?"

Her lips were tight and her narrowed eyes shot darts right through me as she said, "The door!" Taking my hand, she pulled me to the door and said, "Go! Go, right now!"

"No!" And I didn't move an inch. Narrowing her eyes again, she nodded her head toward the opened door as if to say "leave." Shaking my head 'no' and leaning into her face, I attempted to bribe her. "Only if you give me one more kiss."

Lee glanced at the floor, tapped her foot a couple of times, and said, "Then do you promise to leave?"

I nodded, smiled, and stepped in front of her so we were face to face. I laid a kiss on her that could have melted Mt. Rushmore. And, just as she tilted into the kiss, I backed away and said, "Sure do like you, baby," and I headed straight out the door.

Stunned, Lee whispered as loud as she could, saying, "You... you rascal, you've got one coming!"

"And it can't come soon enough for me!"

Entering my place, the phone rang. It was Lee. The first thing out of her mouth was, "I'm sorry, Shannon. You had every right to do something to stop my teasing you. What I did was totally inappropriate. Some of it was honest behavior because of how much you mean to me. But you were so cute with your reactions... Well, I chose to take the kissing a little farther, not thinking how it was affecting you. I'm sorry for being so insensitive!"

"Wow, baby! I'm not the least bit mad at you. To me, you were very cute, and I couldn't help but to tease you back. My actions were on purpose and I am very flattered at your behavior. You mustn't think another thought about it, okay? Just one thing, try to give me that kind attention when we can do something about it, and know that all of our actions were mutual. I love you and there isn't anything you could do to take that away from me. You haven't done anything wrong. Both of us are a lot alike inasmuch as we are big teasers. It could be me starting something with you next time. I have even put you in danger with some of my nonsense. Please, don't cry about this. Are you going to be alright? I can be there in fifteen minutes."

"No you don't have to do that. I'll be okay."

Hearing her sniffling over the phone, I told her, "Sweetie, don't let this incidence hurt you another minute. Okay?"

"You are so understanding. It makes me lo…..care for you more then you'll ever know. Are you going to be coming to Millie's any time soon?"

"Sure am. Unless there is an emergency call early in the morning, yours truly will be there. If we don't see each other tomorrow, then I'll make sure we see each other the next day. It's hard for me to stay away from you for more than twenty-four hours." After telling her again how much I loved her, I hung up the phone and headed off to bed.

While parking the truck at Millie's the next morning, I noticed a man at the curb, leaning against a car and lighting a cigarette. He quickly turned around with his back to me, opened the car door, jumped in, and sped away like a bat out of hell. Shaking my head, I *thought, that man was watching the doorway of the restaurant! I wonder what he is up too.* I went on into Millie's. However, there was a feeling of deep concern as I strolled into restaurant. But, making my way over to the table, where the two mischief-makers were sitting, thought of the mystery man slipped out of my mind.

After greeting them, Grant leaned back in his chair and said, "Hank and I have been talking about having a cook-out and we were wondering if you and Lee would like to come to his house next Sunday. Of course, you're welcome to bring anyone else that you want to."

"It's okay with me but I've made plans to do something with Lee that day. Let me talk to her and see how she feels about it."

Grant, glancing over to the counter remarked, "Looks like she is on her way over here now. Maybe you can talk to her about the cookout."

Before I knew it, Lee had made her way to our table. As I gave her a smile, it felt perfectly natural for me to reach behind her and pull one of the sashes of her apron. Down it went to the floor and slid under a chair. Staring at me, she demanded, "Pick it up!"

Looking up, with my chin tucked into chest and innocently blinking my eyes, I asked, "Pick what up, sweetie?"

Deception or Perfection

Lee put her hands on her hips and glanced at the apron. "You know what! The apron on the floor! Pick it up!"

Hank and Grant were watching every move and listening to every word between the two of us. Glancing down to the floor, I put a surprised expression on my face and acknowledged, "Oh, yeah. You mean *that* apron on the floor? So, that's what you're talking about."

Picking the apron up, I handed it to Lee. Just then, she dropped her pencil, and it rolled under the table.

"Shannon, would you mind getting my pencil for me?"

"Sure will, sweetie." I bent down and picked up the pencil. As I rose up to hand it to Lee, she unexpectedly reached around my body. Pencil still in hand, I glanced down to see what was going on and saw that Lee had tied the apron to my waist. I quickly looked around the restaurant to see if anyone was watching and noticed that everyone had their eyes glued to our table. Stammering like a sailor who had been caught making moon shine, and pointing to the apron, I smiled and asked, "W-wha-what is this for, Lee?"

She smiled back and handed me the check order pad. Then, she sat at the table and began ordering breakfast. "I'll have two eggs over easy, bacon, toast. And, by the way, server, you need to write my order down so the cook can fix the food. Also, the same for my two friends. (Pointing at Hank and Grant) And when we are finished with our meal, please see that Shannon Whitney gets the ticket. Have you got that, sir?" Trying to write down everything she ordered, I asked helplessly, "Lee, what are you doing? You know I can't do this."

She showed no mercy and said, "Well, sir, I can relate to that because there are customers who can't keep their hands to themselves and that can really disturb a server. Now, go on and give our order to the cook."

Hank and Grant were holding back the laughter. Nonetheless, I played along with the little game, placed the order, and returned to the table. Lee stood up and kissed me on the cheek in front of everybody. Then, touching my cheek with her hand, she said, "I sure do like you, baby!" People in the restaurant began laughing. Lee removed the apron and whispered in my ear, "You can't con a con. They will always beat you at your own game. Smiling at Lee, I took her hand, gently kissed it, and replied, "Thank you, great master, for your wisdom."

Turning around, and giving a thumb's up to everyone, I sat back down at the table until it was time to go to work. On my way to the door, Lee caught my eyes. I threw her a kiss and she smiled at me and returned the gesture.

After closing the clinic and crashing in my office, I received a call from Lee. We chatted and teased about the apron incident and talked about Brandie and her "boo" games. Then, Lee remarked, "Shannon, as you know, Brandie is old enough to be starting pre-school this fall. I've got to do something beforehand to let people know about her and Jaden. Do you have any suggestions how that can be done without raising suspicions? No one knows about the two of them except you and Millie."

"I don't have any ideas right now,"

Lee thought for a moment and commented, "It isn't wise to just spring her and Jaden on people."

"I agree. Oh, wait... Hank and Grant invited us to a cook-out at Hank and Vickie's home next Sunday. Maybe that would be a good time to introduce Brandie and Jaden to the people who show up for the barbeque. There has to be some way for people to find out about them. Plus, you don't have much time to get this done before Brandie has to be registered for school. Can you think of a way to start the process of introducing them to Hank and Grant by tomorrow?"

Lee was quiet for a moment, and then suddenly blurted out, "I've got it, Shannon! In the morning when the three of you guys are at breakfast, we'll get things started. There is a little more I need to do, and Millie can help with the plan. Just go with the flow and follow Millie's lead. It is more believable if nothing is rehearsed."

"Okay, baby. You go for it!"

The next morning, after arriving at Millie's, I met up with Hank and Grant, who were already seated at a table. After we greeted one another, I looked around and noticed that Lee was nowhere to be seen and asked "Where's Lee?"

They both shrugged, and shook their heads. Hank chimed in, "We were jus' about ta ask ya tha same thang, Doc. Hope she's okay!"

By that time, Millie had approached the table with our coffee. "Isn't Lee working today?" I asked her.

"Yeah. She's going to be late coming in. She called last night saying that her little girl was flying into Lambert airport early this morning. Talk about a shocker, that one takes the cake. Has she mentioned having a kid to you, Doc?"

Saying the right thing was very important because, not only did Grant and Hank's ears perk up, several people around our table were within hearing range. I responded, "Now, Millie... you know me. Do you think I could keep a secret like that?"

She answered, "Hell no!" and walked away from the table.

Grant, watched me very carefully, and asked, "Are you sure you knew nothing about Lee having a child?" Evasively I answered.

"Grant, how can you ask a question like that? You two know me like a book. You heard what I said."

Hank spoke up, "Why do ya think Grant asked you tha question?"

Right at that moment, Lee came into the restaurant and hurried to the kitchen. After coming out with her apron on and a little order book in her hand, she picked up the coffee pot and began going to the tables where people-needed their coffee cups refilled. When Lee reached our table, she started pouring coffee into Hank's empty cup. My instincts told me to say something; however, she began to chatter excitedly.

"I'm sorry not to have mentioned anything about my little girl. It is hard sometimes to get jobs when you're a single mom. And my daughter's grandparents in Arizona wanted her to come for a visit until I got established. I thought that was a good idea. So, after telling Millie about her, she didn't fire me. I called Brandie's grandparents and they were able to get a late flight into St. Louis this morning. And... this is so neat, guys... my friend Jaden called me and she is flying in tonight to stay with me the rest of the year! She's gone through a nasty divorce and hopes to get a new start in Illinois. She was so excited to come here and live with Brandie and me! Isn't that wonderful? Shannon, will you forgive me for not telling you?"

I smiled at her and said, "Baby, there is nothing to forgive and I am looking forward to meeting your daughter and friend."

She kissed me on the cheek in front of everybody and quickly left the table so that neither Hank nor Grant had a chance to ask any questions. Nevertheless, it didn't stop Hank from questioning me.

"What tha hell jes went on here, man? Somethin' ain't right! Are you gonna tell us why she really didn't say anythang about a kid?"

"There was no reason to ask her if she had a child," I calmly answered. They both kind of stared at me, dumbfounded. But, before they could ask another question, I skedaddled out of Millie's as fast as I could. However, the two them knew there was something going on. They just didn't know what.

Chapter Thirteen

After closing the clinic, I called to commend Lee on her performance earlier at Millie's. "You should have been an actor," I said, "You made a believer out of me, and I *knew* the circumstances regarding Brandie and Jaden."

"Do you think Hank and Grant bought my story?"

"Don't know for sure, babe. But it was very noticeable that the people sitting around us were hanging on your every word. I believe that they swallowed your explanation hook, line, and sinker. Now you can bring Brandie and Jaden out into the open and it will make your life a whole lot less complicated. Won't it be great to not worry about people seeing them come into town with you? You did a great job. I'm confident no one is suspicious about anything. Well, my love, I need to get off of the phone. There is a pile of paperwork calling out to me. I'll be in touch with you later. You know what? I sure do love you, pretty lady."

"You light up my life every time you say you love me. And thanks for the reassurance that my efforts at Millie's this morning seemed to work. Bye, for now."

I went to the mailbox later, and caught another glimpse of a car driving by my lane. It appeared to be the one that was parked in front of the restaurant the week before. However, it wasn't the car that followed me out to Lee's place. "Maybe there's a way to get the license plate number and turn him in as a stalker," I muttered. "What the hell is he doing watching me?" Then another thought crossed my mind. "What if his interest involves Lee?" Not having an answer, I promptly dismissed it from my mind, grabbed the mail, and headed back to the house.

Sitting at the kitchen counter and thumbing through the junk fliers and advertisements, I caught a peek of some familiar-looking envelopes. The Muny Opera and baseball tickets had arrived. After opening the envelopes, I checked to make sure that the information on the tickets was correct. The date for the opera was Saturday, July seventh at seven and the Cardinals game was the next day, Sunday, July eighth at one in the afternoon. "Perfect," I said to myself. "The ballgame is on her birthday and only three weeks from today." I then call Ellen and Vickie to make some arrangements for a birthday celebration for Lee on Sunday evening of the eighth.

I told Ellen about Lee's birthday and asked if she and Vickie would help plan a party and invite only close friends and relatives.

"I'd love to help. Would you like for me to call and ask Vickie?"

"No, I'm going to tend to that as soon as we are off the phone." We chatted just a couple more minutes and then said our good-byes. I dialed Vickie's cell phone and she answered right away. "Hi Vickie, this is Shannon."

She seemed very glad to hear from me, and responded in a surprised voice. "Shannon! How are you? Can you and Lee make it for the cook-out next Sunday?"

I wasn't quite sure how to answer her, so I simply said, "I'm going to have to talk to Lee about it first. I'll probably call her as soon as I'm through asking you a favor."

"Okay," she said, "What's the favor?"

"Ellen has already promised her help in planning a birthday party for Lee the evening of July eighth. Could the two of you work on that for me?"

"It would be my pleasure, Shannon. Do you want us to make it a surprise?"

"What a great idea! Yes. That would be fantastic."

In a delighted voice, Vickie replied, "Well, Dr. Whitney, your wish will be our command."

Very early the next morning, I took a seat at my usual table at Millie's. As Lee approached the table, I said, "Good morning, beautiful. What would you like to do for your birthday next month?"

Giving me a suspicious glance while pouring coffee into my cup, she asked, "How did you manage to find out about my birthday?"

Flashing a boyish smile, I patted the chair next to me as an invitation to sit down.

"Better not, Shannon. As you can see, the place is packed. The cook called in sick this morning so Millie can't help out here." Then she smiled back at me, saying, "So, that flirty smile and calling me "beautiful" will not work this morning. Now, I know why you have been given the reputation as a woman-charmer."

"Who told you that?" Leaning over and giving me a bigger smile, she whispered, "Probably the same one who told you about my birthday, dear heart. Call me later and we can make some plans."

"That sounds great. You know you shouldn't believe everything you hear."

After closing the clinic and finishing my paperwork, I went to the kitchen, poured myself a glass of wine, and made a ham sandwich. After finishing my snack, I treated myself to another glass of wine and retreated to the living room to call Lee. "Good evening, my love," I crooned softly when she answered the phone.

"There you go again with your sweet talk. But don't ever stop. It makes my day. Heck, what woman wouldn't like a man to call her his love?"

Smiling, I thought, *You're right on the nose, baby. The difference is that my sweet talk to you comes from the heart.*

Then, chatting with Lee for a few more minutes, I gave her my good-night wishes, made it an early evening, and headed for bed.

The next morning, I went over to Millie's and sat at the usual table. The restaurant was nearly full when I arrived. Even though Lee was very busy, she managed to bring my coffee with a smile. My primary goal was to get a few minutes alone with her, so I waited until the place had mostly cleared out. Lee swished by me, heading to a couple of customers. I stopped her on her way back to the kitchen and asked, "Do you think you could ask Millie to let you take a break for a few minutes? I have something important to discuss with you."

"Sure. I'll ask her when I give her this order."

Lee was back within two minutes and sat down at the table with me. "Millie said it was okay since we're not busy right now. Do you have something on your mind?"

"What would you say to going to a nice restaurant, then to the Muny Opera the night before your birthday, and to a Cardinals baseball game in the afternoon?"

"That sounds like a whole weekend of fun. I've never been to an outside theater before. And baseball is my favorite sport. You've got yourself a date!"

"That's great, baby. So did you consider the idea of using the cookout this Sunday afternoon to introduce Brandie and Jaden to the community?"

"That is a good idea, Shannon. It will be a welcome change. The two of them have been cooped up in that mobile home for months with no personal contact except you and Millie. Yes. We would love to go with you for the cookout. Where did you say they were having it?"

"At Hank's place. You talk about a beautiful home. They have an in-ground pool, and three acres of trees. Plus, there is a natural creek at the edge of the property. Hank keeps the place looking like a park. Oh, Hank and Vickie have two children. Brandie is a little younger than their kids, but she will love playing with them."

"Are they asking people to bring a covered dish?"

"No, they're doing everything themselves."

Lee was quiet for a moment, and then asked, "Shannon, would you tell me about Hank and Grant? You did say that they were your best friends since kindergarten."

"Okay, sweetie, what do you want to know?"

"Well, how did Hank meet Vickie? They seem to be complete opposites."

"Yeah, she is a classy woman. But I've seen a different side to Hank that he doesn't reveal to just anyone. His I.Q. is off the charts, for example. He skipped the ninth grade and graduated a year ahead of me. Plus, he received scholarships to the most prestigious colleges in the country. But his dream was to go into the navy and that's what he did instead. At one point, I received a letter from him complaining that he was shunned by the other seamen because of his fast advancements in rank. He decided to develop an opposite personality in order to be accepted by his shipmates. It wasn't any fun being shunned by the shipboard sailors. You have only seen him as a redneck."

Lee asked again, "How did Hank and Vickie meet?"

I began to tell Lee about the events that led to Hank and Vickie meeting. "Well, the story is that he was invited to the Officers club for a New Year's Eve party and noticed Vickie from across the room. Hank said that she was so beautiful he couldn't take his eyes off her. It was the same way with me the first time I saw you. Anyway, Vickie caught him staring at her so she walked over to him and asked with a smile, 'What are you looking at, sailor?'"

"He crossed all boundaries, when he answered, 'I'm looking' at the most beautiful and sexiest woman I've ever seen. Would ya like to have a dance with me? I jes might have some moves that will turn you on.' Vickie laughed at his answer but they stayed together the rest of the evening, and Hank has said that she just knocked him for a loop. When it came time for the New Year count down and everyone was yelling "Happy New Year," Hank said he took Vickie in his arms and kissed her. After the kiss, he asked her if she would go to a movie with him and they swapped phone numbers. Then she told him her father was waiting for her, and she was going to have to leave.

"Hank asked Vickie, 'Well, sugar dumpling, where's yer daddy? I'll go over ta him and let him know what a beautiful daughter he has and that we're gonna be datin'.' She pointed to her dad but there were several men in the same direction so Hank didn't know which one she was pointing to. Vickie told Hank, 'I'll take you over to him but don't mention our dating.' Hank asked her if she thought her dad would be upset. Vickie told him no, but he still shouldn't mention the date."

"They started to the other side of the room, holding hands, and Hank said that it was taking so long to get through the maze of people, he thought maybe that there wasn't any daddy. Finally, they reached the far corner of the room where there was a table full of naval officers. Vickie told Hank to stand still for a moment while she talked to her dad, whose back was facing Hank. Vickie then motioned for Hank to come to the table. He said he walked over to him like a cocky rooster and, just as he was going to introduce himself, the man stood up and turned around. Hank said he prayed that lightning would hit because as it turned out, Vickie's dad was a Rear Admiral and the Commander of the base. To this day, Hank says he doesn't remember anything between that moment and waking up the next morning. He told me he once saw a movie that portrayed the same situation of his experience when meeting Vickie's dad, however, there was no way it depicted the fear that goes through a man's head when meeting a girl's father - especially when the father, who also happens to be the Rear Admiral of the naval base where you are stationed, is your boss. After being around Vickie's parents a few times, Hank said you couldn't meet a nicer couple."

"One day, Vickie and I were laughing and talking about some of Hank's escapades and she said, 'You know, Shannon, Hank may have an unbelievably high I.Q. but it was the redneck act I fell in love with.'"

Taking a deep breath, I asked Lee, "Well, what do you think?"

"Wow. I never would have thought to describe Hank as an intellect."

Looking Lee square in the face, I commented, "Don't ever play chess with him."

Lee then asked me about Grant and Ellen and how they met.

They met in college and, at first the two of them couldn't stand each other. She thought he was arrogant and he thought she was a beautiful snob. But then fate stepped in. In his fourth semester, Grant registered for chemistry. On the first day of the class, he was late getting there and when he walked into the room, there was only one empty seat left, and it happened to be next to Ellen. Guess who became Grant's partner when the professor paired off the class for a project? It was Ellen. The week after they graduated he asked her to marry him, and the rest is history."

About that time, Millie motioned for Lee to help her set up tables for a large group who was coming in for breakfast, and I left for work.

Chapter Fourteen

On Sunday, my two girls and Jaden came to pick me up for the cookout at Hank and Vickie's. We arrived at their place about eleven-thirty and Hank welcomed us in. "Come over here, Lee, and meet my kids," he said, pointing toward six-year-old Mindy and three-year-old Gabe. After all the introductions, Mindy invited Brandie to her bedroom.

Brandie looked up at her mom and asked, "Is it alright, Mommy?"

"It's absolutely alright, honey."

About that time, Vickie came through the patio doors. Waving hello, she told us to make ourselves at home and that we would be eating in a few minutes. Then, in an exasperated tone, she told Hank, "Don't you think you should be helping Grant? The meat is about ready to take off the grill, and he could use a couple of extra hands."

"Sure enough, honey pie," responded Hank. He then winked and whispered to me as he walked by, "Thanks for the advice you gave me the other day."

Lee over heard him and quizzed me. "What kind of advice did you give Hank?"

With a nonchalant glance around the room, I answered evasively, "Oh, nothing important."

Then she reminded me of the promise I made to her our first date about honesty. With suspicious-eyes, she asked, "Shannon, what are you hiding from me?"

Trying to evade Lee's question I grabbed her hand and interrupted the moment by announcing that "we are going outside" and asked Jadan "How about joining us?"

She nodded and accepted my invitation.

Jaden had been pretty quiet so far and, as we stepped out of the patio doors, she followed us like a lost puppy. We noticed that there were people all over the place as we made our way to the picnic table. Just as we sat down, Ellen brought the meat over to us, saying, "Hey there, glad you could make it. We have a lot of people who are ready to eat, so dive in and enjoy."

Lee and I introduced Jaden to Ellen, and we told her Brandie was playing with Mindy in the house. Ellen commented, "They're not going to show up to eat any time soon. When kids are playing, they don't like to be bothered. Grant told me about your daughter, Lee, and I'm here to tell you, if she is half as pretty as her mother, it won't be long before you are going to have to keep a shotgun by the door."

Lee appeared to be complimented by Ellen's remark when she shyly smiled and responded, "Thank you Ellen. That is the nicest compliment a woman can receive, especially coming from another beautiful woman like yourself." Ellen responded. "Thank you Lee"

Lee asked her, "Doesn't Grant tell you how beautiful you are?" Ellen lowered her head and softly uttered, "He used to but... what the heck, we're getting too old for that kind of dialogue."

Lee spoke up and suggested, "You and I need to take a whole day off and go shopping. Would you be interested in going Clare View Heights with me this coming Sunday?"

Ellen's chin dropped in surprise and she managed to say, "Yes, what time and where do you want us to meet?"

"How doe's 9:00 sound? I'll pick you up."

Ellen, smiling from ear to ear, confirmed Lee's invitation. "You have a date, Lee. No one in this town has wanted my company for anything." And, with a tear in her eye, Ellen remarked, "We are going to have a great time. Now, the meat platter needs a refill. See you later."

After the three of us had eaten till our stomach was about to burst, we left the table and settled into some lawn chairs under a big tree. There were people milling around the patio and pool, and some of the young ones were playing basketball in the driveway. Looking out at the back of the yard, we saw several men who were throwing horseshoes. Watching all the activity, I asked Lee and Jaden, "Would it be alright with you girls for me to join the horseshoe game?"

"You go and show them how it's done, sweetie."

I gave her a smile, proceeded to walk toward the back of the yard, and spotted the sheriff, Jerry. After meeting the other players, I asked who was winning. Jerry pointed to the opposing team and said, "They are."

"I haven't played horseshoes in a long time," I commented.

Jerry responded by handing me one of the shoes and saying, "Here, take my place. The team will probably be glad to get rid of me."

After I took the horseshoe, Jerry caught me glancing at Lee and Jaden and remarked, "Go ahead, doc. It will be my pleasure to keep a close watch on the girls for you." That made me uneasy. It wasn't what he said, it was the way he said it.

He joined them under the tree, which in my opinion wasn't necessary. I couldn't concentrate on the game for watching the three of them sitting together laughing. They were just having a jolly good time.

I thought. *Who does that arrogant bastard think he is?*

About that time Grant yelled out, "Anybody ready for dessert? Come and get it."

All of the players, me included, dropped the horseshoes and headed for the dessert table.

After eating fudge cake and home-made ice cream, people began to gather their kids up to leave. I asked Lee, "Has Brandie eaten?"

"Yes, she has. Vickie came out earlier and told me she fixed their plates and that they had their picnic in Mindy's room."

Lee, Jaden, and I, along with Jerry, began to help with the clean-up. After we finished stashing the garbage bags in the dumpster, every one began saying their good-byes. As we were about to walk out the door, Jerry filed in right behind us.

"Hey, doc," he said. "You are a lucky man to have three beautiful girls riding around with you. If you ever need some help to chauffeur them around, just call me."

I gave him a look as if to say, "Mind your own frickin' business, mister."

During our trip home, Lee began to tease Jaden about Jerry. "Jaden, Jerry is a good-looking man. And a man like that would be a good boyfriend for you. Did you notice the muscles on him?"

I could feel my blood pressure rise and thought, *What does she mean, "a man like that?"* Before I knew it, I was saying, "Good looking, my ass! He is an arrogant bastard!" Oh, was my temperature ever on the rise by then.

Jaden spoke up and said, "You're right, Shannon. He is just too arrogant for me."

In an assured tone I confirmed her observation by loudly stating, "Thank you. Jaden!"

But Lee would not let it go. "Yes, that's true," she said. "Nevertheless, what if you were the right woman who could turn him into a different person? Don't you think it's worth a try?

That did it. In a very angry tone I told her, "Lee, a short time ago, you were so scared of him, he... he... he made you cry! Now, you're trying to talk Jaden into having a relationship with that arrogant prick!"

Lee seemed shocked and she responded in a hurt voice. "Shannon, how could you speak to me like that? Are you jealous of Jerry?" Clinching my jaw, I stiffly answered, "No, Lee. I'm not jealous. He is not to be trusted." But that was a lie. And I had broken the promise we'd made on our first date again. In my defense, I never cared enough about another woman to become jealous. This feeling was new to me. About that time, we were parking in front of the entrance of my house.

I jumped out of the Jeep, ran around to the passenger side, and opened the door for Lee. She got out of her seat and snapped, "Thank you, Shannon, but we need to have a little talk so I'm going to walk you to the door."

She briskly walked on ahead of me and when we stepped onto the porch, she turned around and said, "Shannon, I'm confused with your behavior. I think you are the most wonderful man alive. If you aren't jealous of Jerry, what got into you to react this way and talk to me like that and use vulgar language in front of Brandie and Jaden?"

After listening to her, I knew she was right about the jealousy and my blood pressure dropped like a deflated balloon. The words kept running through my head. *What have I done?* Twisting my chin and putting one hand on a porch post, I looked into the sky and, with a contrite heart, said, "You are right, Lee. No one deserves to be treated like that. Especially when it is someone you love with all your heart."

She took in a big breath and said, "The assurance I gave you on our second date was from the depths of my soul, Shannon. My main reason for saying what I did was for Jaden's benefit. She has stayed in that trailer for months and if she could be talked into seeing someone besides a little girl and her mother, it would do her a world of good and she wouldn't be so lonely. Plus, I must admit, I was just trying to tease you. Shannon, I know you. And you are a wonderful man. There has to be something else hurting you very badly for your anger to erupt in that manner. Can you tell me the reason you talked to me like that?"

I bent my head down, put my hands in the pocket of my jeans, and shuffled my feet around. Then, I looked up into Lee's eyes and admitted, "You're right, baby, I'm sorry. I guess the Jolly Green Giant living in mind, raised its ugly head. And I bet he is standing in my brain laughing 'Ho, ho, ho.'"

Lee began to snicker. Then she put her arms around my neck and remarked, "You are not going to get rid of me. You are stuck with me for life and if I happen to see a hundred good-looking men, they could never compete with my man."

She noticed the sadness and fear in my eyes. Standing on tip-toe, with her arms still around my neck, she gave my lips an enduring, forgiving kiss. Then she ran to the Jeep.

I rushed into the house and shed my clothes as quickly as possible. Choking back the tears, I stepped into a cold shower and the water splashing on my face seemed to relieve the pain of reliving the scene.

The next morning at Millie's, I sat down at the table with Grant and Hank and complimented them on the outstanding barbeque dinner. "Thanks for inviting us over to the cook-out. We really enjoyed ourselves."

Grant remarked, "Ellen is so excited about getting to go shopping with Lee today. You tell her that is a thoughtful gesture and she will have an extra star in her crown when she steps into Heaven."

"I'll be sure to do that. But she will be working tomorrow. Why don't you tell her yourself?'

"I'm taking Tuesday off to work on the yard and clean the garage before it gets hot. You seem to have something on your mind, bud."

That gave me an opportunity to ask about Jerry. "You are very perceptive, Grant. I definitely have something on my mind. Hank, I have a question for you."

He gave me a 'go ahead' sign and said, "Give it your best shot, Whitney."

"How is it that you know the sheriff well enough to invite him to your home?"

Hank then began telling me about Jerry and, for some reason, dropped his redneck persona in the process. "You know, Jerry is few years younger than us. He graduated a year or so before I got out of the navy. His dad and I worked with the same crew at the plant. One day his dad came to the lower level to ask me a question, and he fell down right in front of me and didn't move a muscle. Kneeling down beside him, I listened to his chest and couldn't hear a heartbeat, so I began yelling, "Call 911!"-After examination, the paramedics said he was dead before he hit the floor. The next day, my crew and I found out he died of a cerebral hemorrhage. I called Jerry's mom to tell her how sorry I was about her husband. After talking to her for a while, and finding out that she didn't know about his insurance, 401K, or any of his other benefits, I offered to help her straighten them out and explain what each benefit was and what it meant for her. Jerry had a job but, when you have a mother and a little brother to support, the money he made working at the Dairy Queen just couldn't cut the mustard."

"One time, Vickie and I went there to get us some ice cream and Jerry asked me if I would mind talking to him about joining the military. I invited him and his mom to come to my home and they came over the next evening. Jerry asked a lot of questions and wanted to know the procedures for enlisting. After telling him about the opportunities and career choices he could have, if he enlisted in the Navy, he asked if I would help him choose a career. After talking to him and his mom a little longer Jerry asked if I would go to the recruitment office with him. I had the next day off, so I took him."

"When he finished talking with the recruiting officer, he joined the Navy, and chose the Military Police as his career path. When his tour of duty ended, the first thing he did was to get a job with the county police force. That's when he got in touch with Vickie and me. We became good friends and did a lot of things together. We went hunting, fishing, and camping. He is a fine man and is very conscientious about his work. It took no time until he became the sheriff of our county. After the kids were born, we lost contact with him for a while and then, out of the blue, he called Vickie and me. We talked a long time and caught up on our lives since the last time we had seen each other. And before we got off the phone, I invited him to our house for the cookout. Why are you askin' about Jerry?"

"Well, Hank, he seems a little arrogant to me," Grant spoke up and asked, "You got a problem with Jerry?"

"For some reason, my instincts are telling me that he can't be trusted,"

Hank smiled and asked, "What's the matter, sport? Is he too good lookin' ta suit ya?" I noticed that Hank had slipped back into his redneck persona, but I was too concerned about Jerry to pay it much attention.

Speaking up with great confidence I said, "There is something about him that is bothersome to me, Hank, and it has nothing to do with his looks."

About that time, Millie came to our table, gave us a refill, and commented, "Boy, Hank, you look as relaxed as a contented cow."

Reaching for his coffee and grinning, he looked up at Millie and responded, "Jes call me Elsie!"

When Millie turned to leave, I asked Hank. "How did your Friday night turn out, you and Vickie have a 'good time?"

He leaned into the table. "I took Vickie to the bleacher section."

Surprised, I asked, "How did you know about the bleacher section?"

Hank gave out a chuckle and informed me, "Ah, Whitney, everybody in Ellisville High School knew about that little lovers' nest. After you and Suanne discovered its usefulness, it became a preferred spot ta make out. Suanne told her friends about it, than those girls told other friends... well, you know how somethin' like that gits around. Us guys knew if there wuz a car parked behind the lunchroom, not to intrude and ta wait till it wuz gone."

"I'll be damned," I remarked. "I thought... Never mind. Go on with your story, Hank."

Hank continued, "You know when we were in high school, that place wuz used more than Bayer aspirin. Vickie didn't know what wuz going on with me taking her to the high school bleachers. But when we got started, she came alive. After we were done, she said, 'Hank, this is the most exciting time we have ever had. Why haven't you brought me to the bleachers before?' I learned somethin' about my wife Friday night. She ain't the prissie pot I thought she wuz. She began thinking of places we could go to besides the bleachers. So, look out, Whitney, because it won't be the last time that we use the lovers' nest."

Grant was very quiet and I asked him, "How many times have you gone to the bleachers, Grant?"

"Never have gone there. As a matter of a fact, the first time I had sex was my sophomore year in college. I've told you that before. I was too bashful to date in high school. Don't you guys remember? You used to tease me all the time about being a virgin."

That really surprised me. "Grant, you were listed in our senior yearbook as being the most handsome guy in school. Not only that, there was... I know at least three very popular girls had a crush on you."

Giving me a dumbfounded look, Grant quickly replied, "You are kidding me."

Hank spoke up. "No, he ain't kidding. Lot of the guys wuz jealous uv you, includin' myself."

Grant shook his head in disbelief, saying, "Man, my bashfulness caused me to lose out on a lot of fun. But thanks for telling me about the girls liking me. It gives me more confidence with my beautiful wife."

We sat quietly for a moment, and then Grant spoke up again. "Ellen and I have some nice plans for next weekend. We have two nights reserved at the swankiest motel in St. Louis. I might not be here Monday if everything works according to the plan. I'll be too exhausted to do anything. And, speaking of work, I had better get my butt out of here. I'm not going to see you guys tomorrow because I've got to take Ellen to see her gynecologist. She is due for a check-up."

I asked Grant if she was okay and he assured us, saying, "Yeah, she is just fine."

Getting up from my chair and gulping down the last sip of coffee, I headed off to the clinic with the hope that Lee would remember about coming to help out. Seeing her Jeep from the driveway, I thought, she is here... and she has taken my parking spot.

Walking through the clinic door I decided to tease her. "Good morning Ronda. Good morning Lee. It's my guess, Miss Lee, that you didn't see the Dr. Whitney sign when you parked the Jeep."

She turned around, and with a sweet smile said, "Good morning, to you, Dr. Whitney. Perhaps if you were here on time, the parking place would have been available. Ronda and Lee looked at each other as though they had never seen me in my professional mode and almost giggling Lee asked, "What would you like for me to do today, Dr. Whitney?"

Now, she knew her question was a loaded one, so I replied, "You can come into the office and I will give you a list of the patients we are seeing today so you can become acquainted with their records."

Lee, in a submissive way said, "Okay, sir."

She didn't think I saw her giving Ronda a wink as she followed me like a little puppy. So we started down the hallway and about half way to the office, Ronda yelled out, "Hey, Dr. Whitney, you forgot something! The list of today's patients is out here. Don't you think you might need them?"

Quickly going back to the waiting room, I snapped the list out of her hand and gave her a look as if to say, "Don't you open your mouth, Ronda." And, just as we entered the office, a roar of laughter came from the waiting room.

Lee sat down in the chair in front of my desk, snickering. I started to close the door and she reminded me, "Dr. Whitney, it isn't professional for a boss to close the door when a female employee is in the office with him."

Clearing my throat and leaving the door open, I responded in a deep voice, "You are right, Miss Lee." Walking over to where she was sitting, I sat on my desk across from her and began explaining the rules and regulations of the office. "As your boss, there are some requirements that the employee has to comply with in order to follow the rules and expectations of this establishment. Number one: the female employee, like you, should start the workday by giving her boss a hug." Then, I took her by the hand and pulled her from the chair into my arms. She gave me a smile. "Now, number two: since I'm the best boss in the whole wide world, there should always be a kiss ready for me."

Looking into my eyes, she softly replied, "Well, Dr. Whitney, are these the rules for all of your female employees?"

"Now, now, Miss Lee. Only for a certain one." Lee walked over to the door and slowly closed it. When she returned to the desk, I stood up to kiss her sweetly. The kiss, however, became more of a discomfort. Lee put her arms around my neck and, pushing her breasts into my chest and gave me a very sensual kiss. She then drew her head back ever so slightly and asked, "Dr. Whitney, have I fulfilled the requirement you requested for the 'helper' position?"

After deeply inhaling, I told her "Let me catch my breath and take a cold shower. Then I'll let you know."

With her chin raised and a mischievous smile on her face, she taunted me by saying, "That'll teach ya, doc." About that time Ronda knocked loudly on the door and, as she opened it, I quickly sat back down on the desk and crossed my legs. It was all Lee could do to keep from bursting into laughter.

"Dr. Whitney," Ronda said, "Are you finished with your staff meeting? Our first patient is here." Then she left to go back to the reception room counter and snickered all the way down the hall.

Well, I thought, At least after that awful jolt, the cold shower can be postponed.

Ronda began to fill the exam rooms and Lee and I went to work. She suggested that she could evaluate the patients and write down the information. Then I'd check out the complaint, give advice, and treat patients, if needed. We took care of twice the number of patients in half the time than what it would have taken me if Lee had not been there. We were finished by four.

Lee locked the door to the clinic and came to the office. We both sat down, me behind the desk, and Lee in the chair across from the desk.

Leaning back in the chair, and cradling my head in my hands, I said, "Miss Lee, your boss must say that, with your knowledge and abilities, you have not only dazzled the patients and their owners, but you have also met all the requirements of this establishment. And I'm willing to hire you for Mondays, if you're interested."

She came around to my chair, turned it toward her, straddled my lap, and began running her hands in my hair. "Oh, my dear boss, you don't have to pay me anything. I just want to be available for your special needs." She continued to stroke my hair.

Swallowing a lump in my throat, I responded eagerly, "Hey baby, I'm ready. I'm *very* ready!" And we laughed. Then, getting serious, I asked, "Well, what do you think about the clinic?"

Lee stood up from my lap and, shaking her head, answered, "It is awesome. Thank you, Shannon, for giving me this opportunity to do what I have wanted to do for years."

"You shouldn't be thanking me. Helping out like you did today… I'm the grateful one, having you by my side."

I got up from the chair and we gave each a loving kiss. Then she informed me. "I've got to go. There should be enough daylight left to play with Brandie before dark."

She waved as she walked out the door and my heart felt lonely again.

Chapter Fifteen

Rolling out of bed on a Tuesday morning, I noticed the date on the calendar, and it was only 10 days before Lee's birthday. And time wasn't waiting on me to buy her a gift. So needing to pick up some supplies for the clinic in St. Louis, my decision was to also go shopping for my little ladies birthday gift.

Taking the day off on Thursday, and on my way to St. Louis my thoughts were, *"I'm going to look in every store that is available until the right item shows up."* Then it occurred to me, *"What in the world could a man buy for the most important woman in his life? The only gift's I have seen men buy for their special lady is candy, perfume, flowers, and other personal effects that are boring. My choice for Lee is going to be something unique."*

After searching through at least 20 different shops and stores, there wasn't any thing that struck me as being special. Giving up my search, than sauntering back to the truck, with a feeling of disappointment, there in front of me was a sign that said, 'The Spirit Of Sports' store. Quickly walking to the shop and stepping into the door way an associate asked me if he could be of any help. Answering him with a, "No thanks I'll be just fine," I began strolling through the shop. Then looking up and down the aisles, there was a shelf full of all kinds of baseball gloves, and one of them caught my eyes. It was black with white stitching. And thinking out loud my comment was *"Lee will like this type of glove, and it is a size that will fit her hand."*

I took the glove up to the counter, and while the man entered the price of the merchandise into the register I asked. "Do you know of any place that has unique things a person could buy for a special woman?"

He told me, "Yes there are some worthwhile shops, but you will have to travel a little distance." After he put the glove into a bag, my reply was, "That won't be a problem. I'll have all afternoon to find them."

The information the man gave me led to South County St. Louis and south west of the arch on I.40. Looking at the name of the street on my directions, and driving a couple of blocks, the shops couldn't be missed. There were several of them in a row that had everything from rod iron furniture to soup. Going into one of the shops and looking around a lady approached me and asked. "Do you need any help?"

Pausing for a moment my response was, "Yes, maybe you can help me. I want to buy a gift for the most wonderful and beautiful woman in the world."

She smiled as though she had heard that request before and replied. "Tell me something about her other then she is beautiful and wonderful. Does she like furniture, clothes, or antiques?"

My answer to her was, "She loves baseball and I have already bought her a glove." The woman turned her back to me with a big smile and snickered. Then straightening her face, and looking at me she said, "I'm sure she will love the glove but it sounds as though you are looking for something a bit more romantic."

"Not necessarily," I said. "I want something that she will treasure."

The woman asked. "Does she live with her family?"

Butting in, my answer was, "She has a little 5 year old daughter." The woman's eyes lit up and she invited me to follow her saying, "Come over here. There is something you have got to see."

We walked to a locked glass cabinet and she pointed to a beautiful ceramic table figurine. It was a young woman lying in the grass surrounded by wild flowers, and holding a story book. She cuddled a little girl that was lying next to her and the little girl had a glow of love on her face as she gazed at the woman reading to her. "That's it." I said "Would you gift wrap it for me?"

The lady assured me saying, "We will be glad to do that for you sir."

When she announced the price of the ornament, it gave me quite a shock. She noticed my stunned look, and quickly gave an explanation."That does sound very expensive, but this living room table piece is the only one of a kind, and kilned approximately 100 years ago. The man who sculptured it lived in Russia just about the time Lenin became the ruler. The artist had to hide his work, because every one of his sculptures was designed to give women high praise. Also he had a deep respect for women's extraordinary intelligence, love of family and love of God. If the Lenin's police had discovered his works of these beautiful pieces, the artist and his family would have been killed, and all his sculptures would have been destroyed. If you want to know more about the man who did the work, you can go to the internet."

I told her, "That's an amazing story. Be sure and cover it with a lot of bubble wrap around it!"

After paying for my girl's birthday gift, my next move was getting in the truck and head for home. It was about 6: 30 before approaching the driveway. Scrambling around in my pocket to find the key to unlock the door, I could hear the answering machine beeping. Lee had left a message asking me to call her back. It didn't take me any time to return her call, and when she answered her phone she immediately remarked in a suspicious manner. "So, you went to St. Louis today."

"Sure did, Baby." I said.

And when I didn't offer her any information about the trip she asked me, "Well...What were you doing in St. Louis?"

My response to her question was, "Didn't Ronda tell you my trip was to buy some clinic supplies?"

Pausing for a moment with a disappointed tone in her voice she said, "I have been sitting around here wondering what you were up to."

Asking her did she think my trip was to see some good looking blonde, she replied. "That never occurred to me. Because you know how lucky you are to have a good looking brunette."

My remark to her was, "You better believe it, Beautiful. I'm the luckiest man alive."

She chuckled and said, "You're a smart man. You know exactly what to say don't you?" All of a sudden there was the sound of Brandie yelling for her mom. Lee informed me that the little princess was about to cry and said, "I've got to go and help my daughter find Goggie."

"Is there anything 'yours truly' can do to help?"

"Don't think so Shannon. I'm sure the pup is close by." Then telling Lee good night and hanging up the phone, I retreated to the bedroom and hit the sack.

Several days had passed since the trip to St. Louis, and Lee's birthday was getting closer. I was eager to give her the baseball tickets before the actual date of the birthday celebration. So driving to the restaurant, my thoughts were, *"I am looking forward to seeing the expression on Grants face when handing the tickets to Lee."*

However, my first stop was the drug store to pick up a card for Lee before going to the restaurant. And walking to the back of the building to the location of the pharmacy, I noticed Grant was working on filling a prescription. And going over to the counter I asked. "What are you doing here so early? You are usually at Millie's by now."

He yelled back. "I'll be there later. Right now a prescription has to be filled for Ellen so she can start taking it today." Asking if she was ok, Grant said, "Oh yah she's fine."

Giving him a quick wave my next move was to go to the greeting birthday card section. I thumbed through several of them, and one turned up that made me think Lee might get a chuckle from it. The outside of the card was an elderly woman taking her blood pressure and heart rate. The caption inside of the card said, "Dearie, don't get distressed about another birthday. As the old saying goes, 'We're not getting older, were getting better.' Only thing is, the question keeps popping up in my mind. Where's the better? Have a happy birthday Dearie."

Leaving the drug store and driving over to Millie's, then walking inside the restaurant, Hank was sitting at our regular table. He spoke to me and then remarked. "Don't know where Grant is. He is usually here before me."

Pulling a chair out from the table my remark was, "He will be here a bit later."

Hank asked. "Why is he late?"

I told Him, "You can ask him when he gets here,"

Lee came over to our table bringing us a cup of coffee. Hank asked her, "How do you like the Jeep, Sweetie Pie?"

Setting the coffee down, she responded. "It is great! I've never thought of ever having a Jeep, but it won't be the last one."

Hank stared at her just for a moment and commented. "That little Jeep is almost as cute as you."

Lee smiled at him and replied. "Why, thank you Hank... I've never been compared to a Jeep before."

Sitting and listening to their comments to one another I remarked. "Hey. Watch it there Nikensary. No flirting with the woman I'm crazy about."

Hank laughed at my remark and proceeded to tell me, "Everybody knows your crazy Whitney, so what was your excuse before you met Lee!" Grabbing a ball cap off his head, I hit his shoulder with it and pitched it on the table next to us. Hank just grinned at me and never moved a muscle.

Lee stood watching the whole scene and with a smile, she asked, "Would you guys care to order any food?" Hank decided on the breakfast special, and just as Lee delivered it Grant walked in. He sat down and seemed to be preoccupied. Asking him if he was ok he responded. "Yah I'm fine Whitney. Would you and Hank like to hear about how Ellen and I made out on our weekend?"

Hank quickly replied. "You bet Bud. We want to hear all about it. Don't we Whitney?"

Shaking my head up and down and swallowing a sip of coffee, it must have been an 'ok' sign for Grant to open up because he began to share.

" Well... Ellen and I had a fabulous dinner, and then after entering the motel room, the discomfort between us was as though we were strangers. Standing around and commenting on the beautiful interior of the motel, Ellen finally walked over to the bed and sat down. She looked so sad and she asked. "Grant, what is wrong with us?" And she began to cry. Going over to the bed, I sat down and took her in my arms saying. "There isn't anything wrong with us."

She pulled away from me with big tears in her eyes and asked. "Then why are we acting like strangers to one another?"

I didn't have an answer to her question. Then she looked at me and shaking her head in disbelieve she remarked. "Grant, you may not realize it, but our marriage has been going downhill for months. Is it me? Aren't you attracted to me anymore?"

Putting my arms back around her my response was, "You are the most beautiful woman in the world. You are intelligent, sweet, caring and talented."

Still crying she uttered in a manner of low-self-esteem. Oh…Sure, I'm great at everything but sex. Maybe if I were a better sex partner, we wouldn't be having this discussion."

I tried to tell her, "Sweetheart, it takes both partners to keep a marriage exhilarating and inspiring. Maybe it's me."

She quickly spoke up. "No Grant. You are remarkable."

After saying that, we kissed and then she brought to my attention about a book she had purchased. "Grant, I've bought a book and wanted to wait for the right time to show it to you. Would you take a look at it? Perhaps if we follow some of these instructions, our love making may become more adventurous to us."

"Shannon… Hank… I'm here to tell you tell you two. Our sex has become the most exhilarating adventure in our lives."

Hank spoke up. "Where did Ellen git the book?" Grant didn't pay any attention to Hank and continued to describe the book.

"The title is '70 Ways To Heaven." Reaching for Hanks hat from the other table Grant took it and fanned himself, and laying it down on the table, he continued his sharing.

"We have already tried 8 of them." Hank butted in and asked. "Grant. Where did Ellen buy the book?"

He again paid no attention to Hank, and kept talking. "Needless to say, those illustrations have given Ellen and me a new outlook on our making love."

Hank spoke up again. "Damn it Grant tell me, Where did Ellen git the book?

Getting aggravated I told Hank, "If you don't shut up and let the man talk, I'm going to take your hat and cram it down your throat. Go ahead, Grant."

He smiled and commented. "Well, looking at the book together there was an eye-opener to the failures of my sexual advances. There are a lot of exciting things that can be done to give Ellen the ultimate experience of exquisite love making and it has been a wonderful adventure. And she is happier than I've seen her in a long time."

"Not much more to tell you guys except we have 62 more ways to heaven and we are looking forward to all of them."

Hank and I set in amazement and speaking up, my comment to him was, "Man that's great." Then I paused for a moment and with a big grin on my face asked him. "Grant... where did Ellen, get that book?"

The three of us laughed, and about that time Lee brought the coffee pot to give us refills and asked. "What's so funny?"

I told her. "Remind me later. And if it's okay with Grant, I'll tell you all about it." Grant said. "It's all right with me. Especially if it helps someone who is having any problem with their love life."

Lee replied. "You have really sparked my curiosity Grant."

As she began to pick up our dirty dishes and while pulling out a chair, I asked her if she could sit down with us for a moment. Complying with my request, Lee sat down and asked. "What is on your mind, Dear Heart?"

Taking the card out of my pocket and handing it to her, she immediately opened it. The baseball tickets fell on the table and Grants expression was priceless. He frowned, crossed his arms and rolled his eyes as if saying, "I can't believe you are giving her baseball tickets."

Lee picked them up saying, "What a wonderful surprise." This is a very thoughtful gift." Putting her arm around my neck she gave it a great big hug and said, "You are remarkable, Shannon. I haven't been to a baseball game in years. Thank you so much."

Giving her a big smile, I responded saying, "You are very welcome, Sweetie."

Grant just sat with an open mouth. And remembering his critical remark a few months back, it was a pleasure to remind him by mocking his statement and body language.

"Oh sure, Whitney. Buy Lee baseball tickets. I'm sure she would really be impressed."

Still a might flabbergasted Grant asked her. "You like baseball? That is pretty unusual for a woman to like any kind of sport."

Her answer was, "I love them. Playing softball all through high school and college became my favorite pastime."

Grant smiled and shaking his head remarked. "It's astonishing that a little fragile woman like you could ever play such a demanding sport."

With a giggle she told him, "Believe me Grant, I'm anything but fragile."

Hank spoke up. "Well... hate to leave such exciting company, but I've got to go to work." Grant and I followed suit in agreement with him and left Millie's at the same time.

The day went by swiftly and I called Ellen and Vickie to confirm everything for Lee's party and they both told me that all was well.

I woke up very early on a Friday morning; the first thing on my agenda was calling Lee. "Good morning my love, I'm missing you and just needed to hear your voice."

She answered in a sleepy agitated tone. "Shannon! Do you know what time it is? What are you doing calling me so early?

Glancing at the clock it reflected in big bright numbers 5:09 and not realizing what time it was, I said, "I'm sorry Babe. It didn't dawn on me how early it is. But it just proves how crazy my feelings are for you."

She yawned real big and said, "You have a smooth talking bedside manner Doc, and you're forgiven. Now would you please hang up the phone so your Baby can get another hour or so of sleep before going to work? We can talk then."

Rubbing my ear after she 'slam dunked' the phone on her receiver, my next move was getting out of bed. After my morning ritual of showering, shaving, and getting dressed, I grabbed a glass from the cabinet filling it to the brim with O.J. Then walking out to the clinic reception room and opening the front door, standing there and watching the Illinois sunrise, the peacefulness surrounded me like a soft warm blanket. The only sounds were birds singing and squirrels chattering in the trees. There isn't anyone who wouldn't have a spiritual experience looking at the colors, and the feeling of awesome calmness. Then the calmness vanished when I saw a car turning around at the end of the driveway. All at once it took off like a supersonic jet. It looked like the same one that was parked at the curb in front of Millie's. In a helpless feeling, my thoughts were, *"This is not a coincidence. But there isn't anything that can be done about it. Whoever the man might be, he is very careful to be discreet. And it's not my imagination that he is watching me."*

By this time, it was late enough that Millie had opened up for business and hopping in the truck and driving to the restaurant my intuition was telling me, "Watch out Whitney! Whatever the game this man is playing, it's not for fun."

When getting out of the truck and looking around, I went into the restaurant. Sitting down in my usual chair, Lee came over and said, "Hey good looking. Would you like a cup of coffee?"

Returning her smile my reply was, "That will be very nice, as long as it is in a cup."

After serving the coffee she told me, "Hank and Grant aren't going to make it here today. Hank stopped in for a coffee to go, and said that he and Vickie were going car shopping. He isn't happy with the gas mileage on the truck. Grant took Ellen to her O.B.G.Y.N."

Having a little concern about Ellen I remarked. "That's the second time Ellen has gone to her Dr. in less than two weeks. Sure hope she is ok."

Lee reassured me. "I'm certain she is just fine. Grant would have told us if there was anything seriously wrong."

Agreeing with her I said, "You're probably right. By the way, it is only 3 days until the two of us will be going to the Muny Opera. The first curtain goes up at 7:00." Then taking her hand, I continued telling her my plans. "If we leave Ellisville early enough we can go to some swanky restaurant and have dinner. How does that sound?"

She had a request. "That is a wonderful plan. But you have got to promise me that you will not have their servers sing the happy birthday song."

Kissing her hand, my assurance to her was, "You have my promise not to say anything to anyone about your birthday."

Staying a bit longer at Millie's, the breakfast hour eased off considerably, and the restaurant became empty. Lee finished a little job in the kitchen and coming back over to the table I asked. "Would 4:00 be too early to pick you up Saturday afternoon?"

Searching the surroundings with her eyes, and making sure there wasn't anyone sitting in a corner somewhere, she bent over and gave me a kiss. And then with a sexy smile she whispered in a soft voice.

"We can leave at any time you choose and do whatever you want to do."

Grabbing her arm and pulling her down to my lap, all that could be done at that moment was to tease her with a question. "Anything I want to do?" Then I kissed her in a longing open mouthed kiss.

About that time Millie came through the kitchen swinging doors and seeing the two of us kissing, she gave an ultimatum. "You two either stop what you're doing, or go down the street to the motel."

Lee stood up trying to keep from laughing and teasingly said to her. "We just wanted to bring a bit of excitement to the place, Millie!"

Millie returned her statement with, "Lee, you're working here is enough excitement! If someone should see the picture of the two of you that I just saw, well… you know… It just isn't good business. The restaurant's name would have to be change to Millie's Sex Parlor." And she laughed saying, "Go ahead you two. Grab every chance of your love that you can, because this old world has a way of stealing it away from you. Just be careful to not let anyone see you in here kissing. Okay?" We nodded our heads in agreement to her rule.

That evening when I drove onto the lane of the mobile home and parked in the driveway, Lee stepped out, looking more beautiful than ever. And as she climbed into the truck and sat down my eyes were glued on her every move. She slid next to me putting her arm over my shoulder. And in a cutesy voice she said, "Thank you, Honey Bunch."

Wrinkling my forehead the thought occurred to me "Where did she come up with such a tacky nickname?"

It seemed as though Lee knew what my thoughts were and she asked. "If a man can call their woman Babe, then why can't a woman call her man Honey Bunch?" I laughed at her and she became a bit defensive and remarked. "So you think that's funny!"

I tried to explain to her about the nickname. "Lee, calling a man Honey Bunch well…its nerdy! And sounds like something that an overbearing woman would call her hen-pecked husband."

In a disturbed manner she shook her head and asked, "Why do you consider Honey Bunch in that perspective?"

Glancing at her my answer was, "I don't know. But that is my interpretation of the nickname!"

Folding her arms across her chest and with an arguing disposition she asked, "Do you think I'm an overbearing, hen-pecking woman when I call you Honey Bunch?"

Trying again to tell her how it affected me to be called that nickname, my answer was, "Lee! I don't like it, and... and... it makes me feel uncomfortable!"

Looking at me she smiled real big and in a childlike voice said, "Okee Dokee, I'll call you, Hunk Zilla!"

"No Lee! Don't call me that either!" Cuddling real close to my body, she went on to say. "Awe, come on Hunk Zilla! You know you like that name!"

The next thing out of my mouth was in an aggravated demand! "Don't call me that again!"

Tilting her head sideways and looking at me she said, "But it makes me feel good when you call me Baby or Babe."

"That's different," I said. "Calling a woman Baby is an endearing nickname!"

Again she asked, "Why?"

That did it! It dawned on me that she was messing with my brain matter. So pulling off the road in a safe place and then parking the truck she softly asked in a knowing voice. "What are you doing Shannon?"

Using my body against her like a bulldozer shoveling dirt, she wound up completely over to the passenger side of the truck, and up against the door. Her eyes got as big as quarters and she said, "Shannon!" And before she could say another word I laid a big kiss on her and every time she would try to say something, I would kiss her again.

Finally she melted in my arms and whispering in her ear in a seductive voice my comment to her was, "You know how much I love you, Baby, and you can call me anything you want!"

She pulled away from me with a clever smile and remarked. "I'll just keep my nicknames to myself! And besides it's dirty pool when you kiss me like that!" Our little confrontation had led us into awakening our bodies to something more than kissing and it wasn't the time, or the place to follow through with anything more than the kissing.

My comment to her was. "When a gorgeous woman calls a man a name he can't handle...Well he has to 'pull out the big stick...Wait, that's not right!" Very quickly another thought came to my mind as to the old saying. "This is it... He has to poke it in the bud!" Lee began to laugh, so I tried again to get the old saying right. "He has to 'Nip it in the bud'. That's it! Nip it in the bud."

Lee suggested there was a need for me to brush up on my 'old sayings.' My reply was, "It's a good thing I like you so much, otherwise we would be heading back to Ellisville"

Sliding myself under the steering wheel we headed for the interstate. By then Lee had scooted next to me as close as the seat belts allowed and asked. "Are you mad at me?"

Glancing into her beautiful brown eyes my answer was. "Mad hasn't entered my mind, and even if you called me, Honey Bunch, there is no way that I could stay mad at you!"

She asked, "What nickname would be comfortable for you?" Then with a coy look on her face she blurted out. "Lover, now that is befitting to your nature! Are you okay with that nickname?"

My answer to her was, "That is a good one. And like you said, it fits! Yah, call me Lover!"

Getting a mischievous, knowing expression on her face she said, "I thought you would like that one."

We had our dinner at the nicest French restaurant in St. Louis. And after we finished our meal, we left for the Muny Opera. The parking area looked as though there might be some difficulty in finding a spot to park the truck. But a young man came to our rescue and directed us to a roomy space.

When the play ended and on our way back to Ellisville, Lee was ecstatic. She began to chatter and then she began to 'try' to sing the play's theme song.

"What kind of love is this that drowns you in delight? What kind of love is this that makes you know it's right?" She stopped singing and admitted that she couldn't carry a tune in a bucket.

Not wanting to agree with her, my condolence was, "You have so many talents with other things that you don't have to sing."

"Yah," She said. "Nevertheless, you have a sweet way of telling another person that they can't sing." She smiled real big and gave me a quick kiss to my cheek.

As we entered the Ellisville city limits I gave Lee a suggestion. "How would you like a glass of wine before taking you home? The evening is still young."

Turning toward me she gave 'The Eye' look, so to speak, and accepted my invitation saying, "Is there any additional item you might offer besides the wine?"

My response was, "Well, how would you like to try out the couch for a bit of a love festivity?"

She answered. "I would rather check out your bed again to see if the festivity is as much fun as the last one." We were totally in agreement with that plan. And that is what we did.

It was only 10:30 when we reached Lee's place and she had her head on my shoulder sound asleep. After parking and sitting for a few minutes and watching her, I slipped my shoulder from her head and softly said. "Babe…you're home." There was no response. Saying to her again with musical notes in my voice, "Darling Heart…you are home." Then giving her a little shake, my voice became a bit louder. "Lee…Lee, we are at your place, Baby!"

Rubbing her eyes, and still half asleep she mumbled. "Oh…I'm home."

Teasing her, my comment was, "Yea, we have been here at least an hour."

With squinting eyes, she gave me a reminder. "Perhaps my body wouldn't be so tired if someone hadn't called me at 4:00 this morning."

I bluntly defended myself. "It wasn't that early!"

Leaning over and halfway giving me a kiss, she almost missed my face and mumbled. "Good night lover."

Quickly getting out of the driver's seat and running around to the passenger side,

I helped her out of the truck and then to the door. Opening it she told me good night again, and almost shut the door on my hand.

Chapter Sixteen

Driving back to my place, I had a strange feeling again that someone was watching me. Glancing in the rear view mirror and not seeing anything, I thought, *Don't worry now. If in fact that is what's happening, sooner or later they are going to make a mistake and get caught.* Then, going into the house and dismissing the thoughts, I went straight to my bedroom and barely undressed before hitting the sheets.

Lee called Sunday morning, waking me up with a cheery tone in her voice. "Good morning, sleepy head. Oh, excuse me…lover." I didn't notice how late it was until I looked at the clock, which showed it was 9:15am.

"What is so good about it when my girlfriend kept me up until 12:00 last night?" I muttered sleepily. "Not only that, she fell asleep on me and said it was my fault!"

Lee chuckled and asked, "You will forgive me, won't you? I promise not to ever wake you again so early in the morning."

By then, I was sitting on the side of the bed and reminded her in a gruff voice, "You forgave me yesterday morning for rudely waking you up, and since turn-about is fair play, you have my forgiveness. Besides, you are the birthday girl today." Then I said sweetly, "Happy birthday, babe."

"When are we leaving for the ball game?"

"How about noon? Would that be all right? The game is going to start at two."

"By the way, lover, have I told you lately how wonderful, thoughtful, and loving you are?"

"That is a nice nickname. It sounds better every time I hear it."

"Lover fits you perfectly."

"You are trying to butter me up for something, aren't you?"

With a shocked gasp, she stated, "I meant every word that came out of my mouth. But I do have a request. Is it alright for Brandie to go with us to the ball game?"

"It's absolutely alright for her to go with us. I should have thought of it myself. We will have a ball."

I paused for a minute but there wasn't even a chuckle. I tried to explain to her, "Get it? That was a joke!"

"You have been around Grant too long. Take my advice, and don't give up your present job!"

"What does that mean? That's a funny joke!"

She giggled and asked, "Shannon Whitney, what planet did you come from."

"Pluto, baby doll!"

"Pluto, huh? Isn't that the one who is related to Goofy?"

"There you go again, hurting my feelings."

"Brandie and I will be ready and waiting for your arrival at 12:00. See you soon, lover boy."

After finishing my morning rituals, I headed straight for Wal-Mart and bought three Cardinal baseball hats and stashed them behind the truck seat along with the glove. I hoped to give the glove to her just before the game started, and we could put on our caps at the same time.

Arriving at the mobile home, I focused on Lee as she and Brandie came out the door, ready to go. Watching my girls holding hands as they made their way to the truck, it was evident that Lee was just as beautiful in her disguise as without it.

I jumped out of the truck, ran around to the passenger side, and helped place the child's carrier in the center of the truck seat. Then I picked Brandie up, strapped her into the carrier, and handed her some dolls to help keep her entertained. When everyone was loaded, we took off for a day of fun!

After driving for a while, I asked Brandie, "How are you doing, princess?"

Giving me a look as though she didn't know how to answer my question, she asked in her little girl's voice, "Why did you call me princess?"

"Because that's what you are. To me, you're beautiful, sweet, and a loving princess. It is usually a special name that a dad might call his little girl."

She still had a confused look on her face and remarked, "But I'm not your little girl."

"Well, is it okay for me to think of you as my little girl?"

She answered in a delighted voice, "Yes! You can call me princess any time you want to, lover boy."

Lee's mouth dropped open. "Brandie! You don't call Shannon 'lover boy!'"

"Why not, Mommy?"

Lee stammered, "Because you—you just don't! That—that's why! It isn't appropriate for you to call Shannon 'lover boy.'"

It was all I could do to keep from laughing. Then Brandie, after thinking for a moment, defended herself. "But I heard you say one time how sweet and loving Shannon is!"

Lee's complexion turned red with astonishment. "When did you hear me say that?"

"It was this morning, Mommy. I heard you plainly say, 'see you later, lover boy.' You also said that the name 'lover' fit him."

Lee was lost for words and with a shocked expression on her face it looked as though she was asking for help.

So I tried to explain it to Brandie. "You know what, princess? Nicknames mean different things to different people. Now...I think I'm a pretty cool man. Do you know what cool means?"

"Do you mean like Ken?" asked Brandie, holding up her Barbie doll's boyfriend.

"Yeah, like Ken. Well...I think I'm cool."

I looked at Lee to validate my statement. She turned toward the passenger window and, shaking her head, she said, "Oh, Shannon is right, sweetie. He is very cool."

You are a cool man, Shannon!" Brandie exclaimed.

Trying to make my point, I continued. "Years ago, when I was just a bit older than you, my friends and I called 'cool guys' daddy-o. We even called my dad daddy-o because he was the coolest man around Ellisville. So maybe you would like to call me daddy-o?"

Brandie blurted out in a giggled. "Yes!" She leaned over and hugged my arm, saying in a soft sincere tone, "I love you, Daddy-o."

A lump filled my throat and tears stung my eyes, but I did manage to say, "I love you too, princess."

Before we reached the interstate, Brandie yawned and fell sound asleep. Lee continued staring out the window, and her body was almost in a fetal position and very withdrawn.

"Lee, are you okay?"

Bursting into tears, and shaking her head, she blurted out, "I'm a terrible mother! I don't know how to relate to my daughter, and I'm careless about what is said in front of her! You have never been around kids, and you relate to her better than me! You are so wonderful with her! And it hurts that she can say I love you and I can't!"

By then we were on the interstate. Being close to a rest stop I decided to pull off and comfort Lee. She was crying so hard, I jumped out of the truck and hurried to the passenger side and opened the door. She stepped out of the truck, put her arms around my neck, and laid into my body, crying her heart out. After a few minutes, she looked up at me, her eyes still full of tears. Handing her my handkerchief, she blotted her eyes and blew her nose (and let me tell you, it was a handkerchief full); and in a shaky, muffled, voice said, "I wouldn't know what to do if you were not in my life. Should something happen to you..."

Butting in and placing two fingers on her lips, I looked into her eyes and said gently, "Shush now, baby. Everything is going to be all right. I'm not Joe. Nothing is going to happen to me. You and I are meant to be together for a long, long time...for at least ninety-five years!"

Blotting her eyes again, and in a quivering voice–she said, "You know what? This is my birthday and we are going to have a ball. Get it? That's a joke."

"You have stolen my joke, missy!"

We smiled at each other and she asked, "Is my mascara smeared? Oh never mind, I'll go to the restroom and fix my face."

When she returned we jumped into the truck and got back on the interstate. After a few minutes, she said, "I'm much better. You might as well know it now, Shannon. When I'm in my monthly P.M.S. time, my emotions have a tendency to elevate."

I tried not to be surprised at her bluntness and hide my

embarrassment. *Well, nature is nature, and I'm glad she feels comfortable sharing that bit of information.* And it explained why she was so upset. Nevertheless, her self-assertiveness still gave me a shock.

We traveled a few miles and I asked Lee, "How are you feeling, birthday girl?"

"Much better, thank you."

Just as we approached Eads Bridge into St. Louis, Brandie woke up, stretched her arms, and asked her mom, "How long is it until we get to the ball game, mommy?"

"We are almost there, sweetie." Lee pointed toward our destination. "See the roof of that big building. We will be there in no time."

Finally, reaching our destination, and finding a parking place, I jumped out of the truck, loosened the straps on the car seat, and lifted Brandie out into my arms. Lee got out of the truck, and by that time, Brandie and I made it to the passenger side, where she was standing. Holding the little munchkin in one arm, my next move was reaching behind the seat to grab the sacks.

Lee asked, "What are these bags for?"

"You will know when we get in our seats."

Hanging the sacks on my free arm, we headed for the ramp that led into the stadium. Working our way through the horrendous crowd in ninety-eight degree heat, we finally stepped into the main hall way to our seats. Seeing a food stand and sitting Brandie down beside her mom, I told Lee, "I'm going to get in line and order our food. What would the two of you like to eat?" I dropped one of the bags and when I bent over to pick it up, someone elbowed me in my eye. Standing straight up and rubbing it, Lee put her hand on my cheek and asked, "Are you okay? That had to hurt."

"Yeah, it did hurt, but I'm all right. I'll probably have a black eye tomorrow. What would you like to eat?"

Lee glanced at the long line and said, "Whatever you want will be fine with us. We will hang back here until you get the food. Hurry, Shannon, the line is growing by the second!"

Managing to work my way through the people, who were packed

like sardines, I finally ordered our food and drinks, and picked up the card board tray that was holding our lunch. With the two sacks hanging on my shoulder and trying to make room to leave the counter, a little boy who was standing next to me bumped my arm and the drinks went everywhere. *Déjà vu! Only this is sodas instead of coffee! Oh well, why not get soaked to the skin? It isn't the first time and it most likely won't be the last.* However, my clothes were soiled from my neck to the belt buckle. The young man that had just filled our lunch tray handed me some paper towels and replaced the sodas.

When I got back over to the girls, Lee asked, "What happened to you?"

Exasperated, I responded, "A little boy had a collision with me." Then Lee grabbed the towels and wiped away as much of the spill as she could and took the tray out of my hands. Then I picked Brandie up again, and we headed for the seats.

It was a nightmare trying to work our way through a mass of people to get to our seats. Thank God, they were the second and third ones in the row. Lee sat down with the hot dogs and drinks and Brandie carefully squirmed into her mom's lap.

Still standing in the row, wiping sweat from my forehead and trying to situate the two sacks that were hanging on my arm, I asked Lee to hold on to my food until it was safe for me to sit down. About that time a man in a seat a couple of rows behind us yelled out, "Hey, you! When are you gonna sit down?"

By this time my patience was worn thin, and I yelled back at him, "When I'm damn good and ready!"

Lee, in a soft whisper, tried to calm my anger. "Shannon, it's all right. Sit down."

"That man is a nitwit, and evidently he is asking for some attention, and I'm just the one to give it to him."

Lee gave me a semi dirty look and added, "What is wrong with you, Shannon?"

There I stood, sweating like a boxer in the ring, one eye almost swollen shut, a shirt full of cola, and two bags on my shoulder that were getting to be like a sore hangnail. Finally, when shuffling my feet around to sit down in the seat, I lost balance. When my butt hit the seat, somehow my left arm hit Lee's arm and sure enough...one of the drinks splashed in my crotch. That isn't all that happened. The sacks hanging on my right shoulder made a U-turn and walloped the little old lady's head sitting next to me. Lee didn't know whether to laugh or be embarrassed.

I immediately apologized to the lady. She began rubbing her head and pinning a strand of hair in place, and nicely said, "That's alright. This stadium has very little room between the seats to move around in. Whatcha got those bags for?"

I tilted toward her and discreetly nodded my head toward Lee and whispered with a hand cupped around my mouth, "She is my girlfriend, and one of the bags has her birthday gift in it."

The lady stood up, looking at the people all around us, and in a delighted loud voice, pointed to Lee and announced, "One of those bags (pointing to me) is a birthday gift for his girlfriend! Isn't that nice?"

Everyone in hearing distance began to giggle. Lee ducked her forehead into her hand and tried to look as though she wasn't paying any attention to me or the little lady. To top that off, the heckler behind us made a taunting remark, saying, "Why don't you give those bags to your girlfriend before you kill somebody!"

Turning around and giving him a look of rage, I angrily told him, "Why don't you mind your own business?"

The next thing he did was laugh like a hyena. That really got to me and I told him, "Listen, mister, you are beginning to piss me off." Starting to get out of my seat, Lee grabbed my arm. "Shannon. This is my birthday. Please don't make a scene. You could get us kicked out of here."

Settling down and turning toward her I apologized. "Sorry babe. I'm feeling a bit beat up right now."

She smiled and remarked, "Not as much as you could be if you followed through with the challenge you were giving to the man behind us!"

Smiling back at her, I whispered, "You are probably right. I'm not a fighter, I'm a lover." She giggled and whispered back, "Yes you are!"

It was about fifteen minutes before the game. Leaning back in my seat trying to overlook the perspiration, soaked clothes, throbbing eye and bruised butt, I felt a tug on my shirt from the little old lady. "When are you giving your girlfriend the birthday gift?"

Trying to ignore her, I thought. *What is this with these people today? Doesn't anyone tend to their own business these days? I planned to give Lee the gift right before the first pitch, and that's what I'm going to do!*

However, the little old lady broke into my thoughts and reaching in front of me she touched Lee's arm and asked, "I bet you would like your gift right now, wouldn't you, sweetie?"

Lee looked at her and then at me with an expression of 'what do I say'? She stuttered saying, "Well…it—it doesn't matter. Whatever (nodding her head toward me) he decides."

The heckler then asked loudly, "What's the matter, bud? Aren't them bags about to break your arm?"

Lee grabbed my shoulder with a firm hold and gave me a look as if to say, "Don't you dare move a muscle."

By now, we had an audience, and the little old lady became more persistent. "Come on, young man! Give your girlfriend her gift."

Disgusted, I surrendered and handed Lee the bag that held the baseball hats. Taking them out, she giggled and placed them on Brandie, me, and herself. Then she reached into the other bag and pulled out the glove. Her face lit up like a candle festival. She put it on her hand and gave it a couple of hits into the palm with her fist, saying, "This is the most thoughtful gift any one has ever given me. Thank you, Shannon."

Then that little old lady stood up, turned around to face the crowd, and waving her arms like an orchestra leader, began singing, "Happy birthday to you, happy birthday…"

Needless to say, I pulled the hat over my face and slid as far into the seat as possible. Everyone within hearing distance joined in on the birthday song. Not only that, we got the attention of half the stadium and a television cameraman. Looking at the large screens, there we were on national television. It dawned on me that someone might see Lee and recognize her because we were being watched by thousands of people. I whispered to her, "We better do something not to be seen

Deception or Perfection

on the T.V." So we stood up and turned around to face the crowd. I was confident that the camera man didn't get a good view of us.

Lee raised her hand in the air so everyone could see the glove, and giving it a couple more hits with her fist, she bestowed a kiss on my cheek. Of course, the prick behind us couldn't keep his mouth shut, and he yelled sarcastically, "Aww, isn't that sweet!"

Again my temper was about to explode. Lee gave me a look as if to say, "Settle down, Shannon!" Taking some deep breaths, I smiled at the people, and it somewhat cooled my anger.

Lee held the glove up to the crowd. They cheered, clapping their hands, and she gave them a bow. And about that time, we heard the celebrity singing the national anthem and the referee saying, "Play ball!"

We sat down and Lee put the glove on, hitting it a couple more times with her fist and she told me, "Thank you, Shannon!" Telling her she was very welcome we settled in our seats and watched the game between the Cardinals and the Dodgers. It was a battle, but the Cards won with a score of nine to eight.

When everyone began leaving the stadium, the moron who was heckling me was right behind us. Seeing him tap Lee on the shoulder made my blood boil and, just as I started to say something, he butted in and said, "Hope you have a great birthday, miss! You've got a smart man there. He knows how to treat a lady." Then he turned to me, offered his hand for a shake and remarked, "You have made this the most enjoyable and interesting game that I have ever attended. You are a good sport, man." He reached to shake my hand, and I stood there with my mouth open, and then he said, "I really respect you!"

Turning my head toward him, with a confused look on my face, I responded, "Thanks...I think."

With a chuckle he reached in his back pocket and handed me a business card and said, "If you know of anyone who might need my services, tell them to give me a call." And he disappeared into the crowd.

Almost half an hour later we were in the truck crossing Eads Bridge, heading for home, and we began to talk about our day. Lee thanked me for the glove again and I apologized for my behavior. She remarked, "When we get to your place if you want to I'll see if there is some way to get the stains out of your shirt and jeans."

"Oh, that's okay. I'm getting used to this sticky, wrinkled feeling."

We were quiet for a moment, and Lee spoke up again.

"I'm inclined to agree with the heckler. This has been the most memorable day of my life. And I'm sure you are going to be very cautious around cola drinks."

With a big smile I told her, "You're right about that." Then, changing my voice, I imitated the heckler, "Isn't that sweet."

We burst into laughter and Lee asked, "What is on the card he gave you?" Reaching in my back pocket and handing it to her, she gasped and said, "You are not going to believe it!"

"What does it say?"

"Anger Management. Roman Sagaisty, M.D. of Psychiatry. That is unbelievable!"

We laughed, and promised that we would never tell another soul about my encounter with a psychiatrist.

About that time, Brandie looked at her mom seriously, as though she was about to cry, "I got scared!"

In a surprised tone, Lee asked her, "Why did you get scared sweetie?"

With eyes as big as quarters, Brandie explained, "It looked to me like Shannon was going to mop the floor with that mean ol' man!"

"But why should that scare you?"

Brandie thought for a moment and spoke sadly, "I woke up real early one morning and could hear Daddy yelling…and…and he was real mad and walking real fast from one end of the hall way to the other! He was real mad! And he said, 'Eddie, you had better be in my office Monday. Or I'm going to mop the floor with you!' Daddy hung up the phone and I ran back to my bed and covered up until you came into my room, and then we got in the car, and we never saw Daddy again."

Lee's eyes began to puddle and it seemed to upset Brandie even more.

She asked, "Did I say something wrong, Mommy?"

Even though Lee knew it was against the law, she took Brandie out

Deception or Perfection

of the car seat, held her in her arms and, rocking the little one back and forth, told her, "No, precious, you didn't say anything wrong. Mommy is sad because she forgot to explain to you why we moved away from our home. I'm so sorry that you heard your father in an angry moment. He loved you so much. When we get to Shannon's house, I'm going to tell you why we are living in Ellisville. Will you be okay until then?" Brandie nodded.

When Lee put Brandie back in the car seat, she looked at me and asked, "Are you still mad at that man, Daddy-o?"

"Nah. Thinking back about the whole thing, princess, I'm sure he might have had too many bottles of beer."

Leaning back into her car seat, she folded her arms against her chest, and looking very grown up, remarked, "Oh you know, daddy-o, some people just can't hold their liquor!" Lee and I looked at each other in amazement at her observation skills.

Then Lee commented, "Some people are going to have to watch what they say in front of this 'little pitcher that has big ears.'"

Brandie asked, "What do you mean, Mommy, about little pitchers having big ears?"

She is her mother's daughter, I thought.

Lee tried to ignore her question and Brandie loudly asked again, "Mommy, what do you mean?"

"That means grown-ups sometimes talk too much in front of their children."

Brandie crossed her arms and said, in an aggravated tone, "Well, that's all I wanted to know, Mommy!"

Lee and I stared at one another in disbelief at the intelligent little girl we had on our hands.

Driving into Ellisville, I thought, *it's going to work out great for Lee's surprise birthday party when she walks into the house thinking she is there to try to get the stains out of my shirt and jeans.*

I asked, "Are you sure you don't mind working on my clothes?"

"Well it might be better to just go in long enough to remove your lovely garments and I'll take them home with me. I'm so tired, Shannon, and Brandie needs to be put to bed. This has been a long day for her."

With an angry pucker, and her hands on her hips, Brandie told her mother, "I'm not tired, Mommy! Why can't we stay at Shannon's house for a while?"

"Young lady! You are an hour past your bedtime. I know how tired you are, and we're not going to have this discussion again. Okay?"

The little princess just sat pouting and didn't say a word. But she sure let Lee know with her body language that she wasn't a happy camper.

When we pulled into the driveway, there were no signs of anyone who might have come to the party. Not even a car. So I parked the truck, went to the passenger side, and opened the door. Then taking my two girls' hands and unlocking the door, we stepped into the house. Touching a switch near the entrance of the door, I turned the lights on, but no one jumped out of hiding to yell surprise. I was beginning to think that my friends had let me down. Before the thought left my mind, Grant and Ellen stepped from the living room into the kitchen and the two of them said, "Happy Birthday, Lee." Then Grant stepped behind her and, taking a blindfold from his hip pocket, he proceeded to put it over Lee's eyes. She backed away from him, and he teased, "You can volunteer to cooperate with us, or we can hog tie you and carry you to our destination."

Ellen asked. "Do you trust us, birthday girl?"

Lee stammered as Grant tied on the blindfold. Brandie looked up at him with a scared look, and she grabbed her mother's legs.

Lee asked, "What are you two doing?"

Quickly, Grant squatted down and whispered into Brandie's ear and, giggling, she put her hand over her mouth.

To this day I don't know what he whispered to the little princess; but she told her mom, "Don't be scared, Mommy, we're going to take you someplace!"

She grabbed Lee's hand. Then Grant took the other one and with Ellen's help, they opened the door. Brandie reached for my hand, which put her between Lee and me. And away we went toward the barn. Doubts began to surface in my mind about asking Vicky and Ellen to plan a party. It was my opinion that the barn wasn't an appropriate place for any kind of function. I thought, *What in the world were Vickie and Ellen thinking about to plan anything out here.*

By then Grant opened the barn door and Ellen took the blindfold from Lee's eyes. A roar of "Happy Birthday" seemed to be coming from every corner of the barn as people came to us, stepping out from behind hay stacks, the loft, and out of the stalls. It had been cleaned from the ground up to the ceiling. Colored lights streamed down from the cross beams to the walls. There was a large table at the far end of the barn with a huge cake and plates and napkins. Across from the table were the town's local musicians, The Hornswoggle Country Band. They began playing the birthday song and everyone started to sing. Lee put one hand over her mouth and she began to cry again.

Hank and Vickie walked up to us with opened arms and hugged Lee and handed her a handkerchief. I teased them saying, "She has already filled one of those today, and I would advise you is get it washed before putting it in your pocket."

With a cute, steamed look Lee slapped me on the shoulder. Then she told Vickie, Ellen, Grant, and Hank, "I can't believe you guys! I've never had anyone in my life who has given me such a wonderful birthday party!"

Vickie spoke up. "Honey, you deserve some special attention, and we want you know how much everyone in this town has grown to love you."

About that time Lee blotted her eyes and blew her nose into Hank's handkerchief. He blinked his eyes and remarked, "That was a big one!"

"Didn't I tell you?"

As we were laughing, Lee gave us a smile. Millie and Jaden came over to give Lee a hug.

Millie remarked. "Charlie, you are one in a million to put up with all of us and especially (pointing at me) this one."

"He is all right, Millie. Little wet behind the ears, but that's what makes him irresistible."

When Lee began milling around, talking to people, I high-tailed it to the house and retrieved her gift. Returning to the barn, Vickie and Ellen were helping Lee open presents and when she finished the last one on the table, I handed her my gift. Grant started shushing the guests and pointing to Lee and myself. Everyone glued their eyes on us.

She smiled and said, "You've already given me a gift!"

"Well...this is a second one. Were you really surprised?"

"Oh yes!"

When she opened the box and saw the figurine, her mouth flew open, and she set it on the table and stared at it for a few seconds. Then she puckered up, started fanning herself with her hands, and I could tell she was getting ready to fill someone's handkerchief again, so I quickly told her, "This has been a stressful but also an awesome day for you. It is okay if you want to cry."

She shook her head no and said, "This is the most beautiful gift that has ever been given to me!" She stood up and gave me a kiss on the cheek. Everyone clapped their hands and someone in the crowd yelled, "You can do better than that. Give the man a real kiss!"

Lee put her left arm over my shoulder, right hand to the back of my head, and slowly pulled it to her face and plastered a kiss on me I never will forget. Whistles and howling began filling the barn.

When she finished the kiss, everyone clapped their hands again. About that time the band leader announced, "Lee, would you pick a partner and honor us with the first dance?" With a mischievous grin she walked to the center of the dance floor and pretended she wasn't going to choose me. So there wasn't a thing left for me to do but to walk straight to her and kiss her in front of everyone. Before we parted from the kiss, the band started playing *The Look of Love*. After our dance, the band cut loose with some great rock and roll music. Everyone seemed to be having a wonderful time, including the kids.

As the party wound down, I glanced around and saw Millie and Jaden, who were the only guests left in the barn. Then my eyes caught a glimpse of Brandie laying on a bale of hay, sound asleep. "This has been a long day for you and the little princess, Lee. Why don't the two of you and Jaden stay here tonight?"

Jaden quickly spoke up, "You are right about Lee and Brandie, but I planned to work on my book for the rest of the evening and don't have anyone to drive me back to the mobile home."

Millie spoke up and said she could drive Jaden home. Lee flashed her pretty smile, slipped her arm through mine, and kissed me on the cheek saying, "I'll take you up on that offer, Daddy-o."

Jaden and Millie laughed, and Millie asked, "Where did that name come from?"

"That's my little girl's nickname for Shannon."

Jaden and Millie thought Brandie was right in choosing a personal nickname for me. They said good night to us and left the barn.

Picking Brandie up and turning the lights out, Lee closed the doors and we headed for the house. Walking in the foyer, and nodding my head toward the master bedroom, I laid Brandie on the bed and quietly whispered, "I'll get some clothes out of the closet and go upstairs. This will be more convenient for you. Also, (pointing toward the dresser) there are sweats in the top drawer if you want something to sleep in. Do you need some help with Brandie?" Shaking her head, Lee kissed me on my cheek. I realized how natural it felt having the two girls under my roof.

The next morning, I woke up at the usual time and there were no sounds to be heard until my feet hit the top of the stairs. Quietly tip-toeing down the steps, and reaching the last one, I could hear Brandie and her mom chattering away. Gently knocking on the door, Brandie said, "Come in."

Standing for a few seconds and staring at the beautiful scene before my eyes, Lee smiled and in unison they sweetly said, "Good morning, Daddy-O," and giggled.

I jumped in the middle of the bed and began to tickle Lee, and she yelled to Brandie, "Help me, Brandie! He is tickling me. Help me!" Brandie crawled on my back and put her hands over my eyes. She was laughing so hard that she fell on the bed and I began to tickle her. Then Lee pushed between us, and I grabbed her feet, pretending to bite her toes. She screamed, and both of them managed a side maneuver and off the bed I went.

"Oh, no!" I cried, and held my arm saying, "Oh goodness! My arm...my arm! Could it be broken?"

They immediately came to my rescue. The second they got on their knees, trying to help me, I pounced on them. Grabbing one at the waist and the other around her shoulders, I yelled "Gotcha!"

Lee looked at Brandie and, in a strained voice, asked, "What should we do with a person who cries wolf, Brandie?"

Releasing my arms, Brandie answered innocently, "We put them to bed without you reading them a story."

Lee gave me a sinister look and asked Brandie, "What do you think about canceling the invitation we were going to give him for dinner next Friday night?"

Brandie stood up and, with a wistful look on her little face, she asked her mom, "Can you punish him another way mommy? Me and Goggy like it when Shannon comes and plays with us."

Lee and I burst out laughing and she remarked, "So much for giving you a punishment, Daddy-O!"

Taking my girls' hands, I made a promise, "I'm sorry for crying wolf! It will never happen again!"

Lee asked, "Do you think we should forgive him?"

Looking into her mom's eyes, she nodded and in a grown up manner told me, "You are forgiven, Daddy-O. Don't ever cry wolf again!"

I responded, "I won't, princess. Perhaps you and your mom will let me make up for my blunder by the two of you joining me for breakfast at Millie's?"

They looked at each other and Lee told Brandie, "I'm pretty hungry. Are you hungry, sweetie?" Brandie smiled at her mom and they decided to take me up on my offer.

After breakfast, heading to the mobile home, I asked Lee, "Do you think we went overboard for your birthday?"

"Absolutely not, Shannon!" she responded. "It was the most incredible day of my life." She gave me a coy smiled and added "Of course the exception is when it comes to our... 'French wine' times."

Smiling back I responded, "Hmm! So, my wine serving is exactly the way you like it, huh?"

She put her arm around my shoulder and said, "It's extraordinary, and I hope you have lots of it in stock."

Giving her an approving smile and a knowing look, I said, "Baby, my cellar can hold all the French wine you want. Just let me know and it will be my pleasure to serve you."

All of a sudden, we noticed the questioning look on Brandie's face.

Lee spoke up, "We have just opened our mouths for a round of questions." But Brandie didn't ask anything, and Lee and I breathed a sigh of relief. It reminded us again that we were going to have to be more aware of what we said around that little girl. She was very smart and had an inquisitive mind.

Parking the truck in front of the mobile home, the two girls jumped out and Brandie ran for the front door. I met Lee at the back of the truck, where she stood smiling at me.

Wrapping my arms around her, I gave her a long, loving kiss. We held each other for a moment and I told her, "There are times when my feelings for you need to be verbalized. I love you so much, Lee, and it becomes tougher than leather for me to leave without you and Brandie."

She touched my cheek and softly kissed me; then, pulling away from my arms, she ran for the door of the mobile home.

Chapter Seventeen

By the time the month of August moved in, I had managed to finish all of the improvements on the mobile home. For some reason, there was an overflow of patients at the clinic. However, Lee helped out Mondays all day and began to work in every afternoon from 3:00 to 6:00 the rest of the week.

One day, after the last patient was as released, I complimented her. "I've noticed that you have a remarkable connection with animals. Haven't figured out exactly what it is, but you are amazing with them."

She smiled and informed me, "Even though there haven't been any studies or anything proven with experiments, my theory is that animals are more responsive to a female. To me, there is a response to a mother's love, and I don't know of any creature that doesn't respond instinctively to a loving parent."

"Well, theory or not, it's as good a reason as anything I can think of."

After cleaning the instruments that were used during the day, Lee left for home. I jumped in the truck, high-tailing it to Millie's for a sandwich. Entering the restaurant, there sat Sheriff Jerry. He teased me about Lee and invited me to sit beside him on a stool.

Everyone in Ellisville knew where Lee lived and that we were in a relationship, so feeling confident that he didn't have any ulterior motives, I sat down. He began to spout out insinuations.

"You know, Shannon, some people tell me your girlfriend doesn't talk much about herself." He released a deep breath and continued, "Yep, that's the gossip! Where do you think she came from, Doc?"

"You know, sheriff…I don't care where she came from!"

Jerry arrogantly patted me on my shoulder and remarked haughtily, "It's my thought, Dr. Shannon, if she was my woman, I would want to know everything about her."

Getting tired of his questions and attitude, I asked him

sarcastically, "You know what 'thought' did Jerry?"

Looking at me with a crooked smile he replied. "Well, that is a question I don't have an answer to, Doc!"

"Thought, thought he had to fart and he shit in his pants!"

The sheriff slowly stood up, pushed the stool under the counter, and said pompously, "You have a good day, Whitney."

"Same to ya, sheriff!"

Now there wasn't a doubt in my mind that he was trying to get information about Lee; and knowing that Millie heard our conversation, I asked her, "Millie, what do you think about Jerry?"

"Well...I think he is a good man. But you break the law; he will throw the book at you. And as far as respecting him...there hasn't been anyone I know of who has been critical or said that they didn't respect him. They say he is honest and will bend over backwards to be fair. I've never known of him not liking anyone. But, for some reason, he sure don't like you."

"Then it's not my imagination. You have noticed his animosity toward me."

Nodding her head and rolling her eyes she said firmly, "Ohhh, yes!"

Immediately leaving the restaurant, I decided to call Lee. After telling her about my encounter with the sheriff, she asked, "Shannon, do you think I should be more visible? Tomorrow I'm registering Brandie for pre-school. Maybe Jaden, Brandie, and I should start going to church. We need to get connected with a place of worship. It also would be a good idea to come into town more often. Hopefully that might stop people from thinking I'm mysterious."

"That sounds like a good idea, but what are you going to say at the registration office when they ask about Brandie's last name not being the same as yours?" Lee assured me that she would think of something.

The following day after registering Brandie, they came into the clinic, and I motioned for them to follow me into my office. Lee walked around the desk to give me a hug.

"How did it go at the pre-school registration?"

Lee told me excitedly, "The only thing they questioned was the birth certificate. Because it had my real name and her dad's on it, the lady who took the registration application questioned me as to why the name I'm using now wasn't the same as on the birth certificate. I told her that my husband died from suspicious circumstances, and the gossip in my previous town became unbearable. So I decided to legally change my name and start a new life in a town where no one ever heard the name Costa. The people here are kind and friendly. Then I asked her to keep this to herself, that she was the only person who knows about this except for my friends, Millie and Shannon Whitney. Not only did she say that my secret was safe with her, she expressed sorrow for the loss of my husband. I believe she will keep her promise. What do you think, Shannon?"

"That is great news, baby. Was her name Mrs. Cline?"

"Yeah! Do you know the lady?"

"Yes, and you can trust her. She is one of the rare ones that won't tolerate gossip. Come here, I've got something to show you." I pulled Lee into my arms and gave her a sensual kiss.

She backed away and stated teasingly, "Shannon Whitney, (she glanced down at Brandie), you should not kiss me like that when you know we can't finish what you have started. Now I'm the one who is going to have to go home and take a cold shower."

Lee quickly put her hand over her mouth and glanced at Brandy. Thank goodness the little one was looking at a picture on the wall of the animals loading on Noah's Ark and wasn't paying any attention to my and Lee's behavior. I told her that my actions could have started a lot of questions from the little princess and I apologized

Smiling and giving me a gentle kiss on the cheek, she and Brandie left the clinic.

The next three months went by quickly. Lee and I did not have any downtime alone. It was my idea that we spend every moment that we could with Brandie. It was beautiful watching the two of them together, and witnessing their constant bonding. My feelings for that little girl became one of the highlights of my life. I couldn't have had any greater love for her than if she was my own child.

There were moments during the next few months, I would occasionally spot a car parked in various places. The driver seemed to be watching me, but he would not get close enough to catch a glimpse of his face.

Going out to Lee's place, I wanted to take some pictures of Brandie and have professional artist paint a portrait for Lee's Christmas gift. Jaden and I took several, and the two of us chose one for the artist. There was a bit of fear that Brandie might reveal our secret. However, Jaden said she would caution her not to tell her mom, and make it a surprise for her. Hopefully, since it was the end of October, the artist would have plenty of time to have it ready for Christmas.

November approached and when Thanksgiving was only a week away, Lee invited me to come to her place for the celebration. She followed up the invitation with a warning. "I have never fixed a turkey or dressing in my life. So…come at your own risk. Jaden is helping, and she has less experience with making Thanksgiving dinners than I do. I plan to go by the library and search the internet for some instructions. Then surely the two of us can figure it out."

The following week went by quickly. While getting ready to go out to Lee's place, I thought, *It has been months since Lee and I have been totally alone. Perhaps we can have some time to ourselves later this evening.*

Parking the truck next to the mobile home, I stepped on to the porch and the door swung open. Out came my little princess and Goggy to greet me. Picking her up and carrying her back through the doorway, she gave me a big hug. Walking into the kitchen area, the aroma of the food was so good, my mouth almost salivated.

Everything was ready, and we sat down to a feast. I have to say, Lee and Jaden outdid themselves because it was the best Thanksgiving dinner I had eaten since my last one with my parents and Jess. Very quickly, I dashed the memory out of my mind to control my feelings before they got away from me.

Thanking them for the delicious lunch, I stood up and began clearing the table. Jaden touched my arm and told all of us, "Get yourselves out of here! I'm going to do this job! The two of you have worked hard all week! Go in the living room and relax!" So we did.

The minute my butt hit the couch, Brandie climbed on my lap.

With a stuffed toy tucked under one arm, she circled my neck with the other, and leaned toward my face to look me in the eyes and asked, "Shannon, when will you be my new daddy?"

With a startled look on her face, Lee exclaimed loudly, "Brandie!" Then she softened her voice and said, "Sweetheart that is not a question you ask Shannon."

"Well, Lee...with all due respect, her question isn't that unreasonable!" She looked at me as if to say, "Butt out, Shannon!" Quickly, I changed my thinking and said, "Princess, it would be my honor to be your daddy. But your mom and I would need to be married. And we have a lot of stuff to talk about to decide if that is the right thing to do."

"Why wouldn't it be right to get married? You love my mommy a whole lot, and Mommy loves you! So...."

Lee butted in. "That's enough questions, sweetie. It is time for your nap."

Brandie wasn't too cooperative with her mother, but after a bit of fussing she gave me a hug and they left for her bedroom.

When Lee returned, she sat down beside me on the couch and with a deep breath, she remarked, "I'm sorry Brandie embarrassed you."

"Sweetheart, she didn't embarrass me. I've wondered myself about asking…"

Lee quickly butted in again and said, "Shannon, you promised that you would not pressure me."

I immediately apologized and agreed with her. "You're right, I won't pressure you."

We set quietly for a moment. My desire was to take Lee into my arms and make love, but instead I whispered to her, "Better get out of here and find a way to stop the fantasy of making love to you. Besides, Mr. Jackson brought his sick nanny goat in late yesterday afternoon, and it needs some drastic attention. She delivered a baby and contracted a milk infection. I kept her overnight in my barn, and her antibiotic is due in about thirty minutes. Do you think you could come over later and spend the evening with me?"

Taking my hands, she gave me a mischievous smile and said, "I think that can be arranged. That is…if you still have that French wine available. And there might be a kiss for you if it is sweet."

"Baby," I responded. "You can have all the wine you want." Then, pulling her close and attempting to get an early kiss, I asked, "How about a sample for your approval of the wine?"

She backed away and sighed. "No samples until my taste buds determine if the wine is sweet or not!"

"Okay, if that's what you want! I'll endure the agonizing moments until you taste the wine." Then I stood up, grabbed my hat, and walked out the door.

Entering my driveway and parking the truck, I went straight to the barn and gave the patient her antibiotic. Evidently the treatment was working because she was running around the pasture frisky as a pup. After calling Mr. Jackson to pick his goat up Friday, my next move was to shower, shave, and lay down for a nap

Waking up about five, I put the wine on ice and looked in my C.D. cabinet for the one that had *The Look of Love* on it and placed it in the player. Noticing a couple of candles in the cabinet, I grabbed them and sat one at each end of the coffee table. While fetching two wine glasses, I heard the sound of Lee's Jeep coming up the driveway. I reached over and turned on the C.D. player, lit the candles, and headed to the door, planning to sweep her off her feet with a sexy kiss. Wouldn't you know, it didn't work out.

When I opened the door, she was so beautiful and the fragrance of her perfume was so enchanting, I stuttered, "You're…you're… here."

She giggled and asked, "Were you expecting someone else?"

Taking a deep breath, I muttered. "Oh no, baby, I'm not expecting anyone but you. I'm just speechless right now. You do that to me sometimes when you look so beautiful! Come on in. The wine is chilled and sweet."

She had on a sexy dress buttoned down front with long sleeves, and it clung to her body like a glove. It had a low-cut neckline down to the tips of her breasts. It made me hotter than a firecracker.

I told her, "There ought to be a law against a beautiful woman like you wearing a dress like that. Women have no idea how crazy they can make a man. Especially since he and his lady have gone for three months without sex!"

Smiling, she looked in my eyes. "Shannon, why do you think I bought this dress? I hoped that you would be attracted to me whether I'm naked or not."

"Sweetheart, I'm attracted to you no matter what you wear. But... will you promise not to put that dress on for anyone except me?"

She gave her assurance that the only man who would see her in the dress would be me. Then, excusing myself, I went to the bathroom and splashed cold water in my face.

Returning to the living room, Lee was seated on the couch, so I sat down beside her and leaned over, all puckered up for a kiss. She scooted away from me and put her hand up to my face, saying, "Ah, ah, ah! Gotta check out the wine to see if it's sweet as you promised!"

You will never see anyone pour a glass of wine as quickly as the one I poured that night for Lee! A magician could not have moved his hands as quickly as I moved mine.

While sipping the wine, she complimented the candles and music. "The room is very romantic."

Trying not to seem impatient for our lovemaking, I nervously responded, "Maybe you should take bigger swallows of the wine, babe, before it gets hot."

She pretended not to notice my eagerness. "Oh, no! Haven't you heard, 'Wine becomes sweeter with time and loving care'?"

"Yes, but no one wants to wait until it grows gray hair!"

She laughed and asked, "Aren't you going to invite me to dance?"

"You betcha!"

Quickly reaching for her hand, I asked, "May we grace the floor with our exquisite dance steps?" Pulling her up into my body, we made a grand, sweeping move. Then, holding her even closer and tighter in my arms, I whispered in her ear, "Lee, you have no idea how much you mean to me. I lo..."

She butted in, "You don't have to say another word, Shannon. One picture is worth a thousand words. Let's show our feelings and enjoy one another with all that is in us." She stopped dancing and, taking my hand, she led me to the bedroom.

Standing beside the bed, Lee began to undress, and by the time I had taken my clothes off, she was lying on the bed waiting for me.

Moving in beside her and taking her in my arms, we passionately kissed one another and united our bodies. The urgency of our movements increased, and we knew it was another binding element of our love. Lee kissed me and whispered, "Can we slow it down, because I don't want it to end so quickly."

We separated for a moment, and I rolled over on my back to catch my breath. Lee shifted her body over mine, and we united again. It was beyond my imagination the way she moved her body in the most caressing way. She stopped for a few seconds and raised my hands to her breasts. I slowly rose toward her and began kissing them, one, and then the other. Sitting upright for a moment, I leaned into our lovemaking and greeted her passion. She then wrapped her legs around my buttocks and began a rocking motion. We knew that the bliss could not be held back any longer and we devoured each other's lips as our desires increased. We slowly embraced the moment with the rhythm of a sea wave. Our breathing escalated and our movements intensified, becoming the ultimate of ecstasy as we fulfilled our pulsating desire.

Leaning my shoulders against the headboard of the bed, Lee and I stayed in the position of our lovemaking for a moment to catch our breath. Then she removed herself and cuddled her body next to mine, and laying her head on my chest, she uttered, "We are extraordinary." Between breaths, I replied, "It's only going to get better!"

She raised her upper body from my chest and shaking her head she softly said, "There are no words to describe it! Why... it could almost be addictive!! Shannon, have you ever experienced... doing or feeling what we have shared tonight?"

I told her, "My precious dear heart, there has never been any woman who affects me like you. It's as though I never want to let you go when we become as one! It's like... like I can't get enough of you!"

She said, "I'm the same way. And yet, those three little words stick in my throat and they just won't come out."

"You know what? You will say them when the right time comes. And it will come. You can take that to the bank! So stop worrying about it. If the only other alternative you have is what we've shared tonight, you'll never hear any complaints from this man."

Relaxing beside me, she smiled, looked into my eyes, and said,

"You're not only an amazing lover—you are also an amazing man."

After thanking her for the compliment, we just held one another for a while. "How would you like to go to the kitchen for a snack?" I asked Lee.

Her eyes sparkled and, with a big smile, she inquired, "What do you have for us to snack on?"

"Oreos and vitamin D whole milk!"

"That sounds great."

Slipping on a pair of sport shorts, I threw her a flannel shirt, and we proceeded to the kitchen. Lee sat down on a counter stool and watched me shuffling around in the kitchen for glasses, cookies, and the milk. Placing them on the counter she poured the milk, while I opened the cookies. Sitting on the stool next to her, we began dunking our Oreos and talked a little bit about Jaden.

Lee remarked, "She never goes anywhere except when I'm at work. Now that we have a phone, I call and check up on her and have encouraged her to do something besides writing that novel she has started. Do you know of anyone she could meet, and we could possibly go on a double date or something like that?"

"Not offhand. But are you sure she wants a man in her life?"

"Well, she needs something besides me, Brandie, and Goggy. She buries herself in that novel she is writing, and it's just isn't good that she isolates herself from the world outside of that mobile home."

"Lee, all of us have to come to a place where we can recognize there is a problem. She doesn't seem ready to do that. It might be better to allow her to do her thing." Lee thought for a moment and agreed with me.

Finishing our snack, she said, "It's past the time for me to be leaving. So, I need to go and check up on the two sweetest females in my life."

I asked, "Would you consider calling Jaden? Perhaps that would make you feel better about staying a little longer." She agreed.

When she got off the phone, Lee came back to the counter and stood in front of me with a smile. "Brandie is fast asleep, so Jaden encouraged me to stay the night." She straddled my lap and began to slip the flannel shirt off her shoulders and said, "That is, if it's all right with you."

"If it's all right with me? You bet it is all right with me. Jaden must have received a signal from my hoping you could stay longer. This is above and beyond my dreams!"

Lee tightened her legs around my hips and launched a kiss that set fire to my whole body. Even though we started in the kitchen, we wound up in the bed, and made love again.

Lee woke me up the next morning cuddling my back and kissing my neck. "Good morning, lover. Are you ready for a final round of making love before we have to go to work? I can't wait too long for your decision because it's only an hour away before I'm due at Mill…"

Before she finished her sentence, I began kissing her mouth and continued down her neck and between my kisses, I mumbled, "Is my decision fast enough for you?" She answered. "Yes! However, I've only got an hour to get home and get to work."

After Lee left, I got dressed and went over to Millie's to have a cup of coffee with Grant and Hank. When I reached our table, we swapped hellos and the first thing out of Grant's mouth was, "Well, Hank, guess what happened to the stars last night!"

Before Hank could answer Grant question, I responded, "Okay, Grant, you've got my attention. What happened to all the stars last night?"

"They're in your eyes, bud. You and Lee must have had sooooome Thanksgiving!" Keeping any comments to myself, I looked around and noticed how busy the restaurant had become.

Hank told me, "Millie's business has picked up so much she has had to hire a new helper and we're here to check her out."

"When did she start?" I asked.

Hank spoke up. "She was supposed to have been here this morning, but we haven't seen hide nor hair of her."

Then a man with an apron on came over to our table, and it shocked the daylights out of us. Taking his order book out of the apron pocket, he asked in a British accent, "Good morning gentlemen. May I take your breakfast order?"

We looked at each other not knowing just what this was all about and finally I spoke up and said, "Ah, ah, we've... just came in for a coffee this morning."

He raised his chin, looked down at us as though we smelled bad and, in a slightly feminine voice, said, "Very well sir." And he went on his merry way.

It was all we could do to keep from laughing out loud. The man was so prim and proper. Grant quietly asked, "You don't suppose, he's (he dangled his hand up and down waving it from the wrist)... you know... one of those people who like men?"

I asked, "Do you mean gay?"

"Yeah,"

The three of us looked at the prissy man and Hank spoke up, "Maybe he is nervous or somethin!"

"He's something, all right!" I remarked.

When the prissy man came to our table to refill our cups, Hank asked him, "Hey, waiter, what's ya name?"

Staring down at Hank and, with a persnickety attitude, he replied, "My name is Wallace. However, you may call me Wally. And for your information, sir...I'm a server, not a waiter. Will that be all, gentlemen?"

All three of us stared up at him, and responded at the same time. I said yes, Hank nodded his head. Grant thanked him and spouted, "That will be all." We began to chuckle.

Hank remarked, "Can you believe that?"

Millie must have been watching us because she came over to our table and asked, "What do you three nitwits see that's so funny about my new server?"

Hank spoke up, "Server? Is that what their called these days?" We snickered. Her complexion turned as red as a firecracker. I tried to calm her down. "Millie, we're not making fun. We just aren't used to a ...classy ... server."

The three of us couldn't contain ourselves, and we burst out laughing! Millie came unglued! Bending at her waist with her hands on her hips, and almost gritting her teeth, she released her anger. "Let me tell all of you, Wallace is a very good friend of mine. He is kind, thoughtful, honest, and he would never assume anything about any of you, because he is not that kind of a man. Also, he is not gay. And as far as him being classy, well, this town could use a little class. Especially since most of the men here are ignorant, self-centered assholes like the three of you. You should be ashamed of yourselves."

Millie walked away from our table in a huff. By then, Lee had come to work and met Millie as she stormed away from our table. She noticed that she was close to crying and asked, "What has happened over here? I have never seen Millie that upset since I've known her."

After telling Lee what was going on, to my surprise, she took up for Millie and Wallace. "I can't believe you guys could be so heartless. From now on, keep your assumptions to yourselves. And, and... shame on you." And she walked off in a huff.

When we went to the register to pay for the coffee, Wallace took our money, and we were glad to be able to use work as an excuse to skedaddle out of there.

As the three of us walked to our vehicles, Grant asked, "Did you notice neither Millie nor Lee invited us to come back?"

Hank spoke up. "Did you notice how Wallace gave our change back to us? Did it make you want to kiss him?" We looked at each other and started laughing again.

Driving back to the clinic and looking in the rear view mirror, there was no doubt that a car was following me again. Nevertheless, it did turn the opposite direction as I approached my driveway.

It was a busy day being that it was a Friday after Thanksgiving. People were getting regular check-ups for their pets before the Christmas holiday. Even though we were busy, it didn't take my mind off of the car that followed me.

After closing the clinic, I hung out at the restaurant until Millie had a free moment. I hoped that she would accept my apology for the rudeness of the three 'nitwits' whose behavior toward Wallace was thoughtless and rude.

Sitting down at the counter stool, I caught a glimpse of a man watching Lee. It wasn't the way most men watch a woman. It looked as though he had business with her. Not able to accept his staring at her, I walked over to introduce myself and reached toward him for a handshake. He didn't acknowledge my gesture or volunteer his name. I thought, *Okay, mister, two can play this game!* So I sat down at his table and asked, "Since Ellisville is off the beaten path, we don't see many strangers here. Where are you from?"

"Here and there."

Looking straight into his eyes with no expression on my face, I replied. "Mister, you need to tell me what business that brings you to our town. We don't rudely stare at our local citizens. Maybe I'll call my friend, who is the sheriff of this county. He just might have some questions for you."

Looking straight back at me, he responded, "Oh really. I wouldn't mind talking to him myself. You see, there are some people who try to disappear. They even change their identity. There isn't anyone around here that fits that description, is there, Dr. Whitney?"

It shocked me that he knew my name. It was evident that he had been snooping around about Lee. I replied, "If there is someone...sir, you wouldn't hear anything about them from me."

By that time Lee brought him a hamburger and a cup of coffee. I got up from the table and said sarcastically, "Nice talking to you, Mister."

He advised me. "Don't size up a man just because he is a stranger, he might be a visiting angel,"

Lee gave me a concerned look. Walking back to the counter with her, she asked, "What was that all about, Shannon?'

To keep from scaring her, I answered calmly, "There is nothing for you to be worried about, my love. Just thought he was someone I knew." When I glanced over my shoulder to get another look at him, he had disappeared.

Lee left me to go and wait on a table. As I was putting my jacket on to leave the restaurant, she flashed me a smile. Then, walking out the door, I saw the man getting into a car. My gut instinct was to follow him.

Parking his car in front of the hotel, he stepped out of onto the curb and turned around and lifted his hand, giving me a wave. *So much for going into the 'private eye' business!*

The next day I decided to see Jerry and tell him about the stranger. Entering the police station, I asked to talk to the sheriff. The man behind the desk pointed to a door down the hall.

Knocking on Jerry's door, he yelled, "Come in!"

When I opened the door and stepped into his office, he looked surprised and asked, "What brings you here, Doc?"

I told him about the stranger. He made fun of me, saying, "The man hasn't done anything illegal. You can't approach someone and threaten to arrest them for coming into a restaurant and ordering a hamburger and drink!" He leaned back in his chair smugly. Rolling a toothpick in his mouth, he continued, "Do you think, Doc, that it's possible you are a bit paranoid about the whole thing?"

"Strangers stick out like a sore thumb in this town, sheriff, and there is something odd about this man. By giving you this information, I hoped you would want to make sure the people here are safe. What are going to do about it?"

Jerry got an obnoxious look on his face and informed me, "If you are questioning my job description, you're a bit out of your league. I'll let you know if anything comes up that pertains to a strange animal, Doc. In the meantime, if you are so concerned about this stranger… well, why don't you go and question him yourself?"

I left the police station. While driving to the clinic, I decided not to say anything to Lee about my suspicions. It would be frightening to her, and there wasn't enough evidence to do anything about it.

Chapter Eighteen

Driving over to Millie's the Saturday morning after Thanksgiving; it was obvious that the Christmas season had arrived. There were empty lots filled with all species of evergreens from spruce to pine. Businesses all over town had decorations in windows, on the roofs of houses, doorways, and sidewalks. It was strange to me that I had never noticed all the hustle and bustle of the season until this year. It also amazed me how beautiful the town looked with lights hanging on the light posts.

Because of the overflow of patients from Friday, I decided to make appointments until noon. After having coffee at Millie's, I went to the clinic. The waiting room looked like a Christmas wonderland. Ronda had put up a tree, and she had decorations all over the place.

"You outdid yourself, Ronda. I've never realized the uplifting beauty of the lights before. Did you go and buy extra decorations?"

"No, it's the same ones that have been used every year."

Going to the office and glancing over the records of my patients, it occurred to me how hard Ronda worked, and I decided to make her bonus this Christmas a big one.

That evening, after locking up the clinic and spending an hour on the phone with Lee, I felt as though my body had been put through a thrashing machine, so it was an early bedtime for me.

The first thing on my agenda the next morning was asking what Lee's plans were for the day.

"I'm cleaning. But I was hoping that you would call and give me an excuse to be with you. What's on your mind for the day?"

"Baby, that's a loaded question."

"What is it with men? They take a simple question and make it into a sexual innuendo!"

"Now, there wasn't anything about sex mentioned in my statement! Maybe it is a woman's perception of what men say. So who is thinking about sex?"

She laughed and admitted, "Technically, you are right. However, you knew exactly what you were insinuating. I'll rephrase my question. Okay... what are you doing today?"

Chuckling, I told her my plan. "I'm calling to invite you, Brandie, and Jaden to go to a movie with me. We can have some popcorn and, after the movie, we can stop off on our way home and have a juicy hamburger."

Lee sounded excited and she yelled out to Jaden and Brandie, "Hey, how would you two like to go a movie and grab a hamburger afterwards? Shannon has just offered to give us a treat."

Her yelling straight into the receiver on the phone gave me a jolt, and I corrected her. "Wait just a minute. There was no offer to pick up any check for our afternoon outing."

Lee giggled. "Listen, Mr. Wise Guy. You should not only pay for our treats, you are lucky that we don't charge you for having the pleasure of our company for the afternoon."

"You are absolutely right, Miss Lee. So, what do you say to my invitation?"

"It sounds great." And we set the time for me to pick them up at three o'clock.

Parking the truck in Lee's driveway, it occurred to me that there wasn't room for all of us and a car seat, so we took the Jeep. When everyone got seated, we voted on what movie to go to and *Shrink III* unanimously won hands down.

After the movie Brandie gave me a big hug and said, "Thank you, Shannon. That was a fun movie."

"You are very welcome, sweetie."

"Can we go to Chucky Bee's?"

"That's where we went and had a supreme pizza. After eating our pizza, we played games and danced the bunny hop with Chucky Bee.

On the way home, Jaden remarked, "I haven't had this much fun since I was a kid." All of us felt the same way. About that time, Brandie began to sing, 'The Wheels on the Bus Go Round.' We all joined her, singing at the top of our lungs. We finished the song, and Brandie told her mom that she was tired.

"I'm sure Jaden wouldn't mind helping you to get comfortable."

Jaden scooted closer to Brandie. "Here, little one, just lay your head right here on my shoulder." It was no time until she went to sleep.

Lee and Jaden began to thank me for taking them (as they put it) out for the day. I responded, "I'm the one who should be thankful. Having all of you in my life is at the top of my gratitude list and makes me thankful every day."

When we turned off the interstate, again there seemed to be a car following us. Jaden, looking over her shoulder, saw the car at the same time.

"Jaden, do you think that car is following us?" By that time, Lee began to watch from the door mirror with a concerned look on her face.

Jaden spoke up saying, "Naw, it's turning around and heading the other direction."

Parking in front of the mobile home, and climbing out of the Jeep, I opened the back door and lifted Brandie from her car seat. After laying the little princess down on the bed in her room, Lee tucked her in and she didn't move a muscle.

Jaden thanked me again, excused herself, and headed to her bedroom. "I'm so tired, but it's the nicest tired I've experienced in a long time. Thanks again, Shannon, and good night to you."

Smiling at her, I responded, "You are welcome." Giving her a wave goodnight, she went down the hall way and into her bedroom, and we heard the bedroom door closing.

Lee and I took in a deep breath, and I headed for the door to go home. Just before stepping out onto the porch, she put her arms around my neck and said, "Thanks for a wonderful day." Then she gave me a sweet kiss.

"Woman, what am I going to do with you?"

"You keep doing what you did last night and you will know 'what to do with me.'"

"And if you keep doing what you did last night… call the paramedics for some extra oxygen because I'm going to need it."

We kissed again and Lee told me what a wonderful man she had. "You are so thoughtful and loving, and I'm a lucky woman."

That was a cue for the John Wayne voice. "Why, shucks, little lady, it's all in a day's work."

She became serious and gave me another compliment. "There has never been anyone in my life who has loved me unconditionally like you!" We kissed goodnight one more time, and I left for home.

The late fall moon shined so brightly it was easy to decide to be a little reckless. Driving out of the lane with my lights off, I again felt that someone was watching me. Getting closer to the blacktop, sure enough, there was a car parked at the end of the lane. When I turned on my lights, it squealed off as fast as it could. *Damn it, they got away before I'd seen the make of the car or the color. It looked just like the one that was parked at my driveway awhile back!*

I loaded my pistol as soon as I got home. Setting it on the night stand, not knowing what else to do, I laid in bed and the mind chatter began. Finally, when daylight came, I got up and looked out the window and there wasn't a car in sight.

The next morning when I went to Millie's and walked through the door, there sat the stranger in a booth. Looking straight at him, he gave me nod hello. About the same time, the sheriff walked in behind me and pretended not to notice him. I thought to myself, *Who do you think you are fooling? You're hiding something.* He ordered a coffee to go and left the restaurant.

Lee didn't notice either of them. When she came over to me, the first thing out of my mouth was, "Lee, do you have good locks on your doors?"

"Yeah. Why do you ask?"

"Just wanted to check with you. Because if you don't have good locks, there are some new ones in the barn. They would be easy for me to install them tomorrow."

She flashed her sweet smile and replied, "You won't hear me complain if you choose to do that." I raised her hand to my lips for a kiss, and then she went on her way to get food orders from the customers who had just entered the restaurant.

About that time a voice behind me said, "Well, look here. There is a Casanova among us." It was Hank. He worked his way around the table to sit in his usual chair.

"Ah ha, so you think I'm a Casanova!"

Hank smiled "Man, you are more hung up on that woman than laundry on a clothes line!"

Grant showed up and he had no more sat down when he began telling us about Ellen chewing him out. He proceeded to mimic her. "Now, Grant, you better put the Christmas tree lights on the eaves of the house, or I'm going to hire someone to do it for you. You have time to do all sorts of things except what needs to be done around the house."

"Then I walked out the door and remarked under my breath. That woman is crazy.' She heard me and asked, 'What did you say?' Man, you talk about thinking up something quick. I told her, 'You're right, honey, I'm just lazy!' She said to me real sullen, 'You got that right.'"

He continued. "Wish she was a robot, then all I'd have to do is unplug her."

After Hank and I stopped laughing, I commented, "Grant, you are the crazy one. You love Ellen more than life and wouldn't trade her off for the world."

Taking in a deep breath and staring at the table, he said, "Yeah, you're right. However, she doesn't have to be such a nag."

We talked a little longer, then Grant and Hank had to leave for work.

Just as I picked up the tab to leave, I glanced behind me, and there stood the stranger. He asked, "May I sit down?"

Pulling out a chair for him, he sank down as though the weight of the world was on his shoulders. "Dr. Whitney, I'm sorry for being so rude to you the other day" He got no response from me, so he continued. "You seem to be a good man; and you are having a relationship (pointing toward Lee) with that lovely lady over there."

My mouth was closed, but he knew by my body language that he wasn't welcome. "How well do you know her?"

Finally my patience ran out and I asked, "Who are you? And what the frickin hell is all this interest in Lee and where she came from?"

He looked me straight in the eyes, with a sincere, earnest tone, and said, "I'm a friend, Dr. Whitney."

"You have a funny way of showing it, mister. You know my name, what is yours?"

"That isn't important right now. But, please believe me, I'm a friend," and he got up and left.

Lee came to the table and asked, "Who was that, Shannon?"

Trying to keep the focus on myself so that she wouldn't get scared, I broke my promise about never lying to her. "Don't know, sweetie. He was looking for the best place to spend the night."

Lee was uncomfortable with my answer but didn't ask any more questions. She brought up the subject about going Christmas shopping. The two of us decided that the best day to get away for that length of time would be November 30th.

When the 30th arrived, we went to the Clareview Heights mall for all our shopping needs. The stores were crowded, and we just went with the flow, having a great time buying toys for Brandie. We also found some special things for Jaden and Millie. We bought Grant and Hank's families' large fruit and cheese baskets. Then we ate a bite of lunch and it was time to go home. Walking out of the mall, I had that feeling again of being watched. Thank goodness there wasn't anyone following us on the way home.

By the time we got to Lee's place, it was late and the lights were out except in Jaden's bedroom. She and I sat in the truck for a while talking. Lee began to discussing her relationship with Joe. "You know, when Joe was killed, there was no closure. Starting a new life and the secretiveness of my identity has been a roller coaster of emotions. There must have been love for him in my heart. But when comparing how my feelings are for you…well, there isn't a comparison, because you are the person who I have dreamed about having in my life. I pray that I'll get some answers someday! Maybe those horrible hours after he died were enough to give me acceptance, and that's why there are no feelings for him. What's wrong with me?"

"Lee, there is nothing wrong with you. What choice did you have? You are the strongest person I've ever met. Not only have you found a way to protect yourself and Brandie, you have also felt responsible for Jaden. You love them and want them to be safe. There is no doubt in my mind that Joe would be the first person to tell you to go on with your life. Even though he had secrets, he loved you and Brandie more than anyone could love a child and his wife."

"Yes, but if it hadn't been for you, Millie, Brandie, and Jaden, I couldn't have made it through the last nine months. If Joe had been an honest man with integrity…you know what, Shannon? There is nothing that can change the past… so help me to not go there again."

There was nothing that could be said to give her comfort. I took her in my arms and gently kissed her lips several times, saying, "You will do the right thing. We would have never met if Joe had not been the person that he was."

Lee began returning my kisses with a yearning that came from her heart. Very quickly this turned into an impelling excitement to make love. We stopped for a moment and I begged, "Baby, don't send me home to a cold shower."

She kissed me lightly on my lips and slipped out of her skirt and underclothes. I scooted to the center of the truck seat and pushed the button that moved it back, to adjust it for more room. She began kissing my neck and then unsnapped my western shirt. Pushing my jeans off to the ankles, she turned toward me and positioned her knees on the seat, centering her hips over my lap. Lee gently placed her hands at the back of my head and kissed me as though it could be her last one. Trying not to be too anxious, taking a deep breath, I slipped her button up blouse and bra off her shoulders. Lowering my head to her cleavage and moving my mouth from one place to the other, it was heaven to devour every peak and valley of her upper body. Then I placed my hands below the waist and guided her hips over mine, and the union was made. With my hands still around her hips, lifting them to the rhythm of our heartbeats, she melted into my chest. Trying to suppress the built up appetite and savor every movement, we prolonged the inevitable by slowing down. Even with the slower pace, our breathing began to increase. Lee took in a quick breath and moaned softly. Then we submitted to our craving and the release became a moment of paradise.

Lee put her arms around my upper body and raised her head, giving me a sweet kiss. "You are magnificent!" Then she settled in the center of the truck seat.

Thanking her for the compliment, trying to catch my breath, we redressed. I remarked, "You are the magnificent one. Look at me. I'm panting like a horse after a Kentucky Derby race. How come women can recover so fast from something like we just experienced?" All at once, it dawned on me what I had just asked! UH-OH! Sure enough, Lee had that terrorist look on her face!

"What do you mean? How many experiences have you had like this?"

My question was a major blunder. I reassured her quickly. "Baby, like you have been told, you aren't just 'a woman.' You're the woman I'm in love with and want to spend the rest of my life making happy. Your lovemaking is out of this world. We don't just have sex, sweetie. We drench ourselves in our passion. You are the first woman to ever make me feel completely satisfied."

She squinted her eyes, licked her lips as though she was about to explode, and turned her head sideways. "Shannon Whitney, you handled this evening like a pro. Don't tell me this is your first time to have sex in this truck!"

I really poured on the charm. "Sweetheart, you are such an unbelievable lover, and every time I'm with you it's like a first time… every time."

"What I would like to know is how can someone lie and sit up at the same time? I can see why women fall at your feet. But this woman recognizes your crap."

Being totally honest, I stated, "Okay Lee, yes, there has been times I've used this truck for sex. But, as God is my witness, there was never, never a time that there was love felt from the depth of my soul like I feel for you. You are my life, darling heart, and hopefully you can believe that no woman on earth could take your place. Please say that you believe me, and can forgive me for all the sexual carousing that I had before meeting you. If you can do that it would mean a lot, because you will be able to trust me. I love you."

She looked at me with an apology. "I'm sorry, Shannon. As you know, the two men in my life were my dad, who abandoned his wife and child for another woman, and Joe, whose life was based on lies. The first time the two of us noticed each other there was a connection that I never felt with Joe. Sometimes I felt more like mother and child, than husband and wife. If there wasn't a fear that Jaden, Brandie, and I might have to pick up and leave at any time... Shannon, I don't have the right to express my feelings for you!"

Giving her a gentle kiss, I responded, "We have talked about this before and my love for you hasn't diminished. If anything it is beyond my wildest imagination that I could feel this way about anyone. My love for you is indescribable. We don't have to exchange words to know what we have. And it's going to be forever."

Lee made me a promise. "I will never question your love for me again! Please forgive me for not trusting you."

"Darling heart, there is nothing to forgive. It's hard for me to see you in such turmoil about something which is totally inconceivable in my mind. And that is thinking about anyone other than you. Sweetie, I'm no good for days after we spend a night together!"

She gave me a big smile and said, "So... every time is the first time when you're with me?"

"Yes."

"This is also my first time."

"A first time for what?"

"To give a man, who is a pro at having sex in a truck, the gift of my body. It was quite an adventure. Can we do it again sometime?"

"Baby, we can have sex in a truck anytime you want... except not anymore tonight. I'm still recovering from the gift you just gave me."

She giggled and asked the damnedest question. "Do you think Jaden could see us making love?"

"Hope so. Maybe she learned something."

Lee hit me on my shoulder. "Shannon Whitney. It doesn't bother you that she may have watched us making love?"

"Well, I didn't care after things got started. It's like the joke, 'I go stone blind once my woman lights the fire.'"

She replied, "I'm beginning to think you aren't the shy man that you appear to be."

"Don't believe everything you see, baby, because there wasn't a shy bone in my body until meeting you. Probably, in a few more mouths, you will know all about my bad boy traits."

Lee took a breath and glanced at the mobile home. "Do you really think we were visible to Jaden while we made love?"

With a grin on my face, I said, "Let me see, (glancing around at the outside of the truck) there are three pole lights, a full moon, and a motion light on the porch. What do you think?"

Her eyes got as big as quarters and, with a shocked expression, she blurted out, "Oh my God, Jaden must have seen us!"

Pulling her into my arms, I gave her a kiss. "Well, now if you want to, I can try doing a repeat!"

Shaking her head, she replied, "The best thing we can do is call it a night. No more exciting pornography for Jaden."

She gave me a quick kiss and looked so cute I couldn't help grinning at her as she jumped out of the truck and ran for the door of the mobile home.

Chapter Nineteen

It was about two weeks before Christmas and walking into Millie's, I noticed the stranger sitting in a corner booth, and he seemed to be waiting for me. Ignoring him while making my way to the usual table and sitting down, Lee brought me a cup of coffee. "You sure do look beautiful today."

She gave me a smile and whispered back, "Bet you say that to all the girls."

As she left the table, the stranger walked over to me, stood for a moment, and asked, "Is it all right to join you? There are a few words we need to have in reference to Mrs. Costa. Ignoring him again, I picked up a menu as though it was my immediate interest and nonchalantly asked. "Who?"

He cautiously lowered his tone, saying, "Christina Costa!"

Smiling pleasantly, I asked him, "Man, who are you talking about? There isn't anyone around here by that name."

He replied with urgency in his voice. "Dr. Whitney, you call her Lee. The business you asked me about a few weeks ago is your young lady friend (and he pointed toward Lee) who is serving a breakfast to the man sitting at the counter."

Pulling a chair from the table, I told him to sit down. "You know by now the dangerous situation she and a couple of her loved ones are in. It is very important that I speak to you about… Lee… as soon as possible!"

"If it is so important, why don't you go over right now and talk to her yourself,"

He glanced around. "It is too risky to take a chance on someone seeing us together. There are other people who have intentions to kill her. Please hear what I'm saying, Dr. Whitney. I really need to talk to… your young lady. If you will be at her mobile home tonight, I will explain everything to the two of you."

Peering at him suspiciously, I asked, "Why should I trust you?

Evidently you know all about Lee and me, and you haven't revealed anything about yourself. What is your name and where are you from? All I know about you is that you're a stranger, and not a friendly one at that."

"At first, the feeling was mutual, Dr. Whitney. However, since our first meeting, and after my research on you, it turned out that you are a good man. Also, both of us have your lady friend in our best interest. You will know all about my identity tonight, if you can convince her to talk to me."

"I'll be at Lee's at seven and don't you get there a minute earlier than seven." He agreed and, after we shook hands, he left the restaurant.

On my way to the register, Lee met me. "Shannon, who is the man you were just talking to? And don't tell me he was looking for a motel."

"Lee, if you can come over to the clinic as soon as you get off from work, I'll explain as best as I can." She agreed to be there.

When I got to the clinic, the first thing I did was tell Ronda to cancel all the appointments scheduled after two-thirty and she could leave at that time.

Dismissing my last patient a little before three, I did a bit of clean up. I heard the sound of the Jeep coming up the driveway and a few seconds later Lee knocked on the door. Letting her in, she noticed me glancing around outside to see if anyone was following her. She asked, "What are you looking for?"

"Come on in, sweetheart, and sit down at the counter." Going to the refrigerator and taking out the orange juice, I asked. "Would you like a glass of juice?"

"Sure. Tell me what's going on with you? You looked worried when you left the restaurant this morning."

While pouring our drinks, I told her, "The stranger at Millie's, well... he wants to come to your place tonight and talk to you."

She became frightened. "What would he want to talk to me about?"

"He didn't say, Lee."

She jumped off the stool and headed for the door. "I've got to leave right now and go home!"

I grabbed her arm and said, "Wait a minute, sweetie."

"No! I've got to get to Brandie and Jaden! Dear God, let them be all right!"

By this time Lee had climbed into the Jeep. Running after her I yelled, "I'm following you."

She nodded. "Thank you, Shannon. You have no idea how grateful that makes me feel knowing you are with me."

When we reached the mobile home and rushed through the door, Jaden and Brandie were working a Fisher Price puzzle. Jaden noticed how scared Lee was and asked, "Is there something wrong?" Lee told her about the stranger and Jaden asked, "When is he coming?"

"He should be here a little after 7:00"

Jaden, with a worried look on her face, questioned me further. "Did he give you any information about himself?"

After I told Jaden no, Lee remarked. "Shannon, you shouldn't have given him permission to come out here!"

"Lee, not only did he know all about you, he also has a lot of knowledge about me. He could have found you at any time he desires. I'm thinking that, if he has all of this information about us, and hasn't done anything to the three of you, he probably isn't a threat."

I went out to the truck to get my pistol. I wanted to put the gun in a place that Brandie wouldn't notice it, so I tucked it under my jacket in between the belt and my waist. She knew something was going on and Lee softly said to her, "Sweetie, company is coming in a little while. There is going to be grown-up talk about grown-up things. It would be best if you would go to your bedroom when they get here and play or color in your new coloring book until they leave. Okay? In the meantime, we are going to eat dinner. How would you like a big hoagie sandwich?"

Going to the kitchen area Jaden and I helped Lee prepare the hoagies and drinks. Finishing our dinner and cleaning up, Jaden asked, "Lee, what if this man is an informer for the gangsters?" Lee shook her head as if she didn't know what to do. Jaden remarked, "I've heard it said that there is safety in numbers. Maybe with the three of us watching every move he makes, it will discourage any thoughts that he

Deception or Perfection

may have to do us harm. Don't trust him, Lee, until we know what he is up to."

Seven o'clock rolled around and there were headlights coming up the lane. Lee told Brandie, "Okay, darling heart, it's time to go to your room and color. That should be a lot more fun than hanging out with us old folks."

About that time there was a knock. Lee glanced at me as I stood against the wall with my hand on the gun. Jaden went to the kitchen area and took a look out of the windows. When Lee opened the door, there stood the stranger who had approached me at Millie's place.

"Mrs. Costa," he said, "may I come in?" Lee reluctantly opened the door a bit wider and he stepped inside and introduced himself. "Mrs. Costa…" Lee corrected him saying that her name was Lee. "Okay, Lee… my name is Jim Preston." He reached into his vest. I placed the right hand over the pistol under my jacket. Jaden started walking toward the door and she nervously swallowed as he handed Lee an I.D. card. Lee took a deep breath of relief and backed away from him.

Preston quickly told her, "Mrs. Costa, I'm not here to hurt anyone. Please believe me. I'm here to help you. The F.B.I. has kept a protective eye on you and your little girl since August of last year. We have times, dates, and even the stops you made at the grocery store and days you went to the gym." Lee was still reluctant to open up to the man and he continued trying to convince her. "Let me tell you this, and if you are still in doubt as to my identity, I'll turn around and leave. Last Christmas you bought Joe a gold chain for his gift. The price was1,246.72. You also bought your little girl a three-to-six year-old computer, and it was blue with white keys and black letters. The computers cost was592.38. Now can we talk?"

Lee stood for a while in a daze. Finally, still in shock, she invited him to sit at the table. She introduced Jaden and me. "These are my friends Jaden and Shannon."

"I have met Dr. Whitney. And it's nice to meet you, Jaden," and shook our hands.

Lee again pointed to the kitchen table with an invitation to sit down and we followed suit as he stated his intentions. "I'm going to skip all the formalities and get down to business. Mrs. Costa, your husband Joe called the F.B.I office in July, a year ago. He asked to speak to an agent and yours truly happened to be the one the agency put him in contact with. He told me that he had enough information and evidence to put the entire Tardino family away for life."

"I asked your husband what made him decide to come clean now. We knew he had been a henchman for the family for over 10 years. And he told me that he went to Matt Tardino and asked him what it would take for him to leave the family."

"He said Tardino was sitting at his desk and laughed. Then he leaned forward and told Joe he would have to die. Joe said that he knew the man was serious. Tardino asked Joe why he wanted to leave the family. He told Joe, 'There ain't no job in the world that you can make the money your makin' now.' Evidently, Joe tried to explain to him that the business they were in wasn't a good thing for a married man. Tardino laughed again and told your husband he should've thought of that before he got married. Joe turned around to leave the office, and Tardino yelled, 'Hey, man, don't do anything you'll regret later. There is no doubt how much you love your wife and little girl.' Joe said that was when he made the decision to call the F.B.I."

"He asked me if I was interested in what he had. I knew he was serious and told him he had gotten my attention. He said he had dates, documents, video recordings of hits, drug trafficking, and taped phone calls of arrangements being made for the prostitution of kidnapped children as young as six-years- old."

"I asked him when we could get this evidence. He said, 'When you can prove that you will protect my wife and little girl.' That is when we began 24 hr. surveillance on you and your daughter. Joe is the only one who knew where the evidence was hidden."

Lee sat in disbelief. Then she asked. "Mr. Preston, are you saying Joe put his life at risk to save Brandie and me?"

'Yes ma'am."

Lee broke out in tears. Jaden put her arms around her and began to cry.

The agent and I sat quietly until they were able to compose themselves. Then he continued, "Mrs. Costa, I am going to ask you a

Deception or Perfection

very important question. Did Joe say, or do, anything that might give us a clue as to where the evidence is hidden?"

Lee blotted her eyes with a napkin and nervously looking at it, she replied, "I didn't even know that Joe was a gangster, much less that he had any kind of information like... like that."

Lee blew her nose as he continued asking questions. "Did he ever say anything out of character, or give you anything that you didn't know what it was for?"

Lee informed him, "No. Joe never said anything that I can remember."

I spoke up and reminded her. "Lee, what about the little black book you told me that Joe gave you just before he left your house the morning he was killed?"

"Oh, yes. The morning before Joe was murdered he gave me a savings account book and cautioned me to keep it in a safe place. He said it would take care of Brandie and me for the rest of our lives if something happened to him. But when I punched the account number into the ATM, it wouldn't accept it."

"That's it! He has a clue in the little black book!"

"All I saw in it is a savings account number and the amount."

Preston said excitedly, "I'm telling you, Mrs. Costa. The little black book has a clue in it that will tell us where the evidence is hidden. We will know right away if any of those numbers has a message in them."

Lee looked at me with a worried expression on her face and she began to stutter, "I... I... don't remember wha-wha-what I did with it?"

Preston became a bit agitated and spoke loudly, "Think, Mrs. Costa, think!"

Quickly butting in, I told him "First of all, her name is Lee. Second of all, you need to cool it. This woman has been through hell and back. There is no need to talk to her like that. Be a little more understanding or get out."

"I'm sorry for scaring you ...Lee. Are you all right?"

She nodded her head. He softly asked her, "Okay.... Now, he gave you the book. What did you do next?"

Lee answered with a sniffle. "Well... oh, yes. After he left the house, I put it in my coat pocket in the foyer closet."

"Do you still have the coat?"

"Yes but it's been worn several times since then, so I know the black book isn't there."

"After you arrived in Ellisville, you are positive that you didn't have it on your possession?"

"No. There was no use for it because when I tried to get some money at the ATM...." Lee paused for a moment and blurted out, "I remember throwing it in the glove compartment of my car."

"Where is the car?"

Lee informed him all about the Mercedes that it was a rental and she had returned it to the dealer.

Then he became concerned and asked, "Did you remove..."

Before he could finish the question, Brandie came to her mom, saying, "Mommy, I'm tired."

Jaden spoke up and told Lee, "You go ahead and finish this business and I'll take care of the little one."

The agent asked again, "Lee, do you remember removing the book from the glove compartment?"

"Why are you badgering me?"

He spoke to her very firmly. "Because there are people out there looking for you and they will kill all of you. The sooner we get that evidence the sooner you will be safe. I promised Joe that your safety would be my priority. However, if we have been able to track you down, then it's only a matter of time before the gangsters find you. Now... can you understand why it is vital to come up with that evidence as quickly as possible?"

Lee took a deep breath. Suddenly, she remembered and said excitedly, "I know where it is! Right after parking the rental car, I got a paper bag and cleaned out the console and glove compartment. I remember putting it in the bag. It's in my bedroom closet."

Lee went to her bedroom and brought the sack into the kitchen and dumped it on the table. Sure enough, there was the little black book. She grabbed it and looked inside. Then, showing it to Preston, she said, "See, there isn't anything in there except the number and the amount of the balance."

Preston took it and laid it open on the table and the two of us worked with the numbers. There was nothing that indicated any kind of hidden messages. Exasperated and disappointed, we surrendered the search. Then, looking at it and picking it up, I noticed frayed edges on a lower corner of the little book. Preston began saying his goodbyes. Glancing at Lee, he headed for the door and said, "I hoped that you might have seen or knew something that would be a tremendous help in locating the evidence." He also told Lee that the FBI would continue to keep the three of them safe as long as it was needed. He then stood-up and headed for the door. I quickly stopped him. "Wait, Preston. Lee, would you get me a sharp pointed knife?"

She brought me the knife. Slightly cutting the corner off the book, I used my thumbnail to pry it apart and out came a folded piece of paper. Preston returned to the table. Handing it to him, he looked at it and smiled. "This is it. It is an address and a map to where Joe hid the evidence."

Lee asked, "Are you sure?"

Preston nodded his head, scanned the paper again, and remarked, "I'd bet my life on it"

He laughed joyfully, flashing the paper in front of us. "We've got the answer to finding the evidence. This is what we have been looking for."

Lee had another question. "What is the address on the paper?"

Preston answered, "It's 38797 Clover Street. And it says south base of the headstone stone. "

"That's the address of the cemetery where Joe bought our headstones and family burial plot. I never went there and have no idea where the plots are located."

Preston asked, "Do you trust me with this information, Lee?"

She looked at me and I told her, "It's your call, baby." Then she glanced at the agent saying, "This would be a miracle if the FBI could use it to put those horrifying people away for years. Go ahead and see what you can find."

"What is your plan?" I asked.

"Dr Whitney, you know I can't tell you that, or anyone else.

Besides, the less you know, the better off you'll be."

"Yeah, you have your evidence. Where is that going to leave Lee, Brandie, and Jaden? Now you have no reason to protect them."

"There are agents on the job right now looking after all of you. And they will stay around as long as needed. That will be until the last of the hoodlums have been put behind bars. If any problems should come up... well... you'll see the agents coming out of the woodwork!"

I asked, "How will we know when all the gangsters, henchmen, and hit men are behind bars?"

He responded, "Dr. Whitney, I can't promise how but I can promise you will know when the last one has been arrested." He hurriedly shook our hand and remarked, "Mrs. Costa—I mean Lee—you have no idea the heroic act you have done." Turning toward me, he said, "And thank you Dr. Whitney, for all your help. Tell your friend Jaden it was nice meeting her."

We were still in a state of shock as he left the porch. I sat back down at the table and Lee went to Brandie's bedroom to check on her. Jaden came to the living room and paced around, looking out of one window, and then the other. She seemed scared. I wasn't feeling so good myself. So, when Lee returned to the table, the first thing out of my mouth was, "The three of you are coming to my house and staying there until we know you're all safe. Saying no to my suggestion is unacceptable. This place is perfect for a sniper to hide."

"Shannon, do you realize that having us stay with you could put your life in jeopardy? Preston is right. If the FBI can find us, then it's only a matter of time before the mafia turns up here."

"Sweetheart, I wouldn't have a life if something should happen to you guys. You will be safer at my house."

She began to pack clothes and Jaden did the same.

As they finished gathering up the suitcases and Goggie, Jaden remarked, "Thanks, Shannon. I think we will be safer at your home." We loaded up the Jeep and truck bed and took off for my place.

Chapter Twenty

The next morning, Lee left for work and I decided to go to the county seat to talk to the Jerry again. Ignoring the front desk, I cruised down the hallway to his office and opened the door, walked to his desk, and confronted him. "Are you aware that the stranger I've been concerned about is an FBI agent?"

Not paying any attention to my question, he asked me. "Isn't it a bit rude, Doc, to storm into a man's office without knocking?"

"I don't have to knock on your door since my taxes pay your salary. You must have forgotten that you are a public servant. Besides, I'm here to talk to you about Lee, her little girl, and her friend's safety."

He arrogantly leaned back in the desk chair, interlocked his fingers across his chest, and propped his feet on the desk. Twirling a toothpick in his mouth, he told me, in no uncertain terms, "Not that it's any of your business, Doc… and like I've said to you before, if I should run into your stranger…. which it is doubtful… and him being a FBI agent or not, he will have to break the law for me to question him, much less arrest him; and, as for as your girlfriend is concerned, she is also a stranger. And how come she took up with you so soon after her arrival here? Tell you what Doc, like I said - if and when your stranger should cross paths with me and he is who he says he is, I'll even tell him that you are a good man if it will stop you from high-tailing it to my office at the drop of a hat. However, because of your mysterious girlfriend, I'm wondering if I should retract my opinion of you. Just want you know, Doc, I'm on to your sweet little lady. She is going to have to convince me a bit more about her identity before I spend 'your tax money' by putting my men on the job to protect your girlfriend. You want to tell me the real reason she is here in Ellisvillle?"

I didn't know what to say so I just stared at him in disbelief. He smugly said, "I didn't think so, Doc."

I gave him a dirty look walked and out of the building. I thought, *It seems as though my trip into the sheriff's office was a waste of time. And it is obvious the bastard can't be trusted to give any kind security for Lee, Brandie, and Jaden. He could even be in cahoots with some underworld people and biding his time when it's clear for a hit man to do his dirty deed. He knows something about Lee. The question is how much does he know. In the meantime, I have really got to be on my toes to make sure that my two girls and Jaden are safe.* My feelings about Jerry were not about to change after this encounter with him.

After leaving the police station, I drove over to Millie's. The breakfast hour was over. I sat down at a counter stool. Lee came over with a mischievous smile and said, "Hey, good looking. Do we know each other?" She took a quick glance around the room to make sure no one was watching us, leaned across the counter, and gave me a kiss.

"If I go out and come back in again, will you give me the same greeting?"

Millie teasingly said, "Funny you should ask Lee that question, because all the men want seconds. But I had to nip that in the bud right away, otherwise she wouldn't get anything done around here."

"I'm the only one who gets that kind of greeting from her."

Lee slyly asked, "Are you sure about that, (and she whispered) lover boy?" Even knowing Lee was kidding, there was a twinge of jealously. Millie caught on to it and walked off laughing. Lee also caught on to what had happened and, surprised, she asked, "You didn't believe that nonsense did you?"

I responded indignantly, "Of course not."

She giggled and gave me another quick kiss. Poking her finger into my chest, she reminded me, "You are the only man in my life, and it's for ever and ever." Then she went on her merry way.

I finished my coffee and was about to get up from the stool. Lee dashed over to the counter and informed me, "Brandie brought home an invitation for her pre-school Christmas play. It is going to be on the twenty-third at seven p.m. in the school gymnasium."

"Great. I'll be looking forward to the seeing my little princess in her first play. What do you want to bet that she will be the smartest and prettiest one on stage?"

"Sounds like a remark a proud daddy would say. However, I don't gamble with an opponent who knows his bet is a sure thing."

Giving her a quick kiss on the cheek and leaving Millie's, I noticed an M.G sports car in front of Scott's Silk Hat nightclub. The sheriff's car was parked alongside of it. There isn't anything the caliber of an M.G. in this town. I thought, *Scott is sure making a lot of money if that car belongs to him, or he sure knows someone who makes a lot of money.* Then it occurred to me, *Bars are where gangsters hang out. What is Jerry doing there? Damn that man! Don't get all worked up, Whitney. Perhaps you have been watching too many gangster movies. Nevertheless, I must not let my guard down.*

Closing time at the clinic was at six-thirty. When I got home, the aroma was fantastic. I stood in the kitchen doorway watching Lee as she moved around tending to the fried chicken and mashed potatoes. Suddenly, my mom's voice rang through my head: *Supper is ready, Shannon, go wash your hands.*

There must have been an odd expression on my face because, when Lee noticed me, she asked, "Are you okay?" I leaned against the door facing and she came over to me. "What's wrong, sweetheart?"

"Lee, my mom's voice just went through my head. She told me to wash my hands." Giving me a hug, she said, "I bet your mom loved to fix this kind of meal." I nodded and told Lee that she would have fried chicken at least once a week. Lee continued, "Perhaps when you walked in, the smell reminded you of your mom. She may have spoken to you to let you know that she is near."

Looking at Lee's beautiful, compassionate face, my eyes began to fill with tears and the memories started flooding my mind—of Mom, Dad, and Jess—and they wouldn't go away. I began to cry hysterically as my body slid down the door facing. The pain was so deep in my chest, it was unbearable, and there was no stopping it. Lee sat down beside me and held my head to her chest, rocking back and forth. She lovingly kissed my head and said, soothingly, "It's all right… it's all right, sweetie… let it all out." Lee hugged tightly to me as I buried my face in my hands and the tears kept flowing like a thunderstorm.

Trying to keep from crying, I muttered shakily between tears, "Why did God take my mom, dad, and Jess from me? They were the kindest and most loving people in the world. They were a perfect example in showing people how to love an-and...."

The tears flooded my eyes again and my chest felt as though it was going to burst. I don't know how long we were on the floor but finally the pain subsided and the tears stopped. Trying to understand why my emotions got away from me, I remarked, "You know Lee... I didn't shed a tear all through my folks and Jessie's funeral or burial."

She took my hand, and kissing it again, she said, "Maybe that's why your mom came to you. This grief has been stored inside your heart for years. And for whatever reason, she chose to come at this time, it is because she knew that you were in a safe place in your life to let go."

I began to cry again and Lee helped me to stand up. We went into the living room and, just as we sat down on the couch, in walked Brandie and Jaden. Brandie ran to me and climbed on my lap with a worried look on her face. Putting her little arms around my neck, she asked, "Shannon, why are you so sad? Did you fall down and get hurt? Mommy can kiss a hurt and make it better."

She tightened her arms around my neck and held on as though I might leave. Tears welled up in my eyes again. So, taking a deep breath and swallowing hard, I replied, "No, princess, I didn't fall down. It is because I'm remembering some sad things."

"Mommy and Jaden, and me were sad when Daddy died and we had to run away because some bad people wanted to hurt us. And I'm sad when I miss my daddy."

Lee put her hand on the back of Brandie's head. She pulled her close to us and kissed her little girl's forehead, saying, "Maybe Shannon can be your substitute dad if you ask him."

Taking a handkerchief from the back pocket of my jeans and wiping my eyes and face, I asked, surprised, "Are you serious, Lee?"

She smiled at me and suggested to Brandie, "If you want to, you can ask him right now."

Brandie's face lit up like an angel's halo and her eyes sparkled as she asked, "Shannon, will you be my sussabute daddy?"

Lee corrected her. "The word is sub-sti-tute, honey."

Brandie smiled at her mom and said, "Okay." Then, turning toward me, she asked again, "Will you be my sus-sa-bute daddy?"

Deception or Perfection

Lee, Jaden, and I giggled and I told her, "It will be an honor, pumpkin, to be your... sus-sa-bute... dad."

"Can I call you Daddy?"

I looked at Lee again and she gave me a big grin, saying, "I hope, sweetie, that it won't be long until you can call Shannon 'Daddy', except it can't be right away. You will know when it's time." Then Lee gave Brandie a hug. "But until then, the two of you can share your love just like he is already your daddy." Lee looked at me and asked, "How does that sound?"

Smiling at my girls, I responded, "That is the greatest news I've had all day."

Lee stood up from the couch and announced in a carefree voice, "Dinner is on the table. Who is ready to chow down?" Brandie raised her hand. Jaden said, "I'm starved. I responded, "I'm ready, teddy." We all had a wonderful meal.

Crawling out of my bed the next morning, I looked out of the window at the Saturday morning sunrise. It had every color of a rainbow. It was so beautiful and there was a feeling of reassurance that Jess, Mom, and Dad were looking after me and my future family. Calmness entered the depth of my soul and peace filled my heart with an acceptance of their death.

Taking a deep breath, I went to shower and shave and put on some sweats. Then, leaving the upstairs bath, and slowly stepping down on each step, every one of them seemed to make a squeaky noise. Lee and Brandie had the master bedroom and I was hoping that they wouldn't wake up from the squeaking stairway. Cautiously going to the bedroom door and peeking in, I found my girls still sound asleep.

The coffee maker had already been set up and all that had to be done was to turn it on. While the coffee perked, I stepped over to a cabinet and reached in for cups. Lee came up from behind and gave me a big hug. Turning around and telling her good morning, she stretched up on her toes as tall as she could and gave me a kiss. When she stepped back from the kiss, my tough John Wayne voice came out. "That ain't fair, lady."

She came back at me with a sweet southern accent. "Why, what evah do yah mean, suh?"

"Well, when a beautiful woman... like yourself,... walks up to ya and lays a kiss on ya like that one, knowing he kant do nothin' about it, well... it just ain't fair."

She batted her eyes and shifted from side to side, saying shyly, "I wanted to warm you up for tonight."

"Is that right, little lady?"

I put my arm around her waist and pulled her into my body, I planted a kiss on her that would melt an iceberg. Just about that time, we heard a little voice saying "Mommy" and then there was a tug on Lee's housecoat. We smiled at each other and decided that we would have to postpone the warm up session and tend to the princess.

Lee asked, "Are you sure you are ready for a wife and little girl?"

"I'm looking forward to it!"

Lee got dressed and left for work. And since there wasn't any patients scheduled for the day, it gave me a chance to clean, organize shelves, and catch up on the paper work.

Finishing the chores, I walked back into the house and found Jaden was vacuuming the living room carpet. Tapping on her shoulder, she jumped and looked around, saying, "Shannon, you startled me!"

"What are you doing? There is a housekeeper who comes twice a week and vacuums."

"When I'm taking a break from my book, this is a good pastime for me."

"Okay, if that is what you like to do. Go for it!"

I hustled up stairs to fetch my dirty clothes and took them to the laundry room. Jaden turned the vacuum back on and then, a few minutes later turned it off, and yelled from the living room. "I'm almost finished, and Brandie needs to eat some lunch. She is such a good child and hardly ever whines or complains about anything."

Returning from the laundry room, I asked, "How would you and Brandie like being treated for lunch at Millie's?"

She smiled and took me up on my invitation. "We would love to have lunch with you."

Jaden had never been to Millie's and I thought we could have some fun during lunch time. And that's what we did.

When we got back home, Jaden and Brandie went upstairs and I stretched out on the couch in hopes of taking a short nap. Just as my body relaxed, I heard the sound of blasting music. Then, all of a sudden, the music stopped. Grabbing the pistol from a locked drawer in the desk and running up the steps, I heard Jaden and Brandie laughing and the music started blaring again. Peeking in the bedroom door, the two of them were dancing up a storm. So I quietly backed away from the scene and went to the living room and turned on the television.

After watching T.V. for a while, I decided to drive to the restaurant. I yelled over the music, "I'm going back over to Millie's to have another cup of coffee. Be sure and lock the door right away."

They yelled back, "Okay."

When I walked into the restaurant it looked empty. Lee wasn't even around. Getting a bit nervous, I stepped to the swinging doors of the kitchen and got the shock of my life. Wallace had Millie pinned to the back wall, and they were in a very passionate embrace. He was kissing her neck, and they were breathing like mountain climbers on Pike's Peak. Smiling and turning around quickly, Lee was standing in my face. "Oh! There you are!"

She stared at me suspiciously and asked, "What are you doing?"

Being a bit startled, I whispered to her, "You are never going to believe what's happening in the kitchen."

Lee crossed her arms and she spoke in an aggravated tone. "Shannon, it is none of your business what is going on in Millie's kitchen."

Still whispering, I muttered, "But- but sh-she and Wallace are in there making out."

"So what?"

Before I had a chance to say something, Wallace came through the kitchen door, and it hit me in the butt. In his English accent, he demurely asked Lee, "Would you mind if I work with you tomorrow?"

"No not at all, but if it's not any busier tomorrow than it was today, there is going to be a lot of sitting around."

He smiled and told her, "That will give me more time to be in the kitchen with Millie." And he winked at Lee, saying, "If you know what I mean."

Millie came through the swinging doors straightening the belt on her uniform. Wallace smiled at her and, smiling back at him, she said, "Boy, things are sure slow this afternoon.

Giggling, I said, "Define slow, Millie."

Looking a mite uncomfortable she asked Lee and I, "You two haven't been snooping through the window of the swinging doors have you?"

Lee said no at the same time I responded, "Yeah."

Millie's face turned red "Wallace and I have been checking the inventory."

Looking around the restaurant and holding back from laughing, I remarked under my breath, "I'm sure you and Wallace did a good job checking out the… inventory."

The two of them stood around not saying a word. Millie kept looking at Lee and I, and she finally spoke up. "Since there isn't anyone around here, the two of you might as well know something." Both of them looked like a kid who stole a cookie from the cookie jar.

Wallace put his arm around Millie and she gave him a big smile and said, "We got married last week."

That was the last thing I would have expected Millie to say and my mouth flew open. Lee threw her arms around Millie, and then Wallace, squealing, "Congratulations to you both. Why haven't you told me you were married?"

"Well, we are legally married. However, later on we want a church wedding with a preacher. We want to share our wedding vows in front of all our friends and plan a big party afterwards."

I hugged Millie and put my hand out to Wallace, saying, "You got a good woman, Wally. Congratulations." Then Millie began to share their history.

"Wallace and I got married when I was eighteen and he was nineteen. Five years later, we got a divorce and had no contact with one another until I called him about the Mercedes. But, as you know, he couldn't help you. When you wanted to do some work on the mobile home, I contacted him for permission to do the work because Wallace owned a half partnership with me. He was so sweet and understanding and we continued to stay in touch. When Wallace said that he had turned his restaurant over to a manager, well...that gave me the excuse to invite him to come and help me. We have grown up a lot, and this time, we're going to get it right."

Wallace looked at Millie and said, "You are right, Shannon, "I'm a lucky man."

They gave each other a kiss and returned to the kitchen. Lee only had about twenty minutes before leaving work, so I stayed around until she was ready to go home. We headed for the parking lot and both of us took a survey around our surroundings. Neither of us saw anything that seemed suspicious.

When we got home, Jaden had a pot roast in the oven but it wasn't quite done. She told us, "Brandie went into my bedroom to play with Goggie and both of them fell asleep on the floor. I covered Brandie to make sure she wouldn't get chilled."

Lee went to take a shower. After she returned downstairs, Brandie came down the steps sleepy-eyed and gave her mom a hug. She walked toward me and I picked her up, giving her big kiss on the cheek. A few minutes later, Jaden called out to us, "Come and get it."

Lee reminded me about Brandie's Christmas play. After dinner I went upstairs to shower and shave and then got dressed again, while singing old Christmas carols.

Just as we were ready to leave, Jaden came from the kitchen and said, "I'm not going to be able to go with you tonight. I only have twenty-four hours to finish my book and get it in the mail." She squatted down to Brandie. "Will you please forgive me for not being able to make the play? I'm so sorry, baby doll."

"It's okay, Jaden. Mommy, (and looking up at me with a big smile) and Daddy-O will take a lot of pictures and it will be fun showing them to you. I'm an angel in my play."

Lee remarked, "You're an angel every day, sweetie."

"Mommy, I'm your little girl and you love me even when I'm not very nice."

"That's right, and don't you forget it."

Sitting in the audience at the auditorium, we could see the teachers placing their little actors; and when they brought Brandie on the stage to place her, it was the first time I realized how much she looked like her mom. My love for that little girl was so overwhelming. Lee smiled at me with a whispered, "Isn't she beautiful?"

With a lump in my throat, I responded, "Just like her mother."

The curtain went up showing all the scenery and a little boy and girl came to the front of the stage with their lines. The boy began, "This is the night Christ was born." Then the little girl continued, "Mary and Joseph had no place to go, but they found a manger. And Jesus was… Jesus was…." A teacher softly spoke to her in the background. "And Jesus was born." Turning around, the little girl asked, "What?" The teacher said the line again and the little girl turned toward the audience and repeated, "And Jesus was bored."

The audience giggled at the little girl's mistake. Then Brandie stepped toward the manger and pointed toward the crib saying, "It was foretold that the baby Jesus would save the world." We were so proud that you could almost hear our buttons pop.

When the play ended, our row was stopped and kept us from leaving. I don't know what happened but we thought that someone might have fallen. Anyway, we were the last ones to get out of the auditorium. Finally, we spotted Brandie standing by a teacher near the exit. When the teacher saw us, she told us what a wonderful little girl we had. Lee took Brandie's hand and the three of us walked through the doors. About that time a man stepped up to me, saying, "Dr. Whitney, this is rude of me, but I have a Boxer pup…"

Brandie was tired and tipping my head to Lee, toward the truck, she went on ahead of me. The man continued talking about his boxer puppy. "That pup chews up everything he can get his teeth into. He also carries his food onto the carpet…"

Beginning to get aggravated, backing away from the man, I told him, "Look, mister, call my office and make an appointment." I walked out of the building just a few feet behind Lee and Brandie.

Suddenly, someone stepped out onto the sidewalk facing my girls with a gun and pointed it toward them. Running toward Lee and Brandie, it seemed as though my body was moving in slow motion as I screamed, "Nooo!" and tackled them to the ground. Looking up at him, I saw him raise his gun again, and then I heard a shot ring out. I thought, "He missed us!" I saw him fall to the ground, face down.

Then another person stepped from the shadows, pointing a gun at the man, and slowly walked toward us. Trying to cover Lee and Brandie with my body, I yelled again, "No, no!" They came closer and closer, holding the gun with both hands. As they reached the light from the street, we couldn't believe our eyes. It was Jaden. She slowly walked over to the man on the ground and, taking her foot, still holding the gun, she turned him face up. He was dead.

There were sirens coming from every direction. Jaden put her gun in a holster under her jacket. Reaching down to Lee and Brandie, she helped them up. I climbed to my feet, and Lee was staring at Jaden in complete bewilderment.

Jaden picked Brandie up and then she put her free arm around Lee's shoulder, saying, "You and Brandie are safe now. No more hiding, no more fear."

My heart ached as the hugging and crying began, and Jaden continued consoling them in a whisper. "It's okay. Everything is gonna be all right! You and Mommy are safe. We got all the bad men who were trying to hurt you."

Lee looked as though she was about to crumble. I put my arms around her waist to support her from falling to the ground while she continued crying.

By this time there were sirens everywhere and five squad cars completely surrounded the school and parking area. Three men got out of one car and came over to us. They were Jim Preston, the sheriff, and a man who we had never met before.

Jim told Lee, "Mrs. Costa, we got all of them except one."

Jerry spoke up and said, "We've had a surveillance camera watching your place twenty-four hours a day. Tonight we caught a man planting a bomb under the mobile home. They were going to get you one way or another." Lee gasped and went as white as a sheet. Hearing two shots ring out across from the parking lot, Jerry and two deputies ran in that direction.

Jim took Lee's arm and he guided us to the center of the squad cars for safety. Jaden's eyes searched the surroundings as she stood over us, and she took her gun out of the holster. We heard a voice calling out to Jaden. "We got the last one." Jaden breathed a breath of relief when

Jerry and his deputies brought back a handcuffed man and put him into a squad car.

I remarked, "That man stopped us in the hallway of the auditorium."

Jerry told us, "Yeah, an informant gave the FBI information about the mafia's plans, and that hood's job was to delay you guys until everyone was gone."

I asked Jerry, "How long have you known about Lee?"

He answered, "From the first week she arrived. My men and I were staked out all over the place. You almost caught me one night."

Shaking my head in disbelief, I said, "I remember but you got away without me recognizing you."

Jerry spoke up again. "We followed you guys everywhere. And please accept my apology, Dr. Whitney. I had orders from the FBI to do whatever was needed to keep you focused on me, and that's the reason my behavior was atrocious. If I could keep you angry at me, it would be less likely that you would notice the FBI at their work. I'm really sorry if my orders hurt you or Miss Lee. They said you are a very smart man, and it was proven the first time we talked to each other. You knew that I was up to something, which made my job even harder. Dr. Whitney, Miss Lee, please accept my apology?" I reached for his hand and shaking it, we knew he was sincerely expressing remorse for his behavior toward me.

I told him, "Jerry, thank you for your efforts in keeping the girls safe. And my friends call me Shannon."

With a shaky voice, Lee spoke up, "And my friends call me Lee."

He nodded his head toward us and said, "It will be my pleasure to be a friend to such fine people."

When Jerry left us, Lee settled down a bit. We were about to leave when Jim came up to us with the other man and introduced him. "Hey, you two, hold up a minute. There is someone I would like to introduce you to." Pointing to the man, he made his introductions. "Lee, Shannon, meet Carl Nester. He is the one who put the rental car in his name. And he also was the contact man for Joe. When Joe and Keith were murdered, Carl contacted... I understand you call her Jaden... who is Sal to us". Then with a grin on Preston's face, he said, "We now will call her Panty Waist, because that's the name given to an agent who becomes emotionally involved with the people they're protecting. Carl called her to get Mrs. Costa out of Chicago as quick as she could. And, even though she was grieving over losing Keith, her job came first. She is one of the best agents we have."

Lee was astounded. She looked at me, shaking her head in disbelief and asked, "Are you sure there is no more danger?"

Nester told her, "There were sixteen mafia members arrested from the west side, which was the gang Joe was in, but also twelve arrested from the east side. Joe had excellent evidence. We watched all of the ones who were the head members for the last three months and got even more evidence that will put them away for life. Sal... excuse me Jaden, is assigned to stay with you a month longer. Then she can decide what she wants to do with her life. Also, here is the little black book. The account was in a Swiss bank."

Lee asked, "What can be done with it? The bank didn't accept the account number when I tried to withdraw some money out of it."

Nester told her, "Yes, because Joe transferred the money to the bank in Chicago the same morning he and Keith were killed, and it wasn't posted until the following Monday."

I asked, "Are you saying that Lee has access and legal rights to that account?"

Nester reassured us. "That's right, Dr. Whitney."

Jim put his hand on Nester's shoulder and told him, "Well, boss, we can wrap this one up." Then he turned to Jaden, smiled and asked, "Hey, Sal. Is it okay with you, staying here another month with this job?"

She nodded her head and said, "Yes. I don't consider it a job. I love Lee and Brandie as though they were my closest relatives."

Everyone got in the squad cars and left. Turning around to pick Brandie up, I asked, "Are we ready to go home, girls?"

It was a beautiful sight, seeing the decorations on the house and the Christmas tree glowing in the window as we entered the driveway. When we walked into the house, Brandie ran to the tree and stood staring at it as though deep in thought. Her mom asked, "What are you thinking about, sweetie?"

"The man who tried to hurt us... is he dead like Daddy?" Lee didn't know what to say.

I squatted down beside her and tried to answer the question in a way that it wouldn't scare her. "Yes, princess. The man is dead but he wasn't anything like your dad. Because your dad loved you and your mom so much, he fixed it so that you and your mom will be safe for the rest of your life. He was the most unselfish daddy in the world to do that. And he would want you to play, laugh, and love the way he loved you."

She put her little arms around my neck and hugged me. Standing up with Brandie still in my arms, Lee and Jaden came over, and we had a group hug. When I sat the princess down, she touched her forehead with the palm of her hand and said, "Shoo wee! I'm sure glad that's over with!" We all had a big laugh.

Chapter Twenty-One

It was nine-thirty before the four of us could relax.

Brandie crawled on the couch between Lee and I. Putting her head on my lap, she went to sleep. Lee started to get up from the couch, but Jaden walked in from the kitchen and offered to take Brandie to her bed so that Lee and I could talk as long as we needed. Carrying the little princess in my arms to Jaden's bedroom was such a gift. Returning back downstairs, Lee was pouring herself a glass of juice. I asked, "What can I do to help you through all that has happened tonight?"

She stared off in to space before she finally answered, saying, "For the moment, I'm overwhelmed. There are a lot of things that are hard to understand. I'm not going to have to be looking over my shoulder anymore, and that is wonderful. However, I've lost my best friend because she is... dear God, Shannon... she is an FBI agent. Our relationship will never be the same!"

Seeing Lee almost in tears again, I called Jaden back down to the kitchen. When she saw Lee, she asked "Are you okay?"

"No Jaden, or is it Rachel, or Sal, or is it Panty Waist? Has your friendship with me been a job? Do you feel proud that I swallowed your act hook, line, and sinker?!"

Jaden walked right into Lee's space and placed her hands on her shoulders. With compassion, she told Lee, "Yes, Lee. At first, all my focus was on making all the right decisions that kept the Tardino family from finding out that Keith and I were FBI agents. Then the two of us began doing things together. I became emotionally attached to you. I love you like a sister and would never detach myself from you." Jaden held her arms out. Lee slowly stepped toward her and threw her arms around Jaden's neck. Both of them began crying. Lee, taking a breath, blubbered out, "I love you too, Jaden (sniff)... and the thought (sniff)... of losing you is (sniff)... so painful. I'm sorry (sniff) ... for being hateful to you."

"I don't blame you (sniff)... for feeling that way."

Pulling two paper towels from the wall hanger and handing each one of them a towel, I put the palm of my hand over my forehead like Brandie and said, "Shoo wee! I'm sure glad that's over with!" They laughed between blowing their noses and sat down on the stools at the counter.

Going over to the refrigerator and recovering the container of orange juice, I grabbed two glasses and filled them to the brim with juice. Handing Jaden her glass, I raised mine, making a toast. "May friendships for the future last, especially the ones from the past." The three of us took a sip and talked for a while longer.

Lee asked Jaden, "Were you in bed the night Shannon brought me home from Christmas shopping?"

Jaden flashed a big grin and then she looked very serious. "Of course I was in bed."

Lee, squinting at her said, "You are fibbing, Jaden. Tell me the truth. Which window were you peeking out of the night we came home from shopping?"

Jaden was puckering her lips and blinking her eyes trying to keep from laughing. She told Lee, "My dear friend, all that can be said to that is wow! Who in their right mind would pass up a chance to watch someone making out? I had to turn the ceiling fan on to cool off. You two know how to get it on!"

Lee was mortified. "I can't believe it! Oh my God! I'm so embarrassed!"

I just sat on the stool and grinned. Lee, with a dumbfounded expression on her face, said with an attitude, "Well, Shannon, say something."

"What do you want me to say, baby?"

Jaden began to giggle. Lee sat with her mouth open and I asked. "Did you learn anything, Jaden?"

Lee hit my shoulder and said accusingly, "What's wrong with you? You don't even care that she saw us making love?"

Jaden spoke up. "Hey! I'm not the only one that saw you two. There was an agent staked out just a little bit east of the mobile home."

Lee's eyes got as big as quarters, and she looked as though she was going to cry. Jaden quickly said, "Sweetie, you got to understand. My job was to keep a close eye on every move you made. And when I wasn't watching you someone else took my place. I'm sorry, Lee, don't be embarrassed. All I could see was that the two of you were safe. And then my head hit the pillow, which is where it is going to be in about five minutes."

Lee spoke up. "Wait, my friend. I have some other questions to ask you. How did you keep in contact with the FBI? We didn't have a phone or a vehicle for a long time, and you hardly left the mobile home."

Jaden smiled and took one of her earrings off and handed it to Lee. She pointed out a small speaker that was well hidden on the back of the earring. "See," she said, "The loop of the earring is the antenna. Now the button at the top of the loop where I clip it to my ear is the receiver."

We were astonished. Lee asked, "But weren't you uneasy about it ringing and being heard?"

Jaden laughed and told her, "It vibrates slightly. And all I had to do to receive a call was mash the little button attached to my ear. I can also talk to the caller without taking my earring off. Something else you might be interested in knowing is that I met Jerry at least once a week at the pond to bring me up to date on the progress of the investigation. You know all the fishing trips were not just for fishing. Jerry also stayed at the pond long enough to help me catch several fish to keep you from asking question as to why I kept going to the pond if I wasn't catching any fish."

Lee just sat and stared at her. With a smile, Jaden asked, "Have all your questions been answered?"

Lee, with her mouth still open, nodded her head. Then Jaden announced, "Well, I'm heading to the bedroom for some shut-eye if you two will excuse me." She turned her head as she entered the staircase and waved goodnight.

Lee and I went back to the living room to sit down on the couch, trying to digest what Jaden told us.

Cuddling in my arms she asked, "Do you suppose Jaden knows where Joe is buried?"

"Before she falls asleep, why don't you go up and ask her?"

Coming back down the steps from Jaden's room, and re-entering the living room, she sat down beside me.

"Remember the address where the evidence was hidden that Mr. Preston read on the little piece of paper? Joe is buried there in the burial lots he had bought for us. The name of the cemetery is Holy Cross and it is in South County Chicago. So is Keith. Shannon, Brandie and I need to go to his grave."

"When do you want to leave?"

"It needs to be as soon as possible."

"I'll get on the computer and reserve tickets on the earliest flight we can get."

"Are you coming with us?"

'Yes, if it is alright with you?"

Reassuring me, she put her arms around my neck and said, "Nothing would please me more. Thank you, Shannon."

"Lee, the only flight that is available has an arrival time in Chicago at 2:37 P.M. on December 24th, with a return flight to St. Louis listed to arrive at 8:21 P.M. That would give us a few hours at the cemetery with enough time to be back at the airport in time for the return flight home. That would also get us back here in plenty of time to play Santa Claus for Brandie."

"Go ahead and reserve our tickets," she told me.

We stepped off the plane in Chicago around three o'clock. After leaving the terminal, we went to a car rental service. Loading ourselves into the automobile we headed out for the cemetery. We reached our destination a little after four. I went to the office to ask for Joe's burial site. No one was in. Turning around to go back to the car, I caught a glimpse of a map posted at the end of the building. Going over to it, I got a better look and discovered it had a list that contained names of the burial sites and their grave numbers. Taking my finger and going through a series of names, I found the information for Joe's grave and the name of the garden where it was located.

Driving through the cemetery, we saw the garden we were looking for. Getting out of the car, Lee and Brandie started searching on one side of the garden and I searched on the other for Joe's grave.

Lee yelled out, "I've found it." Walking over to the lot, she stood staring at Joe's name.

Brandie tugged at her mom's coat sleeve and asked, "Mommy, is Daddy here?"

Lee squatted down beside her and said, "Your dad's body is here, but his spirit is in a place of happiness. That is a little confusing for most children to understand."

"No, it isn't, Mommy. Daddy is in Heaven. Can he see us?"

"I do know if there is a way to watch over us, sweetie, he will find it."

Lee touched Joe's name engraved on the stone. Brandie put her finger right next to her mom's. Lee prayed a prayer aloud as though Joe was standing in front of her.

"Joe, I pray for you to have peace. Please know that you will always be in our hearts. But we must go on with our lives, knowing that you will never be with us again in this space and time. If you haven't gone to the light, then please go now. It will give you happiness forever."

Lee and Brandie took their hands off the gravestone. Then Lee kissed her finger and placed it on Joe's name and we headed for the car

Arriving in Saint Louis a little before nine that night, we drove back to Ellisville with hardly any conversation. By the time we got home, Brandie had gone to sleep. After laying her in the bed, it seemed so natural for me to lean over and give her a kiss on the cheek. Lee stood watching the little angel. Then she reached down, tucked her in, and kissed her hand.

Leaving the bedroom, we went into the kitchen. Lee settled on a stool at the counter. Fetching a bottle of gin from the cabinet I asked her, "Would you like a martini?" She nodded and I gathered the ingredients, grabbed a couple of glasses, and made our drinks. Handing Lee her glass, there was a question in my mind, so I asked it. "Lee, you have been so quiet. Has going to Chicago made you feel differently toward me?"

She answered with a surprised look on her face. "Absolutely not, Shannon! Whatever made you think such a thing?"

Not knowing what to say, I shrugged my shoulders, and went

around the counter to sit down beside her. Then she put her arms around my neck to comfort me. "There are no words that can express how much I care about you. No one could ever take your place in Brandie's and my life."

Lee looked straight into my eyes and gave me a sweet kiss.

Giving her a smile, I kissed her back and suggested, "Santa Claus is due to make his appearance. Are you up to the task of putting the gifts under the tree?"

"It's going to be a pleasure."

We placed all of the gifts except the one that I had for Lee. Then we stood by the tree and she slipped into my arms. She remarked, "Of all the Christmas trees that I've seen, this happens to be the most beautiful one in the world." We kissed each other and decided it was time for bed.

Christmas morning Lee, Jaden, and I were awakened by a squealing little girl yelling, "Santa Claus has come!" By the time we made it to the living room, she was digging into the gifts and saying, "Mommy! Look what Santa brought me. It's everything that was on my list!"

Lee teased Brandie. "He brought you so many gifts, Santa probably had to add an extra reindeer to pull the sleigh. Well, I don't know about you guys, but I'm ready to open my gifts."

We agreed, and Lee started handing Jaden her gifts and then she handed me mine. The only ones that were left under the tree were hers. Grabbing one, she said, "The last person to open their gifts is the loser." We began taking bows off, tearing the wrapping paper, and snatching each other's gifts if one of us were behind the other.

Suddenly, Lee shouted, "I'm the winner! My gifts are all opened first!"

Jaden said, "Well, I don't have any more gifts to open, so I'll take second place."

Both of them looked at me and said in a bragging manner, "You are the loser, Shannon"

We all began admiring our gifts and thanking the giver. Then smugly staring at the two of them, they knew I had something up my sleeve. Leaving the room, I came back with a final gift, and handed it

Deception or Perfection

to Lee. Her mouth flew open and she asked, "You are giving me another gift?"

"Yes, indeed, my sweet loser," I replied.

She narrowed her eyes and remarked, "You cheated, Dr. Whitney. Withholding a gift doesn't count!"

"Oh, yeah?" I said. "If you don't like it, I'll keep it for myself."

She gave me the eye with a warning. "You've got one coming to you, sweet cheater."

Then she began to un-wrap the gift and, when the content was visible, tears began to puddle in her eyes. She said, "I can't believe it. How in the world have you had the time to get Brandie to sit still long enough for a portrait?"

I responded, "Jaden shot a lot of photographs and I took them to an artist who combined the different poses. This is the result."

Brandie heard her name; stopped playing with her gifts and came over to Lee to see the painting. Noticing that her mom was about to cry, she asked, "What's wrong, Mommy?"

Lee put her arms around the little munchkin's waist and told her, "These are happy tears, sweetie."

Lee turned the portrait around toward her daughter and, with a surprised look on her face, Brandie said, "It's me, Mommy."

Lee told her, "It's the most beautiful picture, and the most thoughtful gift, I've ever had." Then she turned toward Jaden and gave her a hug. And she gave me a thank-you kiss. "You know what, Dr. Whitney? Since I've known you, these eyes have shed enough tears to fill a barrel. And having you in my life has been worth every tear that has rolled down my cheeks." Then she gave me another kiss.

We all decided not to fix a big holiday lunch and just sit around and visit. We talked about everything, including the night of Brandie's play. Finally, when we settled down, Lee expressed her feelings about going to work the next day. "I'm really dreading tomorrow's questions and the gossip going around."

"Why don't you call Millie and ask her if you can take the day off? That would give you three days to recuperate from all of the commotion you have experienced over the last forty-two hours. And, if you are not up to it, let me call her." Lee was in complete agreement with my suggestion, so I called Millie.

Millie answered the phone on the first ring. I apologized for calling her on a holiday, and asked if Lee could have the Saturday off.

Millie said, "Shannon, because of the excitement the other night, I'm afraid the restaurant is going to be packed due to what has happened to you and Lee. Wallace is a good server but the two of us will not be able to keep up with the crowd."

"Why don't you call Debbie? She will be good help and will enjoy all the commotion." Millie called back a little later to say she was very pleased to be able to let my girl off from work. After I handed Lee the phone, she gave Millie a little rundown of the happenings the night of Brandie's play. When she hung up, we walked over to the window. Looking outside, there was a blanket of snow and it was coming down so fast that we could hardly see the barn. Then, going to the couch and sitting down, the little one told her mom that she was tired. Jaden spoke up and said to Brandie, "How would you like to sleep with me again tonight?"

Rubbing her eyes and, with a big yawn she said, "Okay"

I picked Brandie up in my arms and Lee gathered her sleep clothes. We went upstairs and tucked the little princess in with a goodnight kiss.

The next morning, the smell of coffee and bacon filled the air. Going downstairs and stepping into the kitchen, I found Lee wearing the fuzzy housecoat that I gave her for Christmas I approached her back and put, my arms around her waist. She looked around from the skillet on the stove and greeted me with a smile and a good morning kiss.

I asked, "Where are Jaden and Brandie?"

"They were up early this morning, ate a bowl of cereal, and are now outside building a snowman. We got about seven inches of snow last night. Hope you're hungry because I've fixed bacon, eggs, and biscuits for you."

After eating the fantastic breakfast Lee had prepared, while picking up the dishes, I commented, "A man could sure get used to this kind breakfast, baby. Thank you."

She shuffled over to the dishwasher and began to fill it with the dirty dishes. Standing up from the table and walking around the counter to where she was working, I pulled her into my arms and gave her a long kiss on the lips. When it was over she said, "A woman could get used to that kind of gratitude, lover boy. Hope I can get this special attention every morning."

"You can bet on it, baby!"

Helping her clear the table, I said wistfully, "Lee, I hope you don't go back to the trailer too soon. Get a little more used to being here. It wouldn't bother me if you never went back." She gave a quick kiss on my cheek and told me not to worry. About that time, a truck pulled up in the driveway. It was a camera crew. Quickly grabbing a coat, I stepped out on to the porch and Lee grabbed her coat and joined me. A reporter and a cameraman started to come on the porch. Stopping him, I said, "That's far enough!" The man with the microphone started firing questions at Lee.

"Mrs. Costa," he said, "What are your feelings about being a prime target of the mafia? What are your plans?"

By this time, two more media trucks parked in the driveway and swarmed the porch, scaring Lee half to death. People were shouting out questions and pushing each other to get closer to Lee.

Quickly taking her arm, I told her, "Get back into the house and don't come out. I'll take care of these buzzards."

Stepping off the porch and lifting my arms, I intended to stop anyone before they got to the porch. However, one managed to get his foot on the first step and I busted him under his chin. The reporters began to get out of hand. I yelled at Lee to call Jerry to bring some of his deputies and clear all of these bloodsuckers off my property. He was there in no time with two other squad cars behind him. All of them got out of their cars and began to push the media away from the porch. Then Jerry grabbed a megaphone out of the trunk of his vehicle and told them, "You folks have five minutes to clear this property and to get out of the county. If I catch even a glimpse of any one of you within thirty miles of these people, you are going to get a fine for disturbing the peace and a visit to the jail. So I'm suggesting that you get in your buggies and ride."

Within five minutes, they were gone; he assigned a deputy to park at the end of the driveway. I walked over to Jerry and said, "Thank you, sheriff."

He responded, "Dr. Whitney, all you have to do is call me if there is another incident like this one."

I reminded him, "Jerry, like I told you, my friends call me Shannon."

He smiled and shook my hand, saying, "Thank you, Shannon, for considering me your friend." Then he asked, "Would it be okay with you if I say hello to Miss Lee and Jaden?"

"Sure, come on in. But you may want to leave off the 'miss' when you greet Lee."

When we entered the house, the girls were in the living room. Jerry gave his hellos. "Good morning, Miss Lee, Jaden, Brandie."

I shook my head, thinking, *That man is so nervous he didn't remember the suggestion I gave him about not calling Lee 'miss'.*

With a shy smile, Jerry said to Jaden, "You were fantastic the other night!"

Jaden replied with a big grin on her face. "Thank you. You weren't so bad yourself."

Jerry shyly looked down to the floor and responded, "Thank you, Jaden. But if it hadn't been for you, we wouldn't have been as successful capturing all of the thugs who were out to kill all of you."

Lee and I gave each other a 'what do you know' look. We were both thinking *Could this be a budding romance starting here?*

Finally, Jerry began excusing himself. "Well, better get to work." Then he took his hat off and blurted out, "Jaden, can I have your phone number?

Jaden, with a big— and I mean a BIG— smile on her face, got a piece of paper, wrote down her number, and handed it to Jerry. While saying his goodbyes, he scooted through the door without taking his eyes off of Jaden. After he left Lee teased her, "Have you got a bucket of water handy, Shannon? We may need it to cool Miss Jaden off."

Jaden smiled and, fanning herself, remarked, "It's going to take more than a bucket…Miss Lee." And she headed upstairs.

Turning around to Lee, I asked, "Is it alright for me to go over to Millie's for a while?"

She said, "Take all the time you need."

Deception or Perfection

The restaurant was full of people and the noise level could have burst a person's eardrum. But when I was spotted, it got as quiet as a mouse. As I made my way over to Grant and Hank, people started talking again. Both of them greeted me, and then Grant asked me a question.

"Can't hear you, Grant, for the noise. Speak up." Even with him speaking louder, it was almost impossible to understand him. Motioning for them to hang on for a minute, I took my cup and walked to the center of the room, tapping it with a spoon, to get everyone's attention.

"Ladies and gentlemen, I'm here because there are a lot of questions that you all have about the police raid the other night. Some people were out to kill my girlfriend, her daughter, and her friend." I began to tell them the whole story and, at the end, they had a chance to ask questions. Half the people walked out of the restaurant once the question session was over.

Millie came out of the kitchen and asked, "Where the hell has all my customers gone?"

I told her what happened.

"That's fine and dandy, but you lost me a lot of business today."

"Millie, my intentions were to troubleshoot what was happening in here because of Lee. She has gone through enough without her having to face a bunch of gossipers when she comes back to work on Tuesday." She patted me on my shoulder and validated my reasons for the show-and-tell session with her customers.

When I returned to the table, Hank remarked, "Man, all of you came close to being killed! Thank God the FBI was on their toes."

Grant asked, "What's going to happen to you and Lee now?"

"Don't know, Grant. She is still a bit in shock."

Grant and Hank left the restaurant for work, and I was right behind them. Walking to the truck, I thought, *I've got to find some way to bring Lee out of her sadness.*

When I got back home, Lee approached me and said, "I'm making a trip to the mobile home to get more clothes and some extra dog food for Goggy. He hasn't had much attention, and Brandie can give him a treat. I'll not be too long."

Chapter Twenty-Two

It was dark by the time Lee returned, and it was apparent she had been crying. I decided to take her someplace where a person could let go. Inviting her to sit on the couch with me, I asked, "Lee, how would you like to take you someplace and have some fun?" She gave me half smile and declined my offer. However, I wouldn't take no for an answer and she finally gave in.

Gathering up gloves, coveralls, a sock hat, and pitching them to Lee, I said, "Put these warm clothes on. We are going for a ride."

"Where in the world would we go that we need to look like bears?"

"You'll see. I'll be back in a minute."

I went to the barn and carried an old sled to the Jeep and tied it on. We were ready to go. Heading back into the house, I stood at the foot of the stairs and yelled up to Jaden, "Is it okay to leave Brandie with you for a little while?" She said yes. I turned around and there stood Lee in her winter garb.

She asked as we were stepping into the Jeep, "Where are you taking me?"

"You will know when we get there."

Five minutes later we were at the City Park. Lee got out of the jeep, and aggravated, she looked around and asked, "What are we doing here?" Grabbing her arm I began to pull her up an incline. Reaching a knoll, she shouted loudly, "Shannon, stop it. I'm out of breath!" She was for sure out of sorts, and said angrily, "Are you crazy? This is a child's play ground!"

Grabbing her hand, I told her, "Come on, Lee, be a good sport."

She backed away from me and complained, "Shannon, no one could move around in this—this garb. What do you want from me?"

Feeling sorry for her and, noticing that it wasn't as cold as expected, I made a suggestion. "You're right; you don't need the coveralls, but keep your boots. You are going to need them."

She was really beginning to get mad and let me know it while she took the extra clothes off. "Shannon Whitney, this is crazy! Adults don't come to a kid's park in the winter, especially when there is a seven inches of snow on the ground!"

Noticing the swings about fifty feet up the hill, I challenged her. "How good are you at running?"

With a sassy look on her face and putting her hands on her hips, she responded.

"I'll have you to know, I'm damn good at running."

She swallowed the bait. So I challenged her again. "I dare you to beat me to the swings." And I took off.

She screamed, "That's not fair!" Then she shouted, "Cheater, cheater, pumpkin eater!"

I returned to where Lee was standing and admitted, "Okay, you're right. That could be defined as cheating so go ahead and draw a starting line."

That's what she did and just before finishing it she took off toward the swings as fast as she could and yelled, "Gotcha!"

I took off as fast as I could, trying to beat her, and fell down face first, and sliding about two feet from the swings. She laughed so hard she was holding her sides. I slowly got up and my body was covered with snow. It was in my face, up my jacket sleeves, and in my boots. Lee kept on laughing while I brushed the snow off my coat and jeans. With my back to her, I bent over to make a snow ball and then threw it at her. Knowing what was coming next, I sprang into a gallop like a quarter-horse and her snowball didn't touch me. My next move was to quickly making another one and taking aim; it caught her between the sock hat and the collar of her coat. It was funny.

She squealed and remarked sarcastically, "You are pretty proud of yourself, aren't you?" She turned around and headed toward me. Brushing my hands together, I thought, *Damn, I'm good!* Clearing some snow off a swing, I sat down on it as Lee approached me with a smile and asked sweetly, "Shannon, would you mind pulling my socks up higher? They keep slipping down into my boots."

Getting up from the swing and bending down to a point of no return, I saw her hand coming from her back and toward me. The next second I was eating snow. I grabbed her, she screamed, and both of us fell. We laughed while rolling in the snow. We finally got our composure, and still lying on the ground, she challenged me. "Do you think you can swing higher than me?"

I accepted her challenge and we got in the swings. She did go higher than me. We also played on the merry-go-round and went down the slide.

Lee noticed the sled on top of the Jeep and, pointing, she asked, "What is that?" That was my cue to unload the sled off the Jeep.

Lee was surprised and exclaimed, "Oh my goodness, it's a sled." She offered to help me pull it up the incline.

"Follow me. I'll take you to a perfect place to for a ride." She grabbed the rope that was attached to the sled and we made it to my favorite hill.

I told Lee, "This is it, and it is the best hill in the county to go sledding."

She stood for a minute as though she wasn't comfortable with the idea. Giving her some words of encouragement, she straddled the sled and said, "I've never done this before

"You're kidding!"

"Shannon, as you know, very seldom does it ever snow in southern Texas."

"I'll teach you."

She was still reluctant to go down the hill. In a sorrowful manner I spoke up, "Well, I'm sure there is someone out there who will go sledding with me."

She gave me the look of an angry cat and loudly replied, "It better not be a woman, because I'll scratch her eyes out!"

Looking all around she asked. "Okay, what do you do on this thing?"

After stepping behind her and straddling the sled, I instructed her, "Put your feet on the wood and hold on tight to the rope."

I yelled "Geronimo!" all the way down the hill. When we reached the bottom, she stood up and said, "This is great. It is as much fun as a waterslide. Can we go again?"

On our third run, just about three fourths of the way down the hill, we must have hit a stump because we went one way and the sled went the other way. Both of us finally stopped rolling at the bottom of the hill. We wound up looking like snowmen. I told her, "You're the weirdest looking snow woman I've ever seen."

She came right back at me. "Oh yeah? What does that make you?"

I started dancing around and singing. "Look at me. I'm so sexy. I'm so sexy."

Running behind me and jumping on my back, she yelled, "Geronimo!"

And both of us landed in the snow again. There was only one way to handle this so I started tickling her. She scrambled around laughing and yelled, "That's enough!" So, there was nothing else to do except to pick the little snow woman up and swing her around. Then, setting Lee down and putting my arms around her, we kissed. After the kiss, she gave me a long serious look and said, "Shannon Whitney, I love you."

Freezing in my tracks I asked, "What did you say?"

She raised her voice and repeated, "I... love... you!"

Blinking the wet snow from my eyelids, my response was, "Say it again."

She began spinning around and around and yelling more loudly, "I love you! I love you!"

Taking Lee's arm I pulled her into my arms and stopped her twirling. Then I began to kiss her forehead, cheeks, nose, and then her lips. After the kiss, I wanted to take Lee home and announce to the world how much I loved her.

Grabbing the rope on the sled, we headed for the Jeep, loaded it, and drove straight home.

After changing into dry clothes, Lee joined me in the kitchen. Brandie and Goggy were playing in the master bedroom. Fixing hot cocoa, I yelled up the stairs and asked Jaden if she would like a cup. "That sounds great!" she responded.

About that time Brandie and Goggy came into the kitchen and she ran to Lee. Then, giving us a hug around the knees, she requested a cup of cocoa. All of us settled in the living room. Lee sat on the couch, Brandie sat down on the floor with Goggy, and Jaden made herself comfortable in a large chair. The only light in the room was the Christmas tree and the fireplace, which gave the atmosphere of soft glowing colors.

I ran up the stairs and fetched my mom's ring set. Returning to the living room, I announced, "There is something that needs to be done and this is as good of a time as any." Kneeling down in front of Lee, reaching into my pocket and removing the engagement ring, I took Lee's left hand and asked, "Would you make me the happiest man in the world and be my wife?"

Jaden and Brandie stared at Lee and it looked as though they were holding their breath. Lee's eyes began to puddle. She placed her hands over my cheeks, gave me a sweet kiss, and said, "It would be my honor to become your wife."

Placing the ring on Lee's finger, I said, "I love you."

She cradled my face in her hands and kissed me again, saying, "And I love you!"

Brandie stood up and ran for her mom. Jaden came over to us and, giving us a hug, she said, "I am so glad the two of you realized that it was time to start planning a wedding!"

Then Jaden's eyes began to puddle. Brandie looked at me and the expression on her face was, "Oh no... not again."

I picked her up and whispered in her ear. Putting the palms of our hands on our foreheads, in unison we said, "Shoo wee. I'm sure glad that's over with."

We all laughed. Then Brandie said to me, "I love you too, daddy."

Lee gave her a kiss and reminded her, "See, sweetheart, I told you that you would know when it was the time to make Shannon your daddy."

Brandie grinned and gave me a hug. She asked, "Daddy, when are you and mommy going to get married?"

Lee and I looked at one another. Without taking my eyes off of her, I suggested, "How about New Year's day?"

Lee grinned and asked, "But can we get a license, invite people, buy wedding clothes, and a dozen other things that have to be done in five days?"

"Don't see why not if we start today with the plans."

Lee became excited, saying, "The first thing we have to do is find a minister who will be open to marrying us on a holiday."

"Leave that to me," I offered. "I'll call Butch Cameron and ask him if he is free to marry us on a holiday. He is the pastor of the Evangelical church here in Ellisville."

"Butch is an unusual name for a minister," Lee commented.

"His given name is Ronald, but he has been called Butch as long as I've known him. You know what? I'll call him right now."

I had good news when I returned to the girls. "Butch said he would be glad to officiate our wedding. And he offered his church for our big day. Now we need to make an appointment for blood tests. I have a number of suits in my closet that are appropriate. But if you need to go shopping, you and Jaden can do that tomorrow. I'm sure we can get a blood test tomorrow too." Lee spoke up. "What about the best man and maid of honor?"

"Let's start asking the ones we want right now. Who are you choosing for the maid of honor?"

"Jaden...no, Millie... would it be all right to ask both of them?"

"Baby! It's your wedding. Why not? That's a great idea. And I'll ask Grant and Hank for the best man job. Or should I say 'best men'?"

Jaden had walked out to the kitchen while we were talking and Lee called her back. She stepped into the living room and Lee asked her, "Would you be my maid of honor for the wedding?"

Jaden squealed like a teenager and ran to her, saying, "Yes, yes, yes! I'll be glad to be your maid of honor! I assumed you would ask Millie."

"I'm going to the restaurant tomorrow to ask her for the same job, so both of you can be my maid of honor. And Shannon is going to arrange for the blood tests."

While the girls were chatting and giggling, I called Dr. Marks. He said that if Lee and I could come into the emergency room early the next morning, he would see to it that we got blood drawn, even though it was Sunday.

The next morning I woke up before anyone else, the first thing on my agenda was to make reservations for a bridal suite at the best hotel in St. Louis. Once everyone was up and awake, Lee and I decided to make an early trip over to Millie's. Of course, Grant and Hank were at the regular table and grinning from ear to ear.

We sat down and Grant asked, "So! What are you two doing here today?"

Then Hank asked, "And who wants to tell us their latest news?"

Lee and I smiled at each other and she asked them, "What kind of news are you talking about? Is it that Millie and Wallace tied the knot last week?"

In an agitated tone Hank responded, "Hell no, little lady, it's about you (he pointed to me) and this pinhead. We heard from a cousin of Dr. Mark's nurse, Pat, who told Debbie, who told Pete the mail man, who told us that the two of you made an appointment to get a blood test."

Then Grant chimed in. "And, besides, Lee is sporting a diamond engagement ring. Now what do you say about that?"

Lifting Lee's hand and pointing it toward the two of them I admitted. "Well, Lee and I are going to be married New Year's day."

Both of them gave us their congratulations and shook my hand and hugged Lee. After they sat back down at the table, I decided to ask them to be my best man for the wedding. "What are you guys doing on New Year's Day?"

Hank and Grant said they were going to sleep in late and snack all day.

"Would the two of you consider being my best man. Or, should I say my best men?"

Hank spoke up and said, "You can't do that. You're only supposed to have one best man."

"Who says I can't have two best men? Besides, there is no way for me to choose between you guys. So, what do you say?"

Grant spoke up. "You can count on me bud."

Hank hem-hawed around and finally told us, "Okay! I'll be there with bells on. This is going to be a celebration I have hoped for since the day you first saw Lee. You know that Grant and you are like brothers ta me and ta share the day of you gittin' hitched..." Hank's voice became hoarse and he cleared his throat. "Well... hell, Whitney. You got the two best men in this state for your occasion."

Lee spoke up, excusing herself, and left the table and went into the kitchen. All of a sudden we heard Millie squeal and knew that she had accepted Lee's invitation to be her maid of honor.

When Lee came back from the kitchen, we left the restaurant and headed for the hospital and courthouse. After finishing that business, Lee called Millie and asked her to get in touch with all of our friends and invite them to the ceremony.

Millie questioned Lee. "Would you and Shannon like to have your guests come to the restaurant for the reception? It is going to be closed for New Year's Day anyway. Leave everything else up to me. You can consider it your wedding gift."

When we got to the house, Jaden and Brandie met us at the door and the three of them ran up stair's chattering up a storm. I heard Jaden ask, "What are you going to wear for the wedding?"

"Don't know, Jaden."

Brandie spoke up. "Can we go to the mall and buy you a pretty dress, Mommy?"

"Yes! We can go early tomorrow morning!"

About another hour passed and I heard Lee say "What!" in a loud voice. They all came down the steps and Lee announced, "Guess what, Shannon! Rachel Ferguson isn't Jaden's legal name! When she and Keith were assigned to protect us, they had to use fictitious names."

Jaden spoke up. "That's right. And I liked my fictitious name better than my legal name. My real name is Sally May Evans."

I commented, giggling, "That name suggests a red polka dot dress and a big bow in your hair. There is nothing about you that looks or acts like a Sally May. Besides, you will always be Jaden to me."

She smiled and said, "I feel a whole lot more comfortable with that name than I do with Sally May. And I just might make that my legal name."

The next morning the girls took off for a shopping spree. I had on my list ordering flowers and calling a photographer. Lee had already chosen one of my suits for the wedding. It was comforting to me knowing that everything was in order.

Since the thirty-first was the night before the wedding, and the next day was New Year's day, we decided to hit the sheets early. However, there were all sorts of fireworks going on and our sleep was disturbed practically all night.

My sense of smell woke me up New Year's morning to the aroma of black coffee. I heard Jaden yelling. "Lee, you're not supposed to see the groom before the wedding."

"Jaden, that's an old wife's tale."

I quickly showered and shaved and went downstairs. Lee met me with a kiss. "What a way to start a day," I commented.

I returned the kiss passionately. There was a tug on the leg of my sweats and a small little voice asked, "Daddy, why do you and Mommy kiss all the time?"

Very quickly Lee told her, "Well, sweetie, when grown-ups love each other, they show their affection with kissing."

Brandie responded indignantly, "Mommy, you love me and Jaden and you don't kiss us all the time."

Lee stood opened mouthed for a moment. So I tried to explain it to her. "Princess, there are all sorts of love. Some don't express the same thing to everyone. A man and woman's love is always ready for a kiss. A mother's kiss is when her little girl gets hurt, or a kiss goodnight, and maybe a kiss good morning. Does that help you understand?"

Brandie smiled and said, "I want my good morning kiss from Mommy and Daddy." Picking her up between us, we gave her a kiss on each cheek at the same time.

Jaden came down the steps and remarked, "That is a beautiful sight!" Lee reached out to Jaden and she joined us in a group hug. Jaden had tears in her eyes and Lee touched her on the shoulder with a caressing smile. Brandie smiled like an angel.

Through the business of the day, I kept glancing at my watch. It was currently 5:10 P.M. and a thought went through my mind. *It's only a few hours away from Butch announcing Lee and I as husband and wife.*

The girls interrupted my thoughts when they came downstairs carrying their clothes out the door to place them in the jeep. Jaden rushed back in the house and informed me that they were heading for the church to finish the final touches to their make-up and to make sure their dresses looked right before walking down the aisle.

Getting myself dressed, while looking at the clock every five minutes, the time finally arrived to head for the church. Entering the little side room from the back of the church, there stood Hank and Grant patiently waiting for me. As we exchanged hello's, the organist came and gave us instructions on when we should walk to the front of the alter.

Becoming a bit apprehensive, I asked, "What is taking so long?"

Hank gave me a big grin and Grant remarked, "Hang in there, friend, the time will come soon enough." And the two of them snickered.

Nervously switching from one foot to the other, I heard the organist begin to play a song and the three of us followed her instructions. Looking to the back of the church, Brandie came walking up the aisle carrying two roses with the wedding bands attached to them. Then Jaden and Millie walked up the aisle and stood on the opposite side from Grant, Hank, and me. Then the organist began to play the wedding march, and I saw Wallace escorting Lee up the aisle. She was so beautiful, my chest filled with love. Her dress was pale blue chiffon that stopped just above the knees. The waist was tight to the top of her hips and buttoned down the front. The skirt of the dress had six large pleats that made her look as though she was standing in a cloud. The fabric flowed softly with each step as she walked toward the altar. To be honest, my mind blanked out because I couldn't take my eyes off of Lee.

Then Butch said, "Do the two of you have special vows you would like to make to one another?"

I turned toward Butch. He could tell that his question was a total surprise. I said, "What?"

People began to giggle and he said again, "Do you and Lee have any special vows you would like to say to one another?" My mind went blank and I heard Butch repeat his question. "Shannon, would you like to share a vow with your bride?"

Lee saw my discomfort and asked, "Would it be alright for me to go first?" She began to tell me how much she loved me and shared her heartfelt emotions.

Butch looked at me. I felt weak, my breathing became shallow and, sure enough, I passed out. Opening my eyes, I focused on Hank and Grant. Then the two of them began to help me up. Lee had a concerned look on her face. Glancing around I saw everyone was trying to keep from laughing. An altar boy gave me a cold wet paper towel and a glass of water. While I was taking a drink, Lee put her arm through mine and whispered, "I love you."

And that's all it took to bring me out of the fog. Butch was about to continue the ceremony and I whispered to him, "Butch, I want to recite a poem I wrote for Lee a while back and didn't get to give it to her."

He asked, "Are you sure you're up to it?" I nodded and he announced, "Ladies and gentlemen, the groom has something to say to his bride." He whispered, "You've got the floor." Looking into Lee's beautiful eyes, I took her hand and began to recite the poem:

My love for you is an ocean's depth.
Since the first day I saw you and we met.
No mountain high, can express my love.
For you are my life, sent to me from above.
When we dance with our hearts and your soul touches mine,
It becomes a reality, which makes our love divine
So awaken, my sweet, to the morning sun,
And in my arms forever, when each day is done.

Tears began to roll down Lee's cheeks and, when our guests stopped clapping their hands, we swapped rings and Butch said, "You may kiss the bride!" I kissed Lee. Then tears came to my eyes as Butch announced, "Ladies and gentlemen, may I introduce to you Dr. and Mrs. Shannon Whitney."

We all went over to Millie's and stayed long enough to do all the traditional things that a bride and groom does at the reception. Jaden caught the bouquet. A little later, we slipped out the door, and went home to change into comfortable clothes and took off for the motel.

I carried Lee over the threshold and set her down by the bed. It was late, so she asked me, "Hey, lover boy, would it be alright for me to lie down for a while? I'm exhausted."

"Of course it's alright," I said. "Maybe I'll join you."

She slipped off her jeans and fell into the bed. She was sound asleep before my clothes hit the floor. Lying next to her, it was hard to believe how blessed my life had become. Letting out a big yawn and closing my eyes, the next thing I knew I was waking up and glancing at the clock. I couldn't believe that it was six-thirty in the morning. Slipping out of bed, and going to the bathroom I stepped into the shower. The water splashing on my head felt like a fresh rain storm. However, before I had time to suds my head and body, Lee stepped into the shower. Putting her arms around my chest, she cuddled my back and said, "This is a good time to keep the promise I made to you several months ago."

Lee took the soap from the tray and began to wash my back. I quickly traded places with her, eager to return the favor. Then, stretching my hands around to her chest, I slowly rubbed soap in a circular motion over her breasts and kissed the back of her neck. She turned around toward me and laid a hot kiss on my lips. That's all it took to arouse our desire. I gently touched her face with my hand and we began making love. The water shimmered on Lee's body. With closed eyes, she smiled, kissing my face neck and lips. Holding her hands behind her back, we swayed in a rhythmic motion. Our breathing escalated with each stroke as she slipped her hands from mine and placed her arms around my neck. Lee whispered, "I love you so much."

"And I love you."

Our movements intensified with every rocking movement and our desire increased with every moment. Lee softly caressed my face and moaned while inhaling a deep breath. The penetration became more deliberate as I tightly pressed her hips to mine. She paused for a few seconds and we held each other, wanting the moment to last. We kissed again and it was inevitable that we reached the point of no return. Holding my breath and swallowing hard, I felt Lee deeply inhale air between her lips. Thrusting against each other, we reached the highest degree of consummating our marriage. As we were getting out of the shower, there was a knock outside our room. When we opened the door, it was room service bringing a breakfast that had been ordered anonymously. They had two chairs for the two of us to sit down at the serving cart, saying, "I'm starving." She lit into the breakfast with both hands. After eating we laid back into the bed and relived our wedding. Lee teased me, saying, "You know, Shannon, my last name hasn't changed." Asking her what was she talking about, she asked, "You didn't notice how we signed the marriage license?"

"No!"

She continued, "Yes, I'm sorry, but that was the thing to do... to keep my maiden name"

Looking at her suspiciously, I responded, "No you didn't."

Back and forth we swapped the yes's and no's until I picked her up, slam-dunked her on the bed and said, "Take that, Mrs. Whitney!"

She began stripping my robe off and remarked, "I'll take it any way you want to give it!"

We made love again and, when it was over, we laid back into the pillows and she said, "We are the most blessed couple in the world."

Agreeing with her I pointed to the clock. "We told Jaden that we would be home before lunch. It is time to get out of here and head for Ellisville."

One month later Lee ran across the little black book. She asked me to go with her to the bank. Driving up to the ATM, she punched in the account number and the screen showed a balance amount of fifty million dollars. After sitting there for a few minutes in a bit of a shock, Lee spoke up, "I can't use this money knowing how Joe earned it."

"Lee, why don't we go home and talk about it."

Returning to the house Lee poured us a cup of coffee. I said, "Sweetheart, let's assume that the money is legitimate. What would you like to do with it?"

She thought for a few minutes. "Well, there needs to be a college fund for our children."

"Okay, there is forty nine million left. What else would you like to do with the money?"

In deep thought, she sat quietly drinking her coffee and then told me, "You know what, Shannon? I've had a dream in my heart to one day have an outdoor park with lots of animals, from elephants to wild geese. There would be places for family picnics and a children's petting zoo! Also... it just dawned on me... this would be a way for the money to be given back to society. Joe would be pleased to know that the money was used for children and their families." Excitement filled Lee's eyes and sitting down at the kitchen table she began planning out her dream.

A few minutes later Jaden came down the stairs with a suitcase and said, "It's time for me to get back to D.C. You don't need me anymore." Lee got up from the table and, giving her a hug, she said, "I will always need you, my friend. How are you getting to the airport?"

"This is Jerry's day off and he offered to take me."

Lee let out a suspicious "Uh huh."

"Lee, don't you start getting any notions about Jerry and me. We are just friends. And I'm going to be busy for a long time."

Lee again uttered, "Uh huh. That's what I kept telling people. 'Oh! Shannon and I are just friends.' But if that's what you want to do then go for it. However, it's my opinion that you are in denial."

After Jaden left, the house seemed to have space of empty sadness. But we knew that we would see her sooner than she thought.

Three months later Lee and I found out the reason Ellen made so many visits to her doctor last fall. She and Grant told us that they were expecting a daughter in July. Hank has been cleaning up his red neck act for some reason. But we love him and Vickie no matter who he wants to be. Millie and Wallace are planning to build a new upscale restaurant. And we found out that Jaden applied for a job with the Veterans Administration in the St. Louis regional office and got the job.

Lee, Brandie, and I… well, we are looking forward to whatever life gives us. We know that God will help with a little bit of Heaven each day. So, what else is left to say? I know! We will live happily ever after.

BLACK ROSE
writing™

CPSIA information can be obtained
at www.ICGtesting.com
Printed in the USA
FFOW05n1436300614